A Place
for
Outlaws

A Place
for
Outlaws

Allen Wier

1817

HARPER & ROW, PUBLISHERS, New York
Grand Rapids, Philadelphia, St. Louis, San Francisco
London, Singapore, Sydney, Tokyo

The author is grateful to the University of Alabama for a Summer Research Grant.

A portion of this novel, in slightly different form, has appeared in *The Southern Review.*

The author gratefully acknowledges permission to reprint portions of the theme song "Ask the Authority" by Walter Garner for "The Friends and Neighbors Show" from Wally Price, WACT radio station, Tuscaloosa, Alabama.

FIRST EDITION

Designed by Alma Orenstein

Library of Congress Cataloging-in-Publication Data

Wier, Allen.
  A place for outlaws.
  I. Title.
PS3573.I355P5   1989   813'.54   88-45918
ISBN 0-06-016113-2

89 90 91 92 93 AR/HC 10 9 8 7 6 5 4 3 2 1

for Donnie

There would always be, in Julia's heart,
a place for outlaws—
a place her mind could not rule.

PART ONE

Huldah and Annabelle

1

JULIA understood the price that sometimes had to be paid for love. Julia's mother, Vivian, had paid with her very life. Vivian had leakage of the heart. She had never been able to exert herself. Carrying Julia had taken all her strength. Vivian had her baby in her mother's house, where she and her ne'er-do-well husband, George, had lived since they married. After Vivian gave birth, she never got out of bed. She could barely whisper, but she saved up enough strength to bequeath Julia to her younger sister, Annabelle, who was home from boarding school.

Before Annabelle had been sent away to school (to see if anyone could teach her some manners), their mother, Huldah, had always made Vivian go with Annabelle on dates—Annabelle was too flighty, and too pretty, to be alone with a man. Huldah said no, when Annabelle announced that she was to raise Julia.

"No," Huldah said. "Not while I'm alive. You're not even married, Annabelle."

"Then I'll get married," Annabelle said.

Huldah snorted. "I wouldn't put it past you," she said, closing the subject.

Julia was born in June of 1924. Forty days later, Vivian, just nineteen, drowned in what little breath she had. It was as obvious to Huldah as it had been to Vivian that George couldn't raise his daughter, but it was almost as bad to think what Annabelle might do with a child. So Huldah took Julia.

Huldah had been named for the prophetess who dwelt in Jerusalem and delivered the stern judgment of God's love as recorded in II Kings:

3

Because they have forsaken me, and have burned incense unto other gods, that they might provoke me to anger with all the works of their hands; therefore my wrath shall be kindled against this place, and shall not be quenched.

Huldah's love was delivered to Julia with similar sternness but accompanied by compassion and forgiveness equally Biblical in its depth.

Because thine heart was tender, and thou hast humbled thyself before the Lord, when thou heardest what I spake against this place, and against the inhabitants thereof, that they should become a desolation and a curse, and hast rent thy clothes, and wept before me; I also have heard *thee,* saith the Lord.

Behold therefore, I will gather thee unto thy fathers, and thou shalt be gathered into thy grave in peace; and thine eyes shall not see all the evil which I will bring upon this place.

"Child," Huldah often reminded Julia, "you have been the recipient of loving grace—the good Lord's grace granted you life and your mother's sacrificial grace fulfilled His plan. It is my grace to forestall senility for sufficient time to instruct you in the ways of God and man. Your sin would be to ever forget God's abiding grace."

Julia had tried not to forget. God's grace seemed to take many forms, chameleon-like, camouflaged as the different people who loved her. Her mother, Vivian, was the first, dying as Christ had, so that Julia might live. Next, there was Huldah, who loved her with the fond sternness Julia associated with the Heavenly Father of the Old Testament. When Huldah died, Julia's aunt, Annabelle, reappeared, married by then but still fanciful and flighty as a fairy, a chimera of love, manifestation of the Holy Spirit. God worked in mysterious ways, His wonders to perform.

O the depth of the riches both of the wisdom and knowledge of God! How unsearchable are his judgments, and his ways past finding out!

Huldah ended every Scripture reading the same way:
"Book, chapter, and verse, Julia?"
"Romans, chapter eleven, verse thirty-three."
"Good, Julia. The apostle Paul's mighty letter to the Romans. God's plan for Jew and Gentile alike."
The ways of God came straight from Scripture, which Huldah understood, word for word, as plain and simple as the nose on Julia's

face. The Bible was a rulebook for avoiding hellfire and could be followed as literally as the rules in the newspaper every winter for avoiding house fires. The ways of man, on the other hand, were not always covered. In which cases Huldah was there to give Julia loving guidance.

The rules of behavior and love were the rules of the time and place: 1924 in New London, Missouri, the heart of the heart of the country, landlocked but just a stone's throw from where Mark Twain had cast off for the unknown territory ahead.

Huldah lived in the one-story white farmhouse she'd been born in at the edge of New London (once a good wagon ride from town), with a slate roof and dark-green shutters. Huldah kept a back bedroom for her bachelor boy, Howard, who was gone most of the time, away following the crops. Heart trouble ran in the family; Howard had a heart valve leak. When he was home, working in the lead mines, Julia heard his breath, all the way from the back bedroom to the living room, a steady, high wheezing. Every time Howard went through the front door, coming or going, he sang, "Yes, we have no bananas." He sang it every time.

Julia was a little afraid of her uncle Howard, with his wheezing heart and loud singing. He ate like a horse. When they had corn on the cob, Huldah put a bushel basket on the floor to catch all Howard's empty cobs. After he ate he always went back to his room and slept, wheezing and snoring at the same time. He had a fit once. Right after they had eaten, he fell on the kitchen floor and twitched and jerked and flopped like a fish out of water. Spit ran out of both sides of his mouth. Huldah put her finger in his mouth and he bit her, blood running down his neck and turning pink with spit. She yelled for a spoon. Julia was scared to move, but she pushed a spoon across the table and Huldah held it in Howard's bucking mouth. His eyes were rolled up all white and stiff like curtains drying on curtain stretchers in spring and fall housecleaning. Then he got so still Julia thought he'd died and Huldah picked him up and carried him, heavy as he was, like a little boy to bed. After that, Julia was afraid to go back near Howard's room.

When she was six, Howard told Julia she was adopted.

"Look at yourself," he said. "You're not like us. Your eyes are slanted like a Chinaman's, and your hair's curly."

"Am I adopted?" Julia asked Huldah. Huldah had the ironing board across two chairs in the kitchen and was ironing one of Howard's shirts.

"Howard's teasing you, Julia. You were born right here in this house." The heavy iron bumped and tumped like Howard's work boots going down the hall. The front door opened "Yes, we have no bananas . . ." The front door closed. Huldah looked up from her work. "Come here, child," she said. And she put her arms around Julia and pulled Julia into the warm, moist, starchy smell of her love. "You are *my* child, Julia. But we are all children of God, and we belong to Him."

From that day on, Julia always called Huldah Mother.

The nearest neighbor, Dutch Shoenfeld, could be seen but seldom heard. His was the two-story across the road and down a ways. Dutch Shoenfeld had a nephew who was retarded and spent warm days in a fenced side yard with a padlock on the gate. In summer, Dutch Shoenfeld's tall house blocked the ends of sunsets.

Behind Huldah's house was a squat henhouse, where she kept a baker's dozen of banty hens, and an old barn that Big Ben—an old draft horse Huldah inherited in '21 when her husband passed on—shared with rusted tools, dirt daubers, and spiders. The barn, like Big Ben inside, leaned southeast, away from winter winds.

In winter the cook stove kept the kitchen warm; Huldah would not light the coal heater in the parlor. When snow piled up against the front door, Huldah wore long underwear and wrapped Julia in sweaters. Every evening after the supper dishes were washed and put away, Huldah turned off the lights and sat in the kitchen rocker, with Julia in her lap. Huldah opened the cast-iron door of the stove to give them firelight, and while Julia twisted the gold wedding band on Huldah's finger back and forth, round and round, Huldah sang to her:

> Lord, when we have not an-y light,
> And moth-ers are asleep;
> Then through the still-ness of the night,
> Thy little children keep.

Julia laid her head back on Huldah's chest and felt the soft singing vibrate there.

> And though we do not al-ways see
> The ho-ly an-gels near,
> O may we trust our-selves to Thee,
> Nor have one fool-ish fear.

And between hymns, Huldah talked, and when Huldah talked it was instruction:

"When I die, child, you will go to your aunt Annabelle, Lord help you. And you have to promise me you'll make sure she does right by you. Don't let her give you dancing lessons."

My hope is built on noth-ing less
Than Je-sus' blood and right-eous-ness;
I dare not trust the sweet-est frame,
But whol-ly lean on Je-sus' name.

On Christ, the sol-id rock, I stand;
All oth-er ground is sink-ing sand,
All oth-er ground is sink-ing sand.

"Promise me you won't let Annabelle take you to theatrical productions or moving pictures."

There were several bedrooms, but it was a waste to use more than one room at a time. Waste not, want not. Huldah and Julia slept together in the double bed Huldah had shared for forty years with her husband, Julia's grandfather, R.T. (Years later Julia was surprised to see her grandfather's name, Randall Tennyson, on her aunt Annabelle's birth certificate—she had always thought his name was Arty.) Huldah told Julia about R.T., who was an Irishman and worked hard all his life on the railroad and farming some on the side. R.T. had been a good man, but he'd had a taste for liquor until Huldah cured him one night with a beating from her broom.

"Promise me you won't let her let you wear lipstick."

Huldah and Julia wore sweaters to bed—it was a waste to heat a room while you were under a feather comforter, and it was unhealthy to sleep in a heated room—and lay very still. Huldah was a light sleeper and would not tolerate whispering or wiggling once prayers had been said and the lights were out. Huldah was asleep almost as soon as her head touched the pillow. She slept the sleep of a hard worker with a clear conscience. She did, however, grind her teeth in her dreams. The spaces beneath the comforter and between Julia and Huldah grew warm, and the dark room grew light with the snow glow in the long rectangular panes of the windows. Julia kept her arms against her sides to hold herself still and listened to Mother ask Arty if he'd like a little bedtime kiss. Who would blame a person for what got said in her dreams? Certainly not Julia, who always drifted into sleep with her eyes shut and her lips sealed but her ears open to receive whatever might come their way.

Mornings began in the dark. Rejoice and be glad in each day the Lord hath made. The coals in the cook stove had to be stirred and wood added. Big Ben had to be given hay in the falling-down barn, and eggs had to be gathered from the nests of the banty hens. Every morning Julia brought Mother a basket of the banty eggs to fry until the yolks were hard as Christmas candy. Breakfast dishes were done before the sun came up.

> I must work the works of him that sent me, while it is day: the night cometh, when no man can work.

"Julia?"

"John, chapter nine, verse five."

"John nine, yes, but verse *four*."

After breakfast, Huldah brushed Julia's curly dark hair, brushed it firmly, pulled out the knots fairies put there while Julia slept. The brush caught and pulled, but when she complained, Mother reminded her, "We must suffer to be beautiful, Julia."

Julia learned what Huldah taught, by lesson and by example, awake or asleep. A little girl was to be seen and not heard except when reciting her bedtime prayers. If your right palm itched, you were going to get money; if your left palm itched, you were going to get visitors. A young lady wore her Sunday dress downtown or to ride in a railway car—even if her great-uncle John Wesley Durham was the conductor. If a bird flew inside a house or a rocker rocked by itself, someone was going to die. A young woman did not, ever, wear rouge or lipstick, and she did not, ever, go to Hannibal to watch a moving picture show. If you took a salt shaker from someone before it had been put down on the table, you would never marry. All respectable people prepared themselves for accident or injury by wearing clean, presentable underclothing.

Julia was six when she got her first store-bought dress. Her aunt Annabelle mailed it to her for Easter. The dress was a pale peach, real silk, with a full inch of ruffle around the skirt. Three rows of picoted lace circled the neck, where there was an embroidered peach-colored rose and a pale-blue ribbon. A matching bonnet was made entirely of rows of lace. There was even a pair of rayon tap pants for underwear. Fifty years later, Julia would remember the dress and the bonnet down to the smallest detail. She had never imagined, much less seen, anything so perfectly lovely.

That Easter in Missouri was cold. Too cold, Mother said, for the dainty rayon tap pants. Julia could wear the lovely dress and bonnet to church Easter Sunday, but she had to have on her warm long johns. Mother helped Julia tuck the sleeves and legs of the heavy cotton underwear up under the sleeves and skirt of the dress, and Julia did her best to forget that the long johns still showed in places.

Some of the rules of behavior were so important Huldah didn't trust herself to pass them on with sufficient authority. Huldah was an old woman; she seldom entertained. Social customs weren't the same as they had been in her day. There was more to contend with. So Huldah arranged for Mrs. Lucretia Moulton, née Stewart, the wife of Dr. Moulton, the ophthalmologist, to instruct Julia in deportment. Julia was seven.

Mrs. Moulton always wore a pink cameo at her neck and always wore gray clothes. And she always *rustled*. Julia asked Mother why Mrs. Moulton always *rustled* so, and Mother said she wore taffeta petticoats. Mrs. Moulton brought a thick, heavy dictionary; a large, velvet-lined box of sterling-silver flatware; and twelve silver finger bowls. The book was for Julia to balance on top of her head while she practiced walking. Before Mrs. Moulton came, Julia thought she already knew how to walk, but Mrs. Moulton found quite a bit wrong with the way Julia carried herself. Place settings were another matter. There were utensils in Mrs. Moulton's polished box Julia had never even heard of. At the end of the week Julia would set the dining room table for twelve, leave the room, return, and spot, immediately, any rearrangement Mrs. Moulton might have made to test her. Julia learned the proper placement and use of the cocktail fork, the salad fork, the luncheon fork, the dinner fork, the dessert fork; the butter knife, the luncheon knife, the fish knife, the dinner knife, the fruit knife; the soup spoon, the cream soup spoon, the ice cream spoon, the iced-tea spoon, the grapefruit spoon, the fruit spoon, and the sugar shell. Mrs. Moulton taught Julia a great deal more, not the least of which was how to carry on socially correct dinner conversation (which Julia practiced, hand in lap, speaking to the empty spaces on either side of and across the table-set-correctly-for-twelve from her) and how to discreetly remove a bit of bone or gristle while dabbing her lips once with her napkin. Julia didn't mind Mrs. Moulton's lessons, but she hated waxing and polishing every piece of furniture each time Mrs. Moulton was coming over.

Julia's favorite thing was to play getting married. Mother let Julia put on her mother's wedding dress, and she let her crank the Victrola till the "Wedding March" led Julia down the hall and out onto the porch, where she stood and listened to an imaginary preacher, who always began, *Dearly beloved, we are gathered together . . .*

One summer morning, while Mother was taking her bath, Julia decided to get married out back so Big Ben could attend the ceremony. A wild rosebush that grew against the barn was loaded with rosebuds just opening. Bright morning sun turned the tight flowers into rubies and made black shadow rosebuds against the weathered barn boards. Behind the barn Uncle Howard's abandoned garden grew wild with weeds. A breeze rattled the dry leaves of his corn, and corn silk turned in the air, turned by the sun into fine strands of platinum. Julia pulled out the silky strands and stuck them into her dark hair, making herself a dazzling blonde. She peeled rose petals from the buds opening on the bush. Ten red petals she dabbed on her tongue, soft but bitter to taste, and stuck on her ten fingertips. What a wedding this would be—a lovely blonde with red-painted fingernails and rose-petal lipstick. She crept up to the back of the house—crept slowly so her makeup would not blow away, crept slowly to watch for Mother, who had made clear her opinion of painted ladies—and stared at her reflection in one of Mother's spotless windowpanes. Julia's changed face stared back, silver-gold hair and lips like a kiss from the page of a magazine.

"Julia? Julia?" Mother's voice called from the porch.

Julia blew her kiss, lips and all, into the breeze and ran her fingers through her hair, shedding her bright nails and blonde locks. "I'm coming," she yelled. She shook her hair and brushed corn silk from the shoulders of the wedding dress as she marched toward the *thump, thump, thump* of Mother's shoes on the wooden porch floor.

"Julia, what are you doing back here? Go out front to play. Willy is out this morning. I bet he's watching for you."

One of Mother's rules was that in warm weather, Julia play on the front porch or in the front yard so that Dutch Shoenfeld's retarded nephew, Willy, could at least enjoy watching.

But when thou makest a feast, call the poor, the maimed, the lame, the blind.

"Julia?"

"Luke fourteen, verse thirteen."

"Good."

I was eyes to the blind, and feet *was* I to the lame.

"Job, but I forget where."

"So do I, child. It *is* Job, but that's in the Old Testament, and ours is a New Testament faith." Huldah stood on the porch, her hands white with flour. Julia followed her to the kitchen, where she was rolling pie dough with her big rolling pin. As she rolled, she sang:

Bring-ing in the sheaves,
Bring-ing in the sheaves,
We shall come re-joicing,
Bring-ing in the sheaves.

She always made enough dough to have some left over from her pies to spread with butter and sprinkle with sugar and cinnamon and roll up to bake for Julia. She called the sweet baked coils tootsie rolls, and Julia loved them more than anything in the world, after Mother herself.

In this fashion the nights and the days passed like dreams. One fall morning there was suddenly frost on the grass Julia ran across to the barn to give Big Ben his hay. Big Ben lay dead in his stall. His big, black body was hard as ice, the dark swells of a shadow cast by darkness, a shadow stiff and substantive. Dutch Shoenfeld came with his hired man. They made a kind of harness around the horse's rump and dragged Big Ben out of the barn and pulled him slowly away with a blue Ford tractor. The round, shallow dent Big Ben left in the soft barnyard dirt reminded Julia of the vaccination scar on her arm. First snow came early that year and drifted into mounds against the barn door. At night the dark mounds looked like Big Ben's frozen shape.

That spring the barn door blew open and banged and banged and banged until it came off its hinges and lay like a lifeless tongue before the dark open mouth of the building. Huldah had Dutch Schoenfeld push the barn over with his Ford tractor and carry off the boards. That same spring, the giant elm did not leaf out. The shadow of its bare limbs came into the house and crossed the floor and climbed the walls.

The following spring, when leaves still did not appear, Huldah had the huge tree cut down. While the rest of the yard was still pale with the memory of winter, grass grew green around the stump.

2

ON Valentine's Day in 1933, in a railway car (returning from a visit to Taylor, Texas, where Julia's aunt Annabelle lived with her new husband, Garner Yates), and wearing a blue suit (new for the trip) for only the second time, and wearing freshly laundered and sunned and pressed underclothes, Huldah died, with Biblical suddenness, of a massive stroke.

Just before she died, Huldah had been talking about Annabelle and Annabelle's new husband, Garner, who was older and obviously wiser. How Annabelle had chanced into him, Mother didn't know. Only the Lord could fathom such fortune. It had, as well as Julia could understand, something to do with angels and idiots and children. The last thing Mother said—before she opened her eyes wide and one side of her face twisted and tilted against the train window—was that it was a good thing Annabelle didn't have any children, because Annabelle was still a silly child herself and wouldn't know the first thing about raising one.

Which was true.

Mother's eyes, in which overhead train lights had jiggled tiny and bright, frosted over like the pond outside that they were slipping past. The train window filled with snowflakes, and Julia looked beyond Huldah's frozen face. A small sign welcomed them (back) to Missouri, where, Julia knew, things were supposed to be seen to be believed. Mother's lips pressed against the window. She wore no lipstick to mark that last kiss; no warm breath fogged a spot on the cold glass. Julia believed her own eyes. Mother was actually, after predicting it for so long, dead.

What would become, Julia wondered, of *her.* Aunt Annabelle

didn't know how to raise her, and she knew Annabelle couldn't *really* want her, not with a new husband and house to look after.

Annabelle was twenty years younger than her husband. Right after they married, she had insisted Garner rent them a house in Waco and take the train the seventeen miles east to Mart, where he worked for the railroad, so she'd be close to shops and movie theaters in downtown Waco. She was distressed when, soon after they'd moved into the house in Waco, the railroad sent them south, to Taylor. Garner made up for the move by having a new house built for them in Taylor, just the way Annabelle wanted it.

Annabelle had been a flapper. She plucked out her eyebrows and drew them back in the way she wished God had made them in the first place. She wore rouge and changed the color of her lips daily. She painted her nails to match her lips. She had a box full of ear clips. And sometimes, to Garner's secret scandal and private delight, Annabelle prepared for the unexpected by wearing no underwear at all.

Annabelle's house (for though Garner had had the house constructed and paid for the lace curtains and the wine-red rugs and the polished mahogany piano, it was Annabelle's house in every detail) was the grandest house Julia had ever been in. There were pictures on all the walls and china birds perched on the mantels. Electric lights and gas heaters burned in every room. A row of flames stood like a regiment of redcoats behind cream-colored rectangular grates that had square holes and looked like waffles or wafer cookies. The grates glowed hot-red a long while after Garner turned the gas off. At bedtime on cold nights Garner turned the heaters down but not off. When Julia said it wasn't healthy to sleep with heat on, he laughed and laughed.

There was a radio—the first one Julia had ever seen (or heard). The radio was in a mahogany cabinet and had a round dial with silver numbers and a compass needle that glittered like a distant star. When the power was switched on, there was a space—a breathless, dark silence—and then one pulse of light and sound, one hum in which all the hidden voices of the world harmonized inside the box and the dial lit up like a living face. Deep red fabric covered the opened-wide, perfect O of a mouth the speaker made, and Garner tweaked the dial-knob nose and pronouncements blared so boldly Julia pictured bright exclamation-points coming out of the open mouth: *Cavalcade of America, Science on the March, History's Headlines, Let Freedom Ring, Time to Shine, Believe It or Not, You Said It!*

Annabelle smiled and curled a red-tipped finger around the knob, caressed that nose—*c'mere,* her finger beckoned—and the lights in the room seemed to dim with *Magnolia Blossoms—the Fisk Jubilee Choir, Ray Sinatra's Moonlight Rhythms, Jazz Nocturne, The Hour of Charm— Phil Spitalny and His All-Girl Orchestra,* and *Melodies from the Sky.* Julia sat on the floor, her cheek against the polished wood, music vibrating against her jawbone, the breathy beat of "It's a Sin to Tell a Lie" or "Moon over Miami" or "When Did You Leave Heaven" warm against her cheek. She ran her hand up the side of the cabinet to feel it curve up to a pointed arch like the top of a window in the Methodist church.

Annabelle gave Julia her own room and let her go to bed whenever she chose. Annabelle bought her a nightgown with a lace collar, something as lovely as a Sunday dress just for sleeping. Julia put the lovely nightgown on and lay still, alone in her own bed, warm without the hills of a comforter rolling over her, and she listened for Mother's voice to come down from heaven to protest all this waste. Was the movement Julia heard in her bed sheets what Garner called "Huldah turning over in her grave," or was it just Julia's own two legs swimming in the luxury of all that space?

Mother had often reminded Julia of the sin of idleness, and when Julia woke before sunup and walked softly to the kitchen, to find it dark and empty, silent except for the shudder of the new refrigerator (a steady vibration that recalled Mother's sleeping breath), she wondered whether Annabelle had escaped *all* Mother's teachings.

The first thing Annabelle told Julia was to speak up for herself. "I don't know the first thing about raising you, Julia; you're going to have to help."

The first thing Annabelle taught Julia was the Charleston. "You'll never be popular with the boys if you can't dance." Julia was nine.

Julia had to keep reminding herself that Annabelle was Mother's daughter. Annabelle had Mother's large, round eyes and the high cheekbones, like Julia's mother, Vivian, in the photograph in Julia's new dresser drawer. But beyond appearance, it was difficult to see how Annabelle could have come from Mother. Julia had loved Mother with the fierceness of a foundling for a foster parent, though she knew who her parents were and knew, too, Mother was her own blood. But though she reminded herself to take care, lest Annabelle spoil her or lest she, under Annabelle's easy tutelage, forget Mother's instruction, she was coming to love Annabelle and Garner with the

14

infectious love that grows from affection and trust freely and openly given.

The land around Taylor was cotton land, and it went on forever. Except for clusters around houses, the trees had been cleared for the cotton. The dirt was black as coffee grounds until the cotton plants came up new and turned the land green. The sun baked the plants until they turned brown and burst like popcorn into white puffs. One day, gazing out over a field white with cotton waiting for pickers to wade through and gather it, Garner told Julia, "Looks like Missouri in February. Down here we get our snow in the summer." The sky, always wide and usually blue, seemed to have come down low to meet the earth and spill its clouds over the fields. Julia saw it as a big piece of light-blue construction paper with a narrow strip of white pasted along the bottom edge.

Garner was a died-in-the-wool Democrat. He was a union man and had a good job with the railroad as car and wrecker foreman. He was in charge of clearing the track whenever there was a wreck. He even made all the arrangements for the crew's food and lodging while they worked. Those men ate plenty. Garner bought all the food from Jimmy White's Market until it became an A & P store, the first chain store in town. Garner yelled at Jimmy White for "selling out" and said the chain store would be the death of small businesses and workingmen. Big chains would be the end of free business, and free business had made America great. Julia had never seen anyone so angry.

Garner didn't believe in buying on time. They paid cash for everything. He'd saved until he had $725 for the new Studebaker Annabelle used to drive around town to visit newcomers. Annabelle had an arrangement with the mayor to welcome every new family that moved to town. Though the job did not pay, Annabelle was due, as his official and personal representative, all the honor and dignity of the mayor himself.

Garner was worried that Julia's daddy, George, might try to kidnap her, so she had to stay in the house after school until Annabelle got home from her visitations. The only times it was hard to obey was when Bill Foley came down the street on the ice wagon. The ice wagon was still pulled by horses, and it had a step-up bumper across the back. Julia loved to catch a ride on the back of the ice wagon, and Bill Foley, who was young enough that Julia didn't have to call him Mr. Foley, was glad to oblige.

Garner gave Julia twenty-five cents a week allowance to do

with as she pleased. Frozen malts cost a nickel at Coy's Drug Store. Julia loved them. When she had lived with Mother in Missouri she had no idea such tastes existed. Nor had she ever let her tongue luxuriate in the sweet-tart taste of a lime Coca-Cola. Annabelle had bought Julia her first one the day after Julia came to Texas to live. Annabelle took Julia to town every Saturday to go shopping, and every Saturday they stopped at Coy's fountain for a Coke on the way home. Julia always had a lime Coke; Annabelle, cherry.

Fanny Knopke, Julia's best girlfriend at school, had a new baby sister, and Julia wanted one too. Fanny told her grandmother Knopke, and she said that if Julia put a cone of salt on the right side of her front door, in one year she'd get a baby sister. Julia did without Cokes and frozen malts for two weeks, saving her allowance for salt. She bought the salt out of a wooden barrel at the Taylor Meat Market. Mr. Swinson filled a paper sack full for her. It was hard to shape the salt into a cone. Julia worked on it for an hour. Finally, she went into Garner's and Annabelle's room and slipped the cardboard backing from a new shirt Garner had bought and rolled the cardboard into a kind of funnel for the salt. It was still not easy, and when she had something like a cone the breeze kept blowing salt away. She hoped Garner wouldn't notice the crinkles in the cardboard she slipped back behind his new shirt. Annabelle got home just a moment later and wanted to know what Julia had spilled on the front porch. When Julia told her it was a salt cone to bring her a baby sister, Annabelle kicked it off the porch with the side of her foot. The salt hit the leaves of a camellia bush with the sound of someone shushing Julia—*shhhhhh*— and when she didn't get a sister a year later, Julia knew Annabelle had kicked the spell away.

Garner, who had begun with the railroad as a cook for road gangs, was teaching Annabelle to cook, and Julia learned with her. Garner liked fried pork chops, so they concentrated on that. Garner made good money for the time and the place, and when the Depression came he was one of the lucky ones. He was temporarily reduced from car and wrecker foreman to car inspector, but even so they were well off. He was generous in his luck, and Annabelle and Julia learned to cook in quantity, for on few nights did they feed less than a dozen jobless men. These men were quiet and polite. Used to hard work, most of them were frightened by their unexpected idleness. Each still wore his overalls and heavy work brogans. If the economy suddenly returned to normal, each one was ready to bend over and lift back up whatever burden he'd been told to set down when he lost his job.

16

Julia carried a plate of steaming pork chops into the dining room; a man in the doorway shuffled his heavy feet and bumped against the wall, his eyes avoiding hers, thick wrists and callused hands uselessly empty. The man reminded Julia of Mother's old draft horse, Big Ben, banging backward and sideways in his stall, unaccustomed to the confining barn. The plates were always wiped clean with the soft middles of biscuits. Annabelle said the plates hardly needed washing.

Making beds was easy, Annabelle explained, if you just smoothed the sheets and quilts and folded the covers down. The hard part was trying to tuck the bedspread under the front of the pillows and then smoothing the spread back over the pillow tops. Annabelle said the beds looked more inviting with the pillows showing.

Annabelle was also good at sweeping. The radio on loud was all sweeping required. The music vibrated up through the floorboards and entered the broom straws and your toes at the same time and got you in sync with the broom. With the right music, Annabelle insisted, anyone could fly on a broom. This theory worried Julia because of its suggestion of Halloween witches, but she had to admit she herself swept much better with the radio on.

The first time Annabelle decided she had to spank Julia, she broke one of her long fingernails. That made Annabelle so mad she grabbed a fly swatter and chased Julia to the other side of the kitchen. She chased Julia around and around the table until she started giggling, and Julia started too. That made Annabelle laugh harder, and, finally, Garner came in from the living room and told them he couldn't read the newspaper for all their racket.

Garner was like a man with two children to raise and no wife to help him. But he had the appreciative love of an older man for a pretty and energetic wife he'd been so certain would not accept his proposal that he'd almost never asked, and he had the surprised love of a childless man for the gift of a daughter he'd long ago forsaken hope of having. He had, Julia realized, the patience of Job.

It was Garner who spoke to Julia when she started menstruating. Julia had told Annabelle, who had given her a box of Kotex, and that night Garner knocked on Julia's bedroom door.

"Annabelle has spoken to me," he said. "You are becoming a lady now. Since you are no longer a child, you may no longer wear shorts. You may wear bloomers in your gym class at school." Julia sat, cross-legged, on her bed. "It is not very ladylike to cross your ankles," he said. She swung her legs over the side of the bed and put her feet side by side on the floor. "Julia, listen to me carefully. Men will now begin to try to lift your skirts. It is up to the lady to set the limits. If you ever get too familiar with a man, that man will not marry you, and you will be disgraced. Don't ever go out with a man you wouldn't be willing to sit across the breakfast table from three hundred and sixty-five days a year—because you never know when you might fall in love. And once you fall in love, it's too late." That was all he, or Annabelle, had to say on the subject. He looked down at her and said, "You look a little thin. A lady doesn't want to be fat, but she wants a figure. Here." He reached into his coat pocket and pulled out a Hershey bar. "Eat this after you get in bed. It'll help fill you out while you sleep." And every night thereafter he came to her room at bedtime and gave her a Hershey bar.

Annabelle was a pretty woman and so much younger than Garner that he grew increasingly jealous of her. Her beauty was partly in her face, partly in her unbounded energy. He would not let her go out alone at night, except to church. She couldn't even go to the high school football games, where Julia was in the pep squad. In spite of his jealousy, Garner loved to tell the story about the time he caught Annabelle in bed with another man. He was working a midnight-to-eight shift and came home for breakfast. He had hired some men to nail flooring in the attic, and one of the workers—a big, heavy youth—stepped between the rafters and fell through the ceiling of the bedroom where Annabelle was still sleeping. Garner was coming down the hall and heard the crash. It scared Annabelle so badly they thought she was going to develop Saint Vitus' Dance. Garner and Julia had to rub her limbs to calm her down. The worker, a Bohemian boy, was so embarrassed he quit the job. Garner told Annabelle he hoped she wasn't planning on going down to Robertson Street to get work. Robertson Street was the red-light district in Taylor, and it was famous all over Texas.

Julia once got to go in a house on Robertson Street; that was one of the most exciting things she'd ever done. Mr. Knopke, Julia's friend Fanny's father, owned a café called the Smokehouse, sort of a delicatessen and barbecue place. One night Julia was there with Fanny when Mr. Knopke got a call from a house on Robertson Street. They needed a case of beer right away. Mr. Knopke winked at Fanny and Julia and asked if they wanted to go with him to make the delivery, "Just so Mama don't tink I'm up to no good down dere." The women from Robertson Street shopped downtown in slacks and high, high heels. No lady wore slacks to town. Julia knew better than ever to mention the trip to Garner, but she did tell Annabelle, who made Julia tell her all about it. There wasn't much to tell about the house—it was like any house except that (like all the houses on Robertson Street) it had a picture window in front, so men passing by could see inside. Men in suits and some still in work clothes sat around the living room, and a Negro boy played the piano. A girl who didn't look old enough to be there leaned over the piano and sang "On the Beach at Bali Bali." Julia had expected to see Robertson Street women sitting around in their underwear, but she saw only the singing girl, who wore a dark-green dress, and the woman who came to the door, a big, fat woman with short hair, who wore a white apron over a brown dress. The fat woman sent Mr. Knopke around to the kitchen, where a Negro maid took the beer and closed the door.

"Did you see anything in any of the upstairs windows?" Annabelle wanted to know. Julia realized she hadn't looked up at the windows; she'd been too busy trying to see past the fat woman in the doorway.

"No," was all she said.

"Well," said Annabelle, "the exciting thing is knowing what you might have seen. It's a good thing Vivian and Mother aren't around. Think what Mother would have to say."

Julia did, and it made her feel guilty.

Whoredom and wine and new wine take away the heart.

But that's Hosea, Julia thought, the Old Testament, and ours is a New Testament faith. She tried not to recall the fifth chapter of Galatians:

Now the works of the flesh are manifest, which are *these;* adultery, fornication, uncleanness, lasciviousness,

Idolatry, witchcraft, hatred, variance, emulations, wrath, strife, seditions, heresies,

Envyings, murders, drunkenness, revellings, and such like: of the which I tell you before, as I have also told *you* in time past, that they which do such things shall not inherit the kingdom of God.

Annabelle attended church every Sunday, but Huldah would have been shocked when Annabelle switched from the Methodists to the Baptists because the Baptists asked her to play the piano. The Baptist church was just a new basement that barely stuck up out of an empty lot. You went up the steps to the stately Methodist church downtown; you went down the steps to the plain, new Baptist church. From the street all you could see was the black roof and those little, skinny basement windows opened out like trapdoors. It reminded Julia of a magazine picture she'd seen of a World War I bunker somewhere overseas. Every Sunday the Baptists took up a special collection for the building fund. They were going up a floor at a time. For the next eleven years of Sundays, Annabelle was there beside the Baptist preacher (there were six over those years) at the front of the sanctuary, playing beautifully and showing off quite a few new dresses. Over the years Annabelle and the piano rose up from the basement to the second-story sanctuary as if they were on some slow elevator of time.

One cold, iron-colored afternoon, Julia came home from school and showed Annabelle her quiz on a fire-prevention unit they had just completed. Her grade, a pointed red *A*, danced at the top of the paper like a bright flame, like the scarlet *A* Hester Prynne had to wear in the novel they were reading in English.

"Come on," Annabelle said. "That's a good enough excuse to spend some money." She took Julia downtown and bought her a new dress. Julia couldn't wait to get home and bathe and put on the dress. She wanted to have it on when Garner got home from work. She was almost too excited to sit still in Coy's for their lime and cherry Cokes, but she managed. The gray day seeped into Coy's through the plate-glass windows, but the fizzy Cokes, and the bright-green and white department store box, and the deep-blue dress Julia knew was inside, beat up on the dreary day and punched it into lively shapes. As they hurried to the Studebaker, Julia's and Annabelle's breaths came out in puffy clouds and bounced along with them. Even the red frown on the parking meter Annabelle had, as usual, forgotten to pay couldn't dampen their mood. And there was no ticket on the windshield.

Julia stood in the bathroom and admired herself in the mirror. The dress was navy broadcloth with white pinstriping. There was a Chinese mandarin collar with white ties that Julia had finally gotten into a storybook bow. All the way down the front were—Julia loved them—big pearl buttons.

"Come look," she called to Annabelle. She reached behind her to adjust the half-belt in back, and she lifted the skirt so it and her slip would flounce and fall even. *Woof,* the skirt lifted on its own, and sudden heat ran up the backs of Julia's thighs.

She had backed too close to the open bathroom heater. She was on fire.

"Annabelle," she screamed, and she ran to the back door. "Annabelle, help."

Flames came up on both sides of her hips and hurt her arms. She reached high and ran. "Annabelle."

Annabelle met her at the door and jerked her. She jerked Julia through the doorway onto the back porch with her. She jerked the skirt, tore it off completely, and flaming, it fell onto the porch floor and kept burning. Annabelle patted up the backs of Julia's legs and patted all over her bottom, patting crisp black leaves off her body. Flakes of burned slip, burned panties, and burned skin fell to the floor like black potato chips.

A fire truck (Julia never knew who called it) pulled into the backyard, its bell clanging, men jumping off the back and running the flat canvas hose with the long brass nozzle up onto the back porch, where the floorboards had caught fire. Smoke was making a black cloud on the sky-blue porch ceiling, and when the fire was out, there was a black-edged hole in the floor.

Dr. Quinn came and doctored Julia's legs and her bottom and Annabelle's hands, which were burned much worse than any part of Julia. Annabelle's hands had to be wrapped in gauze till each looked like a big club, or a torch waiting to be lit.

The next day the house still smelled throughout of wet charcoal, worse even than the worst Annabelle had ever burned Garner's pork chops. That afternoon a reporter from the Austin *Statesman* came out and asked questions, and the very next day there was an article and a picture of Julia in the paper. Julia was excited about being in the paper and couldn't wait to go back to school. But Garner came to her room, where she had to lie on her stomach in bed and turn her head sideways to see him, and he told her she should be ashamed.

"A lady," Garner told her, "gets her name in the newspaper twice in her lifetime: when she is born and when she dies. The rest of her life should be private. A lady is not notorious."

The following week Julia returned to school. She had to carry a pillow to sit on. Garner hired Fanny Knopke's older sister, Beulah, to cook and help clean house until Annabelle's hands got better. He fussed a little about the expense of having what he called a maid, but he ate more than Julia had ever seen him eat while Annabelle was cooking, and even after Annabelle's hands were healed Beulah Knopke continued to cook weekdays.

When Huldah died, Julia had been afraid of starting a new life with Annabelle and Garner. Now, though she would always love Mother, Julia wished she might live always with Annabelle and Garner, the radio softly humming like some patient, grown-up lover who would wait for Julia forever, the regulator clock in the hall ticking loudly but the hands frozen so that Annabelle—one hand on Julia's arm, the other waving a spatula like a pirate's sword (both hands cured of their burns and all her nails painted bright red)—might always look up from the pork chops she was burning, her face shining with grease and bright makeup, and Garner might always stand across from them, trying to keep a frown in place while he patiently told Annabelle to turn down the flame.

3

AFTER Julia had been living with Annabelle and Garner about a year, her father, George, came to see her all the way from California, where he sold automobiles. Garner was afraid he might have some ideas about taking Julia away, but after he arrived, wearing a white linen suit and driving a brand-new 1934 yellow Cadillac, he suggested that Annabelle and Garner legally adopt Julia. He had hired an attorney in Waco to draw up the papers. He took Julia in the new car all the way up to Waco to get the adoption papers. He kept asking what he could get her.

"Nothing," she said.

"Anything you want."

"I don't want anything."

"There must be something?"

She shook her head and looked out the windows of the automobile. She leaned her head back against the car seat to look all the way to the top of the Amicable building; it was the tallest building she'd ever seen. Her father took her to Cox's department store and showed her new dresses and shiny patent-leather shoes and stuffed animals but she continued to shake her head. They ate lunch in the Roosevelt Hotel, where businessmen in suits and cowboy boots nodded and smiled at her. She kept looking at her father's face to see herself there, like a reflection floating on water, but she decided they didn't favor each other.

They talked about the dark-green clouds moving in and whether they would have tornadoes. Then he asked her once more if there wasn't something special he could buy her.

"Well," she said, remembering a beautiful woman in the Roosevelt Hotel, "there is one thing I'll probably never have that would be nice."

"You name it, Julia."

"It would be very special to have a wristwatch, one that tells the real time."

"You got it, honey. First thing I'm going to do when I get to L.A. is find the prettiest, the most accurate, the very best wristwatch money can buy, and I'm going to have our initials engraved on the back, yours and mine, sweetheart, and put it in the United States mail straight to you."

Julia stared at her name on the adoption papers. She was now, legally, Julia Yates. When Annabelle married Garner she had become Yates; now Julia was the second woman to take Garner's name. She liked it, Yates, five letters, just as Julia had five letters; that was nice. Annabelle and Garner and, now, Julia: all three of them under the same roof were under the same name. She liked it a lot.

Before he left town late that same afternoon, her father showed her snapshots of a woman with long, straight, moon-colored hair. The woman was young and pretty. She sat like an exotic bird in the limbs of a big tree. Her light dress was often lifted above her knees to reveal slender legs. This lady, Julia's father told her, was his new wife. They had married about a year ago. She was a model, from London, England; an actress too.

"Yeah." Julia's father stared off into the west as if he could see what was happening in California. "Any day now you're going to have a half-brother or sister." Low, dark clouds were tipped at the edges with the orange light of the sunset they obscured. Her father looked down and blinked as if he had forgotten she was there, as if he had completely forgotten where he was. Then he flashed Julia a wide smile and said, "Well, kiddo, time is money." She watched the yellow car speed down the street.

Julia sat on the front porch every day and waited for Mr. Conger, the postman, and every day Mr. Conger smiled and shook his head.

"Now, Julia," Mr. Conger said, "it might take a while to search Los Angeles for the best wristwatch. And the mail has a long way to come, desert and mountains to cross."

Julia imagined Mr. Conger lugging his leather bag across roasting sands, pictured him drinking water from a canteen beside a tall, stiff cactus, her watch ticking down inside the mail pouch.

One afternoon Mr. Conger put his foot up on the porch and leaned forward to rest on his thigh. He stared at Julia as he tugged his handkerchief out of his tight hip pocket. He held the white wad of handkerchief in his hand and moved his face around in it. Sweat beaded on the tips of hairs that arched above his forehead. When he shook his head, he flung tiny balls of sweat into the bright air. Mr. Conger shook his head and said, "You break my heart, Julia." After that, she quit waiting.

She did get her wristwatch, though. Garner gave her one.

"Not the best one in Los Angeles," he told her. "Not even the best one in Taylor, but it keeps good time."

September 19, 1934, Bruno Richard Hauptmann was arrested in the Bronx, New York, for kidnapping the Lindbergh baby. Garner had brought Julia a puppy, a Boston terrier, born in a box on a switch engine at the trainyard. Julia named the puppy Bruno. She was certain Bruno Hauptmann was innocent.

"How can you think that?" Annabelle said. "They found the ransom money in Hauptmann's garage."

Julia was disconsolate. She stared at Bruno Hauptmann's face in the newspaper photograph. He had the same sad eyes as her puppy, the same proud, softly defiant expression.

Julia read every word the paper printed about the trial. She felt sorry for the Lindberghs, but she was sure Bruno was just a scapegoat. Annabelle got irritated.

"The wood for the ladder came out of Hauptmann's attic. He's a foreigner and a criminal. They've got him dead to rights."

"It was Isidor Fisch," Julia said.

"Conveniently dead," Annabelle said.

"What do you think, Garner?"

"I think it's a sad business, politicians kissing dead babies."

When Hauptmann was convicted and sentenced to die in the electric chair, Julia wrote him a letter:

Dear Mr. Hauptmann,

I am only a little girl but I want you to know I don't think you would take someone's baby. I have seen pictures of Mrs. Hauptmann and little Manfred and I know you love your own family too much to hurt another family so much. Isidor Fisch must be the one. I wish you had never spent his money. I live in Texas where the sky is so wide I think of you in jail where you can't see far. I will pray for you and hope they find new evidence or the governor or supreme court will give you a reprieve or a pardon. I named my new puppy Bruno and I love him very much. God be with you and your family.

Sincerely,

Julia Yates

Julia's Boston terrier was a year and eight months old when, on Friday, April 3, 1936, at 7:48 P.M., Texas time, a special announcement interrupted *Death Valley Days* on the radio with news of Bruno Richard Hauptmann's execution in the electric chair. Bruno cocked his head and got up to follow his mistress to her room, where she lay on top of the quilt and he scooted under the bed. From the living room, six-shooters fired rapidly, followed by the sound of horses' hooves. On the bed above him, Bruno heard sounds he may or may not have recognized as Julia weeping. There would always be, in Julia's heart, a place for outlaws—a place her mind could not rule.

The night before Halloween, 1938, Garner called Julia and her curious dog to come listen. She and Bruno sat on the floor by the radio; Garner was listening to incredible reports about the invasion of the planet earth by conquering Martians.

"Uncle Garner, is it real?"

Garner chuckled and snorted. "Of course not; it's a Halloween trick. But it's a good one—invaders from Mars."

"I almost believe it," Julia whispered.

"Well"—Garner grinned at her—"there are plenty of dumber things people believe." He unwrapped a Hershey bar and gave her half. She gave half of her half to Bruno, and the three of them let the chocolate dissolve on their tongues while the war of the worlds raged on.

On Christmas Eve, 1939, Julia sat alone in the living room and stared at the colored lights on the Christmas tree. Annabelle was at her dressing table, fixing her hair like Hedy Lamarr in a picture in an old *Collier's* magazine illustrating Hedy's story: "Escape to Hollywood." The wooden rocker between the Christmas tree and the open front door began slowly rocking.

"Annabelle," Julia called. "Annabelle, the rocker is rocking by itself."

"I can't hear you, Julia. If you want to talk to me you'll have to come back here. If I let go of this pin curl I'll never get it back the way Hedy's is in this beautiful picture."

Julia talked to Annabelle's face and her own face in the mirror at the same time.

"Annabelle, if a rocker rocks by itself, someone's going to die." Julia stepped sideways, putting their heads together in the mirror.

"Julia." Annabelle pinned a curl in place and turned to face her. "Julia, Julia. Where do you get all your superstitions?"

"Mother said so. Mother said the morning my mother died, the rocker in her bedroom started rocking by itself."

"You can't pay attention to all Mother's talk. I ought to know. She raised me. And if I'd paid attention to all her wild ideas I wouldn't've had any fun at all. Your mother, Vivian, was just like you, girl. Worrying all the time about what Mother said. Now, I know Mother loved us, loved you too, but love can get out of control and smother you. Vivian never learned that. I want you to learn to speak up and to think for yourself. Don't take horse-and-buggy ideas into the future."

Julia tried not to worry about the rocker. Maybe it hadn't rocked at all, or maybe a breeze through the open door had moved it and maybe that didn't count.

Annabelle showed Julia another picture in *Collier's*—a tall, beautiful woman in a black gown, who stared out through a narrow window—and said, "You should try your hair like that." Annabelle made Julia sit on her dressing stool while she stood behind her and gently brushed and pulled and pinned Julia's hair until it looked exactly like the hair in the magazine. Julia didn't see how Annabelle did it.

That night Garner was late, and Julia began to worry. Annabelle turned on the radio, some choir—"live from Chicago"—singing Christmas carols and right in the middle of "Deck the Halls with Boughs of Holly." Annabelle poured herself a glass of sherry and then she poured a glass for Julia. Julia heard Mother's voice, Isaiah twenty-eight: seven:

... they are swallowed up of wine ...

and I Corinthians six: ten:

Nor thieves, nor covetous, nor drunkards, nor revilers, nor extortioners, shall inherit the kingdom of God.

Annabelle read Julia's thoughts. "Child, I'm going to have to show you the good parts of that book," she said. "Jesus, you should remember, drank wine and knocked around with harlots and tax collectors. Here." She lifted the glass of sherry and, with her eyes, dared Julia not to take it.

The sherry, deep brown, held the lamplight the way polished wood held light. A bitter taste was followed by a sweet echo that came close to the flavor of pecans. Julia didn't exactly like the taste, but she kept wanting to try another swallow to see if it really was pecans. She could not *remember* the taste, and as soon as she swallowed it she had a sensation of loss.

Late that night some railroad men carried Garner through the front door and laid him on the couch. He smiled at Julia and pursed his lips to kiss the air in Annabelle's direction.

"He passed out getting off the train. We wanted to take him to a doctor, but he made us bring him home."

Annabelle thanked them and said he'd be fine. She closed the heavy front door and Julia heard the scrape of the men's shoes against the brick steps and the muffled sound their voices made. Annabelle sat on the edge of the couch and leaned her forehead down against Garner's forehead. Julia took his hand, cool in her own. His eyes stared up. Annabelle's shoulders dropped and Julia knew Garner was dead. He was fifty-one. Julia's wristwatch read 10:10.

After he got the news of Garner's death, there was a late-night phone call (he forgot about the time zones) from Julia's father in Los Angeles.

"Hey, sweetie, I'm sorry to hear about old Garner. Do you and Annabelle need anything? How about money: did Garner leave Annabelle fixed okay?"

Julia said they had everything they needed.

Her father said again that he was sorry. Julia didn't know what to say. She listened to the space between his words, not silence but distance, all the distance between them, the roar of time and space in her ear. Was it the seashell sound of the ocean she held to her ear, the Pacific Ocean? She pictured her father in an aqua-blue Cadillac, the color of the ocean, driving up onto the beach, ocean foam white around fat tires, her father's face red through the windshield, fish swimming back and forth behind the windshield as in a fishbowl, her father holding a black seashell to his head, speaking into its fluted opening. A black cord that became a long, swishing eel, then the tentacle of a giant squid, ran from the seashell into the blue depths of the Cadillac's back seat.

"Goodbye," he said. "I gotta go now, Julia. Goodbye. Goodbye."

"Yes," she said, "goodbye."

"He say anything about your watch?" Annabelle asked.

"No."

"Well, he drinks like a fish," Annabelle said, as if that explained everything.

When Julia graduated from high school her father paid another visit. Her seventeenth birthday was just a week away, but he never mentioned it. He drove up, alone, in a 1941 Plymouth. He had left George junior with his mother in California. George junior was seven.

"I thought you would come in a Cadillac," was all Julia could think to say.

"Switched to Plymouths, babe. More money to be made from the common man."

He drove her from Taylor down to Austin to show her the University of Texas. He bought her pancakes at a place just across the river called the Night Hawk, and then he drove her into the hill country west of town. The limestone ledges and rugged hills were like no landscape Julia had ever seen, but it came closest to the pictures in the back of her Bible of the Holy Land. Short, twisted live oaks and dark, bushy cedars dotted the scraggly tan grass. Here and there prickly pear cactus stuck up like the round, flat ears of Mickey Mouse in the cartoons. Her father pulled off the road and out onto the flat top of a rise that jutted into space above a dry riverbed. The dust settled around them. He pulled a paper sack from beneath his seat and peeled the opening back until the neck of a liquor bottle poked up. He unscrewed the cap and took a pull, released an *ahh* hot with whiskey-burn satisfaction. If he offered her a swig, she decided, she'd take one. She wanted to take a big swallow and hold it in her mouth and feel it burn like a jalapeño pepper while she looked out at the green and gold hills that repeated themselves until they turned blue with distance. But her father didn't offer. He rolled down his window and took another swallow and sighed and leaned back against the seat. Then he told her he was going to send her here, to the University of Texas, told her he was going to pay for everything.

"I've neglected you, but you were better off with Huldah and your aunt Annabelle. It's tough that old Garner passed on. I know things haven't been easy. But you cost a lot too, babe. Vivian paid a high price. Don't ever forget how much love has been spent on you."

And Julia had never forgotten. She had never been able to forget. She loved Mother, and then she loved Annabelle and Garner more than any natural child could have. They took her when they didn't have to. Julia knew she had been the cause of her mother, Vivian's, death.

When her father looked at her she felt as if he were measuring his loss against her worth.

Julia enrolled in the university, but when the time came to pay the tuition, her father failed to send the check, so she ended up on scholarship at the state teachers' college in San Marcos. That fall, Julia became engaged to marry Larry Otto, whose family owned cotton land and ran the mattress factory. Larry was goodhearted, and he was the best dancer in Taylor. His father had given him a new Chrysler. He came to San Marcos every Sunday to take her out to dinner.

It took Larry months to kiss Julia. He put his hands on her shoulders and looked her in the eyes and said:

"Julia, may I kiss you?"

She didn't want to say yes—that would seem as if it was her idea—and she didn't want to say no because it had taken him so long, so she said nothing and tried to look receptive but disinterested at the same time. Finally, he raised his eyebrows and paused again, so she raised her lips to his and waited. She wasn't sure when he had done it, or if he was through, because all he did was touch his lips on top of hers. It could have been the damp breeze or a drop of rain.

Julia opened her eyes, and Larry was grinning as if he'd done something wonderful. Apparently afraid to spoil such a perfect moment, he immediately said good night and disappeared.

The dorm mother was waiting to tell Julia her father had telephoned all the way from California.

"You are to phone him, collect, dear. It's not too late; it's two hours earlier out there."

Julia got change from some girlfriends (she'd never call him collect) and used the pay phone in the lobby. He was going to be passing through town with George junior. He thought she should meet her half-brother. He and the pretty wife from England had divorced. He was taking George junior to Shreveport, Louisiana, to stay with some friends who had moved there from California.

George junior was a shy, thin, blond boy who looked like the wispy ghost of the blond model up in the tree in the snapshots. George junior was only eight, but he seemed like a little old man. His skin was pale, and he smelled vaguely of talcum powder. He spoke carefully and clipped the ends off his words. He was sweet to Julia, and when they were alone he told her their father was an alcoholic and wouldn't last long.

"Which won't be any real loss, I guess," George junior said.

They sat in the wooden swing on Annabelle's front porch. Their father and Annabelle were in the kitchen, drinking gin and tonic. Larry had driven over to meet Julia's father. Now he was out at the street, leaning against the fender of his shiny car. Julia knew Larry wished she would hurry up with this kid.

George junior grabbed Julia's hand and held it the whole time they talked. In spite of the heat, his hand was cool and dry, and Julia saw veins, pale blue beneath his skin. It was the hand of a wizened grandfather.

"Don't you love him, George?"

"Oh, I guess I do, most of the time, at least. It's hard not to love your father. But that doesn't mean you have to like him too. Do *you* love *our* father?"

"What about your mother?" she said.

"Well, I love her too. The trouble with her is she's just too pretty for her own good. Any mirror gives her ideas. But she'll be thirty-five soon, and I figure that'll be the end of her daydreams and she'll want me back. She's been giving her acting career one more year since I was born. Once she quits loving herself so much, she might love me too."

While George junior talked, Julia watched a pale-gray pigeon doing a slow business in bugs along the cracked sidewalk in front of the house. The pigeon walked with his chest out and his head tilted back, nodding absentmindedly. He bent to poke his head into a crack and held up something tiny and dark in his beak. He was like one of Julia's professors at the college, his beak a pointer indicating an important detail. The gray, sidestepping pigeon was also like this serious, wise-old little boy—her own half-brother—holding her hand while he spoke. She was sad and happy at the same time. She wanted to hold George junior in her arms. She felt keenly aware of a bond between them. She didn't understand these feelings; she felt the same way when she finished a particularly good novel and a lump rose in her throat and she felt like laughing and crying at the same time.

"I'm glad to finally meet you, George. I wish you could come live here so we could get to know each other."

"I think of you a lot, Julia. Sometimes, in my mind, I call you Sis and things like that. You are sort of my imaginary playmate, you know, like little kids have."

They walked around the block together, and Julia heard Larry popping acorns underfoot, a little ways behind them. Then their father's shoes slapped down the porch steps, and in an exhalation of cigarette smoke, he said, "Well, *adiós,* sweetheart. I guess we menfolks better hit the dusty trail."

As it turned out, that was her father's final visit. She never saw him or George junior again. Her father died the following year, on Easter Sunday.

George junior wrote down her address and said he might like to write her from time to time, and that they would spend a long visit together once he was grown and she was through college and they could come and go as they pleased. George junior did write her from time to time, from a succession of military schools. Eventually he was sent to fight in Korea and ended up missing in action.

Julia told him he would always be welcome to visit her and Larry after they were married.

He smiled and said, "No, I don't think so, Sis."

"Why not?"

George junior stopped to stare at Larry, who stood about ten yards behind them glancing at his wristwatch.

"'Cause my half-sister is going to do a whole lot better than that Larry."

And she did.

PART TWO

Avery

1

WHEN Julia was nineteen, the age at which her mother had died of childbirthing, she met Avery Marrs, and it was revealed to her that this man, Avery, loved her. That God's grace might take such a shape in her life amazed her. God did work in mysterious ways.

When she met Avery, Julia was wearing Larry Otto's engagement ring. Avery had a date with Julia's roommate, Arlene. Julia had told Larry not to come see her that weekend because she was studying for a philosophy exam, and she didn't understand the first thing about philosophy. Arlene insisted Julia take a study break and come to dinner with her and Avery.

Avery picked them up in a big cattle truck he drove weekends. He also worked in the college cafeteria and mowed the college grass to help pay his tuition.

Arlene, frankly, was not surprised Julia and Avery hit it off. Avery was fun to be with. Much later, Arlene admitted to asking Julia along in the hope that Avery would make her think twice about marrying that goody-goody, rich-but-dull Larry.

Avery walked Julia and Arlene back to the dorm and then he said, "Good night, Arlene."

Arlene smiled and said good night.

Julia smiled, too, and turned to follow Arlene, when Avery took her wrist and, in a way that left no doubt about his intention, pulled her down a step until she stood right against him.

"Good night, Avery," Julia said. "It was nice of you and Arlene to let me tag along."

"Hush," he said, and his lips were moving over hers. "Hush,

hush," his lips whispered against hers, and his hand opened wide and flat against her back and moved up and down her spine. She felt the warmth of his palm against her skin as if her blouse had vaporized in the heat of his kiss.

"Avery's kiss was," Julia testified later, to Arlene, "out of this world."

Avery worked late nights unloading cattle at the auction pens. After curfew, Julia wrapped a towel around her hair and put a housecoat on over her clothes and carried a wash basket down to the basement laundry room. Beneath a couple of dirty blouses she carried clean, neatly folded clothes.

Avery backed the cattle truck up to the basement window, and Julia crawled out and slipped into the cab beside him. With the lights out, they coasted down the hill and he popped the clutch. The engine roared, and they took off for a honky-tonk drive-in, where they had hamburgers and cold beer and listened to Ted Daffan's Texans sing "Born to Lose" and "No Letter Today" from jukebox speakers hung outside. Avery drove her back to the college and eased the truck up the hill behind the dorm and cut the motor and took her in his arms. Julia smelled hay and manure from the truck and beer and onion on Avery's breath. Most girls would prefer Larry with his new Chrysler and his minty breath and nice manners. But Avery was sure of himself, and that made Julia feel sure of herself too. She loved his hands moving over her body, and she felt no guilt.

Julia kissed Avery one more time and got out of the truck. She dropped through the basement window, wrapped her head in the towel, and slipped her housecoat back over her clothes. On tiptoes, she leaned up to the narrow window and watched the one good tail-light of the cattle truck dance down the hill. Then, humming "No Letter Today," she picked up her basket of clean, folded clothes and carried them to her room.

Somehow, Larry found out Julia had been seeing Avery, and Larry drove down from Taylor to talk to her.

"I don't mind your having friends, dear," Larry told her. "I want you to go to college functions and enjoy yourself while you're down here. But after all, we are engaged, and certain behavior just doesn't look right. Besides, I don't want you associating with someone like Avery Marrs. He's not your type."

Julia wanted to know just what her type was.

"You know what I mean," Larry said. "Avery Marrs has a reputation as a heller. He's got several low-level jobs because his family won't or can't support him. They're just common. He's wild. He drinks too much. I don't mind your going out from time to time, but I don't want you seeing Avery again."

"Oh, Larry, you should hear yourself. Avery isn't so much wild as he likes to have fun. And he's just about quit drinking since he met me. Maybe I'm supposed to be his friend, to be a good influence."

While Julia spoke, a beat-up old Chevy squealed to a stop in front of the girls' dormitory. Avery rode on the running board, holding the doorpost with one hand, his free hand up in the air like a rodeo rider's. Avery's big mutt, Amigo, lay on the car's roof. The motor died, the tires locked, and the Chevy swerved alongside the curb and slid just enough to bump Larry's new Chrysler. Larry still held both Julia's shoulders, but he was looking at the black Chevy, his mouth open. Amigo, part coon hound and part Airedale, slid down the car's windshield onto the hood, where he stood and woofed and howled. At least six boys came out of the car—two through the back windows—and Avery pulled a lariat from thin air and began to twirl a running noose over his head. Just as Avery let the loop go, Larry let go of Julia's shoulders. The noose fell over the small U.S. Mail box that stood on an iron post. Avery whooped and Amigo howled.

"Y-e-e-e-h-a-a-h," Avery yelled. "I lassoed me the mail." He pulled the noose tight and jumped from the running board, the rope in both hands, legs spread, heels dug in the grass. With a jerk, Avery pulled the letter box sideways, bending the angle iron it was mounted on. "No Letter Today," Avery sang, out of tune and off key, but loud, loud.

Three weeks after they met, Avery told Julia he was going to drop out of school and join the army. He asked Julia to marry him before he enlisted. Julia still wore Larry's diamond engagement ring. She took the ring off.

"I'll mail this back tomorrow," she said.

"No," Avery said. "I want you to take it back in person. I want it on your finger while you sit across from him at the supper table and while you visit with his parents in their fine parlor and when you sit with him on the porch, where you can look out at all the land they own and think about the life you can have with him. I want that ring on your finger when he puts his arms around you and kisses you good night. And then, with his kiss fresh on your lips and the day's visit fresh in your mind, if you think you can live with him, if you think you can live without me, then I want you to leave that ring right where it is. But if you know, right then, you can't live without me, then I want you to take that ring off and put it in his hand."

"You *want* me to go see Larry?"

"That's right."

"But why? I don't want to see him. I don't need to see him. I love you, Avery."

"Good. Then do this for me."

"But why?"

"Because someday, way in our future, somewhere else, maybe, when we've had a rough time and you aren't as happy with me as you are right now, I don't want you to wonder if you made a mistake. I don't want you to wonder what life with Larry would have been like. I don't want to be compared to some dreamed-up memory."

So Julia went back to Taylor and spent most of the weekend with Larry and his family in their big Victorian house surrounded by cotton fields. And on Sunday afternoon, after Larry kissed her for only the second time all weekend, she gave him back his ring. She said what she could to make Larry feel all right. It was easier than she had anticipated. All she could think about was getting back to Avery.

Three days later, Julia and Avery married. Annabelle was their only witness. Avery had saved money for a wedding night in the Rice Hotel, in Houston. But the Rice was full up—Houston was full up. Avery drove to Galveston, where the story was the same, except for a place Avery said smelled bad. After midnight, they drove down the beach, to spend the night under the stars. The shore patrol stopped them for driving with their lights on during a blackout. Two big, mean-looking men in uniforms, with dark bands around their big biceps, SP printed there, came over to Avery's window; billy sticks and pistols and handcuffs fastened to their wide belts rattled as they walked. The biggest one leaned close and yelled at Avery. Avery yelled back, just as mean. Avery said he didn't know about the damned blackout, that this was his wedding night; he had two days before he'd be in uniform too. "Follow us," the biggest one growled.

Soon they were in the lobby of Galveston's Jack Tar Motel, and the big SP was banging a black nightstick on the desk. In ten minutes Avery and Julia had a two-room housekeeping suite, the only room left, compliments of the manager.

Julia had one married friend, Elsie Tutweiler. Elsie had married Joe Tutweiler and moved out of the dorm but stayed in school one more semester to graduate. Julia had confided in Elsie that she was embarrassed to think of undressing in front of a man, even Avery. Elsie told her not to worry, it wouldn't be like that.

"My Joe had to go get cigarettes. Probably Avery will have to go get cigarettes too. Then you can get all ready and be under the covers when he gets back. I wore a cute little dido that Joe just loved."

By the time Julia and Avery got to their rooms at the Jack Tar it was almost four in the morning. Julia went into the bathroom to shower, worried about coming out in her nightie, and Avery called through the bathroom door.

"Julia, I've gotta go get cigarettes. Be back in a minute."

He was gone long enough for Julia to shower and put on her nightgown and get under the covers.

Julia had never made love before, yet the motions her body made with Avery's seemed familiar. Her legs and his legs locked together like old friends embracing. Her hands moved over his skin, seeing his body clearly, her eyes sightless in the dark and in the black blur of Avery's eyes and hair. The warm fog of his breathing moistened her lips and cheek.

Julia's body strained *against* Avery's body and *with* his body at the same time. She felt as if she might pass through Avery's skin as a ghost passes through a closed door and on the other side, the inside, discover wonders beyond her imagination. And there was a moment in which she hung, suspended, on the very verge of flesh merging. Then she lay beneath the wing his folded arm and elbow made, feeling her body cool where air kissed sweaty skin, feeling the tremor of his voice down his rib cage, the xylophone ripple of his words. His hands were folded behind his head, someone ready to do sit-ups, but easy, at rest, and he told her how the world began, the first installment of a nightly ritual of bedtime mythology:

Deucalion and his wife, Pyrrha, of the race of Prometheus, escaped Jupiter's flooding of the earth and prayed for guidance from the gods. An oracle told them to veil their heads, unbind their garments, and cast behind them the bones of their mother. In the darkness of a deep forest they tried to resolve the oracle—how could they profane the remains of their mother? Finally, Deucalion declared that Earth was the greatest mother and the stones were her bones. They veiled their faces and loosed their clothes and threw the stones behind them.

As Julia let herself fall into sleep, the stones grew soft and took shape, the water and slime from the flood that covered the stones became flesh, the stony part became bones, and those thrown by

Deucalion became men, while those thrown by the hand of Pyrrha became women.

"To this day," Avery whispered, "humans are hard creatures, and the hard work men and women do testifies to this beginning."

Julia opened her eyes. Venetian blinds of sunlight striped Avery's jaw and neck. Light polished the red circle on a pack of Luckies like an apple on the bedside table. Beside the Luckies was a Hershey bar with almonds.

"Got that for you last night," Avery said. "I remembered you said Garner used to bring you Hershey bars to bed."

It was the first present Avery had ever given Julia. He'd told her, before they married, there was no way he could compete with all the fancy presents Larry gave her—he wouldn't even try. Larry had sent her a silver tray for a wedding present. The tray was beautiful, but Julia returned it without ever telling Avery she'd received it. For the first year she was married to Avery he gave her something, something he got especially for her, every day. It might be a Hershey bar, or a pint of strawberries, or a smooth branch off a cedar tree, shaped like a wing. He never missed a day.

After they married, Avery was stationed in Leesville, Louisiana. His best army buddy, Tiny Tolar, went out with an older woman, Mary Dimanche, who ran a restaurant in Leesville. Julia spent two weeks in Leesville, where she stayed with Mary's family. Mamère Dimanche, Mary's grandmother, brought Julia a little cup of strong coffee to bed every morning. The boys got off base every night, and the three of them hung out at the restaurant till Mary got off, then they all went dancing. They played "One Dozen Roses" and "Paper Doll" and "South of the Border" on the jukebox. They danced and danced and danced. After the juke joints closed up for the night, Avery and Tiny took Julia and Mary frog gigging. They drove slowly, along back roads, and when they heard frogs they stopped and shone lights in the ditches alongside the roads. They got a gunnysack full of bullfrogs. Back at the Dimanches', they fried up the frog legs, and Mary's daddy got out of bed to eat and drink beer with them.

After Leesville, Avery went to Air Force Cadet School at Kelly Field in San Antonio, and Julia got a job in censorship. Avery couldn't leave cadet school. The first time Julia went out to see him, she cried because they had shaved his hair and it made his ears stick out so. He hated cadet school. A sergeant, he was used to giving orders. Now he was taking orders, silly orders. They had him picking up rocks and sitting on only three inches of his chair at meals. One night he slipped out and phoned the boardinghouse where Julia shared a room. Her roommate had a car and let Julia use it. The only room in the Menger Hotel that night was the sample room, and Julia and Avery made love and slept in a single bed surrounded by big tables for displaying merchandise.

Avery had the highest scores in his class in cadet school, but he washed out for being underweight. Julia had never seen him happier. He was stationed at Brooks Field across town, and they got an apartment and set up housekeeping together for the first time since their marriage. They didn't have a car, but Avery had a pal at Brooks who picked him up and dropped him off daily on his motorcycle. They were near a bus line that got Julia to the Bureau of Censorship.

On the top floor of the federal building, she and a roomful of other women checked the U.S. Mail against watch lists. Every letter to or from someone on a watch list was pulled and read. Anything suspicious, anything that might be in code, was sent to another room, for a closer look. There were plenty of German descendants in south Texas, and all German names were on watch lists. More than once, Julia had to read a letter addressed to someone she knew. The women who worked in censorship had been screened and cleared by the FBI. They left jackets and purses in a cloakroom and were required to wear dresses and blouses without pockets.

On Julia's twentieth birthday, her first with Avery, he took her out to the Kit Kat Klub. In the powder room, Julia opened her purse and saw an envelope. Julia snapped her purse shut. A woman beside her was putting on lipstick. She stared at Julia in the mirror. Julia went back to the table to ask Avery what she should do. He had her telephone her boss, Mr. Webb, at his home. Mr. Webb told them to meet him at the federal building right away. Avery had borrowed his friend's motorcycle for the evening and Julia felt like a spy when they rumbled up in front of Mr. Webb and two men she didn't know. The men questioned her and Avery, and they questioned her boss, Mr. Webb. The letter was addressed to a Miss Brownie Lee in San Antonio. It had no return address but was postmarked Miami, Florida. There was no Brownie Lee on the watch lists, but the letter was sent to the code experts anyway. After about three hours they told Julia she and Avery could go. Apparently, they believed her when she told them she had no idea how the letter got into her purse. Mr. Webb's theory was that someone wanted to get Julia in trouble, because Julia was faster than most of the other workers.

Avery had promised to return the motorcycle by midnight, so they just had time to get an omelet at Earl Abel's. Avery dropped Julia at their apartment and returned the motorcycle. In fifteen minutes his friend brought him back.

In bed, in the dark room, Avery's cigarette was a red-tipped wand in his hand, moving figure eights in the air beside her, conducting some band in his head, as he hummed "South of the Border."

"Let's go dancing," he said.

"What?"

"It's your birthday. I want to take you dancing."

"We don't have a way."

"Get dressed," he said, the red tip of his cigarette bobbing with his words. He was already up, beside the chair where he'd tossed his clothes.

Soon they were walking in the warm June night, headed north along San Pedro Avenue to a little joint Avery remembered seeing. It must have been two or three miles, then Julia heard "Oh Johnny" and saw blue neon through an oak tree: the Bluebonnet Club. Before the place closed, they danced four dances; Avery got them a ride home with a waitress and her boyfriend. Back in bed no more than an hour since she'd left it, Julia told Avery her feet ached.

"Let's forget we walked for half an hour; let's pretend we danced all night and that's why our feet hurt," he said. Then he told her the story of Ariadne, who helped Theseus escape from the labyrinth but was abandoned by him on the island of Naxos. Venus took pity on Ariadne and promised her an immortal lover to replace the mortal lover she had lost. Bacchus found her and gave her a golden crown studded with jewels as a marriage gift. When Ariadne died, Bacchus threw her crown up into the heavens, where the jewels burned so brightly they became stars.

The next night, Avery took Julia out and pointed to a curved line of stars, a backward C, Corona Borealis, the Northern Crown, the crown of Ariadne. He told her the Milky Way is the road the gods walk when Jupiter calls them to council; the sparkling road is lined with the palaces of the gods. Avery pointed to Vega, the brightest star in the constellation Lyra, the lyre of Orpheus, who played music so sweet that all the beasts, even the songbirds, stopped to listen.

"When Orpheus died," Avery said, "the gods put his lyre into the heavens as a tribute to his deathless love of Eurydice, his wife."

Avery gave Julia the stars in the heavens, and never, in all the years of her marriage to Avery, did Julia wonder about a life with Larry Otto.

2

JULIA had grown up with heavenly rules from Huldah's Bible and earthly etiquette from popular books of the time (which Annabelle read and passed along).

Huldah had left Julia the cadences of King James's Bible and the rhythm of the hairbrush. "We must suffer to be beautiful, child. Beauty is difficult," Mother repeated and repeated.

Julia had the example of Annabelle's life, her joy in finding the music in things, her certainty that the facts didn't always add up to the truth. "Julia, honey, try to keep your mind and heart as open as a twenty-four-hour café," Annabelle said.

But between what Huldah had not thought Julia was ready to know and what Annabelle assumed everyone already knew, Julia grew up shamefully ignorant of what Annabelle's books sometimes called the "facts of life."

Julia had, for instance, no idea that men and women, even married men and women, might enjoy kissing one another *down there*. Huldah had never quoted from the Song of Solomon. "Oral sex" was certainly not in any of the popular books Annabelle read in the late '30s, and so it was not in Julia's vocabulary.

When Julia married Avery she was, in the vernacular, "still a virgin." (It had taken Larry Otto months to work up to one, unremarkable kiss, and Avery spent scant days with Julia before he married her.) She knew, without asking, that Avery was, to use the vernacular again, "experienced." In keeping with the popular attitudes of the times, Julia did not consider her lack of experience a deficiency, and Avery's worldliness secretly pleased her. In Avery's arms, much that she had never dreamed of seemed as natural as it was delightful.

Julia had been married two years before she ever heard the word *homosexual.* She asked Avery what it meant, and when he told her she couldn't believe she had never thought of it before.

"It's just another kind of love," Avery said. "The Greeks and Romans, for instance, thought it was natural enough."

"Of course," Julia said. "We should all be able to do that. Men and women, men and men, women and women. It would make things better, wouldn't it?"

"It might, at that," he said. "But it would have to happen to everyone, overnight, like hunger."

Until she met other wives and listened to their complaints, Julia assumed all men and women spent many slow hours learning from each other what their bodies desired. Her friends' stories made Julia appreciate how unlimited was her limited experience with one man. But the stories they told were difficult for her to believe. Men who didn't like to touch. Women who thought their husbands' genitals were ugly. Julia listened to her friends as if they were using a foreign language or speaking in some code or jargon. They made her feel stupefied, as if she had missed a universal experience. Their stories must be true for them, just as the stories she read in magazines and newspapers about brutal murders were true for killers and their victims. She would not ever let their stories, their views, become hers.

For a while, before her death, Annabelle lived with Julia and Avery. Annabelle adored Avery. They were two of a kind, full of energy and fun. The three of them went dancing together at least once a week. Avery danced with Julia and then with Annabelle and then with Julia. If Julia had let him, he would have dragged them both onto the dance floor at the same time. He joked about having two good-looking gals, one for each arm.

Annabelle was just as silly. "Must be entering my second childhood," she said.

Julia smiled in spite of herself. She thought Annabelle had never left her first childhood. Julia remembered how Uncle Garner had put up with her and Annabelle before he gave up his ghost. Julia pictured him reclining on his side on a soft cloud, the side of his face resting in the palm of his hand as he gazed down over the edge of his heavenly chaise longue and smiled at the three of them. Garner's angelic smile was no more benevolent or patient than his earthly smile had been. Julia watched her husband and her aunt and smiled along with her departed adoptive father. Avery and Annabelle cut up so, Julia felt as if she were out with two teenagers.

Julia's next-door neighbor said she sure wouldn't let her husband carry on like that.

"What do you mean?" Julia said.

"I mean your aunt Annabelle is still an attractive package."

"But she's my aunt. And she's too old for Avery."

"She doesn't *act* too old, and they seem mighty friendly to me," the neighbor said.

"Of course they're friendly; they love each other."

"That's just the point." The neighbor raised her cup of coffee and held it to her lips and stared at Julia over rising wisps of heat.

"Oh, Lord. I'm talking about a different kind of love," Julia said.

The next-door neighbor pursed her lips and took a slow sip of the hot coffee. She set her cup back in its saucer so hard the spoon jumped and clinked, but she said nothing.

After the war, in the early years of his job, Avery traveled. He knew everyone in south Texas. Avery would call on anybody, and he sold boxes to little hole-in-the-wall companies and big businesses alike. His territory went from San Antonio south to Corpus Christi, down to the Rio Grande Valley—Brownsville, Harlingen, McAllen—and back up through Laredo, Eagle Pass, and Del Rio. The border was all his; no other salesman wanted it. He spoke pretty fair Spanish, though Julia never knew where he'd learned it, and got along equally well with Mexicans and whites. His customers told Julia, "That husband of yours, he's a born salesman. Got *me* calling *him*. You tell him to come see me; I've got a big order for him."

For years, Julia listened to traveling salesman jokes. She stared serenely over coffee at the incredulous face of the next-door neighbor, an unhappy woman, who found it hard to believe (and vaguely threatening) that Julia wasn't jealous of Avery, a good-looking man, on the road so much.

"Temptation," she told Julia, "is *out there,* like a tragic accident, just waiting to happen." The neighbor said it as if she had invented the idea.

"But Avery loves me," Julia said.

"Love is where you find it."

Which was true.

But Julia knew that she and Avery had found it with each other. No hands were Avery's hands but Avery's hands. Beneath Avery's palms and fingertips Julia's skin knew it had no rival. When

Avery kissed her, her teeth and gums and lips and tongue felt so bright she knew that if she walked where other people were, she would blind them.

"How do you know how to kiss better than anyone else?" Julia asked Avery.

"How do you know someone else wouldn't kiss better?"

"I just know. Now answer me."

"I'm Martian," Avery said with a grin. "Where'd you think I got my name? Ours was a dying planet—we didn't call it Mars, of course. Used to an arid climate, we landed in Texas. There are Marrses all over these hills. We walk among you earthlings disguised as ordinary humans, living ordinary lives."

Which is how Julia came to think of Avery—as in disguise. The ordinariness of the life they lived together kept their secret. Avery lived the perfect double-agent life of a controlled schizophrenic. He was *in* the world but not *of* the world. She lived with a Martian. What color were his skies—red, purple, silver? Did his blood run electric green? She knew how his lips, the petals of man-eating plants, sucked her life right out, how his several deep lungs pumped life back.

Avery told her the story of Melampus, the first mortal to have the gift of prophecy. In front of Melampus's house was an old oak tree in which there was a nest of snakes. The servants killed the grown snakes, but Melampus saved the baby snakes and fed and cared for them. One day while Melampus dozed beneath the oak, the snakes licked his ears with their forked tongues. When Melampus awakened he understood the language of birds and creeping things. Now Melampus was able to foretell the future, and he became a renowned prophet. His enemies captured and imprisoned him. During the night, termites in the walls and timbers talked to one another. Melampus listened and learned that the timbers were almost eaten through and the roof was about to collapse. He woke his captors, who heeded his warning and saved themselves and Melampus, whom they held in great respect thereafter. Julia thought that Avery, like Melampus, understood the language of all creatures.

As Julia lived with Avery, he grew more familiar and her feelings deepened, but making love did not, as the neighbor lady had predicted, get old. The hands holding her were familiar, she knew Avery's touch, but the many ways it felt to be touched by him were always changing. Like physical pain and certain tastes (the glass of sherry the night Garner died, for example), the physical sensations of lovemaking were impossible to remember. She could remember the song playing softly on the radio, the slant of lamplight that angled down the hall from the living room, and the curved gray shape of Avery's shoulder that slant of light cast on the wall beside the bed. She remembered how good her body felt when Avery's fingertips, Avery's tongue, the length of Avery's leg, brushed against her. But she could not recall just how it felt to have an orgasm. As that process began—muscles rolling like waves of their own accord—as it started happening she started remembering how it would feel. Part of the deep pleasure, she thought, was the shuddering recognition of this sweet mystery.

The next-door neighbor worked on Julia. She had made Julia's naïveté one of her main concerns. If Julia wouldn't believe *her*, maybe she'd listen to an *expert*. Such an expert was available. He was in town for one week at the neighbor's church, preaching a revival meeting. This man had run a home for unwed mothers. He had counseled men and women whose marriages were in shambles and helped them stay together. He was God's messenger. The neighbor was convinced it was in God's plan for Julia to hear the message this man brought. She begged Julia to go with her.

The sermon was called "Adults Only: A Christian View of Sex."

"Any man," the preacher shouted, "any man who says he does not have unclean thoughts while he dances with a woman is either a liar or he's a Superman. And outside of the funny papers, there's only one Superman. There's only one Superman, and He died for your lust."

The preacher was a big, barrel-chested man with a widow's peak of black shiny hair. There was a wide banner over the front doors of the church, with the preacher's name, HABAKKUK, one word, painted in red, jagged letters, like fiery red bolts of lightning.

Julia asked her neighbor, "Is that his name, just one word, Habakkuk?"

And her neighbor said yes, that was it, like the prophet Habakkuk.

"You mean," Julia said, "that's his stage name?"

Her neighbor's response was to purse her lips disapprovingly and then to show Julia the Scripture reading for Habakkuk's sermon, from Proverbs, chapter six:

> For by means of a whorish woman *a man is brought* to a piece of bread: and the adulteress will hunt for the precious life.

Julia tried to imagine Avery having "unclean thoughts" while he danced with Annabelle and then with her, and she decided Habakkuk and her neighbor were the ones with unclean thoughts. But she liked the Scripture. She liked the adulteress, whom God had given the longing for bread. Like a beautiful bird, the adulteress. She flew all over the earth, rested in trees and thick brush, searched for one bright bit of bread, pecked at tree bark and hard ground for the white bite, the brief taste sufficient, of the precious life. Was it God's curse or God's gift that the adulteress, a wad of feathers and bright colors and hollow bones, could love only in secret and be loved only secretly? A night bird, she fed in darkness, behind cover, in secret, the way we were taught to pray: to thy Father which seeth in secret. Julia went home and read the rest of Proverbs six and thought that, for all her strange nature, the evil woman that can take thee with her eyelids carried God's own secret power and, yes, God's love too. The adulteress could cause man to take fire in his bosom, and that, Julia decided, was an unholy holiness, a holy unholiness, the sharp sting of love let loose in nature. Strutting His stuff, God must love lust too, the lovely lines of nature's dark back and buttocks.

When Julia had her periods, the red-clay-colored promise of life, Avery pulled the covers off the bed and they lay on the cool top sheet. Afterward, Julia lifted the stained sheet up and played the game she had played with clouds when she was a child. She read dark-red Rorschach stains. The shapes love had taken—God's grace manifested in her life: wing, lettuce leaf, mitten, rose, lake, skull, mushroom cloud, mountain, bell, drumstick, star.

When Julia got pregnant with Coleman, she and Avery watched her body change. Never before had lovemaking been so full of power. There between them was the slowly growing result of their love and their desire. Avery rolled her onto her side and came into her from behind while he caressed the tight, swollen skin of her belly as if it were a third, wonderfully erotic breast, and he lay between her legs for hours talking to their baby, his lips and breath tickling her skin. *Fullness* was the word Julia thought, a sodden sponge, engorged but still ravenous.

3

COLEMAN AVERY MARRS was born August 8, 1947. He wasn't the only one. The war was over and men were back home and it was obvious what everyone had been doing nine months before. The Medical and Surgical Memorial Hospital was crowded with women in labor, punching the air and wailing as if they were keening after some natural disaster. Babies screamed in the crowded nursery and on little carts lined up in the hallway.

"Avery," Julia said, "this is awful. How can they keep them straight?"

"ID bracelets."

"You have to keep watch. Make sure they don't mix up our baby with someone else's."

"Don't worry, I'll know him or her. Remember, this baby is half Martian; the blood is different."

"Avery, promise me, as soon as you see our baby, you make sure there's nothing wrong—you count the fingers and the toes, check everything."

Avery had made the same promise for weeks. He promised once more and left to sign Julia in. She watched him move down the crowded hall, watched as Avery stepped around a nurse to embrace Annabelle, who was hurrying to meet them. He pivoted, Annabelle in his arms, a neat dance step, released Annabelle, and continued down the hall.

"This place is a madhouse," Annabelle said. "Have you been here long?"

"Just got here," Julia said. "And I'm starving. I wouldn't leave till the movie was over, and all I've had is popcorn."

"What do you want?"

"They told me not to eat, but I would *love* a hamburger."

Annabelle winked. "There's a joint across from the parking lot. I'll be right back."

"With lettuce and tomato and pickles and onion and mustard. Lots of onion and mustard."

There was nowhere to sit in the crowded waiting room. Julia found an empty space in the hallway and eased down against the wall to the floor. An orderly stepped over her legs, and she pulled them in as close as her swollen belly allowed. The tile floor was cool against her legs. The heat was terrible, even for San Antonio. Avery had taken her to the movies to relax, try to cool off. Julia hoped the baby came soon, while it was still night and not as hot.

Annabelle returned before Avery. She knelt beside Julia and opened her handbag. Julia smelled the onions before Annabelle got the burger out. Annabelle folded the waxy paper so the bun peeked out like a banana from its skin. It was the best hamburger Julia had ever tasted.

Avery finally came back with a nurse, who led Julia to a doorway, handed her a hospital gown, and wordlessly opened the door. Inside, Julia was surrounded by floor-to-ceiling shelves stacked with rolls of toilet paper, wrapped like her hamburger in white paper. There was a box ripped open to reveal thousands of wooden tongue depressors that looked like extra-large Popsicle sticks, and there were several boxes labeled: STERILE RUBBER GLOVES. In this little storage room Julia changed into a thin cotton hospital gown and stuffed her clothes into her overnight bag.

The nurse got Julia on a gurney and wheeled her through swinging doors where Avery and Annabelle were not allowed to follow. Julia looked for Avery's face and saw a masked, turbaned head. *This place is a madhouse.* Was she in the laboratory of a mad doctor? Everything was white. There was steam; metal clanged. Had they wheeled her into an enormous kitchen? She sniffed, tried to identify cooking smells. A gloved hand came down over her face. The movie had just begun when the pains started. Avery wanted to leave, but Julia insisted on staying. Movies cost money. Rita Hayworth was Gilda; she was taking off her long white gloves. The gloves covered Julia's nose. The air was cold, Julia's breath cold, and there was a smell of glue. Someone had broken something, and Julia had to glue it back together. What a waste. Julia had to fix it.

Julia opened her eyes, and Annabelle's face bobbed into the whiteness. Objects slowly floated down into Julia's view and rested against the walls, on the floor. A crucifix, a light switch, metal side rails of a bed like the stake-bed truck Avery used to haul cattle in. A white curtain walled her in.

Nothing stayed put. The crucifix and the light switch pulsed, the bed rocked faintly back and forth as if Julia were on a boat. Her stomach had been swollen and firm; now it felt like a pillow stuffed up under her chin. She wanted to speak, to ask Annabelle about the baby, but her throat burned up into her ears, and she realized she was throwing up. Down her front, on the white sheet, yellow liquid glistened, reflected light, was sticky and shiny as the trail a snail leaves on a sidewalk. Her teeth—her teeth lay scattered in the yellow slime. Her hand slid into the slippery liquid. Not her teeth. Chopped white squares of onion. Her chest bucked and her throat burned again. She couldn't stop hot yellow spew, out and back, burned back up into her nose.

She was underwater. Above her shimmered the bright white-yellow surface. She had to get up there and break through to clear air. She was sinking deeper; the bright light was going dim.

She could not see. She had to reach her feet to feel if they were there. How many toes? Count fingers and toes. Two tens. Four fives. Twenty ones. Little toes with soft white nails like bits of teeth, chops of onion. Little fingers spread like pink starfish, like soft flower petals, rose-petal fingernails.

Time floated, bobbed about like flower petals on water, hovered more than passed. Edges of flower petals turned brown where they danced in place. Water only swayed, flowed nowhere.

Julia saw white light again, and she thought all this in one instant: Your real mother Vivian died bringing you into this world you know the price you pay for love you will die too bringing this baby small dark pleats darts at the corners of Vivian's photograph album paper thick and crumbly color and smell of shortbread dark pleats darts corners of Vivian's mouth her eyes slanting Oriental eyes see dead Vivian when your slanted eyes open her sliced face you saw with baby eyes twenty-three years ago her face your face she gave you then you gave . . .

"Your baby, Julia," Avery said. "Look at that face."

"Open your eyes," Annabelle said.

It was the ugliest baby Julia had ever seen.

"Our son," Avery said. "Coleman Avery Marrs—Ole King Cole before he's old. All fingers and toes present and accounted for. He's got all his equipment, and everything is in working order." Avery grinned down at her as if he had built the baby himself in some basement workshop.

"He's so red and so wrinkled," Julia said. And he was. Red and raw-looking; skin hung in folds at his little elbows; dark, slate-blue eyes slanted under red folds of skin. Julia pulled his blanket back and let her eyes lick up and down him like a mother bear licking her cub into shape. Wisps of black hair matted like down behind his ears and on the back of his neck. Little white bumps covered his cheeks. Julia touched each tiny finger and toe, whispering the numbers as she went:

One for the money, two blackbirds sitting on a hill, three blind mice, four angels overhead, five catching fishes all alive, six pick-up sticks, seven swans a-swimming, eight for a dollar and all very nice, nine nimble noblemen nibbling nonpareils, ten little Injuns standing in a line. One's none, two's some, three's a many, four's a penny, five's a little hundred. This little pig went to market, this little pig stayed home, this little pig had roast beef, this little pig had none, this little pig went wee, wee, wee, all the way home.

His toenails seemed to be still forming, like a photograph taking shape in the developing fluid, the pale slivers on his two littlest toes translucent as two crescent moons in daylight sky. She turned him over and he held himself still, his eyes steady and unafraid. His back was his best feature, the straight crease of his spine, the smooth flesh curving out on both sides like an opened book. His little butt was flat and covered with clear blisters. His thin bird legs dripped at the knees and ankles with folds of red skin. The sac between his legs was tight and swollen; the penis, smeared with some kind of grease after circumcision, stuck up like a Vienna sausage, the head pink and raw-looking. His belly button was black and also shone with a glob of grease. Julia cradled him in the crook of her arm and put her fingertips on his chest, felt his tiny ribs just beneath the skin. His nipples were two more pale, daytime moons, full moons.

"I imagine he's hungry. He hasn't had a decent meal since he was born," Annabelle said. "You've been out of commission for four days. See what he does with one of those soda fountains. You don't get to have big bosoms just for the fun of it, you know."

"Four days?" Julia held her son close and opened the front of her gown. Her nipple was swollen, looked too large for his mouth.

She brought her breast to his lips and his hands opened and brushed against her. His breathing tickled her skin, the soft prickle of blown dandelion spikes. He opened his mouth. His tongue matched his back, a smooth center line, firm curves of flesh, warm and shining-perfect.

A white page divided by black lines into white boxes numbered 1 to 31, black letters above the boxes, A U G U S T, bulges from behind, the way a sail fills with wind and buckles and lifts silently and pulls loose from its moorings and jerks out of sight, to reveal another white page, boxes numbered 1 to 30, labeled S E P T E M B E R, and it, too, quickly flips and disappears. O C T O B E R, N O V E M B E R, movie time rushes Julia and Avery to scenes of Cole as beautiful as the Gerber baby on jars of strained carrots, as chubby and perfect as the bare-assed boy who grins up from the *Ladies' Home Journal* to recommend Curity diapers. D E C E M B E R, Annabelle gives Cole a teddy bear just the size to be his first dance partner. J A N U A R Y, a new year. Notes in a baby book: "Cole rolls over, Cole pulls up." Flowers poking up, leaves poking out. "Cole's first tooth." Calendar pages turning. "Cole's first steps," outside in the J U L Y heat. "Cole's eyes turn blue to brown." Leaves turning red and gold. "Cole's first words, *Da-Da, Bye-Bye.*" The distant future becomes the recent past. Leaves falling. "Cole's first sentence, *Go, Da-Da, go.*" Time flying.

Cole with a fever, asleep, his skin hot between them in the double bed, their legs veed together below Cole's feet, his little toes curled tight as a little monkey's . . . Avery told Julia about the goddess Ceres, who spent years wandering the earth in search of her daughter, Proserpine, who had been carried off to the underworld by Pluto. Ceres, who had taken the form of an old woman, was invited by Celeus and his little girl to enjoy the hospitality of their cottage. There Celeus's only son was gravely ill. Metanira, the boy's mother, received Ceres kindly, and the goddess kissed the little boy and instantly restored him to health. During the night Ceres took the sleeping boy and rubbed his arms and legs and whispered a charm over him three times. Then the goddess laid the boy in the ashes of the fire. Metanira, who had been watching, jumped up and pulled her son from the fire. Ceres then assumed her divine form, and a heavenly splendor filled the cottage. "Mother, you have been cruel to your son in your love. I would have given him immortality, but you have prevented me. Yet he shall be great and serve man. He will teach the use of the plow and the rewards of cultivating the earth." With that, the goddess wrapped herself in a cloud and rode away in her chariot.

Julia smiled at Avery and spoke softly over their sleeping child. "Are you telling me not to pull Cole out of flames?"

Avery's eyes found some light in the dark room and glinted. "Not if you see a god stick him in the fire. Remember his Martian birthright. Some of our ways are peculiar to mere earthlings. Even now," Avery said, his voice as soft and comforting as the quilt they all three lay beneath, "even now, skin to skin, you and I are drawing the fever from little Cole's body. By morning he will be well."

The next morning Cole's fever was gone, his temperature normal, his smile as wide as his daddy's. His eyes glinted, throwing light back as Avery's eyes did, as if those eyes made their own light.

4

NNABELLE'S not herself,"
Avery told Julia one night as they lay in bed.

"What do you mean?"

"I'm not sure, but I'm worried about her. At first I thought I wouldn't mention it, then I wanted to know whether you'd noticed anything different."

"She's going through the change. She's taking shots, hormones—estrogen."

Julia woke before dawn and slipped out of bed. She went down the hall to Annabelle's room and eased the door open. Annabelle was flat on her back, her arms folded over her chest; she was snoring to beat the band. Julia was afraid the loud snoring would wake little Cole.

She sounds like a man, Julia thought, like some big, drunk man, passed out and sawing logs. Maybe that's what Avery meant—*Annabelle's not herself.*

But, of course, there was more to it than that.

Not more than a week later, Julia got a phone call from a priest over at Incarnate Word. Annabelle was there. She had appeared in his confessional but clearly did not understand true confession. She had not wanted to leave the dark booth. A parishioner was keeping an eye on her. The priest asked Julia to come get Annabelle, and, please, hurry. Julia asked a neighbor to keep Cole, and then she drove to the church.

". . .don't know why I thought a priest could tell me anything about love . . ." Annabelle would not shut up. She had been to every church and cathedral and every honky-tonk bar between their house and Fort Sam Houston. ". . . never been married, never lost his lover . . ." It took Avery coming home to get Annabelle calmed down. Her doctor recommended a psychiatrist, Dr. Neilson, who had his own hospital. Dr. Neilson insisted they admit her immediately so she could be observed overnight. The next day Julia was there when the doctor came to Annabelle's room.

He looked at Annabelle, cranked up in the hospital bed, but he spoke to Julia. "Mrs. Marrs, your mother is not a good patient. She knows she isn't well, but she won't talk to us, she won't help us so we can make her well. We don't know what we're going to do with her, do we?" Several nurses and another doctor stood behind him with clipboards and smiled when he smiled.

"You?" Annabelle said. "You're involved with a lady doctor on your staff who's getting divorced because of you and she has a twelve-year-old son. Your wife still doesn't know about it. If you can't get your own life in order, what makes you think I'd think you can fix mine?"

Dr. Neilson didn't say another word. He and his entourage continued on their rounds, and Annabelle was discharged an hour later. One of Annabelle's nurses led Julia to understand that the scandal was true, though she couldn't imagine how Annabelle had found out.

Next they saw a Dr. Romine. He spent an hour with Annabelle and called Julia into his office.

As soon as Julia sat down, Annabelle said, "Say, Dr. Romine, I forgot to ask you something. Are you still running around on your wife?"

Dr. Romine's theory was that Annabelle was having an affair with some man, that she probably had a history of promiscuity, and that she no doubt had been unfaithful to Garner, perhaps was involved with someone at the time of Garner's death. Her attacks, such as the outburst Julia had just witnessed, were simply manifestations of her own guilt.

Annabelle, who had listened closely to Dr. Romine, wanted to know how he was handling *his* guilt. And she laughed and laughed.

Avery took Annabelle to a psychiatrist in Houston, a woman— Dr. Dorothy Keithly—who diagnosed Annabelle as manic-depressive and recommended sleep treatment.

Using various drugs, they kept her in a deep sleep for twelve days and nights. An IV tube carried food and narcotics into her bloodstream. When they brought her out of sleep, she was Annabelle again. She had no memory of any dreams. She didn't even remember the other doctors or the visits she made to priests and bartenders. Dr. Keithly pronounced her well and discharged her.

One year later, to the day, Annabelle was sick again. When they drove her back to Houston to see Dr. Keithly, Annabelle hid on the floorboard, which made Cole giggle. *Those men* were watching her. She worried about little Cole. *They're after him too.* Cole loved this new game. The night before, she had barricaded her bedroom door with the dresser.

This time Dr. Keithly prescribed electric shock treatment. Julia said she wouldn't sign the consent forms unless they let her try the shock treatment first. Dr. Keithly said that was not possible. She went into a mop room and got a sponge.

"The brain," Dr. Keithly explained, "is like this sponge. All these wrinkles and grooves are memories. Each act in one's life leaves a mark on the brain. The more significant the act, the deeper the mark. The electric current we administer in treatment causes the wrinkles to expand and contract, ironing the wrinkles out. After treatment, important memories return—those are the grooves too deep to iron out. Your aunt's illness is related to recent events; we will smooth out those disturbing impressions in her brain."

Julia cried when she saw Annabelle's bed; it had bars around all four sides, like a baby's crib, and a barred top that came over and locked, effectively turning the bed into a cage. But Annabelle said it was fine, they only locked the top after she was asleep, to protect her from *those men.* Annabelle liked Dr. Keithly: "I think she's pretty. Don't you think she's pretty—for a woman doctor, I mean?"

Dr. Keithly said the treatments would be more effective if Annabelle did not have visitors. She did relent once, after Annabelle's first treatment, to prove to Julia that Annabelle was all right. After just that one treatment Annabelle seemed like her old self. But Dr. Keithly kept her in the hospital. There were three treatments a week, for three weeks, followed by a long period of readjustment.

When Julia went to get Annabelle to bring her home, she took her some roses. Annabelle put them in a vase and put it out in the patients' common room. Every other patient came up to the table and touched the roses, held the soft petals between shaky fingers. Annabelle told Julia no one brought flowers to mental patients. They left the roses, and Annabelle had a flower shop deliver a different arrangement every Saturday for a year. She was back in the hospital in time to see the last of these flowers delivered. Her final order was roses again; she had come full circle.

For the next eight years Dr. Keithly continued to treat Annabelle. She underwent shock therapy five more times. The longest she stayed out of the hospital was three years. Avery always knew, before Julia, before Dr. Keithly—who continued to see Annabelle on a regular basis—when Annabelle was about to get sick again.

The apparatus for the electric shocks looked like an instrument for torture, something off the set of a Frankenstein movie. In the center of a small room stood a white porcelain-enamel table with thick leather restraining straps for both arms and legs and a leather harness that went around the forehead and neck. Insulated black wires ran from a power terminal to two cone-shaped electrodes that would be smeared with a clear, conductive grease, then fastened to the patient's temples, suction-cupped to skin and freshly shaved scalp. A leather-wrapped length of sawed-off broomstick would be inserted between the patient's teeth before lightning clamped hold of her brain—Jupiter hurling thunderbolts. A Y-shaped throw switch, a tuning fork of power, voltage meters with needles that flicked like the tongues of serpents, black knobs, one red bulb that pulsed like a ruby in the sun—Julia had seen these instruments before, in her child's imagination, when Bruno Richard Hauptmann died in the electric chair for kidnapping the Lindbergh baby.

The wrinkles and creases this machinery of memories removed from Annabelle's brain reappeared on her face, her neck, the backs of her hands. Skin lost elasticity, sagged, turned sallow. Annabelle complained that food had lost its taste, yet she ate as she never had before. She grew thick in the middle, her movements, once lithe and quick, were as logy as a slug's. Her Thorazine-thickened tongue crowded her mouth, and she slurred her words like a drunk. She got romance novels from the library, the silly adventures of lovesick schoolgirls, and read them and, without realizing, read them again. Annabelle, once so sassy and vain, Annabelle who wore high heels to show off calves she knew turned men's heads well after she was thirty, Annabelle now bought pants suits and shapeless housedresses and slipped her bare, blue-white feet into silver or gold mules.

Annabelle had inherited a good deal of insurance money when Garner died, and she had his railroad pension. Julia never let Annabelle know that her medical bills used up all her money. It pleased Annabelle to think she was going to leave Julia a lot of money. Avery didn't want Annabelle to find out he had paid many of her doctor bills.

She died the Saturday before Mother's Day in 1958, at four o'clock, eating supper because she said she was too hungry to wait until Avery and Cole got home. They were up on the Pedernales for a day's fishing. Julia carried a plate in to Annabelle's room, where she now spent her days in a brown recliner reading her romances and watching the television Avery had given her. She ate from a folding TV tray, metal painted brown wood grain. Julia sat with her and tried to get her to talk, but her mouth was stuffed full of sweet potato, and her eyes were glued to the TV, where a man leaned over a woman in a hospital bed and yelled at her while tears ran down her face. Annabelle lifted a spoonful of cherry jello to add to the sweet potato she was swallowing—Julia would never forget the mound of red jello, too much for the spoon, wobbling, then falling as Annabelle fell forward. The TV tray tipped over, but Annabelle's plate landed right side up. She had already emptied her glass of milk. Only the jello spilled onto the floor, where it broke into red pieces like congealed blood and bounced on the waxed wood.

Annabelle's eyes were open wide. Julia wished for Avery's help, but she was grateful Cole was not home to see this. Julia cleaned the sweet potato from Annabelle's mouth and got her to the car. The stroke had paralyzed her. Julia sat her up in the front seat and talked to her all the way to the hospital. She had no idea whether Annabelle saw the world looming up to meet them in the windshield, no idea whether Annabelle heard a word she spoke, no idea whether Annabelle was alive or dead. A little smile had frozen with Annabelle's face, and it comforted Julia.

Annabelle never regained consciousness, though she did not legally die for four days. They buried her in Taylor in the space that had been waiting for her, beside Garner. She had survived her husband for twenty years to die, just as he had, at fifty-one. It's a good thing, Julia thought, that people in heaven are ageless.

Julia gave Annabelle's pants suits and house dresses to the Salvation Army. She gave Cole the television, but its picture grew dim and soon went out. Cole took the picture tube out of its chassis and tinkered with wires and switches, but he couldn't make it work again. Julia made him throw away the empty cabinet and loose parts, but he kept the dark glass screen on his dresser for months.

5

WHEN he was a baby, Cole's favorite game was peekaboo. He thought he could make himself disappear, become invisible, if he covered his eyes. Soon he was putting his whole head beneath pillows or under covers. Later, after he was walking and talking, he went from peekaboo to hide-and-seek. He often hid himself so well Julia couldn't find him, but even when she called out and begged him to show himself, he stayed quiet and secret until she located him. Once, she looked for him everywhere. He stayed hidden so long she panicked and went to telephone Avery, who walked in just as she picked up the phone. Avery, of course, found him right away, on the top shelf of the linen closet.

"But I looked there," she said.

"I made myself invisible," Cole said.

He had managed, somehow, to climb up, and then he had covered himself with stacks of folded towels.

"When I was a little baby," Avery said, "my daddy pulled out a dresser drawer and put me in it. That was the bed I slept in every night."

The next morning, a Sunday, Avery was home when Cole disappeared again. One minute they were all in the kitchen, Avery drinking coffee and watching a mockingbird through the window, Julia making rice cereal for Cole, Cole on the floor turning the pages of the Sunday funny papers; Julia spooned the hot cereal into a bowl and bent to pick Cole up—he was gone.

"Avery," she said.

Avery nodded, put a finger to his lips, beckoned her to follow. In the hall they stopped, silent, to watch Cole. He had pulled out a dresser drawer and was trying to climb inside. He wasn't quite tall enough, but he kept trying. He got one foot over the drawer edge and kept swinging the other leg up. Then the toe on his swinging foot caught in the brass curve of the drawer pull, a perfect stirrup. He rolled over into the drawer. When he heard them coming he couldn't keep from giggling. Julia beat Avery to him and lifted him up off Avery's soft, white underwear and cuddled him close. He laughed and laughed, his little body vibrating and his feet dancing against her side. She brought him close to nuzzle his neck and inhale his sweet, clean, soap-and-baby-powder fragrance. When she lifted her face to smile at Avery, her eyes were shining wet.

"He's my joy," Julia said, to both the giggling baby and her smiling husband.

"He's mighty easy to love," Avery said. "I know we'll always love him, no matter what he does, but we may not ever have such easy loving again."

It was clear to Julia that Avery loved Cole as much as she did. Which was why she didn't understand his unwillingness for her to have another child.

"Wouldn't it be nice for Cole to have a little sister?"

"Cole's perfect. Isn't he enough? Aren't you satisfied?" Avery said.

"Of course he's perfect, but couldn't we stand some more perfection?" Avery said nothing. She laughed. "I'd love to dress a little girl."

"Just one, my only begotten son," Avery said. Under his breath, he whispered, "I have only so much love to give—a woman, a son." Julia didn't know what to say to that—wasn't even sure he'd intended her to hear.

Julia *was* grateful, for Cole and for Avery. But for the first time ever, she felt a distance between herself and Avery, and that hurt. She pushed her desire for more children out of her mind, but from time to time, for years to come, the desire came back and made her sad.

Before Cole learned to walk, he danced. Julia changed his diapers on the kitchen counter. Cole grabbed Julia's arms and pulled up. On the yellow tile counter he stood eye to eye with his mother, perfect dance partner, and bounced to whatever was on the radio—Frank Sinatra, Perry Como, Frankie Laine, Billy Eckstine, the Chiquita Banana jingle, or, his favorite, "Pepsi Cola Hits the Spot":

Nickel, nickel, nickel, nickel,
Trickle, trickle, trickle, trickle,
Nickel, nickel, nickel, nickel!

A dozen or so years later, the big double-dresser mirror Avery had carried from their bedroom on the floor against the wall, Julia stood eye to eye with a nearly grown man and remembered those kitchen dates with her baby. She dipped and swayed around the living room, preparing Cole for teenaged girls and junior high dances at the American Legion hall. After he mastered the box step, she went on to show him, just for fun, the cha-cha, the fox-trot, and the Charleston. She heard Annabelle's voice as clear as the song on the record player: "You'll never be popular if you can't dance. *Feel* the music, just let yourself *feel* it." Julia's hand rested in the small of Cole's back and felt Avery's muscles there, her husband's body young in the form of their son. In the mirror, Julia's bare feet were as nimble as a young girl's, years ago, sweeping Annabelle's hardwood floors. That mirror was the silver screen—a movie of her life. She and Cole emerged from the dark frame into the beveled edge that momentarily contorted them; then they appeared, whole and clear, and moved from left to right, animated, improvising, until they entered the distorting bevel at the mirror's other edge and vanished. Julia felt a kind of panic and wanted to look behind the mirror. They danced a circle, now outside the mirror's field of reflection. Mother and son, they were on the dark side of the moon. Cole stacked the records, tried to trip her up with difficult music, but Julia showed him all tunes were danceable.

Cole was four the first Easter he was aware of the Easter bunny. He had been so excited Saturday night, Julia thought he'd never calm down enough to go to sleep. Then she figured he'd sleep late to catch up, but, of course, he fooled her and woke at dawn. She had to stall him while Avery boiled and dyed the eggs and sneaked outside to hide them. Cole wore his yellow terry-cloth robe and real-deerskin Indian moccasins. He wouldn't sit still for breakfast before he hunted Easter eggs. He ran out onto the lawn, his moccasins leaving a trail in the dew, straight to a big hackberry tree on the side of the house. Avery had finished hiding the eggs and came round the other side of the house. Julia heard Avery and felt him step close beside her to watch with her. Cole bent forward, his robe rising up to show the pink backs of his chubby legs.

"Ohhh," he said, just above a whisper. "Ohhh, Mother." And he turned and stood and came toward her, holding a pale-green egg in both his hands. "We *just* missed the Easter rabbit," he said.

"We did?" Julia asked.

"Ohh, Mother, we did. Feel the egg. It's still warm. He must have just laid it."

Julia knelt, and Cole pressed the egg, warm, against her cheek. She held Cole's small hand, so full of the egg, with her hand. Both their hands and the slices of green between intertwined fingers were mirrored in Cole's eyes, every bit as big as two Easter eggs.

The summer before Cole started the first grade, Avery and Julia spent a weekend taking him to see all the Spanish missions in San Antonio. Avery saved the Alamo for last. He drove them down through Alamo Heights and crossed Olmos Dam, because Cole loved crossing the dam with its lantern lights in the rock sides of the roadway. They meandered through Breckenridge Park, where the zoo and the sightseeing railroad were. On Broadway they stopped at a drive-in called the Three Little Pigs and had Cokes. Then they were downtown, standing right in front of the Alamo. Julia didn't tell Avery, but she had never been inside the Alamo either. Of course, she had seen it before, they all had ridden past in the car before, but this was different. It was a hot, clear day, and the Alamo reflected the sun like a perfect, glossy snapshot or postcard. It was hard to believe this was the real Alamo, the actual place where Jim Bowie and Davy Crockett were killed. The limestone was platinum gold in the sun. Julia looked close for the faint stains of blood, but every stone was clean. Inside, in cool, dim light, their footsteps echoed, and she smelled dust and remembered this was a church before it was a fort. They went through the adjacent museum and looked at documents and weapons in glass cases. Later, in the lush, parklike grounds, Cole disappeared. Julia and Avery sat on a shaded bench, and while Avery figured out where Cole would be hiding, she tried to picture this place treeless, surrounded by open space and thousands of Mexican soldiers instead of tall hotels and office buildings. They found Cole down by the little river that twisted through downtown. "I wasn't hiding," Cole told them. "I was too easy to find for hiding. I was thinking."

"About what?" Avery said.

"About history," Cole said.

When he was in the third grade, Cole's teacher announced a contest. The student who brought in the loveliest word would win a prize. They had three weeks, and each day they spent ten minutes listening to trial words. Cole carried a spiral notepad around and stopped in the middle of supper to write down words Julia or Avery spoke: *latticework, artesian well, sombrero, veranda, tangerine, dirigible, cottonwood, undulant, aborigine, eucalyptus, Worcestershire sauce, Endymion, dahlia, shale, Ecclesiastes.* At bedtime, Avery went over Cole's lists with him. They spoke the words out loud, slowly, repetitively, quickly, in exaggerated bass or singsong soprano. *Soprano*—how do you spell that? Avery showed Cole how to divide the words into syllables to spell them more easily. Julia heard them working on *Constantinople:*

"*Con-stan-ti-no-ple.*" Avery sounded it out.

"*Con-stan-ti-no-* . . . why *p-l-e* and not *p-u-l*?" Cole asked.

"It's like *principle, p-l-e,* sounds the same as *principal, p-a-l,*" Avery said. "Remember, the principal is your pal. One of those you have to memorize."

They sat at the kitchen table, and its wooden legs creaked when Cole bore down on his pencil on the sheet of lined manila paper. Avery had made a small pot of coffee and let Cole have enough in a cup of warm milk to tan the milk. Julia went to bed early so she could fall asleep with the sound of their two voices echoing one another in the quiet house, the late-night murmur and the smell of coffee lulling her to sleep with a holiday feel, Thanksgiving in her heart.

Cole finally settled on *Cuernavaca.* Avery had gotten a book out of the library and shown him pictures, traced highways and railroad tracks south from San Antonio through Monterrey, Victoria, Tamazunchale (Cole called it "Thomas and Charley"), to Mexico City and Cuernavaca. Cole had some backup words, in case the teacher outlawed *Cuernavaca* for being foreign. His next choices were *boulevard, canvasback,* and *watermelon,* but not necessarily in that order.

Cole came home disappointed. His teacher *had* allowed *Cuernavaca,* since it was a place name used by English-speaking people. But the winning word had been *treasure* and the prize a small treasure chest (the size of Julia's jewelry box) full of chocolate wafers and mints wrapped in gold and silver foil like doubloons. Cole liked *doubloons;* he hated *treasure.* He insisted his teacher had chosen not the word, but what it meant, as what she thought was lovely. Cole said it wasn't fair. Avery said Cole might as well get used to that.

In the sixth grade, Cole announced that he was nearsighted and needed eyeglasses. Julia thought he wanted glasses because Pat Herman had gotten them. Cole was very taken with Pat, who, Cole said, was the smartest whiz in class. Cole said he had to have Pat, who sat beside him, whisper the words off the blackboard. Pat, Cole said, was farsighted. As fast as he could, Cole wrote what Pat whispered. "It's a good thing I can write as fast as he can read," Cole said.

"But neither your father nor I wears glasses," Julia said.

Cole shrugged.

"Maybe that's why he squints so much," Avery said.

A few days later Julia could not keep from weeping when the ophthalmologist put little glasses on Cole. Cole looked up, out a high window in the doctor's office, and shook his head in amazement. "The tree," he said, "even this far away, has individual leaves. It's like wearing a sleuth's magnifying lens on both eyes. Now I won't miss a thing."

"You never have," Avery said, and smiled at Julia's tears.

Each evening, at supper, Cole told Avery and Julia what he had learned in school that day. Six hundred years before the birth of Christ, the ancient Greeks drew maps of the heavens. They saw that the stars were in different places in the sky during different seasons, and they called some of these stars *planets,* which was the Greek word for "wanderers."

"Did you learn," Avery asked, "why the stars shine only at night?"

"The stars shine all the time. But sunlight is diffused through earth's atmosphere into a blanket of brightness we can't see through," Cole explained.

"The Egyptians believed the stars are lanterns lighted each night by the gods, to make our nights beautiful. The gods let the lanterns down on ropes through holes in the sky, and pull them back up in the morning and blow them out," Avery said.

"If we flew high enough in an airplane, we could get above the earth's atmosphere and see the stars night *and* day," Cole said.

"That would be nice," Julia said. "Starlight breakfast."

"We learned about the *velocity of escape* or *velocity of liberation.* That's the speed necessary to escape from earth's pull. *Seven miles per second.* That's all it'll take to send a man to the moon. Will you let me go to the moon when I'm older?"

"Yes," Avery said, "if you promise to come back."

"What if he met a moon maiden and stayed?" Julia said.

"Don't worry, Mother; there's no life on the moon. There's no life anywhere in our solar system except here on earth."

"What about Mars, the red planet?" Julia said, and she smiled at Avery.

"No, not Mars either. Mars is a cold, rusty old planet. The red color is oxidization on the surface. The Martian atmosphere isn't deep enough to protect living things. There's only one-tenth of one percent as much oxygen there as on earth."

"Maybe the Martians built subterranean cities? Or, maybe, some forms of life don't have to breathe oxygen," Avery said.

"Daddy, all living things breathe oxygen. That makes something alive or dead or just a nonliving thing, like a rock."

Avery laughed. "As a matter of fact—since you seem to like facts so much—rocks inhale oxygen."

Cole's eyes got big. "Rocks breathe—they're alive?"

"Depends on how you define *alive*. They don't have lungs. They don't exhale carbon dioxide. But years and years ago, when rocks were being formed, they absorbed lots of oxygen. There's as much oxygen in a layer of rocks a few feet deep as there is in the air above them. And they're still taking in oxygen, slowly. In addition to erosion, it's the oxygen rocks inhale that makes them crumble away." Avery looked at Julia. "Some folks would call that being alive."

"Wow," Cole said. "I'm going to tell my teacher tomorrow. I bet she doesn't know rocks can breathe."

"Don't tell your teacher, honey, but your mother thinks there's a good chance there is, or has been, life on Mars. Intelligent life, at that," Julia said.

6

A HOT, dry morning in June; it was Julia's thirty-seventh birthday. She had on a pair of blue cotton shorts and a sleeveless seersucker top. She had got some sun puttering around in the flower beds the past few weeks. She decided she looked okay in the shorts, decided she didn't look like a woman getting close to forty. She had the front door open, the screen hooked, and when the mailman delivered the mail she heard the mailbox lid open. There seemed to be a different mailman every week. Julia thought all mailmen should look just like Mr. Conger, who delivered the mail in Taylor when she was little. This one was younger than Mr. Conger. He wore a gray summer uniform—short sleeves and short pants with knee socks. Beneath a gray pith helmet, he flashed Julia a movie star smile. Clark Gable on safari. Julia offered him a glass of iced tea. His face was shiny with sweat, and the Pepsodent smile made her self-conscious about her shorts, glad, again, she had got some tan on her legs. The mailman tipped his head and the glass back so far they both stuck out from the porch shade into the bright sun. He brought his head and the glass back down with a nod and a clink of ice, smiled, and said, "Thank you, ma'am." Julia held the glass of ice and watched him march down the block. He left a fat thumbprint on the side of the glass. No one but Cole's playmates called her ma'am. Certainly no one old enough to be a mailman. Surely she wasn't that much older than he.

One square envelope stuck out from the circulars and bills the mailman had left. It was addressed to Julia Yates. Who would use her maiden name? There was a Taylor postmark. Maybe it was a birthday card, some old friend.

It *was* a birthday card, of a kind. It was an invitation: The Class of 1941, Taylor High School, twenty-year class reunion. Lordy, Lordy. *The Taylor Ducks.* Twenty-years. *Tay-lor High, we hon-or thee . . .* Lordy, Lordy.

Taylor was just a little over a hundred miles away, but it felt much farther. Julia had been back only once since she and Avery married and Annabelle moved in with them. That was when she went back to bury Annabelle beside Garner. She had not kept in touch with any of her high school friends. The only people in Taylor she felt she still knew were in the cemetery.

Cole had a baseball game that afternoon. Julia decided to soak in a cool tub. She ran the water while she undressed. In front of a full-length mirror, she stared at her body. Thirty-seven years in the world. She had a teenaged son. He had had a riddle for her last night:

"I am very polished, but sometimes very brutal. Some curse me, some praise me, yet I treat all alike. Who am I?"

"Time," she said.

"Aw, Mother, time isn't polished."

"The face of a clock is," she said.

"I am your mirror," Cole said.

"Same difference," she said.

Now she turned and looked back over her shoulder. On her butt, the small zigzag scars, little lightning bolts, left from the time her dress caught fire looked like stretch marks on her skin.

She lowered herself into the water, cool enough to give her goose bumps even on this hot afternoon. She leaned her head back against the tub, and water slipped beneath her pinned-up hair, cold against the back of her scalp. Her knees, her breasts, four small, round islands. She let her head slip down until water covered her ears: the sound of the sea, other worlds, time and distance.

Avery's steps vibrated through pipes in the walls and roared out of the faucet into the water that filled Julia's ears. Home early, he came into the cool bathroom, two full grocery sacks rattling in his arms. Chips of ice stuck to a bottle of champagne squeaked against porcelain when Avery set the bottle in the lavatory. He reached into one of the brown paper sacks, and a sweet, damp smell escaped. Then he started dropping strawberries into the tub: "Bombs away— ka-boom, whammo, blawie, ker-bam." Avery was laughing in between the sound effects, and Julia started laughing with him. Before he stopped, he dropped thirty-seven big, ripe strawberries into the tub, where they bobbed like little red buoys to mark every year.

"Happy birthday, sweetheart." He knelt to kiss her, and as he did he pushed a strawberry out of his cheek and into her mouth with his tongue. "One to grow on."

He had driven down to the valley that morning and bought six quarts of strawberries, her favorites, right out of the fields. He got two glasses and opened the champagne, letting the foam run down the bottle into the tub with Julia.

"Where's Cole?"

"Baseball."

"Time's a-wasting." Avery kicked off his shoes and peeled off his shirt, unbuckled his pants and let them drop. In twenty seconds he was naked with her in the tub, water sloshing over the sides. He sat behind her, his legs around her waist, his feet floating alongside her shins. She leaned back against his warm skin, and he ran the slick bar of soap across her belly and the bottoms of her breasts beneath the water.

While they relaxed and killed the champagne, Julia told him about the reunion.

"Twenty years," she said.

"Whooee." He shook his head. "What am I doing with such an old woman?"

"Keeping me another twenty years, I hope." With her toe she pulled the drain plug. Avery drew her back against him and kissed her. His lips moved and warm water slapped against the tub and echoed in her ear. Avery's kiss pulled her entire body and swirled her down into him the way the drain drew water from the tub. "Martian," she whispered, and he kissed her again.

Cole's team had lost. They'd been beaten so badly in the first few innings, the coach let them try new positions. Cole got to pitch an inning. The score was eighteen or nineteen to one. He wasn't sure, but it sure was fun. Cole showered, and the three of them went to La Fonda's on Main Avenue to eat Mexican food and celebrate Julia's birthday.

Avery gave her a sweet cotton nightgown, white with white appliquéd roses at the shoulders. And he gave her a small fossil, a fish, *Gosiutichthys parvus,* from the Middle Eocene era.

"To celebrate the mark you make in time," he said.

Cole said he never saw a fish that small except in an aquarium. That was because, Avery told him, this fish came from the canals of Mars.

Cole gave her a lovely compact, gold, with her initials on the top and his on the bottom.

"That's why I gave you the riddle last night. It was a clue. I thought sure you'd guess."

Julia opened the compact, and Avery handed her his pocket-knife to slit the paper that sealed in the powder. She dusted her nose and turned the compact around so Cole and Avery could see their grins in the small mirror. A candle in a red jar on their table danced red in the mirror and in her boys' eyes.

That fall, Avery took Julia to her reunion in Taylor. Festoons of green and gold crepe paper hung from the ceiling of the new high school gym. A group of old-timers from Austin played "Three Little Fishes," "Bei Mir Bist Du Schön," "Blueberry Hill," "One Dozen Roses," and "South of the Border." Twenty years had passed in one sweet breath.

Julia saw Larry Otto for the first time since she'd given back his engagement ring. Avery waved him over. Larry introduced Julia and Avery to his wife, Pat. The four of them sat and had coffee together and talked like old friends.

Larry and Pat had met during the war. Larry had been stationed with Pat's husband at Randolph Field. Pat's husband died in his sleep one night. Turned out he'd had a bad heart all his life. He could've died at any time. At the time he did die, Pat was pregnant with his first child. Larry started seeing Pat to cheer her up. By the time she had her baby, they had fallen in love. Larry adopted the child, a girl, and then he and Pat had four boys. Julia told Larry and Pat about Cole, fourteen, who was back home in San Antonio, excited about an entire weekend on his own.

Pat and Larry favored one another, both big-boned and fair, both a little red on the nose from the afternoon picnic in the schoolyard. Larry still ran the mattress factory, though business was no longer booming. The Victorian house had been sold when his father died. Larry and Pat lived in a nice new subdivision and drove a tan station wagon. Larry had sold most of the farmland to cover debts his father left behind. He had a partnership in the town's farm implement dealership. He and Pat were happy and, if not prosperous, comfortable enough.

Julia saw nothing she coveted. Neither Larry nor Avery had gone to fat, though both had finally quit smoking. Neither had gone bald. But Larry looked raw and lusterless, like rock dulled by years of sun and blowing sand, while Avery's dark hair shone like metal and his eyes had grown deeper and seemed still to hold secrets, promises, dreams, and schemes for the future.

Twelve years later, Julia opened a letter in handwriting she had come to recognize as Pat Otto's. Since the reunion they had exchanged Christmas cards and important news, though Julia and Avery had not been the hundred miles to Taylor, nor had Pat and Larry come to San Antonio. I'll bet, Julia thought, one of her children is getting married.

Larry had had a heart attack, Pat wrote. It had been touch and go, it had been downright rough. He had lost seventy pounds. Julia wouldn't recognize him now. He was going to have to take it easy from here on in.

Julia felt a twinge of sadness, no more and no less than what she had felt that morning when she read in the newspaper about a little girl from Peru who was in San Antonio for surgery to remove a crippled leg so that she could be fitted with a new kind of artificial limb. Shouldn't she feel more connected to a man she had almost married? But that man, Larry-a-quarter-of-a-century-ago-Otto, had departed as air, gone with a gone-down sun one Sunday afternoon when Julia's own young self had told him to disappear. She had her eye on a tiny speck miles away, waiting to become Avery Marrs as soon as she got back to it. She had left Larry on the porch of the Victorian house his grandfather had built and he had, years ago, sold. Now yet another stranger lived in that house. And here she was, in this house, living this life. She looked around at walls, pictures, tables and chairs, lamps that cast warm and familiar light.

Cole was home from graduate school for the weekend. Julia heard him in the kitchen, and she called to him from the living room, where she had been opening the mail.

"Cole," she called. "Cole, I'll dance at your wedding if you'll heat me a cup of that coffee on the stove and bring it to me."

He did, and when he brought the coffee he sat down and told her he'd take her up on her offer. Dancing at his wedding, he meant.

The girl's name was Jeanette.

Avery got Julia through the wedding as he always got her through tight places. They drove over to Baton Rouge, where Cole was at LSU and where he had met Jeanette. Her family came up from New Orleans. Jeanette was small and dark and very pretty. The wedding was a blur. Julia went, it happened, and she went back home. Later, she got to know Jeanette, who was easy to love.

All Julia could remember from the wedding and reception was talking to the priest who had performed the ceremony. He told Julia not to worry, that these young people were destined for each other. He had counseled many young people, and he could tell. These were exciting times, he said, times when a person could make a real difference. For his part, he confided to Julia, he was leaving the priesthood to go work in a factory in Gary, Indiana. A lay ministry of real meaning. Ours should be a corporeal faith, he told Julia. And she wondered whether he intended that *ours* as all-inclusive, catholic with a little *c*, or if he meant just she and he, Julia and Father—what was his name?—O'Brien.

For years, when she sat at a railroad crossing and watched a train shudder and sway past, when she read about workers behind the iron curtain lining up to buy dark blouses and heavy shoes, when molten metal in hot foundry furnaces fired up a TV beer commercial—whenever she thought about factory towns and oppressed workers, she thought of Father O'Brien, only now he was just Mr. O'Brien, or Dave or Phil. Each time she thought of him she hoped his hand, at that very moment, was on someone's arm and was just as calming and reassuring as it had been on her arm, his steady voice just as sure of the future.

7

SIX months after her only child was married, Julia's period stopped. She was forty-nine. A cold night in December, she woke in the dark, wet with sweat. Avery got up with her, and they pulled the quilt and top sheet back and raised a window to let fresh, cold air in. While the air worked on the damp sheets, Avery filled the bathtub with cool water and they got in together.

The night sweats and hot flashes came and went for the next couple of years, and she had some spotting, but her period had stopped as if someone had turned off a faucet.

"For some women it happens that way," her doctor told her.

Julia had dizzy spells, but since she knew the reason, she enjoyed the floating feeling. At times she couldn't sleep, but that was okay too. She had noticed, before she started going through the change, that she was sleeping less as she got older. That had started after Cole left home the first time for college. She felt a certain sweet sadness about losing the mothering part of her. She was more glad than ever that she had had Cole. Now Cole had his life with Jeanette, and Julia and Avery had theirs. Julia still felt good, and she still looked good.

When the next-door neighbor told Julia she didn't look forty-nine, Julia said, "Yes, I do. I'm what forty-nine looks like on me."

Her doctor offered to prescribe estrogen if Julia felt she needed it. She didn't. She always thought it was estrogen that first made Annabelle sick. She would put herself in her body's hands.

Avery was traveling less, and they spent more time together. Sex was better than ever. With Cole gone, the whole house was theirs.

They made love standing up in the shower, on the living room rug, out in the back of the car with the radio on softly.

Julia felt as if the changes were a kind of passageway, a gauntlet of strange but not entirely unpleasant sensations that led to a new, more peaceful life. She didn't want to grow old and die, but she did like feeling so free and so much more sure of herself than she had when she was younger. And she had the blessing of her man from Mars.

She pictured herself on a high bluff overlooking an endless valley—a scene from a western. Purple mountaintops became clouds, yellow wheat leaned in gusts of wind, and she and Avery stood on a high precipice. She wore a long gingham dress. Avery slapped his hat against his thigh, and a cloud of dust rose in the hot sun. Far below, a blue river eased along between curving banks. Somewhere behind them, tied in the shade of a grove of cottonwood trees, were two strong horses. This was a shared moment of unspoken beauty and understanding before they walked arm in arm back to the horses, to begin a long ride down into that lovely valley that stretched out before them. What sights there were to see. What new landmarks waited.

But something vague worried her. Huldah had brushed the words into Julia's brain: *We must suffer to be beautiful.* Julia's life seemed beautiful now without suffering. Why did she sometimes feel she didn't deserve or couldn't expect life to be so? This was no storybook in which you *just know* things won't, can't, turn out so happily ever after. Surely some lives did turn out that way? Julia wanted to grow old with Avery—more, even, than she had wanted to start off with him, years ago. She knew enough now, had experienced enough, to fully appreciate loving one man forever. And the very intensity of her happiness frightened her. Some imp of the perverse kept whispering, *This is too good to be true, it can't last, nothing lasts.*

But what can you do with thoughts such as these? You can let the music come up through the straws in the broom and fill your arms and legs, and then you can sweep. Sweep fast. Sweep hard. Sweep your fears down the dark hall and across the wide room and open the door to sweep them away down the porch steps and out into the anonymous world. Feel the music and sweep every particle away. When you open the door, watch for sudden shifts in the breeze, any ill winds that might blow uncertainties back in.

Julia knew as well as anyone that love demands a high price. Her list of payments seemed long enough. Her mother, Vivian, had died before Julia knew her. Her father, George, had given her up, and she never really knew him. Mother died before Julia understood all the love in her stern ways. Garner died before he could know Avery and Coleman. Her half-brother, George junior, sent to Korea when he was just eighteen, missing in action, Julia never saw him again. Annabelle, dead before she could grow old—though her mind had already lived more than one life. Annabelle started leaving Julia the first time she got sick, the first time she left her self behind. Annabelle's first journeys into other personalities were practice runs for her final departure. And Cole, Julia's only living flesh and blood, grew up and married, went away, as he should, to whatever life he could invent.

Mother's unthinking acceptance of Biblical Scripture as literal rules to live by had simply never taken, as a vaccine won't take when the body already has its immunity. But Mother's prophecies had been wedded, through time and experience, to the immediate music of Annabelle's dance.

Julia could no longer think of herself as a young woman. Her body would never again carry new life. She was almost as old as Annabelle had been at the time of her death. Yet, in some ways, Julia would never be as old as Mother, nor had she ever been as young as Annabelle.

That Julia found herself remembering Scripture and whispering a prayer would have pleased (perhaps *did* please) Mother. The *sense* of the Scripture stuck in Julia's head, and the *intent* of the prayer repeated on Julia's lips would have pleased (perhaps *did* please) Annabelle. The scripture was from Mark, chapter nine, verse twenty-four:

. . .Lord, I believe; help thou mine unbelief.

The prayer was: *Lord, Jesus, Holy Spirit, grant me, daily, one more day's dance with my best dance partner, my Avery, my Martian. In all your heavenly names, Amen.*

8

JULIA held the small but thick book Cole had brought. It had an oxblood cover, soft vinyl or leather like a Bible, tissue-thin Bible pages: *BEDSIDE Diagnostic Examination*, DeGowin & DeGowin. A former student had sent it to Cole from med school, with the inscription: "Eugene Pearson gives this traditional, much-touted little medical book to Professor Coleman Marrs, keen diagnostician of the manifestations of disease and signs of health in American culture." Julia had read the entry on page 216 over and over:

> CHRONIC LOCALIZED CERVICAL LYMPHADENOPATHY: **Virchow's Node.** Sentinel Node, Signal Node, Troisier's Node. This classic physical sign is an enlargement of a single lymph node, usually in the *left supraclavicular* group, frequently behind the clavicular head of the left Sternocleidomastoideus. Often it is so deep in the neck that it escapes casual examination. A purposeful search requires the patient's trunk to be erect and the examiner facing him; the fingers explore the region behind the muscle head. The node is the site of carcinomatous metastasis from a primary lesion in the upper abdomen. When a primary carcinoma is found in the abdomen, demonstration of the sentinel node is proof of distant metastasis.

Within the frightening technicality of words such as "left Sternocleidomastoideus" and "carcinomatous metastasis" was the lyrical and poetic notion of a "Sentinel" or "Signal" node. High in Avery's neck, it cried a warning of the distant destruction already in progress.

Dr. Barker had trouble getting Avery's x-ray out of a manila envelope and onto the flat light in his office. The sheet flexed and made a shallow version of the sound of thunder Julia had made back-stage in high school, rippling a sheet of tin. The spot Dr. Barker indicated looked like a tiny smudge on the film, and Julia moistened the tip of her finger on her tongue and actually tried to wipe the smudge off.

By the time they did surgery, about forty-eight hours later, the smudge (tumor, carcinoma) had doubled in size. They removed most of the lung. Dr. Barker said they couldn't say whether the lung was the primary site of the cancer. While Avery was still recuperating from lung surgery, Dr. Barker located a swollen lymph node deep in his neck. Avery's black and silver hair was shaved off the side of his head, and his neck and lower scalp were stained orange with iodine, a target painted on his head for the giant radiation machine. After Avery was released from the hospital, Julia drove him back twice a week for radiation treatments. Avery joked with the nurses and other patients. He had been a big hit before and after his surgery, and nurses and orderlies came by to speak to him. The radiation therapist told Julia that Avery's attitude was wonderful. "More and more," she added, "we're learning the importance of mental outlook in treating cancer."

The spot on Avery's lung had been detected in March. In June, after two rounds of thirty radiation treatments on his neck, Avery was back in the hospital with a painful, enlarged gallbladder.

"Might be a coincidental gallstone," Dr. Barker told them. Julia and Cole and Jeanette nodded, each knowing this was a kind lie, but each partially believing: *might be, could be, anything's possible, there's still hope.*

Julia read the entry in DeGowin & DeGowin: DEEP ABDOMINAL PALPATION. "After using light palpation, delve deeper." And a few pages later, she found the heading: RUQ Mass: **Enlarged Tender Gallbladder.** The following sentences stood out:

> In acute cholecystitis the gallbladder is usually exquisitely tender to fist percussion; in the early stages it may not be palpable. When distended, it is felt behind the liver border as a smooth, firm sausagelike mass.

So, Julia thought, the Sentinel Node had the right dope. The enemy had infiltrated, gotten behind the lines. The entry, page 493, ended:

> Carcinoma of the gallbladder produces a hard irregular mass that is moderately tender. *Clinical Occurrence:* Acute cholecystitis, carcinoma.

With Cole, Dr. Barker extended the lie: "We'll just have to wait and see." But he made an opportunity to take Julia aside. Dr. Barker gripped her arm tighter and tighter, his wrapped fingers tight as the pumped cuff of a sphygmomanometer measuring Julia's blood pressure.

"My God," Dr. Barker said. "It's everywhere. Gallbladder, pancreas, liver—even wrapped around his spine. The pain must be . . . We just sewed him back up. There was nothing we could do."

"How long?" Julia asked. The question from every medical melodrama. She hadn't thought, just asked. It was, of course, what anyone would want to know.

"It's difficult to predict." Dr. Barker had become professional again. Then he must have seen something in Julia's eyes, her recognition of the phony tone of voice he had shifted into. Dr. Barker blew air out of his cheeks; his fingers relaxed their grip on her arm, but his hand remained, kind now. "Not long, if he's lucky. We'll give him morphine, but the pain is still going to be intense. I doubt he'll make it till the Fourth of July."

"Thank you," Julia said. Dr. Barker nodded. Later, she would think about the inappropriateness of her remark: *Thank you.*

"I want him at home," she said.

"I'd like to keep him in the hospital, where we can give him the best care," Dr. Barker said.

"*I* can give him the best care," Julia said. Dr. Barker looked at her, and something in her face, some lovely defiance, convinced him, and he nodded. "I don't want him surrounded by machines and hooked to tubes and wires. He doesn't want that either, and you know it. We are going to take him home with us," she said.

Dr. Barker insisted Julia keep a tank of oxygen in the bedroom, "to make Avery more comfortable when he needs it," and he came by the house at least once a week and phoned nearly every evening. He wanted Julia to hire an off-duty nurse, but said he'd give in on that so long as Cole was there to help.

Cole and Jeanette moved in for the summer. It would be difficult, all of them under the same roof, but, of course, Cole wanted to be with his father.

Each morning, while Julia sat by the bed and read Avery interesting bits of news, amusing fillers from the paper, Cole wrapped hot towels on Avery's face and filled in the sunken places with thick shaving lather. Daily, Julia watched while Cole rediscovered the topography of his father's face. And daily the face changed. Avery was the Incredible Shrinking Man. Even as Julia listened to the rise and fall of her own voice and the steady scrape of the razor Cole drew along Avery's jaw, Avery was being eaten, from the inside out. Cole shaved Avery's cheek, and the skin, white with shaving foam, collapsed in toward Avery's dark mouth the way sugar dissolved into black coffee.

None of them dwelt on the obvious, but death was always there, standing at the foot of the bed or relaxing, slouched in a vacant chair. Julia and Cole talked, alone, sitting in the dark-green metal lawn chairs out back, beneath an ancient, gnarled live oak.

"Cole, do you think it's spreading upward?"

"I don't know," Cole said.

"God, I hope not. The lump in his neck is what worries me. If it's spreading upward, I pray he dies before it gets to his brain."

"I don't think it has affected his brain."

"No. No, he seems fine. That way, I mean. He gets sentimental at times—when we're alone. But he's given me instructions about insurance policies and bills, all that stuff. I don't think I could stand it if he lost his mind before he died. I don't want him to suffer that."

Cole said he was glad to know she and Avery had talked, openly. Glad they had been able to face the inevitable.

At times, however, Julia doubted the inevitability of Avery's death. The first of July, Dr. Barker stopped by the house. Before he left, he shook his head and told her, "I don't see how he keeps hanging on. I would have said this was impossible. He may see August, the way he's fighting."

For the Fourth, Avery requested homemade peach ice cream, which Cole and Jeanette made. Jeanette insisted on cranking even after the ice cream thickened and the crank got hard to turn.

Julia felt the tension between Cole and Jeanette. Julia had always been close to her daughter-in-law, but things seemed different now. Of course, things *are* different now, she thought, because *things are different now*. Nothing could possibly remain the same. And whenever Cole and Jeanette had visited, Avery had been the glue that held the four of them together. Jeanette was silent now, her jaw locked, a muscle moving tightly back and forth beneath her ear. But Julia could not, would not, worry about Jeanette and Cole. She had a right, she told herself, to worry entirely about Avery. And, of course, about herself.

The ice cream was good, full of fresh Texas peaches from Stonewall, but the chemotherapy kept Avery nauseated, and he couldn't eat more than a couple of bites. The medicine was so toxic it came in sealed glass tubes. Julia had to break off the end of a tube and pour the clear liquid into a glass of Coca-Cola. There were strict warnings in capital letters concerning the disposal of the opened tubes and the washing of the patient's contaminated utensils. Dr. Barker had explained that the chemotherapy was a kind of powerful poison to kill the cancerous cells.

"Of course," he said, "the chemicals aren't choosy. They'll kill whatever cells they get to."

Movement, even in the rented wheelchair, increased Avery's pain. Nausea made eating an ordeal. Even lying on the sheepskin they had bought, Avery was subject to aches and bedsores. He was reduced to a few simple physical pleasures. The hot towels Cole used with Avery's daily shave brought him inordinate pleasure. When he had the strength for it, a warm bath did him a world of good.

The first time Avery asked Julia to help him get a bath, she was nervous. She was afraid of Avery's wasted body, his weakness. She was afraid for him to see her fear. She bent to lift him from the bed and got a whiff of the baby powder she rubbed on his back every evening. She was shocked by how light his body was. Cradled in her arms, Avery's spine and the backs of his thighs felt no heavier and no thicker than a couple of pool cues. It was like lifting a small child. This body had held her as no other body had or ever would. This man had been her lover, her partner, her strength. For a moment their eyes could not avoid meeting. She hated, for Avery, that she had to see him like this. Samson with all his strength gone. She lowered Avery's body until his white, skeletal feet, the pale, ropy feet of a bird, touched the tile floor. Though Avery was inches taller than she, the pain kept him in a constant crouch, his knees drawn upward, while his shoulders sank downward to meet them.

In the mirror on the back of the bathroom door, Julia watched the two of them, husband and wife, an illustration in a book. She knelt on one knee and Avery reached out and gripped her shoulder to steady himself. Avery's red robe (he had insisted on a new, bright-red robe "to be sick in") was draped over his shoulders regally; his sweat-dampened hair stuck up in points like a crown. Julia knelt before her husband as a loyal subject before a sovereign in some cer-emony of knighthood or blessing.

When Avery's robe fell away, so did Julia's self-consciousness. There was no embarrassment between them, only an unspoken acceptance of what little could be done. Julia moved the bar of soap down the orange iodine stain faintly visible on Avery's neck. The soap bar bumped over Avery's bony shoulders and down his clearly visible rib cage. She soaped the purple scars that zigged like lightning down

Avery's chest and zagged across his side. Avery looked down at himself and then up at Julia. He was grinning. He held his thin middle finger out, and in the oily rainbow the soap left on the surface of the water he traced the shape of his scars, his gesture giving the finger and making the sign of the cross at once. His grin became a soft chuckle that shook his chest and made rings in the water. Julia laughed too. Her hands floated up to Avery's shoulders and slid smoothly over the soapy skin to meet in the wet hair on the back of his head. They stopped laughing, but both still grinned. She leaned close and drew Avery toward her until their foreheads rested against each other, their noses squashed together, their eyelashes touching and tickling, a close-up blur of shadow and light. She had an urge to ease her lover's wasted body down under the water, hold him there until he drowned in a final baptism. Their eyes met. Julia knew Avery saw what she imagined. Something, a sly smile, a twitch of irony, flickered across Avery's face. Their lips met, just touched, as they kissed each other—for the last time?—*goodbye.*

September came and with it a late-summer heat wave. Julia kept the air-conditioning on high. Cole had to leave Texas; classes had started in Alabama. He delayed going. His friend Dalton would meet Cole's first few classes. Julia hated to see Cole leave; he had been a great help, and Avery liked having him around. On the other hand, she wanted time alone with her husband, especially the last of her time with him. She knew Jeanette wanted to leave, and she understood that. Then Avery told Cole that if he was hanging around waiting for him to die, it was going to be a long wait.

"You better get back to Alabama and do whatever it is that university pays you to do," Avery said, "because I aim to be here for Christmas. Right, Julia?"

"You bet," she said.

Avery did make Thanksgiving. Cole came back to Texas and spent four days with them; Jeanette stayed in Alabama. Julia had warned Cole that Avery looked worse, but she knew nothing could have prepared Cole for the devastation wrought on the body he had hugged just three months earlier.

When Cole walked into the bedroom, Avery covered his face and said, "I hate for you to see me looking like this, Cole."

Julia remembered how, when he was little, Cole had believed he could make himself disappear by putting an arm or a pillow over his eyes. If Cole couldn't see Daddy or Mama, he thought they couldn't see him. Every night, Julia had tiptoed into Cole's bedroom to kiss him good night, and, every night, Cole pulled his pillow from beneath his head and covered his face.

"You can't kiss me now, Mama—I'm gone away," he cried.

Avery lay lost in the double bed. He had become Julia's sick child, Cole's wrinkled grandfather. He was a shriveled dwarf, a frightening gnome. Even his voice had changed; it was smaller, higher pitched, gnomelike too.

"I'm nearly gone, son," he said. "Aren't I nearly gone, Julia?"

"You will never be gone," she said.

Julia and Cole sat on the side of the bed, and Cole put his hand on his father's frail arm and gently pulled the arm down: Avery's eyes glistened with tears. But as they sat and talked, Avery got some of the characteristic huskiness back in his voice and Cole seemed to adjust to his father's changed appearance. Julia knew this was the last time the three of them would spend together. Even though this skeletal man with a ghost's voice was all that remained of the man she loved, something essentially Avery still shone forth from the used-up body.

Avery asked Cole to get the movie projector and screen down from the attic. He wanted to watch their old eight-millimeter home movies.

"He's been talking about those movies for days, waiting for you to get here. I almost think that's how he stayed alive, determined we were going to see those old movies together," Julia said.

Most of the movies were washed-out-looking, either overexposed or faded from years of attic heat. In one, Cole, about nine, ran around wearing a two-gun holster over a baseball uniform. He pointed both cap pistols at the camera every chance he got. Julia felt a mixture of embarrassment and loss as she watched their younger selves walk and grin and wave. What recognition, what loss was Avery facing, watching his own, once healthy, body move across the yard to stand beside a newly planted pecan tree. In the home movie the tree and Avery were the same height. That tree now rose above the roof and shaded this room from afternoon sun.

In the film Avery had on Sunday clothes; probably they had all been to church or out to dinner. Wearing his dark suit and tie, Avery walked with silent, jerky eight-millimeter steps on stilts he had made for Cole. Julia had forgotten all about the stilts Avery had planned to manufacture. He thought stilts could make a comeback, catch on like hula hoops, popular at the time. Avery had painted the stilts bright orange, and in the washed-out color of the old movie they glowed like neon. Julia wondered whether Avery or Cole saw that the stilts were the same iodine orange as the dye that had targeted Avery's neck for blasts of radiation.

The end of the film wound through the circuit of the projector and made a steady *clitter-clitter-clitter-clitter* as it came off the sprockets. Shadow and light danced across the white screen and pulsed in the dim bedroom. Avery stared at the screen, but he seemed to be looking far back into his distant past, as if he could locate the instant or the motion that began the curve at which point time twisted like a Möbius strip and might offer some clue to the future.

The Monday after Thanksgiving, Cole flew back to Alabama. That night, sitting in the dark living room alone, Julia sipped whiskey, neat, and realized she was listening not for Avery's call for help, nor for his irregular, labored breathing. She was listening to hear his breath stop. She heard the doorbell.

And three or four minutes later, Avery was dead.

Cole and Jeanette took the first available flight and got to Texas early the next morning. Julia picked them up at the airport.

Traffic was light, and Julia drove fast and effortlessly.

"I'm going to be fine, Cole. Your father told me not to carry on, and I promised I wouldn't. We were luckier than some people; we got to have our goodbyes."

She didn't want Cole to have to ask her the things she knew he would want to know.

"The doorbell rang. It was Dr. Barker stopping by. He was so good to us, Cole. I stepped into the bedroom to tell Avery, and he rose straight up in bed and smiled, then he opened his mouth and blood just gushed out, soaked the sheets. By the time I got to him he had fallen over on his side. Dr. Barker said an artery burst. The cancer ate through it. It was sudden, but smooth, if you understand. The blood made a soft, heavy *whoosh*, and he was gone. I wouldn't take anything for that little going-out smile he gave me. I think he waited until Dr. Barker was there, just to make it easier for me. Dr. Barker made some phone calls, and an ambulance came to pick Avery up. Isn't that funny, that they send an ambulance? I mean he was already dead. They came in ten minutes and were gone in five. They started to take the bloody bedcovers, but I wouldn't let them. Dr. Barker wouldn't leave until I gave him the name of someone he could call to come stay with me. I wanted to be alone, but he said he'd stay if I wouldn't let him call a friend. So I phoned Hazel Vance, the nice widow lady who lives on the corner. Then I went in and cleaned up

Avery's room. Dr. Barker didn't want me to do that either, but I insisted. I closed the door and had a little cry and got up all the blood."

"Wasn't that difficult—I mean emotionally—to do?" Jeanette asked.

"No. It was Avery's blood."

The skies were blue and clear, an unusually warm November day even for south Texas. Hazel Vance was at the house. Covered dishes crowded the table—potato salad, homemade pimento-cheese, a pecan pie, a lemon pound cake—the offerings of neighbors. Hazel had baked a ham. Julia introduced Hazel to Cole and Jeanette, thanked her for being so kind. Before she left, Hazel made a big pot of coffee and told Julia not to hesitate to call if she needed her.

Hazel *had* been kind. She and Julia were only nodding neighbors, not close, but last night she had bustled in and talked about the heat and washed the few dishes Julia hadn't gotten to. Then she poured two stiff whiskeys from the bottle Julia had left out and persuaded Julia to sit with her out under the live oak.

"Listen, honey," Hazel told her, "just because I don't know you well doesn't mean I can't love you when you need someone. I've buried two husbands. Nobody can take away your grief—shouldn't try; that's yours to nurse—but it helps to lean on others just a bit. So you lean, okay?"

Julia nodded and later, after she took the Valium Dr. Barker had left, she hugged Hazel and looked down at the woman's gray hair and her clean white scalp and smelled her cedar-closet smell and did lean on her a moment and felt the reassurance of Hazel's warm hand in the small of her back.

"I don't think I needed the Valium, but it was easier to take it than to argue with Hazel. I slept just fine. Better, really, than while Avery was alive. I was always afraid he might need me and I might not hear him from the couch."

Julia had waited for Cole to go with her to the funeral home. Making the arrangements was surprisingly easy. Avery had told Julia what he wanted. His body was not to be embalmed; the casket was to be sealed. There was to be no service, just a private burial, the three of them at the grave, a few verses of Scripture. Avery had said he wanted the cheapest casket they had, but Julia couldn't stand the cheapest one—it was made of some kind of pressed fiberboard, not even as solid as plywood, and covered with awful, textured cloth that reminded Julia of the flocked wallpaper in motel lounges. She picked the simplest, plainest casket she could find, which was not easy since most were done up with tacky trim and curlicued handles. Julia thought they looked like cheap bathroom vanities. The funeral director didn't argue, as Julia had expected, though he clearly didn't approve. He did protest when she told him she didn't want the tent and folding chairs or the bright-green Astroturf around the grave.

"But," he said, "you'll be able to see the *dirt*."

"We *like* this Texas dirt," Cole said. For a moment Julia was afraid there was going to be trouble. Cole's voice had several months' strain in it, and he was looking for someone to take it out on. The funeral director must have heard something in Cole's voice too; he pursed his lips and nodded.

"No chapel tent, no grass mat," the man noted on his pad.

In a little over an hour, all the arrangements made, they were back at the house. Julia turned off the engine but sat a moment in the car, the engine still running in her ears.

"Did you know, Cole, that when we first married, your father told me a story from Greek or Roman mythology every night after we went to bed?"

Cole smiled, said nothing.

"I remembered one this morning: Once, because Apollo shot his arrows at the Cyclops, Jupiter punished him, made Apollo serve a mortal, the king of Thessaly. This king, Admetus, wanted to marry Alcestis, the daughter of Pelias. (Your father knew all the right names, so I tried to learn them—I'm not sure I remember how he pronounced them.) Anyway, with Apollo's help, Admetus won Alcestis, only to get sick, dying-sick. Apollo talked the Fates into sparing the king, *if* someone would die in his place. But nobody wanted to die for Admetus, not even his parents. Before Admetus could stop her, Alcestis offered her life. As he got well, she got sick. Just in time, Hercules—mighty Hercules—showed up and found out the jam his king was in. Hercules hid outside the dying queen's room, and when Death came, Hercules grabbed him and made him give up Alcestis. Saved her, restored her to her husband. Good as new. Isn't that a good story?"

"It is," Cole said, "a good story."

While Julia and Cole had been away, Jeanette had answered the phone and received callers. Several of Avery's clients had phoned. Jeanette told them that Avery had requested donations to the American Cancer Society in lieu of flowers. She had made a list of all the callers for the thank-you notes Julia would write. A couple more covered dishes sat on the table.

Julia ate a small piece of Hazel's ham (she wasn't hungry) and said she was going to lie down for a few minutes. She had a strong urge to be alone in Avery's bedroom. She closed the door behind her. The room seemed smaller, more ordinary, and so very empty—as if all the furniture had been removed. She couldn't keep from looking for blood. But, of course, she had gotten up all the blood. She had changed the linens and cleaned the floor and the side rail of the bed. She had stared at the last brown smear of blood on a paper towel and had remembered the brown shapes her own blood had left on the sheets when she and Avery made love days she had her period so many years ago. So was this splotch of blood, one narrow streak, the final shape of love in her life?

Julia put her palm on the place where Avery had lain, where he had been alive less than twenty-four hours ago. She expected the bed to be still warm from Avery's body. She remembered Cole, years ago, a four-year-old holding up an Easter egg Avery had just boiled and dyed. *Oh, we just missed the Easter rabbit. It's still warm.* As she sat there with her hand on the mattress, her fingers spread into a star, something wonderful (full of wonder) happened. The windows through which Avery had stared for the last months of his life darkened as clouds from nowhere passed in front of the sun. Julia remembered Avery's nickname for Jupiter: Old Cloud-Gatherer. Julia was not sure how long she sat in the darkening room before she saw it—maybe only moments, maybe much longer—a furious flurry of snow. Cole called her from the kitchen, where he and Jeanette stared through the window over the sink at the falling snow.

Julia stood beside Cole at the window.

"Do you two know," Julia began, "what the name Avery means?"

Neither Cole nor Jeanette said anything. Cole seemed to only half hear Julia; he still stared at the sudden snow.

"Avery is a very old Anglo-Saxon name," Julia said. "Avery means 'the ruler of the elves.'" Little green Martian elves, she thought.

The kitchen window blazed with sun, and Julia squinted up at one lingering cloud. There Avery stood, before a fanciful machine (it looked like a huge slot machine with several arms to pull). Levers were marked: SUN, RAIN, FOG, HAIL, HURRICANE, TORNADO, FROST, SLEET, SNOW. Avery leaned forward and rested on the round blue knob of the lever marked SNOW and gave Julia a secret, Martian grin before the cloud dissipated.

Avery's wasted body would be buried in Texas dirt the next day, but Julia knew Avery was already long gone.

That evening, Julia and Cole and Jeanette had pimento-cheese sandwiches and beer. They ate in the den, holding plates in their laps and watching the news on television. The weatherman explained a rare phenomenon that had occurred that day. The weatherman's explanation wasn't clear, but as well as Julia could understand, it had something to do with colder temperatures at higher altitudes, atmospheric pressure. Wasn't atmospheric pressure the same as the barometer falling? Jeanette wanted to know.

"You weren't imagining things," the weatherman assured his watchers. "That was a real snow flurry, a rarity for south Texas."

There had been no accumulation. In fact, the weatherman explained, the snow melted before it ever touched ground. The records would indicate that there was no measurable precipitation for the date.

Julia smiled. She winked at Cole. She lifted her can of beer and tapped it against his and against Jeanette's.

"Let's drink," Julia said, "to the Ruler of the Elves."

The beer was cold. It tasted bitter going down, but it left a good aftertaste in Julia's mouth.

Jeanette took a small sip and set her can of beer on an end table. Light from the weather map illuminated her face and shone on tears that streaked her cheeks. She got up and quietly left the room. Cole caught Julia's eye and gave her a smile, then went after Jeanette. A moment later, Julia heard their voices, muffled and low, as if the furnace had come on and was mumbling secrets to the two-by-four studs in the walls. She wished Avery, who (like Melampus, whose story Avery had told her) understood the language of all creatures, were there to whisper in her ear and reveal the secrets the house kept.

Alone, Julia looked at the weather map of Texas on the TV.

"To the Ruler of the Elves," Julia repeated. In the empty room, she raised her can to toast the weatherman. She took another long drink and let the ice-cold beer pour down her throat and into her chest.

9

THERE was a dead live oak tree farther up the same hillside into which Avery's body would be lowered. The late-November sky was blue, and the warm sun cast the shadow of the tree over Julia's and Cole's and Jeanette's shoulders and arms and onto the hardscrabble slant of land on which they stood, all three of them leaning against the inclining earth and gravity's pull. The hearse backed right up to the grave, and two men from the funeral home slid the casket out like a drawer from a dresser.

Julia read the words, as Avery had instructed, from Ecclesiastes:

> Go thy way, eat thy bread with joy, and drink thy wine with a merry heart; for God now accepteth thy works.
>
> Let thy garments be always white; and let thy head lack no ointment.
>
> Live joyfully with the wife whom thou lovest all the days of the life of thy vanity, which he hath given thee under the sun, all the days of thy vanity: for that *is* thy portion in *this* life, and in thy labor which thou takest under the sun.
>
> Whatsoever thy hand findeth to do, do *it* with thy might; for *there is* no work, nor device, nor knowledge, nor wisdom, in the grave, whither thou goest.

Julia put herself up in the bare limbs of the dead tree above and behind her. She didn't have to climb; she was just there, the way you are in a novel or a movie. From high in the tree she looked down at herself, Cole, and Jeanette standing beside her, while Avery's casket, the color of an old, spent penny, hovered and then slowly lowered, a Martian shuttle craft disintegrating the hard caliche and limestone beneath it, silently blasting a secret landing place in exactly its size and shape—a kind of nest down in the earth. Millions of miles above, light-years away, other planets and distant stars revolved, invisible in the light of day. There was no telling, Julia thought, what unknown signals were being sent and received, what celestial enterprises were under way.

PART THREE

Cole

1

COLE'S eyes were closed, the sun hot on his eyelids. Through them he saw a blue-white brightness like a long-lasting flashbulb. That made him think of overexposure: of his unprotected skin, of the subject of romance.

A romantic, Cole had borrowed the money from his mother and taken the time (which he had less and less of, he thought) so that he could find himself on a Greek island and think of himself as a kind of castaway: Coleman Avery Marrs, just divorced, almost thirty-nine.

All our stories, Cole had read, began on the beach. An allusion, he supposed, to evolution—that first *in the beginning* when (and where) life crawled out of the sea. A natural enough beginning. You had to start somewhere, Cole knew.

In his ears he felt the sponge tips of the new, lightweight earphones and heard Keith Jarrett moan in the midst of his Bregenz Concerts. Keith couldn't stand it. *Neither can I, Keith,* Cole thought. Keith Jarrett was playing something entitled "Untitled." The piano and Jarrett's moans were startlingly clear and resonant, as was the heat of the Mediterranean sun. Cole smelled coconut oil on hot skin and something fishy carried on the soft breeze.

On his left, Cole's new girlfriend lay on a clean white hotel towel, feeling, he knew, left out. His old friend, Philip, had taken a sketch pad and gone up into the hills behind the beach. On Cole's right, Philip's girl, April, was flat on her back. Cole was connected to this girl—between them on the unfolded double straw mat was Philip's new Sony, two sets of earphones plugged into its side—both of them sharing the same music. Cole thought of umbilical cords, blood transfusions, electrodes sending the charge of life into Dr. Franken-stein's monster's brain, and (as he got into it more) of the shackles and velvet chains pictured in those kinky, all-initials (B & D, S & M) sex magazines. *Only connect.*

Cole thought about the music filling his head and Philip's girl's head at the same time, images slipping from her brain out through her ear, through the earphone wire, around the tape and back out of the Sony, through the wire into his ear and, finally, his brain. He wanted to see himself; he wanted the girl to be dreaming of him. Since that was what came to his mind, who was to say it was not her dream beamed through the circuitry of the tiny tape machine? Cole opened one eye just enough to squint out through his lashes. The girl, April, lay perfectly still. He watched closely and saw her shining belly barely rise and fall.

A shadow darkened his left arm, and he turned to see his new girlfriend up on one elbow, watching. She was not on the large straw mat, nor could she hear the music.

"A penny for your thoughts," she said.

He wanted to pretend he couldn't hear her because of the ear-phones, but he felt her hand, warm and moist, on his elbow, so he slipped the earphones up and let the music push against his hair and skull.

"What'd you say?" He kept his eyes closed and faced straight up. He *felt* the bright sun so clearly it was as if he were seeing through his closed lids.

"I said, A penny for your thoughts."

"I'd be overcharging you."

"Come on."

"Nothing. Really."

"Want to know what *I* was thinking?"

"Sure." Cole turned his head in the woman's direction, but he kept his eyes closed against the heat.

"No, you don't. You don't care."

"Sure I do." He opened his eyes, squinted at her. Her lip was trembling, and he thought she was going to cry. He smiled at her. "Tell me," he said.

But instead of crying she laughed, her eyes squeezed closed.

"I was thinking," she said, "what a good time we could be hav-ing and what a fool I was to bring you with me."

Cole did not say anything. He closed his eyes again and lis-tened to the surf. With his eyes still closed, he said:

"You're probably right about both."

Cole and this new girlfriend had been together only a few weeks. During the separation from his wife, Jeanette, Cole had lost weight. He was lean and tanned. His shoulders, which had always been broad, seemed even wider now that his stomach was flat and hard. His hair was dark, but since the separation he had gotten a touch of gray, which began at his temples and disappeared over his ears. The new girlfriend said the gray hair was like feathers; she said she liked it very much. Funny, Cole thought, that a divorce would make him more attractive. His friend, Philip, whom he had not seen for several years, said he looked younger than the last time they were together.

"Divorce seems to agree with you," Philip said, and he winked at Cole's new girlfriend, which, clearly, pleased her.

The girlfriend was named Charlotte Moore, and she was the first woman Cole had slept with since his divorce. She was the first woman other than his wife he had slept with in thirteen years. The lovemaking had been a surprise. Charlotte was a screamer. Loud shrieks. At first he thought she was hurt; then he liked it. She was so brand-new.

Now when she cried out, there was less surprise, no concern, just newness. Beneath her breasts, over her pale skin, he ran his fingers down her ribs. He slid his hands between her large thighs and felt a muscle rise long and firm like a loaf of heavy bread. Thigh skin, baby soft, over firmness: the word *loins,* Biblical sexuality, animal flesh, horsey woman, Tina Turner's thighs—sweat shiny and pumping, muscles straining, skin slapping, thigh chafing thigh. She yelled and moaned and bucked against him, and the bed moved away from the wall.

"Cole," she said, then louder each time, "Cole, Cole, Cole." She slid her hands down his backside and pulled. Her breasts flattened against him, and then he wanted to roll over, to breathe easily and to feel air down the length of his body, but when he lifted his weight she locked her arms in the small of his back and he almost panicked, then he made himself relax, as if he were swimming. He turned his head and took in air, turned his head and took in air, turned his head and took in air.

Against her pale, soft face Charlotte's curly hair looked black. Up close it was dark brown, and in the sun Cole had seen fine strands bright red as sewing thread. Her voice was husky and low (Tallulah Bankhead, Lauren Bacall), and at first everything she said sounded suggestive. Her lips were dark and full and seemed to promise something. She always looked as if she had just sucked on a cherry Popsicle. With the dark hair, her big blue eyes were unexpected. She was intelligent and she was independent. In those ways, if in no others, his new girlfriend reminded Cole of Jeanette, his *ex*-wife. The term was still strange to him, *ex* stuck onto wife like *alumna* stuck onto a college decal on the rear window of a station wagon—someone not as essential as she once was, or as he once thought she was.

Charlotte rubbed thick sunscreen all over herself, and white streaks dried like fingerpaint on her sensitive skin. April's body, beside his on the straw mat, was coated all over with dark oil that made her skin glisten, made the fine blond hairs on her flat belly catch the sun and shine like tiny metal filings. If Cole put his hands on April's bare belly they would slide, warm and oily, up to the edge of her baby-blue bikini top, down to the top of her baby-blue bikini bottom. Charlotte's brown one-piece suit left only her back and her muscular thighs to touch, and the dried white lotion would put the brakes on movement the way a gym floor squeaks sneakers to a sudden, jerking halt.

He was not, of course, being fair. But Cole felt like being unfair. A cartoon devil throbbed redly by his ear, smirking and encouraging him. *You deserve whatever you feel like,* the little devil whispered. *Go ahead, think mean, think small.* What better time for self-indulgence? Nearing forty, getting over his first divorce, no longer special—"You and Jeanette are a legend," more than one friend had told him, "the only happy married couple in the world"—he was now part of the dominant demographic group of his time. Divorced. Single. So he had proved it to himself by doing just the sort of thing the popular culture demanded: he took off for Greece with a younger woman.

From the first travel-brochure afternoon—drinks in the sunny garden behind Philip's blindingly white stucco cottage, the view of green and gold hills and blue, blue sky and sea beyond, a block of feta cheese as white as the stucco house beside the brown, sweat-beaded bottles of beer, April's hand lightly touching Philip's arm to emphasize a point, her fingers tanned brown as the beer bottles, her nails perfect almonds—Philip's situation had seemed better than Cole's. Philip was dark as a native, he had mastered fair conversational Greek, his girl was sexy and seemed totally uninhibited. She seemed—Cole wondered if this was wishful thinking—to have an eye for Cole. Maybe, he thought, she's just the kind of woman who can't be friends with a man except in a sexual (flirtatious, at least) way. Every time April reached for something and her arm brushed his, every time she leaned and took his hand for assistance, every time she gazed out at the ocean and her eyes passed over his, Cole was pleased. As much as he anticipated and enjoyed these moments, he would not let them become full-fledged fantasies. He kept reminding himself, April is Philip's girl. The temptation of April's flesh was helping Cole develop a moral stoicism. Though he knew he wouldn't get close enough to the fire to burn himself, he was enjoying the heat April gave off. But April's presence made him less comfortable with Charlotte.

He told himself he had had the chance to *start over* and already he had gotten himself into, in the jargon, *a relationship,* the obligations of which felt confining and made him resent a woman he actually liked very much. He would always care for Charlotte, but he wondered if his affection for her wasn't a kind of nostalgia he already felt about his first sexual encounter after thirteen years with one (and only one) woman.

Keith Jarrett finished off his untitled number, and the tiny earphones filled with applause that seemed to roll down the beach and crash into the waves. Cole imagined that the applause was for him, and he felt himself grin. He lifted his right eyelid and squinted out through the feathery shadow of his eyelashes. Heat radiated from April's long, darkly tanned body and made the curve of his hip, precious inches from her hip, feel as if it were glowing. April was just the kind of woman he had pictured himself with after his divorce. Jeanette's opposite. You'd guess California, or Florida: the golden tan, the ass-length blond hair, the frosted nails, fingernails *and* toenails always painted, wet-looking. April kept her firm lips—they were straight and thin—pursed all the time.

April seldom spoke except to remark on the angle of the sun and the temperature of the water. Daily she grew darker, the tips of her blond hair bleached bright as the sunlit rocks and fields of the island.

Keith Jarrett was at it again. An encore? Or did April like this part of the performance so much she'd repeated it on the tape, made Keith play that sad ending over and over so that there were no new beginnings on this tape, just lovely endings repeated and repeated.

Charlotte lifted the earphones off his head.

"Do you want to swim?" she asked.

"You go on. I'll join you in a little while."

"We don't have to wear our suits here," Charlotte said, and smiled at him.

He hoped April couldn't hear with the earphones on.

97

"Not now." He slipped the earphones back on. Charlotte stood over him a long moment, then turned and walked down toward the surf.

At the edge of the water, where the sand was smooth and hard, Charlotte stopped and looked back. Cole imagined he and April looked like giant insects with curved antennae, the black wires connecting them to the tape player like long feelers or feeding tubes dipped into the same bright flower. Charlotte turned toward the surf and then walked steadily out into the water.

Keith Jarrett lifted his hands from the piano keys and hundreds of Bregenz Austrians clapped their hands and cried out (in German, Cole imagined) for more. Cole tried to recall the Deutsche word for *more,* but all he remembered was *más* from high school Español. The German book he had studied was gray, the desk, cheap imitation Spanish, stained dark brown. The landlord referred to all the furniture, because of that desk, as Mediterranean. There were just four rooms in the tiny garage apartment. He and Jeanette had moved in the day after they married. Every window looked out into the limbs of live oaks—it had been like living in a tree house. In the center of the apartment, a post served as the doorjamb for the opening into each room. He had held on to that post and walked a circle through all four rooms, like that place out west, Four Corners. Every evening he and Jeanette had cooked in Utah, eaten in Colorado, studied in New Mexico, and gone to bed in Arizona.

The German applause died away and some new, soft rock filled Cole's head and reminded him just how far he had come from that time and place, that old life. Greece: Heraclitus' Principle of Change, the flowing stream. Greece: thousands of miles, hundreds of years, geographical and figurative distance, a new beginning from each ending. On his back in the warm sun, Cole felt as if he were a soldier, wounded in honorable warfare, sent here to recuperate, regain his strength for future battles. He was on the mend. Through his closed lids the sun burned bright.

April's fingers moved with the new song. Her long fingers made a damp spot on the mat. When Cole slipped the earphones off he heard the music, tinny and distant, down in the sponge earpieces and he heard the soft *tump* of the girl's fingers and the *skritch* of her frosted pink fingernails catching the fibers of the mat. He shifted and felt the grit of sand on straw, thought about the Princess and the Pea, about how an oyster turns an irritating speck of sand into a pearl.

This was supposed to be a nude beach. They'd paid about fifty cents in drachmas to ride an open wooden boat across the green bay.

The beach ran along the edge of a crescent of rocky hills. An outdoor snack bar with a woven straw roof over four or five tables and several chairs sold octopus, squid, French fries, cold beer, and Cokes. A black panel truck faded purple by the sun sat on concrete blocks, its rear end open to reveal the bright sails of windsurfing rigs for rent, with free lessons by two naked, muscular young Greeks. A few goats, ribs showing, nosed around rocks on the hills behind the beach. The windsurfing instructors, as dark all over as most of the sun worshippers were pale, ran up and down the beach. Their feet disappeared in the surf so that their naked bodies ended just above the ankles and perfected the image of hoofed satyrs chasing prey. Back home, Cole thought, they'd hulk over us on the lifeguard tower or jump our legs to catch a Frisbee behind the back or under one dark leg. April's suggestion that they come here "because it's nude" intrigued Cole more than he would admit. He wondered whether it would be to his advantage to bare himself. A slogan came to mind: *Men, do you measure up?* He felt some concern for Charlotte, who was sure to suffer from any comparison with April. *The naked truth,* one of the deadlier dead phrases in the language, come to life. But the only nude sunbathers, except for the Greek satyrs (who flashed in the sun like polished copper), were two middle-aged German couples a few feet away. The women, blond and heavyset, folded their legs beneath them on an orange beach towel and played cards. The men lay face down on the sand, their bare bottoms no paler than their backs and skinny legs. All down the beach, the bodies Cole would have liked to see displayed remained covered, and (probably because of this) April said nothing more about peeling down. Cole avoided the white bodies of the Germans and concentrated on what April's scanty bikini offered.

In the midday heat of the Mediterranean sun, April lay still and silent. When Cole rose she didn't even flutter her eyelids; she had the song on the tape moving loudly in her head.

Charlotte was talking to one of the naked windsurfing instructors, ignoring Cole. She was angry and hurt, and he was sorry, but he was glad when she didn't come after him. He resolved not to ask her what was the matter (as if he didn't know) but to act as if everyone was perfect in a perfect world. Behind and far above them was the shape he knew was Philip with his sketch pad. He wondered if Philip had put them all in the picture. He remembered a novel in which a soldier with a missing leg asked an artist to sketch him. "And when you put me in the picture," the soldier asked, "could you draw my leg back on?"

In his bathing suit, and sandals still so new they hurt his feet,

Cole moved up into the hills. The walk was steep; he had to look for foot and hand holds, his eyes moving ahead, plotting his ascent as when he was a kid climbing a tree. He waved at Philip, who lifted a hand. Below, the sand ran out into the clear, green water—the water like glass, not *as smooth as,* but *as clear as.* A long, lovely sailboat sat motionless on the water, looking like a model or toy boat set upon a glass tabletop. Cole had not seen the boat's approach; it was as if it had materialized *from out of nowhere, a dream boat.* That was how he decided to think of it. When the anchor was let out, he watched it all the way to the bottom, but the water was so clear he could not even guess its depth.

Cole's father, Avery, like so many others, had wanted to build a boat. His dream had not been as flashy as the sleek one anchored below—he had dreamed a houseboat. A salesman for a cardboard-container corporation, he had sold boxes, tubes, custom-made cartons.

While Cole was young, before Avery's houseboat dream, all his friends' fathers helped them build kites—sharp diamond-shaped kites, finny airplane kites, long dragon kites. Avery built Cole a box kite. The vertical struts were as tall as Cole was. Avery cut up a red silk kimono he had given Cole's mother, Julia, during the Second World War and glued the wide bands of red silk around the ends of the kite. They waited for wind to test the kite. Finally, after days and days of calm, Cole suspended the kite from the ceiling light in his bedroom, where it hung for years like a geometric, abstract painting and cast red rectangles on the walls and floor. So, later, a houseboat, a floating box, came as no surprise.

Avery figured flotation, compared metal oil drums to fiberglass pontoons. Using a blue-and-white ballpoint pen with *S & S Marine* on the side in yellow rope letters, Avery drew houseboat plans. When he marked arrows down from a tank on the roof and told his son this would give them running water, he grinned as if he had just discovered gravity. In the garage was iron pipe for the houseboat's railing and a stainless-steel kitchen sink accepted from a customer in lieu of a monthly payment. Avery sat behind Cole on the hassock and, with a steering wheel from a wrecked car, taught Cole to handle a houseboat in any current, in all kinds of weather.

With a worn case knife, Avery made a houseboat model. It floated on toilet paper tubes. A cardboard roof, flat for sunbathing, lifted off to reveal a cardboard table that folded against a wall; a small square of tin foil was the kitchen sink.

Avery built his dream boat. And then he gave it away.

Cole still had a sharply focused roll of Kodak Brownie snap-shots: his father and his mother and his wife and himself up in the new, blond two-by-fours. People speculated on what was taking shape. A bomb shelter? A personal spaceship? Were they going to blast off for Mars? In the photos, Cole and Avery had their shirts off. Their skin was the color of the new boards they were nailing in place, and the summer sky above them was as blue as this Mediterranean sky, as blue as the cross in the Greek flag Cole had seen all over this island.

The houseboat was a wedding gift for a young couple Avery knew. The young man and his wife talked of the family they wanted. The young man worked long hours six days a week, and the couple spent their summer Sundays on the houseboat.

In the fall Cole and Avery went out and replaced the vinyl floor tiles that had buckled in the summer's heat. By then Avery had a new dream: Australia. As far as Cole knew, Avery made all his dreams come true except that one. He dreamed of Australia for years but never got there.

Soon enough, the houseboat became part of the property dis-pute in the young couple's divorce. The woman got the houseboat. She moved away and left the boat to deteriorate. Finally, she sold it to a man who dragged it up onto shore and set it on concrete blocks and turned it into a bait stand. He cut one of the oil drums in half and painted it silver and set it on legs as a barbecue grill.

It *was* funny, what Cole remembered.

What he wanted to remember well, what he tried hard to memorize, was not always easy to recall. He had trouble with Avery's face. He did better with a photograph, remembered more easily the frozen image than the living visage. In Cole's memory it was neces-sary to arrest motion. Things came back as still life and framed shot, when he was able to bring them back at all. And he could not hear, in his mind's ear, Jeanette's voice—not one whispered word remained. At first, after the divorce, he had been tempted to telephone her, long distance, to make up some excuse for a call, just to hear her voice. Once, late at night, after enough Jack Daniel's, he did phone and lis-tened to her *Hello,* sleepy-sounding, then more irritated, *Hello, hello,* until she hung up. Maybe she had never sounded like herself over the telephone; he could not remember.

Across the way, Philip was waving his sketch pad like a sem-aphore flag. Cole waved back. The lovely sailboat was moving. The sailors had decided to go farther or to return to some other place or had stopped only to make some minor repair or to mix drinks in the smooth calm of this inlet or to snap some pictures of this perfect day or to eye April through a long spyglass.

Cole pictured April's shape in the center of the pale-green circle of a telescope's lens and remembered the stationery from Avery's employer, the container corporation, on which Avery had sketched houseboat plans. When Cole was a boy, the stationery, with a circle, a rectangle, and a triangle on the letterhead, had reminded him of his geometry book. Below him now were the circles of snack bar tables, the bright rectangles of beach towels, the boat's sail opening into a white triangle. And Cole could still read, as if he held a sheet of that stationery, the italics beneath the shapes: *We're in shape to fit your needs.*

Cole looked down at the shapes he knew were April and Charlotte stretched out on the sand. He wondered if Philip had been drawing those shapes below or dreaming new shapes of his own. That morning, Cole had lain on the bed and watched Charlotte bend her bare back to him as she dried her feet and ankles after a shower. In thirteen years of marriage Cole had seen the curve of Jeanette's back how many times? More than hundreds; a thousand at least. But he could not remember each time. He tried to count the separate times he had seen Jeanette's bent back, and he could not get to ten.

2

WHAT, Cole thought, had brought him to this and to this place? What happened way out in that sea, way back in time, that brought those first single-celled creatures up onto the beach to lie out and begin the world's first suntan?

If Cole could trace the effects of all his causes back far enough, he would find himself out in that original ocean. But if he looked for the beginning (but not the end) of romance, *true romance,* in his life, he would have to look no farther behind him than the dark, wet earth and muggy air of south Louisiana, where he had met and married his first wife, Jeanette.

They went to Mardi Gras together. Jeanette had a girlfriend who lived down in the French Quarter, a place where they could crash for the duration, and he had a car to get them to New Orleans. The day they were to leave, he stepped on one of his contact lenses and crushed it. Jeanette said it wouldn't matter, that Mardi Gras was supposed to be blurry. For the next three days Cole switched his remaining lens back and forth, from one eye to the other, and balanced his vision and his walk.

Several other revelers joined Cole and Jeanette, to sleep on the floor of her friend's studio apartment in the Vieux Carré. It was at least as crowded as any ocean floor. Dark-green, narrow, ceiling-to-floor shutters covered the windows and the double french doors. The stereo played softly all night long, then woke Cole just before dawn, stuck, momentarily, at the end of the last record stacked on the turntable during the night. The needle rasped in the last empty groove, then the tone arm lifted and a blue light winked out. Through the slats of the shutters Cole heard a door close, or open, but no

footsteps. In the courtyard below, dark with ferns and ivy and orna-
mental ironwork, nothing stirred. The air was as wet and heavy as
any dark sea, fathoms deep. Humps of unfamiliar bodies covered the
floor and pressed against him. Cole felt the length of Jeanette's leg
against his, and he slid his hand beneath her shirttail, where he felt
the smooth, tight skin of her belly. He slid his hand under the elastic
top of her wispy panties. His fingertips moved into her pubic hair the
way he had seen slender fish move into the dark curls of aquarium
plants that fanned up from tight tucks of roots in a gravel bottom.
He poked his finger down and crooked it up into her; he felt the
hardness of one pea-sized pebble that he rolled back and forth
beneath his wet fingertip.

There on the crowded floor, taken up wholly by reclined,
curled, held bodies, Cole felt for the first time how it feels to touch
and to be touched so that you become the static filling the space
between skin and skin, the faint burn, hiss, sizzle of secretion and
suction, the very *kiss* of contact. Never before had he understood
impact. He wanted to bolt, but he didn't know whether to bolt away
or toward. In a moment fully breathless and thoughtless, he chose
toward (or he was chosen by that motion, having for the first time
inclined himself in that direction), and a week later he and Jeanette
married.

That had not been a mistake; the mistakes had come later, in
how they lived together. And, still later, in not seeing those mistakes
for so long that, finally, Jeanette deceived him and, eventually, left
him.

Jeanette's rambling, intimately unimportant talk had, when they
first met, turned the hands of the clock like a finger resetting time,
and Cole would look up from his coffee cup to see that it had quickly
become midnight. At some point in the marriage Cole's mind began
to wander while Jeanette talked. It was as impossible now to remember exactly when this happened, or began to happen, as it is to know
when a virus enters your body, when a tumor begins to grow—you
aren't likely to remember, even, just when you first felt pain. If their
marriage seemed so special to outsiders it was because they seemed
to have so much in common. Jeanette was nineteen, a sophomore.
Cole was a graduate assistant in American studies, assigned to grade
papers in one of Jeanette's classes. They met at an all-night grill to
go over a paper Jeanette had written. Cole had been excited by the
originality of the paper, then surprised by the dark-eyed, quietly pretty
girl who had written it. Around others, Jeanette was quiet, almost shy.
Cole felt as if he had to interpret her. She was Creole, petite and

exotic. She lived on thick, dark New Orleans coffee, ice water, and cigarettes. Cole got her to quit smoking and fed her heavy Tex-Mex meals and barbecued beef brisket. When they married and moved into the garage apartment, she spent days in cutoffs and T-shirts, cleaning, painting, nailing up shelves for books. She was small but strong, and not afraid of hard physical work. From the beginning he admired her strength. They worked well together, hammering with a *bam-bam, bam-bam* rhythm. In the evenings they sat on the floor and admired their handiwork, and she matched him beer for beer.

The doctor who gave Jeanette a required premarital exam said she had an inverted womb, that it would be difficult for her to get pregnant. Cole and Jeanette had never talked about children; it was as if they both assumed children would come when the time was right. Those first few years, while they were still *interested* in one another, they spent all their time together. Students together, they had no jobs to separate them for eight hours a day. Neither ever went out—not for an hour, not for an evening, not for a visit out of town—without the other. They spent over a year traveling around Europe and, for the next few summers, visited all fifty states.

Except for that premarital exam, Jeanette did not see a doctor for the first three or four years of their marriage. She mistrusted all doctors, and she had a primitive, almost religious faith in her body's innate abilities to fend for itself. She ate what she wanted, believing her body would crave what it needed most. She periodically fasted or went on eating binges; she drank wine, beer, whiskey, tequila, and gin, often all in one evening; she would smoke cigarettes, cigars, and marijuana; she had eaten peyote buttons and swallowed speed; but she would not take aspirin. Relying on the doctor's remark about her inverted womb, she refused to take birth control pills. "Don't worry," she told Cole. "I won't get pregnant." And she didn't.

A few years later—could it be as few as three or four, as many as six or seven?—Cole had a teaching job at a state college in Ohio. Ohio was flat as a parking lot, the winter landscape the color of concrete. From their bedroom window they watched trainloads of coal go north, trainloads of new cars head south. Beside the tracks a grain elevator gleamed silver in sunlight, glowed in moonlight, poised like a rocket, aimed at the heavens.

Jeanette was taking graduate courses and publishing in small academic journals. She was no longer quiet. She started smoking again and affected the use of a mother-of-pearl cigarette holder. At parties Cole always wanted to go home before Jeanette did. She found rides back later. It bothered him—he was angry, hurt, jealous—but he came to like the quiet at home alone.

Cole often calculated his age against the likelihood of a second chance, a new life. If, he figured, I were to remarry by forty, I'd have ten to twenty good years left. Maybe enough time for a child.

Time passed, became a few more years. Cole wanted a change. He interviewed with several universities and was offered positions, both better than the Ohio job, in Pennsylvania and in Alabama. Cole had never spent time in Alabama. He'd been to Selma when he was in college, to see where the famous march had been, and he and Jeanette once spent a good night and day in Mobile, on their way somewhere else. He'd never imagined living in Alabama. He thought of Confederate flags and George Wallace. He remembered TV news films of Bull Connor turning fire hoses and police dogs on blacks in Birmingham. He thought of Walker Evans's photographs and James Agee's descriptions in *Let Us Now Praise Famous Men*. He thought of red clay hills and miserable heat. But, in a gray, midwestern January, that heat seemed appealing. He'd seen racism everywhere he'd been; it seemed likely that Alabama was no more mean-spirited than Ohio. Universities in the South were more conservative; they had been slower to accept American studies. During his interview he'd been warned he might be treated a little like an outsider by professors in other departments. He didn't think he'd mind that, and he liked the idea of helping develop a fairly new program. He'd be closer to Texas, maybe closer to his roots. He could get a coon dog and a flat-bottomed boat, hunt and fish, simplify his life. Jeanette was all for Alabama; she was tired of cold and snow and loved the idea of being close enough to New Orleans for weekend trips.

They drove down to Alabama to visit. They sat outside in the March sun and ate barbecued ribs. Out of the corner of his eye Cole saw Jeanette smile at him more than once. In the motel they made love in the morning, then went out for a heavy, Southern breakfast of ham and eggs, biscuits, grits and redeye gravy. Cole ate till he felt drugged and then decided they were making the right move.

They bought a house in Alabama (they'd always rented before) and moved early in the summer, before Cole's classes began. The realtor, Laurie, who sold them the house, and her husband, Chip, lived in the same neighborhood. Chip also taught at the university—Russian. By the end of the summer they were all fast friends. It was the first time Cole and Jeanette had both liked both halves of another couple. That first Alabama summer was backyard-barbecue, all-American fun.

106

Cole felt as if he and Jeanette were at a turning point. Their life together was about to get serious, and good. He insisted they sit down and talk about having a family.

"I thought we were a family," Jeanette said.

"You know what I mean."

She sighed. "Yeah, I know what you mean." Then she surprised him. She smiled and became animated. "I'll see a doctor, a good gynecologist." She giggled. "I want babies."

For at least a year they used a basal thermometer to chart Jeanette's temperature and predict her ovulation. Jeanette used the calendar to try to get pregnant, just as her Catholic mother had instructed her to use the calendar to prevent pregnancy. Sex on the calendar's demand did not please Cole, and he was sure Jeanette didn't like it either, but she worked at getting pregnant with the same determination she used to hammer nails. A year later the gynecologist sent them to an infertility specialist, who suggested medication to regulate Jeanette's cycle.

After Jeanette's examination and several tests, they sat in the specialist's quiet office. "Mrs. Marrs, we've been using this drug for over thirty-five years now. It's perfectly safe and very effective." Jeanette took the prescription and put it in her purse. She said nothing.

In the car Jeanette turned to face Cole. She still said nothing, but her eyes were narrowed, her jaw tight. Cole faced the road. He drove and waited.

"I'm not going to take it," she said. He knew she was waiting to see what he had to say to that. When he said nothing, she went on: "It causes birth defects. Not to mention what it might do to my body. We're messing with my hormones."

"Did the doctor tell you it causes birth defects?"

"Cole, he wouldn't even look me in the eye."

Cole shook his head. *Lord,* he thought.

"Doctors talk about 'acceptable risks.' What's an acceptable risk, Cole? You want to take this shit?"

"I can't help it that you have to take the risks, that you bear the child. Maybe I wouldn't want to take the stuff either. Let's find another expert, get a second opinion." Jeanette's smallness made her seem more at risk. As if one capsule might wreck some delicate balance in her body. He *did* admire her. And he *loved* her too. Maybe they should think about how it would be *not* to have any children. Maybe the fact that they had waited so long meant they didn't want them as badly as you were supposed to. Maybe, being an only child,

107

Cole didn't know enough about babies to make a wise decision. He turned down Lurleen Wallace Lane. The name of the street that took them to the first house they'd ever bought was usually cause for at least a shared smile, but not today. Cole held out his right hand to Jeanette, but she did not take it.

"Go to the pharmacy," she said. "I'll take the stuff."

"Let's think about this," Cole said. "Let's talk to another doctor."

"No, I want to go ahead."

"Are you sure?" This was some kind of test. If he agreed, he was somehow betraying her.

The capsules—there were only five—cost over thirty dollars. The doctor had said she might need to take them for several months. It could get expensive.

But they never bought any more. Jeanette never took them. The plastic bottle sat on the back of the lavatory for the next four months. Neither Jeanette nor Cole would throw it away. The brown plastic container became their private symbol for a cure they would not attempt, a malady they could not heal.

The day they filled the prescription, they learned that Chip and Laurie were getting a divorce. Laurie was moving to northern Virginia, where she had family and could get another real estate job. Chip would continue, for the time-being, to teach Russian at the university.

Everything had gone sour in a hurry. After all the years Cole and Jeanette had spent together, it took only a few months for them to divide themselves back into strangers. The divorce took nineteen days.

And now, just five months after the divorce, Cole lay stretched out beside a friend's, Philip's, girlfriend, a woman with a springtime name—April. He lay beside a lovely stranger and they shared Philip's music and the light and beauty of a Mediterranean paradise. Cole was trying to heal himself. He had taken the time and accepted the loan his mother offered, to come thousands of miles just so he could crawl up onto this slant of sand and begin again.

It had seemed, the night Jeanette told him, there could be no new beginning. Cole and Jeanette, Jeanette and Cole: either way, their separate names had become one phrase. It was now hard for Cole to believe how surprised he had been. It was a week before Christmas. She had been painting their bedroom; sheets were draped over chairs and spread on the floor. The only light came from a lamp in the adjacent guest bedroom. A cold front had moved in; "Blame it on the Russians," the newspaper had said, the cold pushed by a Siberian Express roaring out of the eastern U.S.S.R. The room was chilly, and Cole smelled natural gas as he knelt to light a space heater, that and the smell of new paint. Some association—the space heaters at his grandmama's when he was a child, his grandmama's chilly dining room, the box of silver on her heavy old sideboard, or just something about the smell of paint and turpentine in a cold room—made Cole taste silverware, the cold, flat blade of a butter knife on his tongue. The heater's flames gave the room a historical, sepia tint.

Jeanette sat in her green leather chair wrapped in a quilt, her feet pulled up under her body, just her head sticking out. Each wooden arm of the chair ended in the carved head of a duck. Jeanette's eyes were two dabs of brown paint.

For days they had avoided each other. When they passed in the hall between their bedroom and the bathroom she flattened herself against the wall, made sure their bodies did not touch. When Cole could no longer refrain from asking, What's wrong?—the first of a list of clichés—she told him to let her be, give her time, this had nothing to do with him, give her space. So he tried to let things ride, tried not to force the issue. Soon the distance between them, and the not knowing, seemed worse than anything he had imagined. But—and this now seemed impossible—he had never imagined the obvious.

"Jeanette, I have to know what's wrong."

Her head cocked above the high collar of the blue-and-yellow quilt; fanciful appliquéd birds rested on her shoulders.

"Tonight, Jeanette. Now."

Cole's right leg, near the heater, was hot, the rest of him, cold. One of his father's friends, hit by a bus crossing a street, had been paralyzed from the waist down. He sat in his wheelchair one Christmas as the family opened gifts. The man's wife smelled something burning and ran to the kitchen, when their son saw smoke rising off his father's leg, which, too close to a heater, was roasting. The man, of course, felt nothing.

The flames reflected on Jeanette's face were a movie image, the wavy lines that suggest the passage of time or give the illusion of memory or the beginning of a dream or invite us to enter a character's thoughts.

"I don't think we should live together anymore, Cole."

"Is there someone else?" He said it before he thought it. Where was he getting the lines for this scene?

"Yes. Yes, there is someone else."

"Someone I know?" Even as Cole spoke and watched her

mouth move to speak her lines, the truth was *dawning* on him. That was exactly it: dawning, slow revelation, diffusion of light into dark corners, increasing clarity and a sense of urgency.

"Yes, you know him."

"Is it Chip?" Is it larger than a bread box? Is it animal, vegetable, or mineral?

Jeanette nodded and stared at the heater flames.

The moment Cole asked, he knew it was Chip. Friends a long time. Cole and Jeanette, Chip and Laurie. As often as not, it had been Cole and Laurie, Chip and Jeanette. Cole and Laurie in the kitchen making a big salad for the four of them, Chip and Jeanette out in the garden picking roasting ears. Cole and Laurie at a table talking—about what? Chip and Jeanette dancing. The four of them on vacation, Cole and Laurie gone half the day, hiking a steep trail up Lost Man Mountain, while Chip and Jeanette stayed in camp to read and loaf. Not even *a look* had ever passed between Cole and Laurie, and, somehow, Cole thought that meant it was the same between Chip and Jeanette.

"Have you slept together?" There it was, before he had time to stop it, leaping without looking. He wished he could suck the words back into his mouth, vacuum them up. Jeanette had once told him that all the words ever spoken on earth are still in the universe, that, theoretically, they could all be drawn back into some super tape recorder and replayed. All the world's secret whispers still vibrated for those with ears to hear. Somewhere far in the dark of outer space Eve's voice persuaded Adam over and over again. Jeanette's first spoken words to Cole were still out there. What they were—what they *are*—Cole could not remember. Everlasting words, beautiful and ugly—what were Jeanette, Cole's wife, and Chip, Cole's friend, saying to each other forever? Did Chip whisper classroom Russian in Jeanette's ear? What sounds were their bodies eternally making, the soft sounds of moisture, tongues and lips, suction of skin kissing skin. *Have you slept together?* Cole wished he had not whispered, wished he had said *fucked.* And while you slept together, any snoring? tossing and turning? memorable dreams? did you talk in your sleep? any incidence of sleepwalking? *Slept,* euphemism for the noises Cole heard, his answer from outer space.

Jeanette sighed.

"More than once?"

"Yes, Cole, more than once."

. . . *more than once . . . more than once . . .* The words bounced

110

against the high ceiling, slipped through the attic, out into the dark-ness above the roof.

When Laurie left town, after she and Chip split up, she hugged Cole goodbye and told him to call her if he ever needed someone to talk to. Had she been warning him? Had Cole been blind, or had he been secretly conspiring with Jeanette, conspiring to betray himself?

"Cole, I know you want a family. We aren't a family, the two of us. I know now I won't—I can't—have children. I don't think I want to. You've still got time with someone else."

Cole drove out to the interstate, where places stayed open all night. A bright-red Texaco star led the way. He passed the Huddle House, Journey's End Motel, and the First National Bank's lighted time and temperature sign: 11:01, 33°. He drove down a ramp onto the interstate and passed a big Roadway truck. He wished he were not from here. He wished he were only passing through. He wished he were a traveler asleep in a room at the Journey's End and that the next day he would get up and drive to Arkansas or Wyoming, where he had a log cabin on a lake and a wife and children who were happy he was finally home.

He had never imagined, when he imagined starting over, how miserable he might feel. Why was he so miserable? He had not been happy for some time; how could this be any worse? Was he so unhappy just because Jeanette was leaving him, or was it because she had betrayed him—not only she but Chip, too, had betrayed him—or was he sad because he'd spent thirteen years, not all of them unlucky, with one woman and, now, they were giving up, now they were fac-ing their shared failures.

A little before dawn, Cole drove back home. Jeanette was not there. He drove the short distance to Chip's. The white clapboard house and the trimmed lawn were glazed blue with frost and a full moon. Two cedar trees, perfect teardrop shapes, framed the front porch. Dark-green shutters and a Christmas wreath on the red front door completed the Currier and Ives scene: *Season's Greetings, from our house to your house.* In the drive, snug, nestled side by side, were Chip's car and Jeanette's car. The front room on the right side of the house had a bay window. That had been Chip and Laurie's bedroom. Now, Cole knew, Jeanette and Chip lay there, side by side, touching—shoulders, arms, hips, thighs, ankles—at rest, vulnerable, their ghosts given up for the night.

And that night, in his white Ford pickup in front of the neat little house, the house Chip and Laurie had lived in until their divorce, the house in which Cole and Jeanette had eaten so many meals and had spoken and listened to so many words, sitting there, very late at night—there, very early in the morning, with the engine off and the cold seeping into the truck cab, Cole gave up Jeanette, felt her slip away like a held breath escaping.

Cole fancied he heard carolers, their candles held high, flames dancing on the bay window of the bedroom where his wife and his friend lay, the carolers' cheeks rosy and round as the cheeks of cherubs or the cheeks of clouds in drawings of Winter, their words wafting from another century, ancient a cappella, *in thy dark and dreamless sleep, the silent stars go by.*

Cole pressed in the clutch and released the emergency brake. The truck rolled silently backward, the frozen house and its sleeping occupants receding in the windshield. The house slowly moved away, grew small, the shore slipping from a sailor who has cast off.

That night he gave himself up fully to an inevitability. This is how this feels. This is how things are. *So be it.* Melodramatic as it seemed, what he felt that night was innocence going out of him.

Cole had been twenty-five, Jeanette twenty-one when they married forever. Cole knew he would love again, and he hoped he would love better, but he knew he would never love for the first time again, and he was afraid of coming back to love. He was afraid of touching some new, second skin and feeling also, beneath that skin, Jeanette's bones.

COLE'S eyes were closed, the sun hot on his eyelids. Through them he saw a blue-white brightness like the midday sun over the Mediterranean. The lovely island of Paros in the Cyclades in Greece, and Philip and April and Charlotte, and the sleek sailboat on the clear water, were now memories. Like memories of his father, Avery, who was long gone, dead and gone, and of Jeanette, his wife for thirteen years, who was also gone, remarried and gone (for good? he wondered—for bad?) to Oregon. Cole's first summer, after his first divorce, gone by.

Cole was back in Alabama now, and the woman's name was Rachel, and she and Cole were from two different worlds. They had met at a party.

A September night in Alabama—air conditioners couldn't keep up with dancers, doors and windows were opened, jackets and ties tossed over chairs. On the front lawn, people cooled off. A man's sweat-soaked white dress shirt stuck to his skin, which glowed pink, like mother-of-pearl, through the material. Cole nodded to a couple on the front porch and stepped into the living room.

Rachel sat alone on a green hassock by the open front windows. She reminded Cole of some princess in a fairy tale, someone in a soft, pink princess dress sitting on a big green toadstool with something like glitter in her long golden hair.

They talked about divorces, his and hers. Her estranged husband, Bobby, was being nasty about money, which he had plenty of.

"Bobby Vickery Chrysler-Dodge," Rachel said.

"I've seen the ads on television."

The ads began with quick close-up views of new cars from

Dutch angles or through a fish-eye lens: a headlight, a taillight, a streak of chrome trim, a sexy girl's face reflected in window glass; then a large man with a blond pompadour smiled and turned his face sideways, the screen filling up with his ear, his jaw moving as he said, *Bobby Vickery Chrysler-Dodge. Talk to Bobby. . . . He's listening.*

"That's Bobby, in the ads. He thought it up himself."

"The big guy with the ear *is* Bobby?"

"That's him. He was a football star in high school. He blocked a field goal and won the state championship. Broke the kicker's foot. People remember that and buy cars from him."

"*You're* still talking about it."

Rachel smiled her melancholy smile but said nothing. They danced and she held him close. When the party began to break up, he asked her to go for coffee, something to eat.

"It's late; I'd better not."

Cole walked her to her car, parked down the block.

"Neat little MG," he said. The convertible top was up. The plastic rear windshield reflected a streetlight.

"I hate it. Bobby got it for himself on a trade. Thought he had to have a convertible. Then he got a new demo he liked better, so he gave it to me. It's always breaking down; the top leaks and whistles in the wind. It probably won't start now."

"I sorta hope it doesn't. I don't want you to leave."

Rachel took his hand. "Thanks for talking to me tonight. I hope you'll be my friend. I'm probably going to need some good friends, with this divorce business. You know what that's like."

He took her other hand. "I don't want to be just your friend." He held her in his arms, and then he took her face in his hands and put his lips on hers. For a long held breath they stood, lips touching, then Rachel's arms moved across Cole's back, and her mouth moved over his.

He thought perhaps he had never before kissed a woman, had never before been kissed back.

The MG, God bless its little British soul, would not start. Rachel got out and held the door open, for him to try. He wanted in that moment to know all there was to know about getting a car started, wanted to make everything work for Rachel, just to show off here in the deserted parking lot. And, of course, he wanted the car to fail miserably so he would have more precious time with her. He held the gas pedal down and let it up, held it down and let it up, then he turned the key, and the engine fired and caught.

Rachel slipped behind the wheel. He leaned in, and, with her hands on the wheel and his hands on the metal door and with her foot racing the engine, their mouths clung together again. Wordlessly, Rachel let out the clutch, and the car whined backward. Cole's face was cool and empty where her face and mouth had been. He stood there until her taillights winked out of sight.

4

COLE sprayed water from the hose in an arc that splattered the grass in front of Shots, his golden retriever. She barked and snapped air where the water fell. Cole washed leaves and pine needles from his flat-bottomed fishing boat. Tomorrow morning he was taking Rachel fishing. He went ahead and hitched the trailer to his truck, hooked up the lights and the safety chain. He hoped he wouldn't have to go out again—he'd have to unhook everything or drive around pulling the boat. That afternoon, the air conditioner on full blast and the stereo just a notch higher, he went over his fishing tackle and drank one of the Mexican beers he'd splurged on. He'd take a fly rod, in case bluegill were hitting in the shallows, and a couple of bait-casting rigs. A little reel oil and WD-40 had them working smooth as silk. This time of year they'd probably want plastic worms and deep-diving crank baits, but he untangled poppers, buzz baits, and spinner baits just in case. Some of the lures were beautiful, lures that had caught *him* with their shapes and colors, silver or gold lips, bits of glitter, rattle of BBs or tiny propellers, multicolored plastic hula skirts, and their *names:* Snagless Sally, Jitterbug, Broken-Back Rapalla, Hula Popper, Lunker Lure, Shad-Rap, Zara Spook, Hellbender, Devil's Horse.

That evening he skinned and fried chicken breasts, boiled and deviled eggs. He had Cheddar and Swiss cheese, green olives, French bread, red grapes, chocolate cookies, and white wine. He cleaned the cooler and set it on the counter to dry. He had two bags of crushed ice in the refrigerator freezer. For supper he sampled the picnic and had another Mexican beer, Corona, in the clear, long-necked bottle.

The next morning Cole woke before six and took a long shower. He walked a couple of blocks to get a newspaper. It was nice out, warm already, but not miserable hot as it would be soon. There wasn't a cloud in the sky.

Back at the house, he flipped on the radio, WACT, ACTion-Radio, the local country station. The early-morning gospel show was on, and, while his coffee brewed, he listened to Lester Flatt and Earl Scruggs sing "Who Will Sing For Me?"

At seven-fifteen, "Ask the Authority" came on, a high-pitched chorus singing the intro: *Ask the Authority, he'll tell you what to do / Why don't you ask the Authority, he's got some good advice for you.* The voice of the DJ who hosted the show came on,

"Hey, when we gonna get us some rain?"

"We could sure use some, all right," said the Authority.

"You doin' okay this mornin'?" said the host.

"I'm always doin' okay."

"There you go. Before we take some calls this mornin', you have something you want to tell the folks about?"

"Talking this mornin' about all-purpose Nu-Life, *N-U-Life.*"

"Just what is Nu-Life?"

"Good for your horses, your dogs, cattle, hogs. It'll clear up a bad open wound. It's good for swollen areas, lameness. Put it up under your hounds' leg pits, on their bellies, where those ticks and fleas bite on them all summer. It stops the mange, cures all kinds of eczema, makes cut places heal up faster. Put it on wore places, it promotes hair growth, slicks over bare spots."

"Ever try it on a bald man?" The host was chuckling.

At least, Cole thought, I don't have to worry about that. Not yet, anyway. Avery's hairline had receded some, but he died with plenty of dark hair on his head.

Cole put on his fishing cap, black and gold, with a white patch outlined in red; embroidered red letters said BAMA FEEDS. Cole liked to think of FEEDS as a verb. While he was tightening (for the umpteenth time) the bright-yellow nylon rope on the trailer crank, Rachel drove up. She waved and pulled the MG smartly, grill to grill, against his truck. Now he'd get a chance to prove how well he could back a truck and trailer. She slid over her gearshift into the passenger seat, opened the door, and swung her legs out.

Cole followed Rachel's tanned legs up to bright white shorts and a red cotton blouse. She reminded him vaguely of April, but she seemed softer, more vulnerable. Her tennis shoes were as white as her shorts, with no socks. Her blond hair was knotted in a bouncy ponytail. Cole held the truck door handle with one hand, a mug of coffee in his other hand. He had opened his mouth, but nothing had come out and he had forgotten to close it. How did he feel at that moment? The way he had felt the time he decided to go off the high dive in seventh grade.

When Rachel had said she loved to fish, she was loving a shady spot on the bank with a cane pole, a line to a bobbing cork. By ten of a September morning in Alabama, in a metal boat, learning to bait cast a graphite rod, to squeeze and release her thumb so that a six-inch plastic worm with a mean hook buried in its side would drop quietly into the lake near cover along the shore—even the most avid aspiring angler might have wanted a separation if not a quickie divorce from the sport. But Rachel was stubborn. Over and over she cast, reeled steadily and nudged the worm along the lake bottom, and lifted it dripping, covered with mud and milfoil, to start over again. Not until her thumb was raw and her blouse sweated through could Cole convince her they had sacrificed enough to the fishing gods.

Thirty minutes later, Cole's boots sat beside Rachel's muddy tennis shoes on his front porch. He adjusted the volume on a Keith Jarrett album, then sank beside Rachel on the couch.

"Wait," she said. "I know this house has a bedroom, and I know there is a lovely double bed in that bedroom."

Rachel leaned against his bed and unbuttoned her red blouse. Never taking his eyes off her, Cole took off his shirt. Rachel wore a bra the color of her tanned body. She unsnapped her shorts, pulled the front zipper down, and stood out from the bed to let the shorts drop to the floor. She stepped out of them and let them lie. Her string bikini panties matched her bra. Cole pulled his jeans off and walked over to her. She dropped her arms to her sides, and he put one hand between her breasts where the bra fastened. He had no idea how to get the damned thing off, but the plastic clasp opened magically and he brushed the soft material off and touched each breast with his fingertips. Rachel hooked a thumb in each side of his shorts and pulled them down, half kneeling. Then she skinned her panties off and stood against him.

They pulled the coverlet down to the foot of the iron-and-brass bed and lay down together on the clean, cool sheets. Cole looked Rachel over, touched every place he looked at. They watched one another without speech. There were the sounds of their arms and legs sliding over the sheet and of their hands moving over one another's skin and of the window air conditioner's motor and the vibrations it made in the window and of piano melodies repeating themselves all afternoon.

The clock in the kitchen range said 6:00 when they sat, naked, at the table and finished the fried chicken. Then Cole dressed as he watched Rachel on the edge of his bed talking to Bobby, who was supposed to meet her at a lawyer's office. He pictured Bobby, the man in the TV ads, the face turned away, a huge ear tilted down to hover over Rachel, naked on the edge of Cole's bed. *Talk to Bobby. . . . He's listening.*

Cole wondered whether Chip had stood and watched Jeanette, naked on a bed, telephone to see if Cole was home. Rachel and Bobby were already separated, and Bobby was not Cole's friend, but Cole wondered how much that would change things. Standing there watching this woman zip up her shorts, Cole wondered if anything made much difference once you thought you had fallen in love.

Some spot in Cole's heart that had hardened against Jeanette and against Chip softened again, and some other spot in his heart turned to stone. A whole new set of clichés had a moment of truth for him. He wondered what he was hardening himself against.

5

COLE pulled up to the drive-through window at the doughnut shop, where orange neon blinked, FRESH NOW, FRESH NOW. Rachel wanted coffee; a doughnut sounded good too. The doughnuts were hot; the sugar coating came off and dried on their fingers like sweet wax.

Not more than twenty minutes out of town, they got stuck behind a log truck, but neither of them minded. Easing along behind the slow load of logs, they were able to leave off the air-conditioning and roll down the windows without being blown away. The moist, warm air carried into the truck the smells of fresh tar from recent roadwork and burning trash from nearby. Somewhere farther north it was already autumn.

Rachel's family lived in northwest Alabama, near a place called Pilot Point, not far from Waterloo. Pilot Point was almost in mountains; Rachel's father told her it might be cool enough at night for the fireplace. That sounded optimistic. Cole pictured an evening of manly talk with Rachel's father, glasses of bourbon cold in their hands, a fire warm against their faces.

Cole pushed a cassette into the tape deck. George Jones, the only country singer Rachel liked. "He's so bad," Rachel said, "he's good." George was singing "Her Name Is . . . " a funny song, supposedly written about Tammy Wynette. Since Tammy was married at the time, George couldn't sing her name, so he put in some instrument that went *d'wang k-wunk.* Cole turned up the volume, then he lowered his hand to touch the grip of the .38 resting beneath the seat. Rachel gave him a look he couldn't read, and George Jones wound it down.

Cole had bolted the camper cover—an aluminum shell with sliding side windows—onto the truckbed. Shots was back there on a foam mattress. Her tail wagged in the rearview mirror. Cole reached over his shoulder and opened the sliding rear window of the truck just enough to let her poke her cold nose into the cab and nuzzle his neck and ear. She whined, and over the sound of the music he heard her tail banging. Shots hated riding where dogs were supposed to ride. When Rachel wasn't with them she rode up front, stretched out across the seat with her chin on Cole's thigh. Yesterday, at the drive-through car wash, Cole had spent a pocketful of quarters to vacuum all the dog hairs.

George sang "He Stopped Loving Her Today," with honky-tonk desperation, wailing about placing a wreath upon a man's door and carrying him away, when Rachel put her hand on Cole's thigh and, with her other hand, turned down the volume.

"Talk to me," she said.

Cole was enjoying the music and the feel of the road. He could think of nothing to say. Ahead, the log truck shifted down to pull a long hill. A red rag tacked to the longest log bobbed and flared like a tiny bullfighting cape. "About what?" he said.

"Nothing special. I just want the sound of your voice." Rachel's smile melted him, zapped him, a spacewoman's ray gun. Cole was oh so willing to be zapped, fried, jellified. How did he feel? He felt the way he was going to feel when he passed this log truck and floored it over a hill and his bottom dropped to his knees: dream-falling, sudden-elevator sensations. He had once felt that way with Jeanette. When and where did that get used up, worn out, lost, thrown away? He didn't want to wake from Rachel's spell. He understood why Odysseus had himself strapped to the mast so he could suffer the song of the sirens.

Cole felt the subtle strain in the engine as they began to climb. The land had become wilder, the woods thicker. Eroded red clay hills had given way to steeper elevations, rock cliffs. Ridges thick with pine, taller and darker than the trees they had left behind, enclosed the road. In the hollows between the ridges were huge hardwoods, leaves bright green in the sun, and here and there a hawk peered down from the top of a telephone pole.

"Up ahead, take the left fork." Rachel rolled up her window. The ridges cast long shadows. The air was cooler. They had entered a different geography.

Cole rolled his window up, too, and made it quiet in the cab.

The cassette had reversed itself, and, faintly, they heard Merle Haggard: "It's Not Love, But It's Not Bad."

Rachel crossed her legs and flexed her toes, popping the back of her shoe off her heel and pulling it back again. The suction of the shoe against her heel made a soft kissing sound. Off to their right, a river spread wide as a lake, gray and cold-looking, heavy and solid as a whetstone. The highway stretched straight over a massive dam. Below the dam, water roiled and foamed, rose as gray-green thunderheads and stormed back down onto huge rocks. Beyond the rocks, water became a river again and meandered off between the hills as if it had nothing to do with all the energy it left behind, its fury strained out by mysterious parts of the dam deep underwater.

They crossed the Natchez Trace and followed the river. The last town with a sign was Waterloo. Then a narrow county highway took them toward Pilot Point and, finally, to an oak-shadowed gravel driveway. This was a perfect setting for a Southern mansion or a roomy farmhouse, but instead, in a clearing the oaks surrounded, was a rambling, ranch-style, brown-brick house, with an attached three-car garage. Concrete fanned out from the garage and sported a basketball goal on one side and a gas grill on the other. A bed of azaleas stretched across the front of the house, pine straw spread around the azaleas. The garage door opened magically.

"Pull on in," Rachel said.

In the side yard a V-hulled boat sat almost vertical, its bow resting in the crotch of a pecan tree, a faded canvas cover roped over the boat. Closer to the house were the stumps of recently cut pine trees, the exposed wood still raw yellow, pine chips scattered on the ground. A satellite dish sat where the trees had been.

Rachel's mother was coming through the back door into the garage. "Now the test begins." Rachel laughed. "You're about to see my roots. I'm reformed redneck."

Cole and Rachel got out of the truck.

"Rachel, honey." Rachel's mother talked over Rachel's shoulder as she hugged her: "And you're Cole. Everybody just calls me Willie, Cole. You come on in now and make yourself to home."

"Don't you want to let Shots out?" Rachel asked.

"She's fine for a while. Give her time to settle down."

"What a pretty dog." Rachel's mother peered through the side window of the camper cover. Shots whimpered and licked the window. "Is he a Lab?"

"No, not a Lab but a retriever, yes. A golden."

"And *he* is a *she,* Mama."

"Well, she sure is pretty. I love that long hair."

The back door led to a laundry room, where a brand-new-looking washer and dryer were both busy.

"Isn't that awful, doing the wash when company comes. But I had to get it done. Cole, come on in here and meet Rachel's daddy. Can I get you some ice tea or a cup of coffee?"

Rachel's father, Chet, held Cole's eyes with his before he released Cole's hand. "Pleased to meet you, Cole. Sit down."

The kitchen opened into a large den, where a console TV was on, a Saturday-afternoon movie: World War II fighter planes strafed a battleship; black-and-white flames and clouds of smoke and bullet dashes filled the screen. Through sliding glass doors Cole saw pecan trees and pines, rows of fruit trees, and, a good hundred yards behind the house, an enormous garden area. A fair-sized tractor, John Deere green, sat beside the garden, a canvas cover over the engine. Chet turned the sound down on the TV.

"I bet you two are hungry?" Rachel's mother said.

"We've eaten, Mama. We had a big breakfast."

"You'll have to forgive me, Cole. I don't have my dinner ready yet. Hope you like roast. I'll get you some ice tea and a piece of cake. I've got a fresh coconut cake and some pound cake and a real good fruit cake. My pies are still in the oven."

"Tea would be good, Willie." Cole had made up his mind to be relaxed, be friendly. Calling Rachel's mother Willie so easily was the first step. He took the tall glass of iced tea.

"Cole likes his tea unsweetened," Rachel said.

Willie looked confused. "He does?"

"This is fine," Cole said.

"You never drink sweet tea," Rachel said. "You *hate* sweet tea."

"This'll be fine, for a change," Cole said. But Willie was already getting out another pitcher. She could make up a pitcher for him in two minutes with the microwave. Before he could taste the tea, Rachel took his glass and emptied it down the sink.

"Mama's sweet tea is *real* sweet. She puts the sugar in while the tea's hot and stirs it in good."

Cole wanted to taste the sweetened tea. That was how he had drunk it as a boy, but several years ago he had gotten out of the habit of sugar or salt. Now, watching Rachel stick fresh green mint into her glass, he longed for the sweet, minty taste. But Willie already had an unsweetened pitcher brewing.

Cole sat in a straight wooden chair. Rachel looked in the refrigerator, stood with the door open letting all the cold air out, until

Willie fussed. Chet sat in a brown plaid recliner and looked out the sliding glass doors.

Rachel straightened one of several framed photographs over the couch. Most were of men in uniform. There was also a certificate of some kind.

"Daddy's navy pictures. Where's the one with your ship's dog, Daddy?"

"You're looking right at it."

"He looks just like the RCA dog that looked into the Victrola. What kind of dog was he, Daddy?"

"Just dog dog. We didn't know for sure. Didn't know where or when he got on board. He'd been living on garbage from the galley. Probably one of the cooks knew about it but didn't let on. We made him our mascot. Called him George Washington." Chet turned to Cole. "Ship was the U.S.S. *Washington.*"

"What's that?" Cole pointed to the certificate. It looked like a diploma of some kind.

Rachel handed Cole the framed certificate. "From when they crossed the Arctic."

70°38N'   April 15, 1942   00°17′W

All seamen wherever ye may be, Greetings . . .
Know all ye By these presents that __Chet Weaver__ did
appear in my most Northern Realms, embarked in the
U.S.S. WASHINGTON bound for the Dark and Frosty wastes of the
land of the Midnight Sun, and did, with my ROYAL permission,
enter this dread Region by CROSSING THE ARCTIC CIRCLE.
By Virtue Whereof I, NEPTUNE'S REX, ruler of the Raging Main,
do declare him to be a LOYAL and TRUSTY BLUENOSE and do
call upon all CEBERGS, Sea Lions, Narwhals, Polar Bears,
Whales, and other creatures of the FRIGID NORTH to show him
due deference and RESPECT.

DISOBEY UNDER PENALTY OF MY ROYAL DISPLEASURE.

signed _Lord Neptune_
signed _Davey Jones_
signed _Cmdr. W.W. Harrette, USN_

Cole read the certificate, then Chet took it and studied it a minute, handed it back to Rachel.

"It *was* cold up there, let me tell you. But beautiful."

No one spoke. It was as if each of them, Chet and Willie and Rachel and Cole, was picturing that icy, white, bright beauty. Rachel tilted the framed certificate in her hands, and it caught the overhead light and became an incandescent shape, brightness itself. She moved the square of glass, and the dazzling reflection left blue-bright streaks in the air. Rachel's head eclipsed the overhead fixture, and a gold nimbus surrounded her face. The picture on the television changed, and a sparkle of pink, then blue, danced through the light Rachel gave off. She took a step, a little dip of her hip, and the colored light fell down the length of her body like pixie dust, trailed behind her like the dazzling tail of a comet. In that instant Cole saw Rachel as a glittering ice fairy, an Arctic angel, and he knew he was lost.

6

RACHEL had told Cole about her life with Bobby—at least a version of it. We all revise our histories; Cole knew there were other versions. For example, there was Bobby's version. There were the various versions of friends and relatives who were on the outside looking in. And there was God's version—some True Story of Rachel and Bobby.

Now that Cole saw where Rachel came from, had met her parents and seen the view from their windows, his view of Rachel was differently focused. Cole's version of Rachel's life with Bobby began with what Rachel told him and included details he filled in himself.

"We snuck off," Rachel said. "Didn't even spend the night together. It was two weeks before we told anyone."

Bobby rented them an apartment in a new complex in Waterloo. Rachel and her mother went shopping together at least once a week. The whole family had dinner together every Sunday. Later, Bobby bought Rachel the house she wanted in a new subdivision south of town. (Cole and Rachel went for a drive, and she showed him the house, right after she showed him her high school and the country road where she lost her virginity.)

For a couple of years Rachel fooled around with new appliances and drank coffee with other wives. The days began to drag. Daytime television was depressing, and the neighbor ladies were goody-goodies. All they talked about was church and children.

"Plain and simple, Cole, I was bored."

Bobby bought her a piano and she took lessons. Her teacher told her she had a natural gift, but that only made her sad. She thought she might have been a musician if she'd known, if she'd started earlier.

Bobby was selling new cars at Dixie Dodge. He didn't know a thing about cars, but he knew how to listen to people and they all knew him; he'd won a state championship pretty much by himself. A high school cheerleader, Rachel had always dated football players. She wanted the boys other girls wanted. Friday-night dates became either wonderful or awful on Saturday afternoon (preparing for Saturday-night dates), when details were exchanged with other girls, their hair in big pink rollers, their giggles choked into the necks of frozen Coca-Colas that fizzed back up their noses in snorts of envy or anger. It never occurred to Rachel that one morning years later, she would look across the Formica top of a breakfast bar in a new house and watch a new husband wash down toast and eggs with a glass of Florida orange juice out of a Tupperware pitcher and be anything less than proud and fulfilled.

How, exactly, *did* Rachel feel? As if she were an actress in a TV commercial (for orange juice or milk or bread, for a refrigerator or dishwasher or microwave oven, for detergent or floor wax or air freshener, for toothpaste or denture cream or sanitary napkins), and beside her, looking at the camera, was the man Casting had sent to play her husband.

What, exactly, did Rachel notice about her husband? That his neck was too thick.

The more she thought about it, she didn't like big bodies. She didn't like Bobby's thick neck, his heavy thighs and calves, the meaty feel of his middle. She couldn't get her arms easily around him.

"We didn't fit together well," she said.

In bed, Bobby loomed darkly over her, rolled on top of her, panted and lunged as if he were trying to block a kick. When he finished, he collapsed; his weight pressed her down. The mattress rose around her, and she wanted to be swallowed, to disappear from beneath him.

Rachel's body was shrinking, dividing into compartments. A tiny, clearheaded Rachel lived in one of those compartments. She was high up, somewhere in the back of her head. Up there, beneath a thatched roof of hair and an arched white ceiling of skull bone, she sat on a pale-green seat and thought about the rest of her body. Her body was moving, but she was sitting still. She was in a roomette on a long train, and stretched out before her, on a long downhill grade, was the rest of the train. Rachel's long body stretched out, constantly moving—rocking and swaying—but Rachel could not see ahead or behind. Her endless body contained several separate compartments, in which other, different Rachels thought different thoughts and dreamed different dreams. Rachel tried to explain this to Bobby, and he got upset and yelled and even cried.

"I had never seen him cry before," Rachel said. "I had never seen any grown man cry before, except on TV."

Bobby's suit coat was tight around his biceps, his shirt collar pressed a red ring in the skin around his neck, and the knot of his red tie pulsed with his sobs like a swollen, second Adam's apple. Rachel was surprised at how he disgusted her. He was large and healthy and full of appetites. He ran through his life, and hers, as if he were chasing a ball the way he'd been taught. Now it was little more than habit, second nature, instinct.

"A man like that had no business crying."

They fought. All the time, they fought. Rachel quit cooking, and they ate out most of the time. Then Bobby started coming in late, either tipsy and smelling of cigarette smoke and perfume or silly and suddenly horny. Rachel felt as if they were both locked in a tiny roomette, and Bobby's flesh and the flat walls pressed against her.

Bobby was doing well at Dixie Dodge. He got a chance to go partners on a new dealership in the university town, a few hours away. Maybe a move would do them good.

"It was better at first. Different, and different was better for us. But soon different was the same."

Bobby begged her to *get some help*. From her roomette in the back car of her brain, Rachel thought she saw the conductor, a chance to change her ticket, alter her destination. She cut a deal with Bobby. She would see a psychiatrist, but if that didn't help or if the doctor agreed it was for the best, Bobby would give her a divorce.

In the waiting room at the mental health center, Rachel met a psychology graduate student named Tim. He was there every Monday and Wednesday when she came in for counseling. They agreed to meet one night at a club near the university.

"Tim was small and cute, a wonderful dancer. He was five years younger than me."

Rachel left her car on campus and went with Tim to his apartment. She asked him to turn off the bedroom light. He thought it was because she was shy, but she didn't want to look at the dirty, gray sheets. Tim made love the way he danced, with light, intricate moves, following a music in his head, leading Rachel effortlessly, never forcing her backward or jerking her forward. Afterward, when he tried to talk to her, they were lost. He was too full of words. But from time to time she phoned him to pick her up at the mall, where she left her car. She forbade him to phone her, and he never did. When she saw that he was falling in love with her, she quit calling him.

After being with Tim, Rachel realized she might learn to love a man in ways she had thought possible only in stories and movies. Surely Bobby was not happy either. He always had a girlfriend. But he refused to discuss a divorce.

"I'll never let you go," he said. "You're my wife, till death do us part."

"He doesn't want me," Rachel said. "He's just worried about his money."

Cole wondered how the story would end. Till death do us part? In Rachel's dreams, Bobby died again and again: Rachel received phone calls from the state police (there were so many ways a car could crash); Bobby slipped and fell down the stairs, his head split open, blood on the cream-colored tile; as Bobby slept, tumors spread, lungs collapsed, arteries clogged and burst; ambulances came screaming down their street night after night. Rachel woke time after time and stared at the large, still body beside her and slowly reached her hand toward Bobby, expecting to touch cold, unyielding flesh. Different takes of one particular scene were filmed over and over, by Rachel, by Cole. All versions of this scene ended with Cole holding the smoking gun.

7

WHEN Cole went out to his truck to check on Shots, she sailed over the dropped tailgate, out of the garage, and across the yard. Cole whistled and slapped his thigh, and she raced back. He rubbed behind her ears. "Okay. Go on." She moved from azalea bushes to oak trees, nose to the ground, sniffing and snorting, feathery tail held high. The sun was down, the yard in deep shadow from the hills. Full darkness would come soon. Headlights danced through trees—a car passing on the highway. In the silence that followed, Cole called to the shape of ghost light he knew was Shots.

He and the dog returned to the garage, where Willie was spreading an old quilt beside her freezer. She had set out water in a big stainless-steel mixing bowl.

"She'll be comfortable here." Willie said. She knelt and stroked Shots while the dog lapped water.

Shots lay down on the quilt and looked up at Cole. Willie looked up, too, and gave Cole a warm smile. There was something in her look that embarrassed Cole. It was her unguardedness. He forced himself to smile, and he held his hand out to help her up. His gesture was one of gentility, steadying a lady as she alights from a carriage, prelude to a bow and a curtsy that began a minuet, a motion that called to mind powdered wigs, scented handkerchiefs, and uplifted pinkie fingers.

Willie took Cole's hand with the self-assured grace of nobility. She put her hand against his back and guided him ahead of her. "Let's get you back inside," she said, "before it's too dark to see."

Cole wondered if he could ever be part of this family. He wondered if he wanted to. Did he want to marry Rachel and try to fit in with these people? Was he afraid of them, or did he see this as a safe, warm place to be? His visit, polite as it might be, was a rite of passage. Would Cole be declared a Loyal and Trusty Bluenose? What did these Cebergs and other creatures of the Frigid North really think of him?

Rachel and Chet sat in the den, with the six o'clock news on softly. Willie began quietly wiping the kitchen counter, the last of the kitchen cleanup. Chet adjusted a box on top of the television, then tilted back in the recliner with a newspaper. Rachel sat on the couch, flipping through issues of *Country Living.* Cole sat beside her, and she showed him pictures in the magazine, rooms she liked.

Outside, the satellite dish whirred and turned, a jealous ear inclining toward signals ricocheted from space. Shots heard round the world. The news of tomorrow bounced over the international date line.

On the TV news a jumbo jet sat on a runway barricaded by olive-drab trucks and jeeps. A man wearing a gas mask filled the screen, replaced in a blink by the local newscaster in a blue suit, his mouth moving. Over the newsman's shoulder was a picture: a brown face under a white turban that was mirrored by a white beard beneath, the face inside a red circle with a red slash diagonally across it. Beneath the face was the word HOSTAGES.

Willie sat down and began giving Rachel hometown news— who had had babies, who had got divorced.

Chet hid behind his newspaper. A woman with long dark hair stared at Cole from the back page, the headline: SURROGATE MOTHER THREATENED. When Chet laid the paper on his footstool Cole saw that Chet's hand had hidden the rest of the headline: SURROGATE MOTHER THREATENED BABY.

Willie and Rachel disappeared down the hall. Cole heard Rachel laugh. Willie carried a thick brown book. "Look what I found. Look here, Cole." Willie slipped a photo out of the heavy book and handed it, over Rachel's head, to Cole. Rachel posed in a high school cheerleader's outfit with her arms outspread, white pom-poms like big chrysanthemums in each hand. Her short skirt had alternating black and white pleats. Gold letters outlined in black spelled P I R A T E S above a black skull and crossbones on the front of her white sweater.

"My cheerleading picture." Rachel grabbed the photo. "What else is in there?" Rachel and Willie sat together on a love seat.

Chet came and leaned over them. He turned pages in the album while Willie and Rachel went through a stack of photos.

"Here it is," Chet said. He pulled a photo out of the little black arrowhead corners glued into the album. "What's it worth to keep me from showing this to Cole?"

"Daddy, don't. I mean it." Rachel grabbed for the photo, but he kept it out of reach. Rachel reached and Chet dodged. Finally, he laughed and gave her the photograph. He bent down beside them in the cone of yellowish-brown lamplight. Chet and Willie and Rachel, frozen in sepia. The lamp went out. Across the room the television threw light like the fire of a furnace, illuminating in chiaroscuro the family tableau, father hovering beside wife and daughter, and, off to the side, Cole, a solitary figure, silent interloper, Icarus, unnoticed subject of the painting.

"Damn it to hell," Chet said, reaching for the lamp cord he had caught with his shoe. He plugged the cord back in and sat on the arm of the love seat.

The TV screen was awash with blue-green ocean, pink-orange sky and beach. A tanned, muscular man and a nearly naked woman cavorted on a tropical beach, while the titles of Nat King Cole's Greatest Love Songs rolled up with the waves and into the sky:

FOR ALL WE KNOW

LET'S FALL IN LOVE

PRETEND

A BLOSSOM FELL

TOO YOUNG

RED SAILS IN THE SUNSET

UNFORGETTABLE

PARADISE

WILD IS LOVE

Nat sang a few words of every third title, an abbreviated medley, while a mellifluous voice-over guaranteed these songs would bring back untarnished memories and golden moments. This special collection of the world's most cherished love songs, sung as only the unforgettable Nat Cole could sing them, was not available in any store, but could be ordered direct, right now.

"Daddy, here's snow on Christmas."

"No, sweetheart, that's the time it snowed for Mamaw's birthday. There's Uncle Booker's Cadillac. We told him not to park down the hill. But you know Booker—nobody could ever tell him anything.

Of course he got stuck, and of course we had to get out in the cold to push him."

Cole stepped into the kitchen and got more coffee. "Willie," he called, "do you want me to turn off the coffeemaker? It's about empty."

"Just help yourself," Willie said. "Rachel, can you believe we used to dress like that?"

Cole turned the coffee off. On the TV weather map, a series of satellite photos that began at 6 A.M. showed clouds moving out of the Gulf of Mexico in sudden jerks across Alabama. Cole looked for his truck down between the clouds, spied in the lens of a satellite camera, Cole and Rachel and Shots moving through the weather up to the northernmost edge of the state. The barometer was falling; so was the temperature. Dry Canadian air was moving down from the northwest, and a low-pressure front was coming up from the Gulf of Mexico, bringing warm, moist air. If these two systems collided there would be thunderstorms, the possibility of tornadoes. The weatherman was betting on it. He expected the low to stall, allowing the upper air mass from Canada to blow across the warm, moist Gulf current. He predicted an 80 percent chance of thunderstorms by morning, with conditions favorable for severe weather.

Chet stepped over and switched channels. This weatherman was hedging his bet—a fifty-fifty chance of thundershowers.

Cole slipped out the back door to check on Shots. As soon as he stepped into the garage she was up. She put her two front paws together and stretched, bowing and taking a few steps backward, her uplifted rear ending in her merry tail.

"Hello, girl. You doing all right out here? I guess I'm doing all right in there. How's your water?"

Her water was fine. She hadn't eaten her chow. On cold nights, when Cole let her sleep inside, she woke him in the wee hours, crunching. She ate on her own schedule. Eating never seemed as important as greeting him, sticking her head under his hand to get it rubbed. Cole wondered if dogs felt loneliness.

When Cole returned to the kitchen, Rachel looked up and smiled. "You have to see these." Then she was absorbed again in the photos.

Something fell from the back of the album. Willie picked it up and scrutinized it.

"Look, Chet, your old buddy from the navy. The one who was with you at the Arctic."

"Walt Dillard?"

133

"No, this says Mason T. Blessing."

"Mason T. Blessing? I never knew any Mason anything."

"Sure you did, Chet. He was with you on the U.S.S. *Washington.* Have you got so old you can't remember?"

"Let me see that." Chet took the picture, a newspaper clipping sealed like a driver's license in clear plastic. "This guy was one of your boyfriends, Willie. I remember you talking about him."

"Chet. My goodness, I guess I know who my boyfriends were."

"Hard to keep track, many as you had. You wrapped him in one of those Saran Wrap machines to save his cute smile."

"I don't know him from Adam. You sure he wasn't on ship with you?"

"Nah. Look at the insignia. This guy was a seaman apprentice. Walt Dillard was a petty officer. Besides, this guy was on the *Enterprise.*"

"I wonder who he is."

"I wonder what the hell he's doing in our scrapbook," Chet said. "I still say he's one of your old boyfriends."

Chet went to the kitchen for some pie. He put the clipping on the table as he went. Willie shook her head behind Chet's back and smiled at Rachel.

Cole picked up the clipping. The face in the newsprint photo looked lost, as if he, too, wondered why he was here. His was not the baby-faced innocence Cole had often seen in wartime photos of soldiers and sailors, boys snatched from behind a plow or off a bicycle or out of a ball game. Mason T. Blessing looked experienced but wistful. Cole read the caption beneath the photo:

SOMEWHERE AT SEA. Seaman apprentice Mason T. Blessing is somewhere at sea in secret maneuvers on the U.S.S. *Enterprise.*

Chet said he was going to go feed the bedbugs, but first he'd show Cole which kitchen cabinet held the bourbon.

"In case," he said, "you're of a mind to have a toddy before bed."

"I might just do that," Cole said, genuinely grateful this was not a Southern Baptist, teetotaling family.

Chet went on to bed, and Cole found a glass and poured himself a good three fingers, neat. He drank a silent, ironic toast to these folks—in spite of their smug security and who-knew-what secret fears—who had produced Rachel. Cole said his good nights, leaving Rachel some late-night talk time with her mother, and escaped any new revelations about where or what Rachel came from. It was as easy to imagine Chet pulling her from a black hat, surprised that the trick worked, as it was to see her as made in her father's image. Maybe Cole didn't know enough about her.

In the guest bedroom, once Rachel's room, Cole undressed. He stood in a space he'd never filled before. He was in a house like any house he might whip past on a country road late at night, where he might see, beyond the sea of darkness, a light and might wonder who was up, thinking what thoughts.

Cole hung his shirt over a chair. A mirror above the dresser cut him off at the waist. He stepped out of his jeans and put his keys, change, and pocketknife on a doily centered on a mahogany dresser. Polished wood smelled of lemon oil and reflected Cole's hand. A family Bible and two rows of photographs were arranged on the dresser top. One row was photos of a little boy, Rachel's brother, Doug, who, Cole knew, had been killed in a car wreck. The other pictures were Rachel. Sticking out of a quilt, baby Rachel has the round bald head of Ike, the jowly face of Winston Churchill. A pigtailed Rachel wears shorts and strikes a fifties pinup pose on the fender of a big tractor. Teenaged Rachel in a shiny green dress (the only color photo) and green high heels (dyed to match the dress?) holds the arm of a boy in a tuxedo (rented, judging from the fit), who sports a stiff flattop and a bandage over the bridge of his nose (football injury?). Purple orchid tentacles reach, like a lurid Venus flytrap, for Rachel's ear, for her parted red lips. Finally, Rachel, really Rachel, smiles like a model watching Cole watch, watching with the same eyes as the bald baby girl of the first photograph. Rachel to Rachel to Rachel to Rachel.

In flowery, antique script, the names of Rachel's forebears were inscribed in the Bible. The names of men and women now dead who had lived near here and given Rachel her past. Who knew but what some man or woman among them had waked in the night and felt his or her heart thunder and faced, here in this dark clearing, the absolute, inescapable dread of the next dark wilderness.

Tonight Cole would sleep beneath quilts Rachel's grandmother and aunts had made with their own hands—what else, in lifetimes of moments, had those hands gripped?

This room, once Rachel's but now anonymous, *the guest room*, with the decorative Bible and the chronological rows of framed photographs, seemed to tell it all. All there was to say about life as it had been lived here. The dresser, Willie had told Cole, belonged to Rachel's great-grandmother. It looked as unused as a reproduction in a furniture store. The prints of Cole's bare feet showed up, dark, on the carpet that, like a lawn freshly mown, displayed the even swaths of Willie's vacuum cleaner. By the time Cole finished his first cup of coffee in the morning, Willie would have passed the vacuum's wand over the room again, sucking up all traces of his steps. No one could track him here. Willie took pride in the family tale of the time Chet rose early and went to the bathroom. He returned to the bedroom, but Willie had already remade the bed. The heirloom quilt on the bed looked brand-new, looked like the blue-ribbon winner of a recent crafts fair.

Cole popped out his contact lenses, put them in solution in a plastic case. The room was a soft blur of blue. He picked up a photo of Rachel's long-dead brother, Doug, and held it close to his face, their noses almost touching. There was something grim in Doug's aspect. Was it pretense, mannered meanness, that low-down look, a pose to cover something secret?

The corners of the big four-poster bed rose like the masts of an ancient ship, and when Cole crawled aboard, the mattress sank with his weight and the bed seemed to drift away from the solid wall into the dark center of the room.

High above, cool air from Canada was drifting south ahead of schedule. By the time warmer air holding Gulf moisture made it this far north, there would be no system to collide with, no energy for storms, just more muggy, late-summer days. Outside Cole's window, the satellite dish glowed, a low moon tethered to the house. Silent signals, electronic hieroglyphics, beamed down from space all night long—messages, for those with ears to hear.

8

COOT'S was a throwback to the sixties. When there wasn't a band they played classical or jazz on an eight-track tape deck behind the bar. There were a couple of pool tables with dark stains on the felt, an assortment of wooden tables and chairs, several one-armed school desk-chairs. A rack by the front door held newspapers on wooden sticks as in a library. During the day there were usually a couple of chess games going. Tonight, a jack-o'-lantern sat on the bar, a toothy grin flickering on its face. Halloween was still a month away.

Two pinball machines sat against the back wall. Winner Take All had stylized cowboys and dance hall girls with great cleavage looking down at an elaborate casino layout. Cole had learned the amount of body English the machine tolerated: it didn't tilt if you treated it right. Pinball was a life-and-death struggle, the forces of light and noise against the forces of darkness and silence. No game ended more suddenly or hopelessly, the machine alive and blinking and binging one moment, then one small word, TILT, glowed, and the ball rolled down through dark, silent pathways. More than once Cole had worked a steel ball through the maze of chutes and onto the revolving roulette wheel of Winner Take All, keeping it alive, lights flashing and bumpers dinging and buzzing, the glass top atremble with vibrations, his fingers extended inside the machine as rubber flippers that saved the ball time after breathless time, until he got the numbers and heard the *thwock* of a free game tallied. Redemption. Another chance. New life. All the lights came back on, the old score rolled off, black numbers were replaced by squares as clean and white as teeth without cavities. Winner Take All was an antique. Sitting beside it was a new machine, Controllers of the Universe, computerized, all electronic beeps and flashes. Controllers of the Universe featured black and purple aliens, a combination of Darth Vader and Tyrannosaurus Rex. Cole was bemused by his strong feelings for the smiling cowboys and optimistic slogan of Winner Take All, his disdain for the corrupt creatures that ruled the absolute and unforgiving nature (breathe hard and it tilted) of Controllers of the Universe. Not to mention that a quarter bought just three shots at Controllers of the Universe but gave you five chances for Winner Take All. Pinball wizards lined up at the new machine, so the old cowboys were always waiting patiently for Cole to deal himself in. One day he would come in with a few quarters and time to spend, and the smiling dance hall girls would be gone, replaced by some adult-fantasy creature with an unpronounceable name like Ktron or Thalx or Valvd.

The new wave was upon him. Old age, Cole thought, was a sense of superiority of experience tinged with sadness because everyone else, especially those too young to understand, didn't share one's values, one's taste, even in pinball.

No one sat with Nathalie and Dalt. Dalt and Cole taught in the same department at the university—American Studies. Dalt had started seeing Nathalie after he got divorced, almost five years ago now. Cole held out his hand, and Dalt reached into his jeans pocket and slipped a tiny brown bottle into Cole's fingers. Under the table, one-handed, Cole unscrewed the black cap and tipped the bottle against his moistened finger, which he dabbed beneath his tongue. After four or five times, the medicinal taste of the cocaine spread, his lower lip and the tip of his tongue tingled, went numb. Cole liked the taste and the way the beer couldn't wash it, or the numbness, away.

"How are they?"

"Haven't started yet," Dalton said. "Don't know if they're here yet. They were in Hattiesburg last night; their bus broke down coming up here."

"Usual fuckups," Nathalie said.

They were Cole's good friends. He trusted them and liked being with them. But right now, they had forgotten him. Knowing how good that could feel—forgetting where you were and who else was around—made Cole want Rachel. So simple. Two people wanted to spend time together, nothing more. And it was everything. They were still trying to follow her lawyer's advice not to see each other—at least not to be seen seeing each other. Cole thought how nice it would be to be out in public with Rachel, to be *normal* again. He felt as if he had not been normal for a long time. Since before his divorce; probably a good while before, if he was honest.

Was Rachel thinking of him right this second?

Cole felt the subtle lift of the cocaine. He had already emptied one of the beers, but he felt alert, wide awake. He tossed off a shot of tequila. It tasted the way he imagined hair oil would taste. *True* magazine, a cartoon ad, a man with gleaming black hair slicked down, shellacked, every hair held in place, high in the air on the arched back of a bucking bronco right off the Wyoming license plate, a sombrero in one upheld hand, a grin on his face: *His Wildroot gives him confidence.*

The sombrero brought back Pancho Villa, in Boquillas, Mexico, just across the Rio Grande from Big Bend National Park. Cole had been back there when he went out west after Jeanette told him about Chip. Perversely, he made his camp at the same campsite (number 58) up in the Chisos Basin where he and Jeanette had camped with Chip and Laurie. He had always liked secrets, liked playing at espionage, from hide-and-seek to watching Chip's house the night Jeanette confessed their affair. Alone, in campsite 58, he wanted to show himself how much his life had changed. He left Shots tied up at the campsite for the afternoon and rode across the Rio Grande with an old Mexican in a dented boat. He rented a burro and rode it the mile or so into Boquillas, where, in a bare adobe room, there was an iron bed in which, so the story went, Pancho Villa once slept. Virgins came from all over Mexico to sleep in that bed and give themselves to the ghost of Villa. Cole had stood in the open doorway of the room, which was white with a blue border painted around the top of the walls where they met the ceiling. The floor was painted green. A child's drawing, the innocent blue line of sky was drawn straight across the top, the straight green line of grass across the bottom, but instead of the house and tree sticking up into the white reality of the world, Pancho Villa's bed was crayoned there. The room smelled like wet cement. Cole and Jeanette had slept together in an iron bed. Jeanette liked to put her bare feet against the cool iron on warm summer nights, said it cooled her whole body. Cole was moved by how connected, how timeless lives were. Surely Villa, in the hot, muggy cottonwood canyons of northern Mexico, put his bare feet, surprisingly soft from being always inside heavy boots, against the iron bars of many beds. Surely each virgin, her skin burning, was surprised at the coolness of his touch.

"Hey. Hey, come in, world." Nathalie waved a hand in Cole's face. A speaker by their table was going full blast, and it was hard to hear anything else. Cole smiled, nodded. Nathalie smiled, nodded. She closed her eyes and gave herself up to the music. Dalton was emptying another beer. He reached behind Cole's chair as if he were going to embrace him, patted his side, leaned over so close Cole felt his lips touch his ear.

"Carrying your roscoe?"

Cole straightened so he could feel the .38 against his kidney in the small, inside-the-pants holster clipped to the top of his belt. For a few minutes he'd forgotten the gun.

"That shoulder holster is okay," Bennie Broadnax, owner of the Blue Point Pistol Range, had told him. "But you got to reach across, and then you got to pull it back across to shoot. Look—go for your gun." As Cole pulled the pistol out, Bennie pinned Cole's forearm to his chest. The pistol barrel was still caught in the holster. "Besides," Bennie said, "it's too damn hot to wear a jacket over that thing. I sell you this little deal, clips tight over your pants top, under your belt. Let you have this, four bucks. What'd you pay for that fancy shoulder holster?"

Cole grinned a good tequila grin at Dalt and moved Dalt's hand down the back of the chair to the hard knot that was the pistol handle snug in the small of his back. Bennie was right: "This little thing, you get where you don't know it's there." Cole was getting used to carrying a gun.

In a moment's quiet between songs, Dalton said, "You know, in Texas it's a felony to carry a gun anywhere they sell liquor. Don't know about Alabama."

"That's probably the least of my worries," Cole said.

He did have a license:

This does not permit you to carry a gun openly as an officer

STATE OF ALABAMA A37313

Pistol License

License to (CARRY A REVOLVER OR PISTOL CONCEALED ON THE PERSON) or (CARRY A REVOLVER OR PISTOL IN A VEHICLE) is hereby granted

To <u>Coleman Avery Marrs</u>

The license was in his wallet right now. It didn't mean much. Plenty of people carried guns, especially in their cars, without bothering with a permit. Rachel had insisted Cole get the license. She told him where to go at the courthouse and that he'd need ten dollars, cash. Rachel said her lawyer thought it might help if Cole had to shoot Bobby. Cole admitted to himself he liked it.

After spending five days and close to three hundred dollars at the Blue Point Pistol Range, Cole knew that an assailant and his victim exchanged an average of one-point-nine shots with, on the average, less than six feet separating them. Considering the close range and the number of shootings, the number of U.S. handgun fatalities was not so large. Something less than six thousand this past year. The figure was, nonetheless, over one hundred times the handgun fatalities in Great Britain for the same year. Cole had asked Bennie whether that meant Cole should move to England, but Bennie had not seemed amused.

"You find you something to concentrate on, a button or one of them little 'gators knit over the tittie on his shirt, and you take your time and *aim*. You'll have your body turned to the side, like this, so he's got less target. Brace your weapon in the palm of your hand and squeeze off two quick rounds. Always two at a time."

"Why?"

"Gives you two chances at the little 'gator. You don't get a kill shot by then, he's already hit the deck, dove behind the couch, or killed you. You carry six shots; you got two more chances, two bursts each. Remember, the average handgun exchange consumes one-point-nine shots. And that's all."

"One-point-nine."

"Right. Now, if he's real close, keep your elbows snug to your rib cage—like this, see. Can't slap the gun away; you're using all your body weight."

Cole bought hollow-point bullets.

"Sure, they more expensive, but you figure if you have to use force you want ever' little edge available. Say you just wing him, hit a shoulder—with a regular thirty-eight he's still capable, still viable. This baby *explodes* inside his shoulder. Any hit is deadly."

The last day, Cole filled the target, a life-size silhouette of a man, with holes. Ninety-eight kill shots out of a possible hundred. Bennie retrieved the target.

"Deadly," he said. "You could be good at this, my man. You already shoot better than my security guards, and they come in ever' week. What's your dude's name?"

"Bobby," Cole said.

"Okay. Bobby." Bennie took a black marker and printed B O B B Y across the bottom of the target. "Now . . ." Bennie held the target out, and light filled the holes in the head and neck and chest of the dark figure. "You tack this fucker on the outside of your front door. Sonofabitch'll think twice." He rolled the target up and handed it to Cole as if it were a diploma. They shook hands. "Wicked," Bennie said.

The Real Stuff, Cole thought.

As soon as he'd heard the band's name he'd liked them. Now that he saw their stuff he liked them even more. Two young guys stood up front and played—two electric guitars. A big guy with fingers big as bananas and a face that could have invented sadness was on keyboard. One older guy sat in a chair behind them and played congas, bongos, tambourine, maracas, and other, homemade-looking wood-and-leather instruments. A four-man basketball team, tall, lean, and mean, dark as mahogany. They wore their hair in dreadlocks and had on loose-fitting smocks and pants that looked like surgical suits except they were bright red, yellow, and purple. The guy in back looked like a lion, his dreadlocks a thick, dark mane around the fine features of his face, his muscled arms and shoulders tapered down to a thin waist and small hips and legs. From under his chin stringy hair curled and dripped like Spanish moss. He sat very still and stared straight ahead, moving only his arms and hands, and he looked like every maharishi on every paperback about yoga. They sounded Jamaican as all get-out, plenty of dems and dats and mons, and they sang about redemption and revelation, innocence and defiance, love and seduction.

Cole polished off another beer. He was enjoying the soft rush of the cocaine. His heart was beating fast, and he felt a sweet distance above his arms and legs. His arms were light, his legs almost weightless. Yet, he knew, when he got up and walked around he'd feel fine. Coke was like an especially smooth several cups of coffee— the energy of caffeine without the jangles. He did not like marijuana, the sense of tunnel vision, the filter it put between him and the world. The only times he'd ever enjoyed it were sexual. Pot was nice then, when you could focus on something close at hand and then drift into sleep. But Cole had always had trouble with sleep. Sleep was a small death, and he knew every time he slept he was missing something.

Sorority girls looked at one another covertly, unsure how they were supposed to respond to The Real Stuff. A few scruffy-looking graduate students and punk rockers swayed to the beat as if they were in cahoots with the rasta men. Some began to dance in the narrow spaces between tables, nodding their heads like pigeons, communicating with knowing looks with their friends still seated, who nodded back in some code of the hip. The lead singer, who had the high cheekbones and long fingernails of a lovely woman, encouraged them with his wide smile and sweet voice. The singer laughed softly between the lyrics, and Cole wondered if he was laughing at them or at himself. A potato-white, heavyset girl, with close-cropped, silver-dyed hair and a dingy, sleeveless man's undershirt that stretched when her heavy breasts bounced, moved close to the stage and raised her arms above her head, her wrists touching. Several silver bracelets on each arm made her look handcuffed. She gyrated, lifting first one foot, then the other, her thick socks down over her short black boot tops. The lead singer stepped to the edge of the low platform that served as a stage and danced opposite her, like a shadow cast thin and tall against a wall. The musician moved to different music, wispy and sad in his insight. The husky dancer seemed intent on making the music do what she wanted it to do. She jumped like a caricature of a peasant stomping grapes. The rasta man had become a lovely and innocent girl using her charms and her wits to keep a clumsy and potentially brutal man at bay. The stomping girl did a slow revolution, her arms still upraised, and her teeth, revealed by her fixed smile, were illuminated and exaggerated by the stage lights. Cole felt a purely physical chill when the lead singer wrapped his long fingers around the microphone and sang "Could You Be Loved?"

Was Rachel thinking of him at this very moment?

Cole got up and began to make his way back to the bathrooms, where water stood an inch deep from a stopped-up toilet. The two bathrooms, side by side, had been recently painted with some kind of cheap latex paint. The ceiling and walls, the baseboards, the pipes and light switch, even the wooden toilet seat, all turquoise. A bright, bare bulb lit up graffiti, most of it from the same black pen, most of it verse about drugs and war, few drawings, and no phone numbers.

He went around the standing water to the rear wall of the building, where he stepped through an open back door into the sticky night. A black square slowly became ankle-high grass surrounded by brick walls. Above the buildings hung a slice of summer moon, *hook*, unaccountably his word as a child for cantaloupe. There were stars too—stars Cole could name but not find, constellations Cole knew but did not recognize.

Again and again Avery had shown his son the shapes stars made, told Cole the Greek and Roman myths. Orion, Avery said, is the most beautiful constellation. He told Cole how Orion was blinded for his violent efforts to posses Merope, how he regained his sight and dwelt with Diana, the huntress, whom he was to marry. But Diana accidentally killed Orion and, weeping, placed him among the stars, a giant in a lion's skin and girdle, a belt of stars and a bright club. Sirius, his dog, follows him, and the Pleiades, daughters of Atlas, fly before him.

Was Orion visible now, the end of September? Cole could not remember. Looking north, he found one of the dippers, Big or Little: he couldn't tell. Whichever, it was tipping to the west, spilling darkness down over this square of dirt and grass. The end of September, the night was warm, but cool compared to the sweatbox Coot's had become. Cole barely heard the lead singer inside softly wailing "Is This Love?" Cole pissed against the building next door and listened to crickets in the grass. There had been talk for a long time that they were going to put tables out here and make this walled-in lot Coot's courtyard. The grass ended at the rear of a two-story building that housed a furniture store facing on the next street over. In a lighted upstairs window Cole saw what appeared to be a weaver's loom, a large blue-and-white floral design on the loom. An old man stepped into the square of light. He was as sharp and finely detailed as a slide focused on a screen. He had white hair over each ear, wore a white shirt and a dark vest, and held a yellow pencil between his teeth. He turned and appeared to stare directly at Cole. Then he grabbed the loom and it became a mattress he was moving. The blue-flowered mattress slid across the window and blocked the bottom edge of the overhead light, and a bright nimbus rose over the man's bald head like the glow off a distant planet, golden in the lens of a powerful telescope. The mattress moved out of sight, and the man turned his back to Cole and leaned a moment against the windowsill, exposed and vulnerable. The telescope could just as easily be a rifle scope, Bobby's head in one end, a black cross hair and Cole's brown eye in the other end.

Back inside, the smoke and heat were more oppressive, but Cole felt kindlier toward the crowd, even the sorority girls, who were beginning to snap their fingers and jerk their shoulders as the lead singer laughed and led them on. Cole stood beside a cute brunette. She was small, like Jeanette, with a tiny waist and pert breasts. The girl wore a striped Izod shirt and phosphorescent-white shorts and danced by herself between the bar and the wall. She had her back to Cole and kept throwing her hips, tight in the shorts, in his direction. The shorts rode up into her crotch; she bent over and revealed a good deal of her bottom, pink-orange slices of *hook*. Her friends laughed, her ass juxtaposed to Cole's crotch. She thought they were laughing *with* her, and she accentuated her motions. The lead singer gave Cole a conspiratorial grin and suddenly stopped the song. The girl, surprised, fell backward into Cole's arms. Cole held her, her elbows in the palms of his hands, his chin against her hair, soft hair that smelled, even in the sweaty, smoky bar, like strawberry jello. She tried gamely to pull the moment off. She reached up to touch Cole's cheek.

"Thank you, Ramŏn. You dance beautifully, as always," she said.

Then she pulled Cole's face to hers and kissed him wetly. With the quick probe of her tongue, Cole felt the girl almost give in to the kiss, felt her almost forget where she was. He laughed with her and thanked her, and they parted forever.

Cole had his goodbyes ready for Dalton and Nathalie, when he spotted Betty Meriwether in his chair. The Real Stuff was pounding out "I Shot the Sheriff," and Betty's dark head was bobbing back and forth. Where had she come from?

Betty held up a beer and a shot of tequila and gave him a toothpaste-ad smile. Nathalie turned so that Betty couldn't see, and gave Cole a perfect imitation of the smile.

"Where's Dalt?" Cole said.

"Waiting for me. We gotta go," Nathalie said. "See you, sweetie." She leaned close and kissed him and whispered, "Now, you behave yourself; Rachel's watching."

Nathalie disappeared into the crowd, and Cole was suddenly sitting alone, after midnight, with Betty Meriwether—the *much* younger wife of Professor Neil Meriwether—whom he barely knew. Several beers and three shots of tequila waited on the table. He started working on the tequila and chased it with one of the untouched, warm beers.

"So, how you doing, Betty?"

"Better, now." She tossed back the last two shots of tequila, and Cole went for more. The Real Stuff were stuck on Bob Marley. They were doing "Stir It Up." Cole had no idea how the evening was going to turn out. What the hell, he thought. His daddy, Avery, always said it didn't matter what time it was if you weren't taking medicine.

In khaki shorts and a cotton blouse, tossing back tequila and beer at Coot's, Betty seemed more natural than times he had seen her at university shindigs. She was Cole's idea of cute, with short, curly brown hair and an open, round face. Leaning close to be heard over the congas and guitars, Cole saw more freckles than he'd noticed before. The smile Nathalie had down pat *was* a bit much, but Betty's teeth were straight and pretty. Cole imagined her in braces, Professor Meriwether paying some orthodontist plenty for that smile—the cost of beauty, one of the expenses of having a child bride.

"You know, Cole—I hope you don't mind my saying this?" She paused so he could say no, he didn't mind, but since he didn't know what it was she hoped he didn't mind, he waited, and she went on. "Well, anyway, I just thought you might like to know, I—we—a lot of people, actually—weren't sorry to see you and Jeanette part company."

Cole immediately felt defensive. No matter what had gone on between him and Jeanette, he still distrusted people who bad-mouthed her to him. Maybe they thought that's what he wanted to hear.

"In fact"—the smile, tongue moving over straight white teeth— "*I* was especially pleased. I hoped we might be able to be friends. Jeanette never liked me—I guess you know?"

Cole was sure Jeanette had never given Betty Meriwether much thought. He shook his head.

"I think it was because I understood her too well. And"—Betty put her hand on Cole's shoulder: it was damp from the bottle of beer and warm through his shirt sleeve—"I think she knew I was attracted to you."

"*Was?*" Without exactly wanting to, Cole was playing this game with Betty. Flirting? Not exactly. More like reading his lines, completing some ritual ceremony. For the first time, he felt sexual anticipation.

"*Am,*" she said. "Though you move so fast I may be too late. Am I acting too forward? From what-all I hear about you and Rachel Vickery, tonight may be my last chance." Betty had not moved her hand from Cole's shoulder. She let it slide inside his elbow and her fingers played with his shirt sleeve.

Vickery. Rachel Vickery. Bobby's name. Cole hated hearing it. Bobby Vickery Chrysler-Dodge. The big ear on the TV screen, *Talk to Bobby. . . . He's listening.* Cole had yet to even see the guy in the flesh. "Maybe he and I should meet, try to talk things out." Rachel had pitched a fit. "How many times do I have to tell you he wants to kill you. Believe what I say. Keep your gun handy, all the time." That story, the same one, over and over.

The Real Stuff was doing a thudding, slow, sexual number, the maharishi rattling maracas like rain sizzling in the background, their lean leading man crooning, his voice way up near the ceiling. Cole and Betty danced in a narrow space between the toilet water on the floor and the end of the bar. Betty was not as tall as Rachel. Betty's breasts pressed against the bottom of Cole's rib cage, and he could see over the top of her head. Already he was used to the way Rachel fit against him, missed her size and the effortless way her body merged with music.

As The Real Stuff began their last set, Cole and Betty left. She gave him the keys to Professor Meriwether's new, block-long Pontiac, and he drove, following her directions, to a bluff that overlooked the river. The pavement ended in a gravel turnaround.

"I didn't know this place was here," Cole said.

"We used to come here to park when I was in college. These days kids have their own apartments, cable TV and dirty videos, king-sized water beds."

"You went to the university?"

"I was in Neil's class, Milton seminar. We caused quite a stir. Neil was married. Even worse, his wife was the daughter of the then dean of arts and sciences. They had three kids, the whole bit. He's twenty-three years older than me, you know."

"What happened?"

"Oh, everything and nothing. It was a big scandal for a while. Dr. Porter, that was the dean, Neil's wife's father, tried to get Neil fired for moral turpitude, said Neil would never teach again. Things were stricter in those days. Eventually the whole mess just blew over. End of tale."

"Professor Meriwether too. Everybody, it seems."

"Divorce, you mean? Yeah. Just like assholes—everybody's got at least one."

It was strange to hear Betty say *assholes,* strange to picture her as the femme fatale in a love triangle.

"Any regrets?" he said.

"Sure," she said. "I don't think I've ever done anything important I don't have some regrets about."

Betty put her hand on Cole's cheek and turned his face toward her.

"Neil is good to me, and I have long ago accepted my situation. But sometimes I get lonely. If I had just one special friend, I think I could get through those lonely times."

Betty surprised Cole with the force of her lips, her tongue moving against his, pressing against his teeth. She gripped his thigh and ran her hand up into his crotch. She was turned sideways on the front seat, her left foot folded beneath her, her right foot on the floor mat. What was the joke about keeping one foot on the floor? Cole

147

sat behind the steering wheel. Betty leaned against the passenger door and unbuttoned her blouse. Cole ran his fingers over the pebbled skin of her nipples. He wanted her and didn't want her. She rose on her knees and unbuttoned her shorts. He heard her zipper open. Then he put his hand over hers and held her. Beside the edge of her hand he felt the slick top of her panties.

"Not in a car," he said.

"Here. Now," she said.

Then the car filled with light, headlights topping the hill behind them. Betty looked at Cole for a long moment.

"Damn you," she said. And he did not know whether it was the approaching car or him she cursed. Her body sank like a cushion giving in to weight, her shoulders dropped, and she drew her blouse together. The car, a city police cruiser, made a slow circle, spotlighted the brush at the edge of the clearing as if the police were jacklighting game. They did not shine the light into the Pontiac. Cole watched the taillights of the police car disappear down the hill.

"I feel like I'm back in high school," Betty said.

There was something new in Betty's voice when she said that. Cole couldn't decide if what he heard was anger or regret or wonder.

He drove back to Coot's and pulled in next to his truck. He got out and Betty slid behind the wheel. She rolled the window down.

"If I had known I was going to meet you I might have waited," she said.

He leaned in and kissed her freckled nose.

"Good night, Betty."

"Yes," she said, and rolled the window up and backed into the street and drove away. Cole was sure Neil Meriwether was deep in a dreamless sleep.

9

COLE drove home and let Shots out. She squeaked and thudded her tail against his leg so hard it hurt. He'd named her Shots with whiskey in mind, before he was pistol-packing. In the bathroom he popped out his contact lenses, let things blur a little. Without the contacts, even close to the medicine cabinet mirror, his face was slightly out of focus—a romantic effect photographers created intentionally. It softened his look.

He got a glass and filled it with ice cubes and carried it and an unopened fifth of Jack Daniel's to the living room. The glass and the fifth in one hand, he punched the power button on the stereo receiver and lifted the tone arm with the other hand. He didn't know what he'd left on the turntable. Whatever.

Flat on his back on the floor, he felt the .38 press uncomfortably against his spine. He slipped the pistol, in its holster, out of his jeans and set it on the floor by the phone. Shots came and lay down beside him, got as close as possible and rested her chin on his chest. She watched his eyes. If he met her eyes or gave the slightest smile, any encouragement, she'd lick him in the face. He watched her out of the corners of his eyes and concentrated on not grinning. He ran the blade of his pocketknife around the plastic seal of the unopened bottle. The album started, Billie Holiday, "Body and Soul." Cole set the glass flat on his chest and poured, watching the spaces between ice cubes fill up, the whiskey swirling like oil on water. Ice popped and clicked.

Cole took a long pull on the Jack, set the glass on the floor, and topped it off again. Then he put the telephone against Shots's cold nose on his chest and dialed the number Rachel had written on a sheet of blue notepaper, her friend Beverly's number. The blue paper, with Beverly's name and number in Rachel's writing, smelled like leather and had the curve of Cole's hip from riding in his wallet. Rachel answered on the first ring. On the phone her voice was deep, almost husky.

"I miss you," he said. "I want to see you."

"Make sure Bobby's home, then come see me. Don't come in your truck. Bobby knows your truck."

"How?"

"I guess I mentioned it. What difference does it make? Can you get another car?"

"Dalt's."

"Good. Go make sure Bobby's car is at the house. I'll give you directions. It's not easy to find at night. Write this down."

Rachel made him repeat her directions twice.

"You'll have to park and walk around the side so you can see the garage."

"You mean I have to prowl around your house at three in the morning? If he spots me he can kill me, legally."

"If he's home, he's asleep. If his car's not there, he may be roving around. Probably watching over here. I don't know if he knows Beverly's house, but my car is right across the street."

"He knows you're at Beverly's?"

"I had to tell him."

"Why?"

"In case something happened. An emergency. Anyway, it wouldn't be hard to figure where I'm staying."

Cole sighed. Shots stood on all fours and waited to see what he was going to do.

"He always parks in the space nearest the house, and he never closes the garage doors. If his car's gone, drive straight home and call me back. If he's watching this house and he sees you, he *will* kill you. He really will; I know him."

"Can't let that happen. I'll see you soon."

"You have your gun? Just in case? Promise me you won't go without your gun. Remember, you shoot first and let the lawyer ask questions later."

"I'm not planning on shooting anyone. Not tonight, anyway."

"The lights will be out. I'll leave the front door unlocked."

Cole phoned to tell Dalton he needed the Volvo, and when Dalt didn't answer, Cole knew he was over at Nathalie's, and, one more time, Cole silently cursed her foreign soul for refusing to have a telephone.

He splashed cold water on his face, rinsed his contact lenses, squirted wetting solution on them, and stuck them back in. In the mirror his eyes were bloodshot. They burned too, but he wanted to see clearly tonight, even if it hurt.

He gave Shots a couple of dog biscuits and checked her water. She ignored the dog biscuits and watched him.

"You be good, girl. I'll be back before long. Lie down. Eat your dog bones."

Shots lay down but still ignored the biscuits.

Outside, Cole stood a moment in the quiet darkness and looked up at the stars. The whiskey had left a nice, slightly sweet aftertaste in his mouth. So many stars, yet not nearly as many as he would see without all the reflected lights of towns and cities. Imagine the empty plains a hundred years ago, a covered wagon anchored out in Nebraska, that night sky. Or the endless sky a thousand years ago, a sailing vessel becalmed on the Tyrrhenian Sea, stars to steer by. He wondered if this was anything like the way soldiers felt before a night patrol. There must have been a million moments down through time when someone had thought: I cannot believe that I am here, about to go out in the night into unknown territory, where there might be a person I do not know, a person different from me yet the same, who may actually hurt me, may actually kill me, cause my death. Cole would drive tonight down unfamiliar streets, but the street signs would be in English, the architecture recognizably Southern-subdivision-brick-and-siding rather than mist-shrouded castle wall or snow-quiet German bridge or steamy-yellow thatched hut. That Cole was going out with a loaded pistol in a university town in Alabama made it all the more difficult to believe.

Had Cole asked himself when he had become irrevocably committed to the chain of events he was following tonight, he would have said it happened after he and Rachel went fishing, that afternoon when he stood in his bedroom and watched Rachel, on the edge of his bed, her legs together and straight—from the lacy crotch of her panties down to her red-painted toenails on the smooth hardwood floor—telephone to see if Bobby had checked up on her. That's when, Cole would say, he had crossed over some line, some demarcation of what he was willing to risk. What was harder to acknowledge was how much he liked the image of himself as a man given over, wholly, to the dictates of his own passion. He was no kid; he'd lived (if he was lucky) half his life, and suddenly he was on a razor's edge. Something was happening.

10

THE lights were out in Nathalie's apartment. Her orange VW bug was parked sideways on the grass against the nandina bushes under the living room windows. Dalton's ancient dark-blue Volvo station wagon was squeezed up against the Beetle.

Cole opened the door of his truck and forgot, one, how loud he had the Eric Clapton tape going and, two, that the nickel-plated .38 Smith & Wesson Special was in his lap. He tried to hit the volume knob and grab the pistol at the same time and ended up crouched beside the truck with the gun pinned by his thigh against the rear tire and one arm smeared with grease from the door lock. With his clean hand he lifted the .38 from between tire and leg and put it back on the seat. He pushed the volume knob off with the elbow of his greasy arm. The pistol reflected a security light on the corner of Nathalie's apartment building, and Cole thought it had been a mistake to buy the nickel-plated model instead of the blued version. Doubly a mistake since it cost thirty dollars extra. But when he bought the gun he was thinking cowboy, and now he was thinking self-protection.

Cole found the keys under a floor mat that covered a square of plywood he helped Dalt tack down after the Volvo's floor rusted through. The car spent its early years in Vermont and winters of road salt had left the lower body freckled with rust. Age spots. The bumpers, front and rear, were missing, one the victim of an overloaded U-Haul trailer, the other stolen—God knows why—when Dalt lived in Boston. The car had so much character he wouldn't consider getting rid of it. A true bomb. It cranked first time, bless it. Loud. Muffler, of course, long gone. Lucky for Dalton Alabama still had no safety inspection. A state trooper once told Cole that if they inspected, they'd pull half the cars in the state off the road, and all the poor folks'd be on foot.

All us poor college professors, Cole thought. He always felt like an impostor when someone called him Professor Marrs. American studies was the only academic department Cole knew of in which you could study comic books and matchbooks and get paid for it. That was what most people thought about the Popular Culture folks, anyway. Cole was a Symbol-Myth man. Simply stated, the symbol-myth school treated myths seriously. They were interested in the history of the American mind, the power of individualism, the development of superheroes. Cole had published a couple of pretty good essays on the American West. He had a long article, "The Legendary Western Outlaw as Hero," forthcoming in *Prospects,* a top American studies journal. The cowboy myth was not so far removed from the Greek and Roman myths Avery had loved so much. And though he might make ironic, self-deprecating jokes about being a "perfesser," Cole enjoyed the research and liked his students. The pay was not so hot, but Cole liked the hours, the academic sense of time. An hour-long class lasted fifty minutes; a week was either Monday, Wednesday, and Friday or Tuesday and Thursday; a year was two semesters long plus summer off, and those semesters were broken up by Thanksgiving break, Christmas break, and spring break. Every semester he could change his schedule. Cole had read an interview with a well-known Texas writer in which the writer was asked how he liked teaching up at Princeton. He said he liked it fine; it paid better than jobs in Texas and the work was mostly indoors.

Cole left the Volvo rumbling out in the street and pulled his pickup into the space where the Volvo had been. Why had Rachel told Bobby about Cole's truck? He couldn't figure it.

He pulled his blue-jeans jacket and the empty shoulder holster from behind his seat and tossed them in the back of the Volvo. The .38 he slipped into the little clip-on holster and tucked it inside his jeans.

His first class tomorrow was not until 7 P.M., so it didn't matter that it was after 2 A.M. when he set out to see whether Bobby was tucked in. He had Rachel's directions on a sheet of university stationery. Don't take chances, she said her lawyer said. It was taking a chance to cross a street. Again and again, Rachel made him promise to carry the pistol.

Cole grabbed Dalt's cowboy hat, sweat-stained and cracked, off the back seat. The straw brim folded low over his forehead. Mean hombre. Cole and Dalt joked about Dalt being one of the Dalton Gang and him being Cole Younger, desperado. Lately he'd been feeling a lot like a desperado.

The Volvo radio was, of course, long dead, but the Clapton tape in Cole's truck still played in his head: "Wonderful Tonight," one of the songs Clapton supposedly wrote to win George Harrison's wife, Patti Boyd, the model. According to the story, Clapton saw her at a party, and that was it. "I'm in love with your wife—what are you going to do about it?" Clapton said to Harrison. "Whatever you like, man," said Harrison. "At that point," Clapton said later, "she became disillusioned with George. So I don't think I stole her." Harrison had Clapton out to his Oxfordshire mansion "for proper conversation." They had a duel. Guitars at ten paces, winner take all. Harrison insisted that John Hurt, the actor, a friend of both men, witness the duel. Harrison gave Clapton an old, beat-up guitar and amp, but Clapton played the juice out of it. A man driven, obsessed, he played with *passion*. According to the tale, Harrison got rattled and tried to be too clever, while Clapton concentrated on what Hurt called "a few meaningful notes." Clapton won "by common consent of those present" and left with his lady. Still driven, Clapton kicked his heroin habit for Patti, for whom he wrote "Wonderful Tonight" and "Layla." Later, after Clapton and Patti got divorced, Harrison said he had never been angry. Harrison said Patti was still the greatest and that Clapton had always been one of his best mates. Harrison made them all sound very chummy and civilized.

Doing a bad imitation of Clapton, Cole, singing cowboy, passionately out of tune or off key, he knew (though he didn't know which), headed east for Forest Lake, a sprawling subdivision he always wanted to call Forest Lawn. Expensive, look-alike houses surrounded a man-made lake and an undulating golf course, where, Rachel complained, Bobby had spent all his weekends for the last eight years, and where, Rachel had told Cole, Bobby frequently made love to her, in broad daylight, bare assed on the clipped grass.

At this time in the morning, two-thirty, late September, in west central Alabama, the air had finally begun to cool. When Cole rolled down the car window, air poured in like water from a faucet. Through the vents (in Dalt's Volvo, winter or summer, the vents were permanently open), air swirled around Cole's ankles and up his legs, rising like cool water in a tub. The moisture made the heat of the day unbearable and justified the vague adjective *soft* to describe the night. Odors borne on such currents were palpable. Cole breathed a resinous scent of pine he knew probably emanated from a chemical plant that discharged waste into the river late at night. A tracker reading sign, Cole detected another odor, an oily echo, carried on easterly breezes from a paper mill an hour's drive away. And he smelled skunk, faint enough to be almost pleasant, similar to the good, bitter smell and taste of Heineken beer. Feculence and fecundity were closely related. Cole bought Shots' dog chow at Bama Feeds Store so he could walk through the strong smells of feed and seed, pesticides and fertilizer. He knew a couple at the university who had moved to Alabama from Flagstaff, Arizona, and talked for months about the smell of dead things in the air. Above the timberline in Arizona they breathed the absence of odor, rarefied air Cole associated with oxygen tanks and outer space—crystalline and cold. All life began in water; this wet Alabama air testified to those origins.

This part of Alabama, the very tail end of the Appalachians, was rolling, red-clay country. Highway cuts through hills left steep, bare faces. Rainwater turned red with earth until, eventually, the raw sides of these cuts resembled a cross-section of some giant root system. Stalactites of clay ran downhill, stalagmites of dark, vertical gullies ran uphill. In the wooded hollows between hills, fog seeped from tree limbs to float in thin, ghostly clouds. On a moonlit night, the tin roofs of barns and sheds turned the color of the fog, and the countryside looked like a grotesquely Romantic painting.

Tonight there was no moon, no Romantic landscape. Cole felt the weight of the .38 against his back, always there, firm and relentless as a tumor. For the second time in his life, Cole considered the possibility that he could kill another human. The first time was when he expected to be drafted and sent to Vietnam. Then, when he thought about killing, he'd been safe at home, the enemy still vaguely "the enemy," thousands of miles away in a dense nightmare jungle. He was not drafted, and that enemy receded into a world of words and TV newscasts. Tonight, the enemy seemed no more real.

It was two-thirty in the morning, and the streets were empty. Cole was wide awake. In the faint green glow from the dash, his hands on the wheel looked strong and sure. With no muffler, the Volvo sounded like a tugboat. Cole watched the shoreline change, breathed in the odors of decay and mold and manure, sure signs of life. With each deep breath the very real machine for killing pressed against his tailbone.

Cole wasn't sure how far back he'd have to go to determine the events that caused him to be on this particular road in Alabama at this particular moment. He did not believe every hair on his head was numbered and the smallest sparrow had been taken into consideration. The universe *did* seem, most of the time, fairly indifferent. Cole was not fatalistic. He tended to believe in free will as more than a foregone conclusion. He was satisfied that whatever turns he had taken had been choices freely made, choices that led him here, to this time and this place, a quarter to three in the morning, driving a borrowed car down the deserted streets of a fancy subdivision called Forest Lake looking for a street named Sylvan Way.

He stopped at an intersection and peered at the street sign, a redwood plank with routed letters hard to read at night. Car lights approached, and he waited for the car to cross the intersection. It was a tan Ford LTD with a metallic gold badge painted on the door, Forest Lake Security. Cole turned down Land-O-Pines Lane. The Volvo sounded louder than ever. Would the night patrol believe he was a yardman getting an early start? By the time he found Sylvan Way the LTD had disappeared. He drove past Rachel and Bobby's house twice but couldn't see the garage from the street. He stopped the Volvo several houses down and put on the emergency brake (though he was sure it no longer held). Motor running for a hurried getaway, the Volvo chuffed loudly, and smoke drifted from under the body. Cole carried a flashlight and kept one hand on the pistol holstered in his pants.

Rachel and Bobby's house was one of those partial imitations of a French château, brick with a dark overhang of fake mansard roof. It looked like a mausoleum—an unfortunate comparison. There were no shrubs along the drive to hide behind. The grass was close-cropped, perfect as Astroturf.

Cole knelt on the warm concrete. His flashlight beam sparkled on the fenders of a chrome-and-blue bicycle. No car.

He ran, close to the ground, for the cover of a stacked cord of firewood. He heard the Volvo, faintly, between the sounds of his own breathing. Every second he expected the high-pitched *pa-ching* of a bullet hitting the woodpile. He took a long look down the drive, then made a run for the garage.

The bike was a girl's Schwinn—Rachel's or some neighborhood kid's? Cole's own Schwinn had been a bright-green three-speed. He pictured Rachel, in shorts with a ponytail flying out behind her, pedaling toward him. He stepped close, felt the faint hum, the vibration of central air-conditioning in the glass panes of the kitchen door.

Sometime between parking the Volvo and crouching behind the firewood, Cole had decided that if Bobby's car was gone, he was going in. He wasn't sure why. He'd always had a penchant for hide-

and-seek, surveillance. Tonight the risks were great, more real than ever before. He wanted to discover what more he could about Rachel, but part of his desire to enter, to look and to listen, was the desire to take the dare the risk offered.

He wrapped his shirttail around the doorknob and twisted. Locked. He toed up the edge of a straw welcome mat and shot the flashlight down. A brass key glinted. He couldn't believe Bobby stashed a key under the mat.

Did he begin, now, as a burglar, a murderer?

The door opened with a sucking sound, followed by the low whine of the air-conditioning. Cole's boot *thunk*ed on the kitchen floor. He walked slowly in the dark, feeling along the wall for the light switch. His hand touched a louvered door; he smelled detergent and felt the faint warmth of a hot-water heater. Beside the door he found a light switch and flipped it on. A blue-white glow dimmed, then came back to stay, bright with a low hum, a long fluorescent tube over a serving counter. The kitchen was right out of a commercial for gleaming tile floors and designer paper towels, the kind of kitchen in which all the colors had two names—harvest gold, sunset orange, teal blue—a room in which Rachel had spent hours of her life.

A neighbor might see the light. But it was long after midnight; the lots were deep and wide, the light not very noticeable. Bobby might come suddenly down the stairs Cole now saw against the opposite wall. He almost wished Bobby *were* home: settle things here and now in this clinical light that ate up shadows.

Cole flipped the light off and used his flashlight. On one wall were large ceramic pieces of fruit, a maroon apple, a blue bunch of grapes, a banana as long as his arm—a Fruit of the Loom ad. Rachel had put these things on the wall. How little he knew about her.

He stepped onto thick carpet into a formal dining room filled by a black-lacquered Oriental table and chairs. A dimmer switch on the wall controlled a brass chandelier. Cole made the chandelier appear and disappear in the polished tabletop. He imagined himself at this table, Rachel dimming the lights as she entered. There was a mat, clear plastic like the seat covers of a maiden Aunt's Chrysler, covering the carpet by the front door. Cole crept down a hall past a bedroom and a bath and stopped before double French doors. He opened the doors and sent a beam of light over depressing dark wood paneling. Cole admired the fire tools, heavy iron, not the cutesy Early American kind with flimsy handles and brass-plated eagles. He hefted a poker, the curved hook cooked white at the tip. Kill a man easy with this sweetheart.

157

There wasn't much on the built-in bookshelves: pop psychology—*You Can Be All Right Too, Marriage the Modern Way, Learning to Love*—a book called *Investment Opportunities*, a study guide for a real estate exam, and several tennis and golf magazines. There were no paintings, no photographs on the walls.

The air-conditioning shut down, and Cole froze. He switched off his flashlight. In the silence, the noise of his body shifting in his clothes, his boots on the carpet, his breathing, was amplified. He consciously relaxed, then started up the stairs, the flashlight (off) in one hand, the .38 in the other.

Cole went along the upstairs hallway, feeling the walls until he came to a door. He pulled the door open, fast, and poked the barrel of the .38 into a soft stack of sheets in a linen closet. The next door opened into a bedroom, empty, the bed made. It looked as if no one lived here. There was a study, a desk wide and flat as the Texas plains, a chrome-and-vinyl desk chair, a chrome floor lamp arched over the desk like an expressway streetlight. Cole shone light over the desk: some papers, a black NADA used-car price book, a framed photograph of Rachel in a bouffant hairdo.

A heavy, four-poster, king-sized bed did not quite fill the master bedroom. This bed, too, was neatly made. Cole threw light into the adjacent bathroom, where a lace-trimmed peach shower curtain hid a deep tub, and a bowl of pink, shell-shaped bars of soap sat on the back of the toilet. There were two shell-shaped lavatories in a soft-pink fake-marble vanity top. Light bulbs surrounded the mirror above the vanity, something out of a movie, backstage: a star on the door, Rachel sitting at a white stool, her gown open at the thighs, her legs crossed, one foot swaying up and down, dangling a high-heeled slipper with fluff over her toes while she dabbed at her face with a powder puff and smiled at Cole in the mirror.

Cole stepped into a walk-in closet, closed the door behind him, and flipped on the light. He smelled sizing and leather. Rachel's dresses, her skirts, her blouses, her slacks, were organized perfectly; pairs of high heels and sexy strapped sandals waited patiently beneath the outfits. Cole flipped through the dresses and blouses, none he had ever seen her in. He took a blue jersey dress off its hanger: cool and slippery, water in his hands. He could almost compass the waist with his fingers. Something felt soft and thick, like a pincushion, and he turned the dress inside out to see two soft shoulder pads, white triangles with crimped edges, uncooked pastries. These pads and the narrow black straps that held them in place looked like strange prostheses. A frightening melancholy settled over Cole.

Bobby's shirts were mostly slick rayon, flowered as the tropics. He had a long line of shoes: brown, black, cordovan, sporty two-tone jobs. There were shoes with leather tassels on the toes, canvas slip-ons, electric-blue jogging shoes, red-and-white golf shoes with silver spikes sunk in the carpet. Cole put his foot beside a heavy wing tip. Cole's boot became a kid's. The row of suits was a dozen ushers at a wedding or a line of waiting pallbearers. There were colorful polyester slacks, designer jeans, a stack of plaid shorts and a stack of knit shirts on a shelf, little knit alligators to aim at. Cole switched off the closet light.

On a heavy double dresser Cole saw *The Joy of Sex* and *More Joy of Sex,* saw more than he wanted to. He'd watched a TV show once, *Perry Mason* or something, in which a man who thought his wife was cheating on him followed her to a motel, where another man met her. The husband waited until his wife and the man left, then he slipped the desk clerk some dough to rent him the same room. The husband sat on the bed and wept, and the picture jumped to a close-up of his fist gripping the bed sheet.

A noise: something tearing, ripping. Cole switched off the flashlight.

"You coming in, or what?" The ripping noise was the seal of weather stripping separating.

"Why don't you come in a minute?" Cole recognized Bobby's voice from the TV and radio ads: *Talk to Bobby. . . . He's listening.*

Cole crept to the bedroom door. A triangle of light from the stairwell crossed the hall.

"You're not gonna be long, are you?" Another voice, a man's.

"Nah, but there might be a cold one or two in the refrigerator." Cole heard soft steps on carpet, then louder on tile. Then the sound of the refrigerator door peeling softly open, the jingle of glass touching glass. "Got a Coors in here, some orange juice. Want to split the beer?"

"Sure." The other voice, louder. More footsteps on the tile. Brighter light came up the stairs.

"The cash is in an envelope. Won't take a minute," Bobby said.

The carpeted stairs groaned softly. Cole backed up beside the bed, silently put the flashlight on a pillow. He turned himself at an angle to the bedroom door, one foot slightly in front of the other, and, elbows against his ribs, raised the .38, his left hand bracing his right. This was it. In a few seconds the room would fill with bright light and Bobby. He'd catch himself in midstride when he saw Cole, not ten feet away, the mean black hole in the end of the barrel. Cole had the advantage of surprise. Jesus.

"*Wait* a minute. I put that envelope in the freezer." The quick *thump, thump* back downstairs, the *slap* of shoes on the kitchen tile again. Bobby laughed. "*Cold* cash."

"Hurry up, Bobby. We got a lot of ground to cover," the other voice said.

The air-conditioning came back on, and Cole heard voices but couldn't make out meaning. The light up the stairs went dark, the front door closed, the voices stopped. Cole sank down on the bed and breathed in cool air from the vent. He looked out a window—nothing. He eased down the stairs, worked a beam of light around the kitchen, stopped on the counter where a brown Coors bottle and a bottle cap sat beside an empty glass. A line of foam clung to the inside lip of the glass.

Cole locked the back door behind him and put the key under the mat. He expected Bobby to jump in front of him like the killer after blind Audrey Hepburn in *Wait Until Dark*.

What was Bobby up to? Did the cash have anything to do with him? Maybe Bobby was paying someone to get him. What did the other guy mean, *a lot of ground to cover?* Would they be waiting for him at Beverly's? Maybe it had nothing to do with Cole. They sure weren't selling cars this late. The smart thing, the safe thing, was to go home and phone Rachel and be content with her voice on the phone. But Cole had known all along that Bobby or no Bobby, he was going to see Rachel tonight. Dalt's Volvo waited, no longer running, the red alternator light shining a silent warning. Cole turned the key, and the engine caught and shuddered loudly back to life.

11

THE fog had become heavy. Cole drove out of Forest Lake and passed Memory Gardens Cemetery and the Veterans Hospital, took the back way into Beverly's neighborhood. He crossed a deep gully and went over a set of railroad tracks, passed a lumberyard beyond the tracks, and climbed a long hill, up which monstrous dark shapes loomed, kudzu gone berserk over trees and telephone poles and looking, this late at night, in the fog, like ooze from outer space.

Beverly's neighborhood was working-class neat. White cottages with dark-green or barn-red trim sat on oversized lots where large gardens produced Big Boy and Better Boy tomatoes. There were no curbs; the lawns gently gave way to blacktopped streets. It was a neighborhood of Fords and Chevys, fishing boats and pickup trucks, a nice place to take late-afternoon walks and listen to dogs bark you past as neighbors nodded from lawn chairs on concrete front porches. Tonight every house was locked in sleep.

The Volvo never sounded louder. Rachel had said Beverly's house was across the street from a school. Cole saw basketball goals first. He cruised slowly and spotted Rachel's MG in the school parking lot. He resisted an impulse to pull in beside her car, slam the Volvo door loudly, and sashay across the street to the house he figured was Beverly's. Instead, he eased down the street, on the lookout for the finny black demo Rachel said Bobby was driving.

And there it was, a Charger or Chaser, some new idea from Chrysler. Two rows of brake lights glowed bright red. Cole stopped to see what he could through the rear window. A streetlight revealed a dark shape leaning from the passenger side toward the driver. The guy who was with Bobby at the house? A buddy to help take me out, Cole thought.

Enough was enough. Cole pulled on the emergency brake, wondering again if it worked, and got out. Holding the .38 against his thigh, he approached the car. The two shapes inside merged. Cole grabbed the car door and pulled it open.

In the instant light, Cole saw the driver's red hair, the girl's unbuttoned white blouse, her blinking eyes.

"What the fuck, man?" The boy's voice trembled.

Cole shoved the door shut and the light went out. He rapped the window twice, and it lowered a few inches. Through the opening Cole saw the girl buttoning her blouse, saw one dark nipple.

"You scared the shit out of us. I ought to call the cops."

There was a moment in which Cole knew the boy was deciding what he had to do, what his girl expected. In that moment Cole slipped the pistol into the holster in the back of his pants, made sure the boy saw the gun in the streetlight. The girl put her hand on the boy's arm.

"You got better things to do than waking her old man with a lot of police questions." Cole said. "Good night, now." Cole got back in the Volvo and drove past them. In his rearview mirror he saw the license plate on the front of the car, a snarling panther's face, the Eastside High Panthers. There were probably half a dozen new black cars like that in town, and Bobby could be driving anything. Cole's hands sweated, and the backs of his knees jumped softly on the accelerator and clutch pedals. His heart kept time to the Volvo's fast shudder.

He drove a couple of blocks to calm down, then headed back. The black car was gone. Cole drove around to the far side of the school and pulled into the space reserved for the principal. The spelling rule his father had taught him years ago repeated itself in his head, principle, p-l-e, and principal, p-a-l: *Remember, the principal is your pal.* Cole shut off the motor, but it still ran in his ears. He eased the car door open. The dome light had, of course, long ago gone out for the last time.

Cole tugged Dalt's straw hat down low and snug, as a disguise and for confidence. He pulled the clip-on holster out of his pants and worked his arms through the leather-and-elastic straps of the shoulder holster. (Bennie, my man, this ain't likely to be hand-to-hand combat; I'm after quick-draw capabilities.) Warm as it was, he slipped his jeans jacket on over the shoulder holster. His boots crunched gravel. At the edge of the parking lot he stopped, looked, listened. In front of him was the asphalt parking lot, Rachel's MG hunched into the far corner, and on his right, a playground with monkey bars, see-saws, and swings, their chains hanging perfectly still. Not a breath of breeze. The parking lot was a jungle clearing he had to cross. Cole wondered if the school had a night watchman and wished now he hadn't parked in the principal's space. A siren wailed in the distance.

In the third grade, a friend who went to Catholic school told Cole nuns pray every time they hear a siren because someone, some-where needs help. As he had every time he'd heard a siren since third grade, Cole said a silent prayer, and he began to cross the open space.

On film, a flute or an oboe *dum-de-dum-dum*ing, he was a car-toon wolf or fox, his knees and feet lifted high, his shoulders up, his head dipped, turned left, then right, his dark pupils rolled in the whites of his eyes, left, then right; a piano *plink plink plink*ed his quick fox steps. His hands floated at his sides. The house waited dark and silent.

He heard the roar of an engine turning over, and his heart turned over with it. Bobby.

Boss Head makes your arms and legs behave—advice from Bennie at the pistol range. In one fluid motion Cole had the .38 in his right hand, the butt braced in the palm of his left hand, the fin-gers of his left hand holding his right hand steady. His left leg was in front of his right, presenting his assailant with his side, a narrow target.

Boss Head says, aim first—there's plenty of time—then squeeze off two rounds. What did you aim at on a speeding car? No buttons, no knit alligators. The windshield wiper on the driver's side, Cole decided. He waited for the car to come hurtling out of the shadows, then realized the engine was running steadily, realized it was, in fact, the huge air-conditioning unit outside the school's offices. He ought to complain—an irate tax-payer—that they left the damned thing on overnight. He knelt and rested, wiped his hands on his jeans, stood and walked across the street, stepped onto the front porch of the house he hoped was Beverly's.

The doorknob, slippery in his sweaty hand, turned silently, unlocked, as Rachel promised. Cole thought, as the door moved inward without a sound, *What if this is the wrong house? What if, by chance, pure coincidence, the people who live here forgot to lock up tonight? What if?*

Cole stepped over the threshold into total darkness and closed the door behind him.

He thumbed the lock into place. The room felt close. *What if?*

Then Cole *felt a presence,* a warmth, a rising heat, and a familiar scent, and he began to see, or thought he saw, a pale cloud approach. His eyes adjusted, and the soft shape of heat and scent slowly materialized as Rachel in a short, white terry-cloth robe.

Wordlessly she extended an arm, slipped it around his waist, and brought her body alongside his. Her motions conjured up the memory of a boat gliding up to a dock after the motor has been cut, the way the bow turns so the stern swings around, and, ever so gently, the length of the hull comes along behind, sideslipping against the length of the dock, no waves to knock wood against wood, just the perfect, soft kiss of the complete maneuver.

Rachel led him across the dark room. Neither of them spoke. He felt a rug underfoot, felt the grate of a floor furnace in the hall, saw the dark rectangle of an opened door that, from the damp smell of soap and perfume, he knew led to a bathroom. In a room at the end of the hall, in the cool green light of a digital clock radio, Rachel reached up and lifted Dalt's straw hat off Cole's head. She opened his jeans jacket and pushed it off his arms. Gripping the pistol handle, she slipped the shoulder holster off onto the floor and placed the .38 on the bedside table. She handled the gun matter-of-factly, treated it as if it were natural, an ordinary part of their world. She unbuttoned Cole's shirt and pulled it off. Her palms were cool on his bare chest. She pushed him down onto a bed.

Green, underwater light outlined the curves of Rachel's profile as she knelt to remove Cole's boots and socks. Her fingers deftly unbuttoned the fly of his Levi's. The covers had been pulled off the bed. Under his bare back the sheet was warm with what Cole knew was Rachel's heat. She tugged his Levi's off, and the mattress gave under the pressure of her knee beside his hip. Against the green glow of the clock radio, 3:39, the .38 shimmered like several cubes of ice stuck together, and Rachel's body, as she let the short robe drop, was tipped with cool, green flames. Her other knee pressed the mattress against his other hip and she leaned over him, her hair hanging down around his head, tenting their faces in darkness and the warmth of their breathing.

Cole drew Rachel down on top of him. The length of her body was so warm she might have had a fever. Cole remembered a detective novel in which a private eye told a divorce lawyer, "Always give 'em a half hour before busting in; by then there's something worth popping the flashbulbs." The clock read 3:43. Four minutes was all they needed to give us, he thought.

At 4:48, Rachel asked about Bobby's car.

"It wasn't there."

She didn't ask why he'd come anyway.

"I wonder where he is. Keeping tabs on me."

Keeping tabs on me, a line from a detective novel.

Rachel's cheek rested on Cole's chest, her hand moved slowly, idly touching him. The sheet over them breathed when they breathed, lifted when they lifted a foot, shifted when their bodies shifted. The cool skin of Rachel's belly moved against him with every breath she took. Cole liked the length of her against him, but he felt anxious. His contacts were giving his eyes fits; his head ached. He had to leave before daylight, before Beverly's neighbors started leaving for work, before Bobby came cruising by—if he wasn't outside right now.

Cole slid his hand down Rachel's shoulder and took her nipple between his thumb and finger. He stroked it until he felt it rise and stiffen. Then, in an instant, the window beside the bed turned white. Cole's hand was on the .38 before he knew he had reached for it. *Guy I knew in Saigon,* Bennie told Cole, *left his piece under his pillow and stepped into the bathroom to shave. They got him. Through that little frosted window. No shit. When someone's after your ass, you take that piece everywhere.* Cole never asked Bennie who "they" were. To Cole, "they" are all the same enemy. The same ones grunts ran from in Germany and in Korea and in Vietnam. And this one too, Bobby— he was "they." Bobby was there shattering shards of frosted glass and blowing blood onto the thick white lather Bennie's friend had brushed over his cheeks and around his mouth and down his neck.

"It's okay," Rachel said. She stretched up on her knees against the window to peek out the edge of the curtains and the shade. "It's Bev's neighbor who works for the railroad. He leaves early. That's his floodlight. He puts his dog on a chain every morning."

The light through the shade illuminated Rachel's breasts, the flat tuck of her belly beneath her ribs like a sudden intake of breath, the tops of her thighs, hard and smooth as polished stone. She looked like a mermaid: her back curved out from her shoulders and in at her waist and back out into the swell of her ass, then disappeared under a long shape of sheet, where her bottom half seemed to taper into tail fins. A statue of a mermaid, that statue of the Copenhagen mermaid.

To say Cole and Rachel made love would be only part of the story. Sure, it was an old story, but one that kept reinventing itself, and since Cole was in this version, it was new for him every moment. It was more a story of impulse than any Cole had been in before.

12

COLE picked up his ringing phone, expecting Rachel, but it was his mother, Julia.

"How are you, Cole?"

"Fine, Mother. Good, even."

She was calling to let him know she was considering selling the house. She might retire somewhere else; she wasn't sure. First she wanted to travel, poke around the country some. She hoped Cole didn't object.

"Of course not," he said. "Sounds great. Besides, you don't need my permission to do anything you want to do."

"Oh"—she laughed, a good, familiar laugh—"I wasn't asking; I was telling."

"Let me know if it sells and if you need my help," Cole said. "And why don't you arrange for your travels to bring you by here? I'd like you to meet Rachel."

"I might do that," she said. "I just might."

PART FOUR

Adam

1

AVERY had been dead almost ten years—a decade. While he had been alive, growing old gracefully had seemed a charming possibility. Now it seemed like unconditional surrender. The strange and terrible nature of time was the paradoxical way it changed everything and changed nothing. The time and the place changed. People grew older and wore away, gave in and tired out, lay down and gave up, came along and passed on. One day you were here as you always had been, the next day you disappeared. You changed on the outside, but the you that lived inside you stayed the same. Julia's arm, which rested now on the cool top of a kitchen table, was the arm of an older person, almost the arm of a stranger. The hand that moved over the tabletop, tracing the whorled wood grains, was an older hand, but the hand inside that hand, the hand making those motions, was steady and sure, making the motions of 1933, or 1958, or 1976, or 1986, all the same.

Ten years after his death, Julia missed Avery as much as she missed him the night he died. When she was alone in their double bed, curled in the dark under the same sheet and quilt that once covered them together, the same way she was (inside her changing body) the night they married (the same way she knew she would be *inside* her body until she died), she slowly froze from his absence. She ached with the relentlessness, the inevitability of her aloneness. Not a night had passed since Avery died that Julia had not gone, finally, into sleep wanting and hoping to dream of Avery, to be with him again in whatever strange ways her dreams rearranged her world, to see him, to hear his voice, to feel his hand, for the split second that a dream took all night to make.

169

One dream began with the rocker rocking. A hand pink as a baby's hand gripped the back of one rocker rung, moving the chair. The hand joined to a wrist, and a long forearm, bare and smooth, stretched flat across the floor. The arm disappeared beneath the closed front door. Julia opened the door; a man stood there, his right arm stretched from his shoulder down to the porch floor, where it flattened like Plastic Man in Coleman's comic books and slipped under the door. He rubbed his arm, and it retreated backward across the floor, slid back like a snake over Julia's foot; the man's hand backed up his leg, the arm shortening until it stopped and the hand rested against his thigh. Julia knew this man but didn't know him. His was a face from old photographs. He looked like her son, Coleman.

"Julia," he said. It was Avery's voice the man used.

"But you're too young," she told him. "You're too young."

The man, the young Avery, looked down at his smooth, pink arms and turned to see himself reflected in the windowpanes.

"I'm sorry, Julia, I didn't realize . . ." He reached out and patted the air. "You wait right here," he said, and he turned and ran away. Receding down the street, he looked light and nimble as some small animal. Then he was back, light silvering the edges of his dark hair, skin tanned, more creased, the way he looked before he got sick; Julia reached for him, *Oh, Avery,* but he stopped her, his palm against the air between them. "No, I'm sorry; that's not allowed."

He sat in the rocker, one dark arm on each chair arm, and smiled at her.

"I can't stay long, sweetheart. You wouldn't believe how hard this was to arrange."

That's where the dream ended. Avery was in the rocker and he disappeared, went black from the outside edges in, just like the picture winking out on her TV screen.

Coleman, her only child, was the only person Julia had ever loved who had not disappeared. Julia had loved Cole's wife, Jeanette, and when Jeanette left Cole, she became one more person who vanished on Julia. All the others—Vivian, Mother, Annabelle, Garner, and Avery—were already gone. Avery, at least, never left her while he was alive. Thirty-three years Avery put up with Julia.

If Julia had any regrets—besides the total agony of his absence—it was that Avery had let her talk him into postponing some of his dreams.

" 'The aborigines call the time of creation Dreamtime,' " he read to her from *National Geographic.* " 'Their first ancestors rested in the forms of rocks and boulders that later became the bare-wallaby men, the poisonous-snake people, and other creatures who created the landscape.' "

What a landscape. Avery knew it well from words and pictures. Some red-hot spark of Australia, some flint speck of Martian-red rock (homesickness?), some ruddy grain of Australian sand, some sorrel bit of Australian tree bark, had blown down the nautilus spiral of Avery's ear canal or up the dark passages of his nostrils and sinuses or through the very pores of his skin, directly into his veins and the chambers of his heart.

The grit of the faraway and the unknown rested on Avery's tongue, where he continually tasted it and shaped it into something whole and lovely the way an oyster shapes a pearl. In dreams he walked the gibber plains. "Gibber," he told Julia, "is from an aboriginal word for stone." In dreams he scrambled over rocks, finding goanna lizards and grubs to eat. In dreams he knew exactly where to dig for water. In dreams he ran a sheep station in the vast, vacant outback, and his children listened to a teacher's voice over the radio, words carried like hawks riding the hot thermals for miles and distant miles, from the School of the Air.

" 'There, beneath tropical eucalypts, are giant mud slabs, twenty feet tall, like giant prehistoric tree stumps. Made by Australian termites, these mounds point north and south. Magnetic nests, giant tombstones—like Stonehenge in England—Australians call an area of the slabs a cemetery. Inside the giant nests, in tiny cells, termites store the bodies of their dead.' Someday"—he must have said it a thousand times—"I'll take you there. We won't get thirsty because I'll know where to find water. We won't get lost because we'll steer by the termites' magnetic nests."

Someday, sometime, one of these years, soon became *the past.* When Avery got sick, Julia thought about taking him, so he could walk those hot gibber plains before he died. She imagined winning a contest from some ad with a cute koala bear, or a newspaper story with the plea *To Fulfill a Man's Last Wish,* a mason jar by the cash register of the City Café, *Help Send This Man Down Under,* Avery's xeroxed photo taped to the jar, an airline offering free airfare. Of course, Avery was too sick. Of course, he wouldn't have wanted to go in his condition. Neither of them would have been comfortable with the publicity of a contest prize or a charitable fund. And, Julia knew, dreams are for the living, not the dying.

"I just wish we'd gone to Australia," she said. "I'd rather we had done that than spent our money on a house, or clothes, or a car.

I am sorry for that, Avery. Sorry I was always the practical one. One should never be practical about life. And I promise you I won't ever be practical again. I promise, from now on, I'll follow my impulses."

"No, Julia, you were right. Dreams unfulfilled are always unspoiled. Besides, I've walked the continent, New South Wales up through Queensland and the Northern Territory to the west and back through the south and Victoria." His finger in the air traced a circle, counterclockwise, the way, he had told her, water runs down the drain in Australia, the Southern Hemisphere, everything upside down and contrary. "Maybe," he said, "you'll get to go, after I'm dead, and you can see it for both of us."

"Yes," she said, "I might do that. I could never see anything, especially Australia, without seeing it through your eyes too." She did not really expect that she would ever travel very far, surely not as far as another continent, never as far as Avery's luminous origins on the red and distant planet Mars.

Avery had always cooked on the weekends, when he was home. He did all the grocery shopping. (When he died, Julia so dreaded going to the supermarket she ate out for almost a month.) Avery washed Julia's hair for her and sat her on the floor in front of him and wrapped it in the big curlers to dry. Every morning he was home, he brought Julia coffee in bed. Even after they'd been together thirty years, his hands moved all over her with a gentle urgency that convinced her night after night and year after year that her body was brand-new.

Almost half a century later, Julia could not recall the taste of sherry, but she could remember exactly how she had felt, at exactly 10:10, when Uncle Garner died. And now, ten years after Avery's body disappeared forever, she could not recall *exactly* what her orgasm had felt like, but she still caught her breath with the memory of Avery's warm tongue tip, the wet tip of her nipple. Contact, connection, to be *touched.*

She knew she'd never find another man with ways like Avery's; she wouldn't even try. But she had a vague idea that in a man *unlike* Avery she might again find ways that would take her breath away. She knew better than to look for him. Love had to catch you, Julia knew, unawares.

2

JULIA never did travel as far as Australia. But, ten years after Avery's death, she still believed dreams were for the living. Her friends—the scared widows, who tinted their hair blue and moved to retirement homes in cities near their children, and the few husbands still living, who advised her about taxes and the upkeep of the house in San Antonio—all told her she should get rid of the house (expensive maintenance, accidents waiting to happen, poor security) and sell her car (mechanical problems; wrecks even; it's not safe for a woman—especially a woman of your age—to be out alone; where do you ever drive, anyway—to the store and back, that's all) and move somewhere in Alabama, near Coleman, in a nice retirement home. All these old ladies and old men harping at her to give up, as they had. They wanted her to join them. If she gave in to what they called "what's best for you," then, somehow, their losses were diminished when hers were added to them. It was old math: as you added years you based your formulas on subtraction. Well, she was gonna be contrary. She was a Martian's widow. Her heart was in the gibber plains that ran through the Australia of a dead man's dreams. Her blood ran counterclockwise.

Beginning now, she might live as long as the thirty-three years she'd spent with Avery—another lifetime. Annabelle had told her to keep her heart as open as a twenty-four-hour café. Everyone said she didn't look her age; why should she act it?

Before Avery died, he explained to her that he had made financial arrangements to take care of her.

"Besides," he said, grinning, "time you get home from burying me, there'll be suitors lined up at the front door." She laughed too, told Avery there weren't any men who could measure up to him. "Well," Avery said, "in a way, I hope that's true. I hope I'll always be a man of property in your heart. But you'll find another man, somewhere, who'll give you what you need after me. You shouldn't be alone. You're too *vital.* I hope living with me has been so much fun you're sort of addicted to a man's company."

It wasn't until after Avery's death that Julia discovered how well he had provided for her. He had taken out several large life-insurance policies over a period of years, all long before he got sick. In addition to leaving her quite a lot of money, the policies paid off the mortgage and the car. Avery had two independent health policies—she actually made a few hundred dollars on the medical expenses. Soon, she'd also have social security. She wasn't filthy rich, but she was free to do whatever she wanted without worrying about how she'd pay for it. She wasn't sure, at first, what (if anything) she wanted.

When Avery died, Julia was fifty-two. The Widow Marrs. She spent six months handling insurance claim forms and final bills and transferring papers and credit cards to her name. She went to dinner parties where well-meaning friends tried to pair her off with available old widowers, and she dodged phone calls from the husbands of those same friends. That these married men called did not surprise so much as disappoint her, because it confirmed how impoverished their imaginations were. She wanted something *different* in a man. She knew how unusual Avery had been. He'd spoiled her. It was no longer possible to be interested in the ordinary. Men her age had nothing to talk about but certificates of deposit and retirement tax laws. They were ordinary *and* old. Few of them tried to kiss her. She kind of respected the ones who did, but when (out of curiosity, mainly) she let them have their way with her, they didn't seem to know what they had in mind. None of them had Martian kisses to offer.

She thought a lot about traveling, about where she wanted to spend the last years of her life. She thought about Australia, but she wanted to preserve the Australia she and Avery had imagined, wanted their shared dreams to remain untarnished.

She thought of driving to visit Coleman, a preliminary trip to test her wings for a long solo flight. He had invited her to meet Rachel, but Julia didn't think he really needed visitors right now. He had his life to lead, and she had hers.

Coleman and Jeanette's divorce had been one more separation Julia had suffered. Julia had been less surprised than Cole seemed to be. She had seen the tension between Cole and Jeanette ten years before, when Avery was sick. She knew Cole felt betrayed in the worst possible way, but she still had a measure of sympathy for Jeanette, who had always had a Catholic sense of penance. Contrition led to absolution. Jeanette had, whether she knew it or not, found a way to endure guilt, to make sure she paid for her actions. The punishment must fit the crime.

Julia's feelings were hurt that Jeanette did not ever speak to her. She thought they had been closer than that. Not even a phone call or a letter. Julia had shared Cole's sadness, and now she shared in the healing expectations of new possibilities in his life. The best she could do was to let Cole alone to find his own answers. Julia wondered if Rachel, whom Cole mentioned often, was one of the answers.

Julia saw Avery in Cole, but not as much as she would have liked to. She saw herself too. And she saw traits she could not account for. Avery would have known how to help Cole through the divorce. Avery had possessed the power to bind up wounds, to heal—except he couldn't heal himself when his time came.

It was hard to believe Avery had been gone ten years. Now Julia needed something new in her life, wanted something. She didn't know what she wanted, but she knew she wanted.

She put a brown rinse on her hair. She bought new clothes. She sold her seven-year-old car, though it had only 36,000 miles on it. Bought a new, foreign sports car, black as the "back of beyond," and learned to shift the five-speed transmission. Hazel Vance walked down, the afternoon Julia drove the new car home.

"That's a hot number," Hazel said. "Where are you headed?"

"I don't know." Until Hazel asked, Julia hadn't been sure she was headed anywhere. "Somewhere I've never been before," she said.

"Good for you. If I were young as you, I'd take off," Hazel said. Then she opened the passenger door and winked. "Give me a quick spin. I'll daydream the rest of *my* trip."

Julia listed the house with a realtor, priced it low, and sold it in two weeks. At a garage sale, she took cash for everything she hadn't packed behind the new car's bucket seats. She felt sad seeing one or two special things carried off, but she felt good at the same time. Avery always said, "Things belong to those who want them most," and she enjoyed seeing people so happy *buying* things. She didn't count the cash, wrapped stacks in rubber bands, and put it all in the glove compartment. Because it was mostly small bills, it felt like a *lot* of money.

An October sun was warm through the tinted glass. Loud electric guitar came out of an FM rock station. She wasn't sure where she was going, but she felt better than she had in years.

On the passenger seat were covered dishes two of her neighbors had brought over: chicken and dumplings, soft and chewable; banana pudding the same color as the chicken and dumplings but topped with a perfect white meringue that stood up in crusty brown peaks. Each bowl was dishwasher- and microwave-safe plastic, each was wrapped liberally with heavy-duty aluminum foil. Tiny beads of condensed moisture rested on the foil like silver beads of mercury from a broken thermometer.

Early in Avery's sickness she had broken a thermometer and knelt and with the edge of her palm tried to sweep the wobbly, continually dividing silver drops together. Someone had told her that blood ran blue in our bodies, turned red only when it met oxygen. In the glass measuring tube the mercury seemed to rise red, like blood in air, but in fact the line was, they said, deadly gray metal. Metal, yet soft and jiggly; liquid, yet hard to absorb. She had knelt on the cool bathroom tile and wished she could pick up the rolling bits of Avery's body heat and drop them one by one back into the tiny broken tip of the thermometer and see the red line take shape in a perfectly normal way and register a perfectly normal number for the degrees of heat in that body in the next room. Kneeling there, she had heard Avery cough and cough again, and she watched her tears hit the tile, where they did not roll away.

Julia whipped the car into a shopping center and swung around the end of a speed bump. Behind the stores, out of view, were the parked cars of store employees; here stacked and sagging cardboard boxes overflowed dark-brown Dumpsters. She wheeled a tight circle and pulled close to the open side of a Dumpster. Stenciled words warned that anyone dumping garbage would be prosecuted to the fullest extent of the law. Julia wondered, as she rolled down her window and pitched first the chicken and dumplings and then the banana pudding, bowls and all, into the Dumpster, what was the punishment to fit such a crime?

She pulled up to the drive-through window of a Burger King and ordered a Double Whopper and a large coffee, black.

"No catsup. Give me mustard, and heavy on the onions."

"Cut the catsup, add mustard, extra onions."

"I like a hamburger with my onions," she said.

Julia drove past houses, streets, and buildings she'd never seen before. Nothing looked familiar. Everything brand-new.

She followed a graceful arch of pavement and found herself on an elevated expressway, a loop surrounding San Antonio. The road curved close to an office building, her car swimming the waves of second-story windows. She felt completely anonymous. She could be anyone, could be anywhere. Was this Texas? She could not be sure. Somewhere far behind the streets and office buildings and shopping malls and warehouses she passed was the Alamo, dwarfed by hotels and banks; buses and cars pulled up where Mexican troops once attacked. Touristy restaurants were crowded along the Paseo del Rio, and modern-day Texans prowled El Mercado and La Villita, where Mexican curios were sold alongside Bowie knives and cowboy hats in a kind of movie-set, old-timey Texas. Gone, too, she was sure, were the Kit Kat Klub and that joint she and Avery walked to, out San Pedro, dancing with Avery through the parking lot, blue neon pulsing to the beat of "Deep in the Heart of Texas." *Well, okay. Time,* she thought, *to put all that behind me.* In her rearview mirror she saw a sign for Houston; that sounded good enough. She took the next exit and turned around. She liked the air against her face and lifting her hair.

Well out of town, she saw cattle grazing and fenced, rough pasture scattered with horses down both sides of the interstate. At least she was back in Texas, even if time raced by like the green exit signs. She felt as if she were stopped, the car engine softly respiring while someone rolled film of the flat Texas landscape: telephone poles and short mesquite trees slid by, receding in her rear windshield.

Three hours later, by the digital clock in the dash, the blue mirage of downtown Houston approached. On the interstate, city limits sign to city limits sign, west to east, Julia clocked the width of Houston on the car's trip odometer: fifty-three miles.

Fifty-three miles gone in a glance, just like that, the highway emptying, moving like a river, smooth as glass. Beyond Houston she passed the glittering lights and space station shapes of Texas City refineries. She wished she could fill up with rocket fuel for a journey to Mars.

In Lake Charles, Louisiana, high on a bridge the interstate became, she looked down on ships, cranes, and cargo nets, more refineries. The perspective of the bridge, the reflecting water all around her, made everything new. She saw everything for the first time, a foreign sailor on liberty.

In Lafayette she was hungry and stopped at a place her neighbors would have warned her not to enter, especially at night. Neon beer signs lighted up the windows; there was a pool table inside. She ordered seafood and okra gumbo and a draft beer. The bartender, a big man in a sleeveless shirt, gave her a spotless white napkin and suggested she add a dash of Tabasco sauce. The beer was cold, the Tabasco hot, the gumbo delicious. There were a crab claw and two oysters in her bowl, along with bits of crab meat, shrimp, slices of dark-green okra, and other tasty bits she couldn't identify. She couldn't wait to tell Coleman she had eaten oysters, rich, dark brown, almost the color of the okra seeds. A boy playing pool stepped back to let her pass and told her to "drive careful, now." He was cute. Young enough to be her grandson, but she gave him a smile and winked just the same. She pushed the door open with her rear end, and the boy grinned and gave her a salute.

The cool night air, the beer, and the lingering heat of Tabasco on her tongue were a great combination. She nosed the car along, faster and faster.

Before midnight she whooshed through Baton Rouge and a sudden, light shower. She had been to Baton Rouge for Coleman's wedding, but all she remembered was that the state capitol looked like the Empire State Building. She and Avery had never even met Jeanette. Avery had gotten her through that one, and it had turned out okay. At least for a while. A pretty good while by today's measure, she guessed.

Outside Baton Rouge she got gas at a convenience store and bought some crackers packaged with a square of cheese and a dill pickle in a plastic bag. She pulled a sixteen-ounce can of beer out of an icy tub by the cash register. "Lady gets a tall boy," the clerk said. Julia liked that, a *tall boy*; she'd remember that. She ate while she drove and listened to country music from a Baton Rouge station. After the tall boy she had to stop at a rest area to pee. The beer had made her drowsy too. It was a little late in the year for mosquitoes, so she left the window down and tilted her seat back and slept.

In the dream she was kissing Avery. He had on a gray hat with a wide brim, and she couldn't see his face. She reached to brush the hat off his head and saw that he was not, or was no longer, Avery. The man unbuttoned her blouse and kissed her breasts. She lay back on some kind of mattress that was floating, drifting around a lake. Warm, wet lips moved down her body. She put her hand on the man's head and felt a woman's long, silky hair. She looked down at a naked woman. Above her, in the limbs of a tree with giant leaves, sat the man who had been kissing her. Naked, he smiled down at her. She let her head loll to one side, and her cheek slipped into the cool water. On the shore, Avery stood naked, with an erection. The woman between Julia's legs lifted her face and saw Avery too. The woman began swimming toward Avery. The man in the tree grabbed a limb and swung down, his feet splashing beside Julia. The limb bent with his weight, and his body sank until water came halfway up his thighs. As he sank, the man's penis floated, growing thicker, a floating log, a gliding alligator, coming right at Julia.

A dive-bombing mosquito woke her from the dream. It was still dark. She slipped her fingers between her legs, pleased by her wetness. She got out and stretched, washed up in the rest room, where, in a metal mirror, she could barely make out two pink welts on her neck. The car clock read 4:30. Good enough.

Julia hit New Orleans at dawn, ahead of morning traffic, and drove straight to the Vieux Carré, where Coleman and Jeanette had spent their honeymoon. She had café au lait and beignets at the Café du Monde. Shops opened, men swept ancient slate doorways, a couple in evening clothes got out of a white Cadillac tinted pink by early-morning light.

New Orleans was a place where Julia and Avery would have been content. She drove out to Lake Pontchartrain and crossed the twenty-four-mile causeway and then drove twenty-four miles back. She went out St. Charles and looked at beautiful old houses; twisting live oaks; dark, twisted ironwork. In the garden district she gassed up, though the tank was not near empty, and was directed to a neighborhood café and bar called Parasol's, where she got a roast beef po'-boy sandwich and took it with her into Mississippi. By sundown she sat with her bare feet wedged into soft sand a few feet above the waveline, eating her po'-boy, drinking a cold tall boy, and listening to the gulf.

She spent the night in Pass Christian and the next day crossed the state line: Alabama the Beautiful. She intersected a highway that would take her north to Cole, but she drove on. She ate in Mobile and put a quarter in a phone to call Cole, then changed her mind. She was hours away—why phone just because she was in the same state?

For the next three days Julia puttered along the coast, stopping when she felt like it, eating when she got hungry. In Florida the interstate was crowded with spotless Howard Johnsons, new Burger Kings, and long, creamy Winnebagos. She cut over to an old two-lane that hugged the coast just a few miles off the interstate, and she moved back in time. This was a different landscape, one she'd never seen but still recognized. She stopped at a wooden stand and bought oranges and pink grapefruit. Concrete-block houses with tiny front yards outlined with oleander and hibiscus crowded the shoreline. Julia eased south, and the world grew brighter. Driveways and parking lots and the shoulders of the highway turned white with crushed shell, and the pavement itself was streaked white with sand. Silver flashes of bays and inlets dazzled her. She had slipped through a blinding time warp and driven into some old vacation snapshot, overexposed in the glaring sun.

In a place called Pirate Harbor, she watched brown pelicans float over water. The sun outlined their beaks and tipped their feathers with light. They were creatures from an animated film superimposed on the landscape, escapees from Disney World, some seacoast *Zip-a-dee-doo-dah.*

She passed Aquarama Waltzing Waters, Everglades Wonder Gardens, and Jungle Larry's African Safari Park. In the Everglades she crept through zones where signs announced that the Florida panther, an endangered species, might be crossing.

Julia drove as far as she could drive. She took U.S. 1 to Key Largo and on through Islamorada, where she passed sprawling shell shops and funky washeterias; through Duck Key and Marathon and No Name Key. The road ended in Key West, where a sign pointed to Cuba, ninety miles of water away, and reminded Julia she was at the southernmost tip of the United States. She knelt and rubbed white dust and the coupled bodies of lovebugs off the car so she could put on an *I Went All the Way* bumper sticker.

Constantly in sight of ocean or gulf, she headed back north, the highway she had come down, the only way back.

Born in Missouri, then living in central Texas, she had never spent any time near the ocean, though wide open spaces seemed the way she had imagined ocean would be. In the Texas countryside, at night, an occasional distant farmhouse light had made her think of a boat anchored on some wide, dark sea. Maybe it was the open spaces and great distances in her previous life that made her respond to wide water. Her previous life—that's how she was coming to think of all the years before the past few days. Nothing in that life—not the limitless horizon nor the infinite blue skies of Texas—nothing had prepared her for the perpetual motion of the sea. She was sure the feeling was not new; many must have felt it. There was something life-enhancing, life-prolonging, in the now thundering, now lapping waves. Eternal, yet madly, dependably irregular: a dog's long tongue slapping the surface of his water; a rocker runner tipping way, way back, then dipping once more to creak a porch board; the factory pound and hiss of heavy-metal stamping and compressed air; an endless list of breathing rhythms. Here, truly, resting her weight so surely on the weight of the earth, inhaling the sea's exhaling, she might continue to live, might never die. The warm, moist, odorous respiration of the sea resuscitated Julia.

Back on an expressway, she looked down on the tile roofs and treetops of Miami. At her eye level, an elevated monorail passed over a narrow river below. The river was crowded with yachts, tugboats, and skiffs and lined with squat shacks that were wholesale seafood stores and the office buildings for small shipyards cluttered with rusty hulls and scrap metal. Ahead, a sleek blue train slid silently over the monorail and disappeared among the tall shapes that were downtown Miami. The river below looked like some ancient Asian port, while the city ahead conjured up the stylized Martian metropolis of a 1950s movie set. But this was no Mars Avery would recognize.

Julia got off the expressway and back on Highway 1, then A1A, keeping as close to the ocean as possible. She stopped for gas at a station flanked by enormous banyan trees opened like umbrellas, to spread a canopy of limbs that dripped vinelike roots and covered an entire empty lot. The boy who pumped Julia's gas got up from books spread over a green metal desk in the station, and told her, without unclenching his teeth from the pencil held there the way Tarzan held a knife, that a single banyan tree would cover acres if allowed to grow unchecked. Napoleon's entire army, the boy said, once camped beneath a single banyan tree. Julia wondered if that was what the boy was studying in his several opened books.

North of Miami she sped past the sculptured hedges of Gulf Stream Race Track, the shadow of her car supple and willowy as any thoroughbred. She felt as if something were up. She realized she was a betting woman, and she felt lucky. The road sign said Hollywood, Florida, but she wasn't sure it wasn't California. She could've just crossed the continent. The sun was setting and not over the water, but on a day like this, who could trust the solar system? That night she drank coffee, not decaffeinated, and sat on the balcony of her motel room, facing the ocean. She stared out at the water and knew it did not have to be the Atlantic. She watched the waves foam white, phosphorescent in the evening light, and searched the dark horizon for the lights of Japan.

The next day she cruised down a wide boulevard lined with giant palm trees and pastel pink and blue and yellow cottages with red tile roofs. From the car radio Aretha Franklin was singing "Freeway of Love." Julia rolled down her window to smell the ocean. Sunlight bounced like an incandescent beach ball off metal and glass. Julia felt the way she imagined it felt to be high on drugs. The boulevard, Hollywood Boulevard, ended, like any good rainbow, at the entrance to the flamingo-pink hotel of anyone's postcard dreams. The hotel loomed, tall and rounded, a many-layered, pink-frosted cake, surrounded by a white swatch of beach and the psychedelic green ocean. Like racing silks, the blue, blue sky displayed perfect white polka dots of clouds.

Hollywood Beach was exactly Julia's idea of the perfect beach. Miles south were the tall hotels and condominiums of Surfside and Miami Beach. Here were stucco bungalows, low cubical hotels with glass bricks and turquoise tile, art deco shapes and colors, the Wonderful Time Apartments, the Blue Marlin Apts., with an orange fish on the sign, the imitation turrets and towers and curved stairways and arches of Morocco. Along the beach were wooden lifeguard stands, clusters of leaning palm trees, a yellow bandstand with metal folding chairs ready for a Sunday-night concert. A clutter of souvenir shops sold lamps made of conch shells and starfish; bright-orange, quilted, fish-shaped, beaded coin purses; playing cards with fifty-two different naked women in every deck. The tiniest bikinis Julia had ever seen hovered in a storefront window like tropical fish in an aquarium. Along the boardwalk (which was asphalt, not boards) were beer joints and eateries with crank-out windows opened to the ocean: the Starting Point Lounge, Al's Pizza, Ice Cream Delite, the Dog Cart. People Yankee-white and tourist-tan at wooden outdoor tables ate hot dogs, French fries, and gyros. Many spoke French, Hollywood Beach being favored by French-Canadian vacationers. Julia figured this was what teenagers would call funky. Funky, she decided, often turned out to be what appealed to her. She would find a room in one of the hotels that crowded the boardwalk. There was one, the Turret Inn, (apartments, efficiencies, rooms by the month, week, day) with a row of windows in a round tower facing the surf, that she especially admired. A low white wall enclosed lush green Bermuda grass, on which a family was playing croquet, hitting the bright red and yellow and blue wooden balls with loud *clacks*. The lawn furniture was made of wood slats fanned out wide and angular as stylized palm fronds. The flat chair arms supported tall banana-yellow or cotton-candy-pink drinks adorned with bright slices of oranges and limes and fingernail-polish-red cherries. From each frosty glass a pair of skinny, striped straws stuck up, flashing a V-for-victory sign. Julia wanted to climb the curving stairway to that turret room, wanted to sleep there with the rush of the ocean and the *clack* of a croquet mallet and the wind-chime clinks of ice in tall drinks with long names. She wanted to sit in that row of windows and stare out at the ocean.

That particular apartment, as it turned out, was reserved, by a couple from New Jersey. But, as it also turned out, the phone rang while Julia was talking to the innkeeper (Mr. Fox, Percy Fox, a natty little man in seersucker trousers and suspenders). It was the very couple from New Jersey on the line, forced at the last minute to cancel. They realized, Mr. Fox told them, they would forfeit their deposit, the first week's rent? Mr. Fox's worried look was replaced by a smile at Julia's good fortune, not to mention the double rent he could now collect. Neither he nor Julia mentioned this. Both were pleased at the way circumstances had turned out. Percy Fox followed Julia out to her new car. She paid for a month in advance with cash from the glove compartment.

3

ON Hollywood Beach, at the Turret Inn, Julia met Adam Smith.

Julia sat in a low lawn chair, the sun bright through her closed lids, ice melting in her glass, the sea roaring in her ears. The brightness softened, and she opened her eyes expecting one of the occasional cottony clouds, but looked up, instead, at the dark shape of a head surrounded by light. In the glare, Julia couldn't tell whether the head was a man's or a woman's, young or old; it looked like the vague illustration for some flowery verse in a *Christmas Ideals* magazine, rays of sun radiating out like stained glass; it looked like the familiar cartoon version of the devil himself, dark points (ears? hair? some kind of crazy hat?) sticking up like horns.

The head moved and the sun shone on white teeth; the horns were wraparound mirrored sunglasses. A man, definitely. Good-looking. Young.

A man's hand emerged from the brightness. A man's voice introduced itself.

"I've never met anyone named *Smith* before," Julia said. Then she smiled. "*Adam Smith,*" she said. "It sounds like an alias."

The man smiled, his teeth whiter than the sunstruck sand. "Who knows what it was when my grandfather landed at Ellis Island? Probably had a -vich or -ski or something worse, hard to say and hard to spell, on the end of it. I don't know. More to the point, I never cared enough to find out. I'm Adam Smith, native-born American."

After the disappointments Julia's real father had brought her, the sadness of Avery's departure, Julia understood a decision to let the past lie, to go with the here and now. It was a stance she had embraced the day she'd sold the house in San Antonio and started driving somewhere. Adam Smith was as good a name as Julia Marrs, as good a name as any.

"What do you do, Adam Smith?"

"Today, or tomorrow?" he said. When Julia just continued to look him in the eyes, he went on: "Different things. Build boats. Race boats. I used to be a drug smuggler, like everybody else in south Florida. I make deals; I do what is profitable for me to do."

"Sounds like an exciting life," she said. Was he making fun of her? She didn't think so. She didn't know whether he was telling the truth, but, she realized, she wasn't sure it made any difference. He was watching her. Looking for a reaction? No, something else. "My late husband built a boat once," she said. "A houseboat."

"May I get you another?" He took her glass in his dark hand.

"Why not?" Julia said. For a moment the man stood holding the glass and stared down at her. For that silent moment there was no expression on his face, then his smile flickered and caught the way the sun flickered and blazed when it came out from behind a cloud, flickered like a flame dancing on the head of a candle. Julia closed her eyes; when she opened them again, Adam Smith was gone. She looked north, then south, along the boardwalk; she looked out at the empty surf. A woman held a little boy's hand, leading him toward the ocean. The boy walked stiffly, shaking his head from side to side but laughing. Each time a wave came in, the boy backed up, kicking his feet, jumping the roll of water, which drowned out the sound of his laughter. Adam Smith was nowhere in sight. Had she imagined him? She turned to look behind her just as the man emerged from the Turret Inn office, a drink in each hand. He came toward her, his hands extended (with the drinks) like a sleepwalker. He walked like the little boy, chest lifted, ass out, stiff-kneed.

With one hand Julia shaded her face from the sun; with the other she took the drink the man offered. "Where'd you get these? And so fast?"

"I know old Percy. Keep a couple of bottles, glasses in his desk drawer. Ice from the ice machine."

"Mr. Fox, the landlord?"

Adam nodded, sipping his drink.

"What about you?" he asked. "Vacation or what?"

Julia saw a small copy of herself on each of Adam Smith's mirror lenses. Like carnival mirrors, the lenses distorted Julia's body; her breasts stuck out voluptuously. As she told Adam Smith about herself, she imagined that he saw her, from behind the glasses, just as

185

she saw herself reflected on the front. She did not tell him about Avery, only that she was widowed. She listened to herself—she sounded more intriguing than she would have thought. Twice, she paused, gauging his interest. Each time, he waited for her to continue. When she did not, he asked a question, indicating not only that he wanted to hear more but, also, that he had listened to every word.

Julia had not talked so much for a long time. Perhaps not since Avery had been alive to listen.

"Few tales," she said, "interest us as much as our own lives. Forgive me for going on so."

But no, he wanted to hear more. The sun was sinking and the top of the Turret Inn threw a long shadow over them. The shadow curved along the bottom and came to a point, like the blade of a long knife, at the edge of the waves.

"Not much more to tell about an old widow. Tell me about yourself. What made you stop and talk to me?"

He had not "stopped" to talk to her; he had seen her from Percy's office and been *drawn* to her as he had been drawn to Florida by its constant heat and beauty. And she did not look like anyone's widow.

Julia laughed. "You'll keep the whole state warm with hot air like that. Don't flatter me. I may intentionally forget to act my age, but believe me, Mr. alias Adam Smith, I know how old I am."

Julia learned enough to know that Adam Smith had been drawn here like so many others looking for something faster, something better, something newer than whatever he had left behind. *South Florida, man, where they build year 'round.* No one, she had been told, was *from* this place. People who weren't bolted down too tight just got loose and rolled down here, all the way down till there wasn't anywhere else to roll.

"My father was a businessman who ended up in Boston. He ended up well enough, I guess. He made his in Boston, so I decided to make mine elsewhere. Miami might be my elsewhere."

"How long have you been in Miami?"

"Oh, just a while. I like it, though."

"I think I do too, though I'm not sure why."

"Sure. You drifted here, like me. Floated over a border. That street, Eighth Street, for years just a numbered street, right? Now it's Calle Ocho, even in *Time* magazine. And it really starts right there. Old men talking Spanish, crowded around street corners, playing dominoes under the trees in Little Havana. Get in some big old Buick, a rusty oil-burner, boat of a car, and cruise a few blocks; no border patrol, but you change countries. One side of the street you got jive talk and rap music, regular Afro-American scene; cross over to the other side, skin the same, hair just as nappy, but it's *les Mystères* and *le Bon Dieu*—Little Haiti, where everyone's black as burned toast and talks Creole. Cross the bay, Miami Beach, New York Jew country—Jew talk, Jew food, flocks of old people waddling down sidewalks like pigeons. Up here in Hollywood, French-Canadian invasion—coconut-white skin and coconut suntan oil and coconut-rum drinks. And water everywhere: ocean, canals, river, more ocean. Water makes the land tilt and sway, something loosey-goosey. What's that poem—'Water, water everywhere, and not a drop to drink'; so much water makes the land less important, there to hold the water in place, at bay. Little pink houses, white houses, pale-green houses—little pastel ice cubes floating around in a tropical drink, palm trees sticking up like fancy straws. Like me, you like floating."

"Water, water everywhere, and all the boards did shrink," Julia said.

"Oh, you know poetry too. I read a lot of poetry. Find out lots of stuff I already knew but didn't know I knew it."

"That sounds like something my son, Coleman, might say. Maybe worded a little differently, but close enough." Adam's smile twitched, like a light dimming, just missing a beat, one dark pulse when you saw the filament inside, then bright again so fast you weren't sure what you'd seen.

"So. You have offspring?"

Offspring? Julia laughed. "One son, Coleman. Pushing forty (gives you an idea how old *I* am) and just divorced. I worried about him at first; now I think he's going to be okay. There's not much I can do for him now. I hope I did whatever I could years ago."

"What kind of business does your son do?"

"He teaches something called American studies. Which seems to cover just about anything."

"Poems too?"

"As long as they're American poems, I guess."

"High school? College?"

"College, university. In Alabama."

Adam Smith looked at Julia as if he were not familiar with the word: *Alabama?*

"Alabama, a southern state, sits up thataway, over by Florida's panhandle. They do have universities there." Julia was teasing, but this man, Adam Smith, didn't seem to understand her tone.

"Yes, I know of Alabama. Football—Bear Bryant—and George Wallace. Rough on niggers."

Now it was she who was unsure of his tone. Every now and then he seemed to say something (*offspring, niggers*) that wasn't quite right, as if he'd learned English by reading strange texts or over-hearing conversations. The rest of the time he was silky smooth, articulate. Quoted Coleridge.

"If I were your son I would come to Miami to teach. There are probably many new Americans here who would benefit from learning about American studies, their new culture. And I would want to be close to my charming mother."

"Actually, Coleman doesn't know I'm here. I mean, he knows I sold my house in Texas and hit the road—sort of an extended vacation. I sent him a postcard from Key West."

"You're like me," Adam Smith said, his voice quiet, not as play-ful as he'd been. "You come and go as you please. Something hap-pens, you change directions. I had an accident in Massachusetts, motorcycle accident. I got repaired, then I came down here because of the water, the boats. Then a boat accident turned me into a busi-nessman. My father's death, his interment, was my last reason to ever return to Boston, and with him dead, there was no reason to stay. This is a good place for business, a good climate." Adam Smith swept his arm out toward the darkening ocean. The beach had emptied, and the waves sounded louder. "Wide open. Lots of movement. Power. Energy. Heat. Isn't that what you like about it, Julia?"

Listening to Adam, Julia had an inkling of the impulse that led so many Cubans and Haitians to set sail for Florida, each with a dif-ferent state in his mind's eye. Tomorrow Land stretched at least this far south of Disney World. Julia, too, was a kind of immigrant on this finger of sand beside this endless sea. For days now she had listened to the mysterious sounds of ocean and softly spoken French words in a place foreign and new. How had she come so far from her origins? She was more than miles away from the little girl Mother, Huldah, had held and rocked and sung hymns to. Just the two-piece bathing suit would be enough to keep Huldah from recognizing Julia. Annabelle, on the other hand, might even approve of the almost giddy way this stranger, Adam Smith, made her feel. She had come here, to this time and place, the same way most people move through their lives—she had drifted here, floated across borders. Unknown in a for-eign land—she liked the anonymity. Here she had no history. Any-thing might happen. A good place for starting over. Now she found herself alone on an almost empty beach where she had spent most of an afternoon talking to a strange man, a man as alien in his own way, she speculated, as Avery had been. She felt as wide and open as the ocean. She felt the possibility of a new beginning, another life. Adam Smith took her hand in his, and for the first time since she kissed Avery goodbye, her heart raced as something in her blood stirred.

4

A FRIDAY morning in October, Vincent "Vinny" Ayala, a.k.a. Vince Adams, a.k.a. Adam Smith, stopped at a pay phone in the Miami airport and phoned Percy Fox, manager of the Turret Inn in Hollywood.

"Connect me with the lady," he told Percy.

Five minutes later, Ayala sat in a redecorated airport coffee shop eating a gooey Danish and sipping coffee into which he had stirred four spoons of sugar. He flipped through a Miami *Herald.* Pink neon flamingos and turquoise neon palm fronds reflected in a glass brick wall that separated the coffee shop from the airport concourse. Its polished stainless-steel tables put Ayala in mind of a medical laboratory. A faint odor of new carpet reminded him of a woman's vaginal scent. For Ayala, that scent was neither pleasant nor unpleasant; it was the smell of money.

Even through tinted plate-glass windows, the sun glare off acres of concrete runways was harsh. October in Miami, not yet noon, and the temperature and the humidity both in the high eighties. Houston would probably be as bad. In Boston it was already fall: leaves so red and gold they looked freshly painted, still wet, jerking on cool breezes.

April is not the cruelest month. T. S. Eliot, Ayala thought, had he lived in Miami, might have written about the cruelty of summer sliding into winter with only the calendar to prove the change.

Ayala knew a lot of poetry, lines from college literature classes. Yesterday he'd checked a poetry anthology out of the Miami Beach

Library with a stolen library card made out to Daniel Rubenstein. He intended to brush up, memorize.

He had used Daniel Rubenstein's Visa card to pay for the new linen sport coat he was wearing, for his new shirt, tie, eelskin ankle boots and matching eelskin belt. The Cuban salesman had whipped a sport coat off the rack and slipped it on him. He held the coat in the small of Ayala's back, his hand at rest where Ayala's ass started, while he chattered about the fit. A slight frown, a barely perceptible shake of Ayala's head, and the salesman flung the coat on the floor. They walked along a mirrored wall, leaving a trail of crumpled sport coats on the polished tile. A parrot in a brass cage cawed and whistled and called out *Loverboy, oh Loverboy*. They came to a linen Ayala didn't frown at. The salesman gave the lapels a soft tug and slowly shook his head, couldn't believe how perfect. Speaking to the mirror, the salesman offered Ayala a glass of wine. A blonde in teal-blue high heels and a matching suede bikini brought the wine. Through the glass, her red thumbnail was a maraschino cherry. She bent, to give Ayala a view of her nipples.

He had been tempted to buy more, but then they would call in the amount on the Visa, and he wasn't sure whether Daniel Rubenstein had discovered the stolen card. This morning he had used the card to pay for a round-trip ticket to Houston, then shoved the card into a vent slit in the side of a water fountain.

The Miami *Herald* listed famous birthdays for the month of October: Virgil 70 B.C., Erasmus 1469, Sir Walter Raleigh 1554, Bolingbroke 1678, Jonathan Edwards 1703, Samuel Taylor Coleridge 1772, John Keats 1795, Friedrich Nietzsche 1844, Mahatma Gandhi 1869. A fairly impressive month. Go all the way back to 70 B.C., he thought, and any month would be impressive.

He wiped his fingers and left dark prints of newspaper ink on the napkin. Vinny, he thought, leave some fingerprints for the FBI or the DEA—give the dumb sucks a break.

He crossed his legs and felt the thick padding of a zip-lock plastic bag inside the top of each boot. Each bag held eight ounces of cocaine. Ayala had ground up the rocks, sifted the powder through a screen, and weighed it. He usually paid $60 to $70 a gram for rocks. This time he was in for an even $30,000.

He had learned what he could. He kept five-plus grams for himself and stepped the remaining coke down a fourth, sifting in 150 grams of mannitol, a baby laxative. Joe, the Houston dealer, would pay $50,000, then step on it with more mannitol or with inositol ("muscle sugar," a B vitamin) or speed (crystal meth from a basement lab; cheaper than coke, it jacked up bad stuff). Joe made $10,000 to $25,000 a deal.

In spite of what the sucker trade thought, coke was adulterated by Colombian cooks before it got to the States. As demand increased, farmers in Peru and Bolivia harvested all kinds of shit. In Colombian kitchens any alkaloid was cocaine. Pasta was made into base and sent to crystal labs in Colombia, where it was cut with lidocaine, cheap and available over the counter in Colombia and Venezuela.

It was a safe bet that at some River Oaks party next week, lawyers and doctors would be snorting powder that was less than 30 percent coke and calling it *good blow.* Most of them didn't know, or care. Dealers cut cocaine with anything white—lactose, caffeine, even quinine, which had terrible side effects. Ayala did a foil burn and Clorox test before he bought. Not like a lab, but he eliminated really bad shit. He never light-weighted grams. He cleared $20,000 for a round trip to Houston, plus a little over five grams for his own use— enough for a nice party; he had no habit.

Eight months ago he had sent a quarter to Joe by National Express. They'd used National Express without incident for over a year. He sealed the coke in seven zip-lock bags, a gram each, those in a larger zip-lock, and that in a manila envelope he sealed in a Jiffy bag mailer with a phony return address. The package didn't arrive on time. National Express said to give it one more day; weekends caused delays. Monday, Joe got the package. He left it on his kitchen table, unopened, for a week; if DEA came knocking, he could claim he didn't know anything. When he opened it, no coke; a printed form in the envelope: IT IS ILLEGAL TO SHIP CONTROLLED SUBSTANCES. NATIONAL EXPRESS CANNOT BE RESPONSIBLE FOR ILLEGAL SHIPMENTS AND STRONGLY DISCOURAGES SUCH PRACTICES. Ayala shut down for a couple of months. Nothing happened.

"Some fucking stiff at National Express is enjoying plenty of free toot," was Joe's guess. "Think of all the contraband those fucks rip off. That's the kind of job I need—some courier service, Post Office, UPS."

Ayala tried to make all his deliveries in person now; when he couldn't, he used the U.S. Postal Service. Then, six weeks ago, the evening nonstop back to Miami had been full. Rather than fucking with the Atlanta connection, he stayed overnight in Houston. Joe picked up a package, and Ayala locked $12,000 cash in a fireproof bank bag, slit open a pillow, and stuffed the bag in with the feathers and made the bed back up. Joe took him out to eat Mexican food.

When Joe brought him back, the doorknob and lock had been smashed in, feathers everywhere.

He left the room key on the bed and caught a cab to the airport, where he got the next available flight, which stopped in Cincinnati and went on to Boston. At Logan he sat up the rest of the night and read the *Globe* and thought about his old man.

His old man had arrived in New York when he was nine. By the time he was eleven he'd worked his way up the coast to Boston, where he went from loading fish into trucks to unloading stiffs at a funeral home. Ayala grew up above a funeral parlor. In a few years they owned two parlors, and the old man had plans for him to finish school and take over the business of the dead.

He managed three semesters at Northeastern. That was more than he needed. The main thing was to read—anything he couldn't learn on the streets he could find in a library. He dropped out of school and, for lack of something better to do, one afternoon, after sitting through two showings of *2001: A Space Odyssey*, he joined the Marines. He ended up in Vietnam, but spent most of his time working on engines in a motor pool. He did not make friends but earned respect for his way with trucks and jeeps.

When he got out, he looked up another ex-Marine, Ronnie Tuma, whose old man, Tony Tuma, had fallen, hit his head in the tub, and killed himself, leaving Ronnie a wrecking yard and auto-parts place in Somerville and a used-car lot in east Boston. Ronnie gave Ayala a job at the car lot and let him use the garage and tools to tinker with motorcycles, which Ayala started racing on Sundays. When he wasn't racing or tearing down an engine, he stayed stoned and listened to the Grateful Dead. He hated living at home but not enough to pay for a place of his own. His mother was sick in bed. His sister screwed nights and slept days. He was biding his time, but he didn't know what for. He got good with bikes, won most of his races. His mother died, and that took most of the fight out of the old man, who, one night, came to watch him race.

Showing off—trying to get back at his father, to hurt him in some way by being good with the bike—Ayala got the feeling he was in control, got the feeling he could force the machine beyond its limits. Had the race been big-time, they would have replayed the crash on the TV news. In slow motion it would have been almost beautiful: the front tire raced away and kangarooed over the railing, tilted like a flying saucer and disappeared; the forked frame that had held the tire vibrated like a tuning fork, some kind of inverted dowsing rod; it jerked down into the asphalt in a fireworks spray of disintegrating

193

metal. Sparks ignited gasoline, and the fuel tank exploded. Flames shot into the sky and pieces of fire fell into the bleachers. Spectators scattered, and Ayala watched his body separate from the machine and float up, horizontal, weightless as an astronaut, the blue crash helmet reflecting light like a star. The body fell to earth on the grassy infield, which saved Ayala's life. The emergency room intern said he had no right to be alive.

"Hey, man, you sure you're not from some other planet? It's not human to survive such injuries."

He did not feel lucky or grateful, nor was he surprised to be alive. Detached from his body, he lost his fear of it. His body was a suit of clothes he could put on and take off. Fuck it, he would come and go as he pleased.

His father came to see him in the same hospital where his mother had died. They talked about the quick and the dead, about Ayala's need for speed, about the lively and profitable business of dealing with death. They made a pact, struck a deal. There was a piece of property ideal for the location of a third funeral home. This property extended to the bay; the bay, to the ocean. Ayala would run the funeral home and behind, in a large boathouse, he would spend his spare hours converting his lust for land speed to a lust for water speed. Racing boats, his father felt, was safer than racing bikes, by virtue of a boat's liquid landing places. His father had just buried a wife and felt a new sentimentality about his only son.

After a nine-month course at the College of Mortuary Science, Ayala became a licensed mortician. The new parlor his father financed had all the latest equipment. The preparation room looked like a first-class hospital surgical unit: sterile white tiles, stainless-steel gurneys and tilting preparation tables, shiny new scalpels, clamps, scissors, needles, augers, pumps and hoses, bowls and basins.

He had excelled at the mortuary college, and at first he did all the dermasurgery himself. The incision he made (usually in the femoral artery or the subclavian vein, since they were hidden by burial clothes) would have been hardly noticed had the person been alive. He had a good eye for the best tints to blend with embalming fluid, the right lighting to use in the Slumber Room (rose-colored light, for example, took care of green skin caused by embalming fluid when the deceased was jaundiced), and he was careful to color-coordinate burial clothes with skin tone.

But it was the restorative artwork he most enjoyed. Accident victims offered the best challenges. With plaster casts and wax, he replaced missing parts. He reattached heads with splints wired through holes drilled in jawbones. He removed tissue to correct swelling; he worked a syringe of massage cream up into hard-to-reach cavities to fill sunken spots. With a stippling brush, he added texture and pores to a wax ear or lip, then applied masking paste and cosmetics. After the business grew and he hired more assistants, he still did the mangled corpses. He dissuaded those who requested closed-casket services.

His boat race winnings were equaling his funeral home profits when he met a Cuban boat designer named Jaime Ramirez, who pointed out that there were more boats registered in Florida than in Massachusetts. Ramirez needed a test driver, someone smart who knew motors, someone who would push a boat and his body to the limit. Ayala went to Fort Lauderdale to see Ramirez's machine shop and boatworks. Ramirez offered him a partnership, and he left the funeral business with his father and flew south. The first year was a struggle, then they turned the corner and money started coming in. Ayala got involved with design. A test boat, *Pegasus,* chose airspeed over water speed, got away from a new driver, and rocketed over a pleasure craft bearing tourists toward supper at a sassy seaside spot on the Intracoastal. One of three propellers (how to figure the odds?), churning air where something heavier was wanted, found the solid head of Rebecca Ann Lawless, a former Miss Ohio, and separated it from her body so suddenly you missed the moment even when the super-eight movie (made by one Mel Royster, who'd turned from a blur of sea gulls to the roar of three nine-hundred-horsepower engines) was shown frame by frame in the silent, dimmed courtroom. The coroner's photographs revealed difficulties for the dermasurgeon. Ayala wished he could do the restorative work. He imagined Rebecca Ann's cold, naked body and wondered how it would be to screw a headless woman, a modern Legend of Sleepy Hollow.

Negligence was proved, insurance canceled, bankruptcy filed. Ayala needed money, and he knew boats. Smuggling was the natural next step, tilt, or twirl of the dance; he followed the music.

His first run was in an old Magnum—souped up, she'd do sixty knots—with a police radio and scanner on board. He ran after midnight without lights. A man called Ortega rode shotgun with an M-16. Ayala was never told the names of two others, there to help load and unload the cargo. These two rarely spoke, and when they did, it was Spanish or Portuguese. Off Duck Key they rendezvoused with a freighter from Colombia and loaded the Magnum to the gunwales with bales of marijuana. They put in at Cod Sound, where a panel truck and a closed U-Haul trailer waited to carry the load north.

Two other speedboats loaded at the freighter and disappeared. He learned later that the other boats had unloaded above Big Pine Key.

He made many night runs. He had excellent night vision, and under his hands any old tub sizzled. Hot—*caliente;* he was hot. The Cubans called him El Diablo.

Cigarette boats and Scarabs replaced the old Magnum. Ortega and his M-16 were always there, and now there were radio scramblers on the boat and on shore; they could communicate without being picked up. A stolen DEA radio crystal made it possible to monitor DEA and police transmissions. When the DEA and Customs were looking for them, they put out a little boat with a transmitter taped on the talk position. DEA and Customs boats homed in on that signal while Ayala's cigarette picked up a load miles downocean.

Ortega was replaced by a guy named Mitch. A car bomb had gotten Ortega's legs, one hand, and the right side of his face—taking his right eye and jawbone and most of his teeth. Doctors were trying to save his arms and remaining hand. The car's sun roof had saved Ortega's life; most of the concussion had gone through the opening.

Ortega lived, but Ayala wondered if he wished he hadn't. A little Armstrong Face Former and Denture Replacer would have fixed Ortega up for casketing; what would restore his life? Ayala wanted away from the crazy Colombians. He made a good contact, a supplier in Miami who would front him cocaine until his buyer paid off. He became a mule, or courier, and started free-lancing. He had contact with only two men, Rocky Himaka in Miami and Joe Russo in Houston.

It still galled him to think about the $12,000 ripped off in Houston. Every time he picked up the paper he read about more arrests, special drug task forces, new government crackdowns in the war against drugs. They busted a ring of stewardesses and pilots who'd been bringing in tons of coke on flights from South America. There was a black dude who roamed the Miami airport, claimed he could look you in the eyes and *know* if you were trafficking. The cops checked him out; he nailed drugs 90 percent of the time. The dude's eyes were better, one cop said, than the noses of trained dogs.

"We're not above accepting the help of any citizen to help win the war against drugs," some DEA inspector was quoted in the *Herald,* but, Ayala knew, it rankled the narcs every time that nigger busted someone with his hoodoo eyes.

They'd never win the war, of course. It was as stupid as Vietnam. Politicians got mad and made more speeches and shoved a few more million dollars down. The DEA paid a quarter of a million for a cigarette boat to outrun smugglers. The *Blue Thunder* was mean-looking; with a top speed of ninety, it could corner at sixty. The boat builder was offered half a million for a boat that cruised at a hundred and twenty and cornered at ninety. The government was encouraging free enterprise, competition in the marketplace, the American way.

Drugs even made the *Herald*'s Fishing Report. Captain Thomas Vic out of Islamorada had recently reported that the dolphin were back. According to Captain Vic, the dolphin liked shade.

"Look for them," he said, "under floating bales of marijuana."

If they decriminalized or legalized and controlled drugs, they'd put all the smugglers out of business. Every time they had a big crackdown it hurt guys like Ayala but didn't faze big operators. He did not intend to end up in the pen, butt-fucking his life away. He'd learned something about himself in that hotel room in Houston, feathers all over the bed and floor. He'd been more pissed than scared. He'd been totally, physically furious, and—this was the interesting part—he'd *enjoyed* that feeling. It was almost sexual. The last time he'd felt such a rush was the day he cracked up that bike, with his old man in the grandstand.

He knew most breaks were just that. Chance. How to figure the odds? Had an overpowered *Pegasus* not gotten away from an inexperienced driver in a test run, who knows? Ayala and Ramirez might have been the designers of *Blue Thunder*, might right now be hard at work on its faster, more expensive nemesis.

Breaks, good or bad, made the odds more interesting, harder to divine. A motorcycle crash landed him, intact, in a private morgue where he rejoined torsos and heads. A boat test in Florida hurled him into smuggling. Smuggling connected him to old Percy Fox, and Percy led him right to Julia Marrs, right where he was now, making his last journey as a mule, right up to the edge of a precipice, about to begin a new story.

5

JULIA'S phone rang. Like a young girl, she let it ring three times before she answered, breathed deeply to still the quaver she knew would be in her throat.

Already Adam's was a special voice, deeper over the telephone than in person. The voice did not say hello, did not make any introduction; it began immediately talking to Julia.

"You have slept without dreaming, you woke early, you feel wonderfully rested. You have not gotten out of bed. You didn't want to dress before you heard from me. But, sadly, this will be a long day for us both, Julia. I have business today and cannot be with you until this evening."

After Adam's call Julia stayed in bed. She wanted to drift back into sleep, but could not. Finally, she gave up and went to the kitchen, where she opened the windows wide. The noise of the waves increased as if she had turned up a volume knob, and the grassy smell of ocean mixed with the smell of coffee she spooned into a pot. While the coffee brewed, she ran hot water in the tub. Soon she was in up to her neck, the pink knobs of her knees and one hand (holding a mug of hot black coffee) sticking out of the water. Steam, heat waves rose from the tub, from her coffee. She took a mouthful of coffee and set the mug on the side of the tub. She leaned her head back until she felt the hard, cool tub, water lapping up the back of her neck, coffee warm in her throat and down into her chest down under the hot water. Her arms floated, and she let her mind drift. She would not *think* about what was beginning with Adam Smith. For once she would indulge her appetites, follow, like any good dancer, her body's lead.

She intended to be very purposeful all day about doing whatever she wanted, whatever she *felt like* doing. She might do nothing, just absolutely nothing. She might go back to bed, if only to slide around between the cool sheets, her arms side-stroking, her legs scissor-kicking across the double mattress. She might then get out of bed and take another bath. She might walk to the beach and eat a Greek gyro, or she might stop at a little store and buy fresh strawberries and real cream, a carton of eggs and some thick-sliced bacon, a loaf of bakery bread and real butter, and make a whale of a meal. Or she might not eat at all today, just drink coffee to get a good caffeine buzz and later have a glass or two of wine on an empty stomach and enjoy how quickly she would feel light-headed and imagine that not eating was making her body slender and firm, young again.

6

───────────────────────────

AYALA caught the waiter's eye. He was the all-American type, tall, blond-haired, and blue-eyed. He had nice shoulders, a trim waist, a cute ass. Ayala asked for another cup of coffee and a glass of water. When the water came, Ayala accidentally on purpose knocked it over on the tray so it spilled on the boy's crotch. The boy sucked in air and bent at the waist as if someone had punched him in the balls. Ayala apologized. He put a twenty on the tray. *Keep the change.* Through the wet white waiter's pants he saw the outline of the boy's briefs. *Thank you, sir.* Ayala smiled, stirred spoonfuls of sugar into his fresh coffee. Money talks, he thought, gets you anything you want, just when you want it.

A headline in the *Herald* caught his attention:

FLORIDA SOON TO BE 5TH LARGEST STATE

JACKSONVILLE (AP)—It may be a corporate executive, a shipyard worker, or a retired widow, but someone will soon move to Florida and push the state's population past that of Illinois, making the Sunshine State the fifth-largest in the nation, a researcher says. And, based on the Census Bureau's provisional estimates, it won't be long before Florida passes Pennsylvania to become the fourth-largest state. One effect is a rapidly expanding market, making Florida a more favorable location for many types of businesses.

Each day, 895 new Floridians arrive. Each day, Florida needs an additional 140,000 gallons of water. Each day, Florida produces 120,000 gallons of waste water and 4,800 more pounds of solid waste that must be disposed of. Each day, Florida needs two more miles of highway, two more classrooms, two more teachers, three more police officers, and four more jail beds.

There you have it, he thought. A favorable location for many

200

types of businesses. The illegal drug business brought over a billion dollars a year into the state's economy; bigger business than tourism. Every day, three more cops and four more jail beds. Ayala was making up a different kind of bed to lie in. He had in mind another business for which this state was a favorable location. Of the 895 Floridians who had arrived on a recent day, one was a wealthy widow (in a state that likely led the nation in wealthy widows), who was going to lie in that bed with him. After her, others would arrive. The supply of widows was sure always to outstrip the demand.

Percy Fox had given Ayala the tip. Ayala wholesaled marijuana to Percy. Percy was small-time, but he had good eyes, like the airport hoodoo nigger.

Most of Percy's hotel guests were middle-class French Canadians down for a week in the sun. This gal, Julia, was different. She had class, something Percy couldn't put his finger on. Not bad-looking for her age; Percy guessed she was in her early fifties. Percy kept thinking she was something good, if he could figure the angle. She wanted the three-room apartment, ocean view. When the phone rang, some blind guy selling light bulbs, Percy acted like it was a cancellation. He jacked the rent a hundred, and the dame didn't flinch. He asked for cash and followed her out to a new black sports car—an expensive job, Porsche or something. There was a stack of bills three or four inches high in the glove box. Percy figured thousands. That was pocket money. No telling how much she had salted away. Percy was thinking quick, one-shot score, wham-bam-thank-you-ma'am.

But Ayala wanted to break out of the cycle, living hand to mouth, robbing Peter to pay Paul or however that went, starting over every time his dough ran out. Why not marry Julia Marrs and spend the dough before her sonny boy inherited it? He'd been irritated when he found out about the son, but pleased there were no other heirs. Just one guy to figure. Julia Marrs wasn't bad for an old lady. There was something there he had not expected. He was going to eat her right up and enjoy doing it. He'd find her dark side and roll her over and make her take a good long look at her underbelly.

As Ayala approached the metal detector, a man in a brown J. C. Penney FBI suit stepped up and touched him on the elbow. The man flipped open a wallet, flashed an official-looking ID, some kind of seal and a metal badge clipped to it.

"Would you come with me, please."

Ayala stiffened. The man put pressure on his elbow, inclining him away from the metal detector. The badge meant nothing. Could be anything—FBI, Miami-Dade cop, retired-men security service.

"No," he said. "I decline your offer. I have an airplane to catch." He shrugged free of the man and stepped through the detector's empty doorframe. The man was totally surprised.

"You'd better stop," the man said.

Ayala's new eelskin shoes snapped on the tile floor where the new carpet ended. At Gate G-11, the final boarding call was being announced. He hurried down the enclosed ramp onto the airplane. He had to squeeze over a big guy sitting on the aisle. Through the window he saw nothing unusual. The engines whined; cool air hissed out of an overhead nozzle. He screwed the silver ring open, the way he had twisted the brass nozzle on a water hose when he was a boy, making a wide bell of spray that caught the sunlight and threw rainbows on the side of the funeral home.

It took longer than usual to taxi, and then they had to wait in line for a runway. Ayala imagined the pilot getting a police call. He expected one of the stewardesses or another cheap suit to head his way. But nothing happened.

Once they were at cruising altitude and the seat-belt light blinked off, he headed to the toilet. He locked the door, and a fluorescent light flickered on. He took off the new linen jacket. His shirt was wet against his back. He patted cool water on his face.

Maybe some narc was waiting in Houston, hanging out in the airport lounge with a pocketful of warrants. Should he stash the cocaine on the plane? Wash it down the drain? He sat on the toilet and lifted his pants cuffs. The coke was soft and cool through the plastic. Thirty grand—plus twenty grand profit waiting in Houston. A three-hour flight—time to think this out. If they were gonna snatch him on the plane, they'd have already done something. Why risk scaring him, why give him a chance to ditch the coke? Another fucking glitch. The DEA were real fuck-ups, they were astonishingly stupid, or they were so sure of themselves they were toying with him and could nab him anytime. Odds were he would waltz right off the plane in Houston.

"Business trip?"

The fat fuck sitting next to him wanted to talk. Ayala looked at him for a long moment, then said, "Yes, it is. *My* business. *Comprende?*"

The man nodded and studied a plastic-coated sheet of safety instructions.

They landed in Houston, the huge Intercontinental Airport north of the city. Eight minutes ahead of schedule: he wondered if that had anything to do with him. He waited until the fuck beside him heaved himself up, blocking any view of Ayala from the aisle, then he stuffed the bags of coke under a seat cushion.

He deplaned; no one approached. He went to a pay phone and held the receiver to his ear until the area was completely empty. No one. He hurried down the ramp, back onto the plane. A stewardess was leaning over an empty first-class seat, picking up a napkin, her ass sticking out into the aisle at crotch level. Ayala imagined pushing her skirt up over her behind and humping her from the rear. She looked over her shoulder.

"May I help you, sir?"

"Forgot something; going to check my seat."

He entered the coach section. Two stewardesses and a tall guy in a uniform—captain, copilot, one of those—back near his seat. Fuck. They'd found the shit, or they were so near his seat they'd see him if he pulled the bags out.

"What's the problem?" Was he imagining the threatening tone in the guy's voice?

"No problem." He spotted a man's hat in an open overhead bin. "Forgot my hat." He picked up the hat and gave a wave with it. The stewardesses looked at the captain. Ayala walked back through first class. A cowboy sauntering out of a saloon, he half expected a bullet in the back.

He took a cab to Hobby Airport, downtown, and phoned Joe, who was pissed. Ayala told him to fuck himself.

He got a flight out of Hobby to Miami through Dallas–Fort Worth. With the hour he'd lose to the time zone, it would be rush hour when he landed in Miami. He'd have to shower and dress, then haul ass up to Hollywood for Julia Marrs. So he'd hump it. She was more important now—$50,000 more important.

The hat he'd stolen off the plane was an expensive fedora, five-X beaver. He inspected the sweatband. The hat did not look much worn. He'd prefer a panama straw for Miami, but this was October, and the fedora was a light gray. He could wear it now, according to the calendar, wear it at least through February or March, in spite of the heat. Fashion was dictated by the calendar, not by the climate.

He smiled into the men's room mirror. The hat sank over his forehead and rested on his ears. He arched his eyebrows and they disappeared up behind the brim. One of the three stooges.

Julia Marrs was looking better by the minute.

7

ADAM SMITH was not the kind of man Julia had ever imagined herself with. She was a different woman now. She wasn't sure what kind of man the *new* Julia would be with. She wished Adam were a little less attractive. She was afraid to learn exactly how much younger Adam was than herself. He couldn't be much older than Coleman. But he was oh, so different from Coleman.

Adam's thick black hair was always combed straight back, always shiny, wet-looking, as if he'd just emerged from the surf. Long in back, it reminded her of Elvis Presley's hair, except that Adam's sideburns were short and trimmed to sharp points like those of the space travelers on *Star Trek*. Adam's body was tanned a rich, deep red-brown, the color of the oyster and the okra seeds in the gumbo she had eaten that night in Lake Charles. His bathing suit, a shimmery, silky black brief, left a red line visible in his skin when he sat or leaned over. His muscles rolled tightly beneath flesh the way waves move at low tide, the way sunlight over the sea sometimes appears to dart, trapped beneath waves.

The first time Adam took her out, he wore a light-blue linen suit that turned his eyes blue. His yellow shirt was open at the collar, and a flat coil of gold circled his neck and reflected the late-afternoon light. That evening, Julia held the back of her hand to Adam's throat and felt the gold chain cold against her skin. When he bent to brush her cheek with his, she inhaled his odor, something sweet and barbershop strong, mixed with the faint scent of sizing from new clothes.

Adam Smith picked her up in a blue convertible, a small two-seater, and took her to a fish market and restaurant near downtown

Miami, on the Miami River. They drove underneath the expressway, through the shadows of concrete pillars cast by tall, amber expressway lights. The black shapes of steel cranes and the curved bows of big boats loomed up into the deep-blue evening sky. One wall of the restaurant was lined with white butcher cases, whose glass windows displayed the creamy-white, silver-gray, orange-pink bodies of fish, oysters, and stone crabs spread over glittering ice.

Julia and Adam Smith drank cold beer and ate spicy smoked-fish appetizers. Julia heard five languages at tables around them: English and Spanish (of course), but also German, and French, and something she thought was Chinese or Japanese but Adam told her was Vietnamese.

"Were you in Vietnam?" she asked.

"Yes."

She nodded. How young did that make him? He changed the subject.

"Let me order for you," he said.

Adam Smith ordered them each Miami-style stone crabs, cold, with mustard sauce, and whole grilled yellowtail. The fish were beautiful, two side by side, golden, striped dark brown by the grill, their fins and tails dark and crispy-thin; one eye on each looked up at the mounted fish that swam the white walls of the restaurant. They had more smoked fish, spicy coleslaw, and another round of cold beer in dark-green bottles. For dessert they had key lime pie and cortado, Cuban coffee mixed with boiling milk, loaded with sugar, and topped with a sprinkle of cinnamon.

"Real key lime pie," Adam told her, "is pale yellow and made from fresh key limes. There's food coloring in the tourist stuff to make it green."

After the meal, Adam drove her down Bayshore through Coconut Grove and down Main and then Old Cutler Road, under a miles-long canopy of banyan trees, to a park in a hammock of mangroves. The park was closed. Adam pulled off the road and parked the convertible in some trees. At the park entrance he wedged the gate open and they slipped inside. They walked holding hands. Julia heard waves in the bay she could not see, a breeze through the thick mangroves, and the sound of their footsteps. She smelled the ocean and felt its closeness. They stepped into a clearing and the dark sky curved down to meet the dark water curving up. Somewhere in front of her, in the moist darkness, was the serrated line of the horizon, where jagged waves made the tracks of the zipper that fastened the sea to the heavens. Julia wanted to stretch her arm all the way to that zipper, to feel the cold metal joining of the planet to space.

Later, Adam took her dancing at an after-hours club in the Mayfair. The doorman turned away a couple that could not produce a membership card. The same doorman greeted Adam (what was it he called Adam?) and ushered them in. Adam had not shown a card. Perhaps he had slipped the man some money? That, or he knew some secret sign, Julia thought, smiling at how nosy she was.

The place was packed. Fast-dancing had changed since she'd last been dancing with Avery, but the slow stuff never changed much. Adam was not as natural a dancer as Avery had been. Adam was almost too professional, like a dance instructor, but he was smooth and knew all kinds of moves.

The band played several Latin tunes, and Julia followed Adam and picked up the steps. Two women danced together. One was tall and thin; her long black hair hung straight down the open back of a glittery silver jumpsuit fastened tight around her legs below the knees, like a bullfighter's pants. She wore very high heels, black with silver bows. Her partner had close-cropped platinum hair and wore a soft aqua sweater dress that came only to the tops of her thighs. The band started a sassy number with a pounding conga beat, and dancers moved back to give the two women more room. They never touched, but the tall, thin woman's body haunted the body in the short sweater dress. The tall body bent and swayed like the long shadow of its partner. Someone whistled, and a woman in the crowd called out in Spanish. Adam Smith's hands moved up Julia's sides and held her breasts. It felt nice. Everyone watched the two women. When the song ended, the women kissed each other on the lips. The tall one turned and looked at Julia. The woman smiled at Julia and threw her hip sideways, slapped herself there, and laughed.

Long after midnight, Adam took her to a restored art deco hotel on Miami Beach. The hotel bar spilled out onto a wide, L-shaped porch crowded with people dressed to the hilt. This was a slightly older crowd than the one dancing at the Mayfair. On the small, round table, her hand on the glass was so close to Adam's hand that the fine hairs along her wrist touched his knuckles; beneath the table, his leg rested against her knee. A breeze rattled palm leaves on the wide beach that began right across Collins Avenue and stretched for at least a hundred yards out to the ocean.

"Come on," Adam said. "The sea is calling." They were drinking brandy from bell-shaped snifters, and he slid the long fingers of one hand around the stems of both glasses and held them up, where they clinked together like glass castanets. A waiter eyed Adam and the glasses, but smiled and nodded when Adam dropped two twenty-dollar bills on the table. He led her across Collins Avenue and through a grove of palm trees to the beach. In the dark, she couldn't tell where the wide strand ended and the ocean began. Adam spoke, but the breeze and the noise of waves blew his words back into his mouth. It sounded as if he said *fear blows lower keep hotter.* Then they were closer to the ocean, the sand firmer underfoot, and he repeated himself. "This pier goes over deep water."

Julia carried her shoes in one hand, her brandy in the other. The rough, sandy boards of the pier were hard, solid after the sand, and she pressed down with every step, feeling the weight of her body on first one foot, then the other. Had she bent her knee and pushed up with all her strength, she would have sprung off the end of the pier, as a diver off the end of a board, and catapulted up into the darkness far out over the ocean. Adam's shoes slapped the gritty boards, and his steps merged with the slapping of water against pilings. They sat at the end of the pier and faced the breeze that came at them from the dark. Adam's shoulder rested against Julia's. She lowered her face to the snifter of brandy and slowly inhaled the warm flavor. When she lifted her face to the dark sky and water beyond, the sea breeze replaced the peppery fumes of the brandy with the familiar but exotic smell of the sea.

Adam drained his glass, and so did she. He toasted her with a wink and pitched his glass up into the air, and so did she. She listened to hear the glasses splash, but they did not, and she pictured them taking flight in the salt air.

Adam stood and pulled her up. His right hand touched Julia's back—the heel of his hand rested in the declivity of her spine. His left hand moved below her hip, her skirt came up in gathers as he worked his hand beneath the fabric and found her skin. He brought the tips of his fingers up a muscle in back of her thigh which spread into the cool roundness of her ass. She saw a darker darkness, his face lowering to hers, and she longed for the press of his mouth over hers but felt, instead, the soft moistness of his lips brush her forehead. All the walk back down the pier and across the beach, her forehead felt as if he had left a mark there, a bit of soft ash.

*   *   *

Adam started to put the car top up for the drive back to Hollywood, but he caught her eye and smiled, shook his head and left it down. "We feel like being blown away, don't we?" he said.

And they were blown away. The car sped along; only snatches of music made it from the radio to Julia's ears before wind jerked the sound away. Had she or Adam spoken, neither could have heard, but that was fine; she was content to be hurtled through the early morning, her hair whipped back and tugging at her scalp, something (insects?) stinging her elbow poked out into the buffeting air. Headlights swam steadily past them on the other side of the expressway while they raced along in a sea of glowing shrimp-eye taillights.

Adam pulled up beside the Turret Inn, came around, and opened her door. In his warm palm, Julia felt how cold her right elbow was.

At the door, Julia knew Adam knew she wanted him to kiss her, but she also knew he was not going to. He was putting himself in control. He didn't know how much he was already controlling her responses. She had not wanted a man in this way for a long, long time. Her body was making demands it had never made before, not even when she had her Martian lover.

"Again, tomorrow," Adam said, and it was not a question. In the near dark, his eyes were black as bullet holes.

8

JULIA saw Adam Smith's silhouette all the way from the beach. How was it that she already knew his shape so well and from such distance? She stared at the unmoving shape as she walked, one hand shading her eyes from the bright sun.

He stood at the top of the outdoor stairs that led to the second-floor balcony. When she got to the stairs, Julia saw that the door to her apartment was open behind him. She had not left it unlocked. How had he gotten in? His friend Percy, the manager? Barefoot, shirtless, Adam stood in jeans so faded they looked silver in the brightness. The sun shone up the length of him, shining the metal button above his fly and turning the few curled hairs on his chest into bright wires.

"I didn't know whether I was going to see you today," she said. "You're a nice surprise."

Adam neither spoke nor smiled. He turned, and Julia climbed the stairs and followed him into her apartment. He did not go into the kitchen, as she expected, to offer her something cool to drink. He went into the bedroom.

"Here," he said. He stopped beside the bed and waited. She walked up to him, and he unfastened her damp bathing suit and peeled it off her breasts and down over her hips and let it drop, a softness down both her legs at once, then lying cool over the tops of her bare feet.

He put his arms around her and kissed her, his mouth kneading her mouth. The metal button of his jeans, warm from the sun, pressed into her abdomen, cool and damp from her bathing suit. Her arms greased his back with suntan lotion, her fingers rolled fine grains of sand into his slick skin. She smelled the fragrance of lotion, salt in her hair, and sweat—hers and his.

"I need a shower first," she said.

"No. Shower later."

"I can smell me."

"So can I, and I like it."

Julia woke to the noise of the shower. The sheet had stuck to the lotion on her back, and when she rolled over to look into the bathroom, it peeled off like a Band-Aid. She watched Adam's shape through the foggy glass door of the shower stall. Through the rising steam and the fall of water, she said, "That's a nice way to be put to sleep."

Adam said nothing, and she wasn't sure he'd heard her over the shower. She waited until he turned off the water and stepped out. He was dark and dripping wet. She wanted him again, wanted wet skin against her and sticking to sheets.

"How long did I sleep?" she asked.

"A couple of hours."

"Did you sleep too?"

"I watched you."

He reached for a towel and rubbed his hair, bowed his face into the wadded towel, lifted his head and combed through his hair with his fingers. He opened a black shaving kit that sat on the back of the toilet. She wondered what else he had brought with him. A change of clothes? A suitcase?

He turned on the hot water and held a shaving brush under the tap. When he rubbed the brush in a shaving mug, muscles moved in his arm and beneath his shoulder blades. He brushed soap onto his face, then began shaving beneath the sharp point of his left sideburn. The razor cut smooth, skin-colored swaths in the lather. He opened his mouth to speak, and it looked like a breathing hole opening in a bandaged head.

"I keep an extra razor, a few things, in the car. Just in case." He cocked his head just a little and smiled at her in the mirror, then looked down where he held the end of the razor under running water. Steam from the tap clouded the corners of the medicine cabinet mirror, leaving his face framed in the silver oval like an old-fashioned daguerreotype.

Julia got out of the bed and, still naked, walked on the balls of her feet across the cool floor to press herself against him and feel

211

the wet places of his body touch hers. In the fluorescent light from the medicine cabinet, Julia saw things she had not seen before. A scar followed Adam's hairline down the side of his face, as if he had been scalped or his hair had been placed over his head and sewn meticulously, perfectly in place. An accident? Surgery? Tiny veins spread red and thin from the sides of his nose into his cheeks. A sign of what? Alcoholism or drug abuse or, worst of all, age. Adam smiled a malevolent, undertaker's grin, almost a grimace, bared his teeth, straight, white, artificially healthy-looking, and gave her a leering wink.

He splashed hot water, then cold, on his face and wiped the mirror with his forearm. The bathroom window was full of sunlight, and that bright rectangle was reflected in the mirror and from there to the white bathroom wall.

With a snort, Adam stepped between the mirror and the window as into a spotlight on a stage. In the brightness, the places on his body that were still wet gleamed. He took Julia's nipples in his fingertips and drew her toward him, pulled her into the reflected glare with him.

A tiny ball of water rested in a cleft in Adam's chin, a cleft Julia had not clearly seen before, and beads of water clung to the ends of his hair. Julia took his chin in her mouth and sucked and tasted soap and felt the faint prickles of his just-shaved skin against her tongue.

His hand moved down her side, and she breathed deeply to keep from being tickled. She moved her hand between their bodies and her fingers searched his skin as her lips slid up over his and her tongue filled his mouth. Her fingers moved into his damp pubic hair, then she held the thick weight of him. Her hand seemed to squeeze tighter around him, but it was his swelling she felt. He leaned back against the smooth glass shower stall and took her weight above his bent knees. With a hand under each of her thighs, he pulled her up until she felt the heat of his tip end. Against the smooth bottoms of her thighs she felt the muscles that ran over his thighs tighten, and he pulled her down onto him. A thick warmth penetrated her just as her bare feet touched the wet, cool tile floor—completing a circuit. For an awesome instant she expected the black sizzle of her electrocution, the smell of burned hair and charred flesh. She thought of Annabelle being strapped onto a table for electric shock treatments, Annabelle's body jumping with repeated jolts. She thought of Bruno Richard Hauptmann, his body arching up from the electric chair, burned places where the lightning entered his body. Unlike him, Julia thought, I go willingly to my execution. She looked across the steamy bathroom, looked for Jupiter with a jagged, white-hot thunderbolt in his upraised arm. What she saw was the wet, black shiny back of Adam Smith's head reflected in the shower glass.

Julia pulled her face back and looked at Adam Smith's face. That face bore no expression, a description she had read in novels but never before believed. She put her lips to Adam's neck, red from the razor, and rested her head against his shoulder as he walked, tilted back, carrying her on his thighs to the bed.

9

The Turrett Inn
Hollywood, Florida

Wednesday afternoon

Dear Coleman,

I'm still here in Hollywood, where I feel strangely at home. Strangely because it is such a foreign place, so unlike any place I've lived before. I feel some weird combination of energy and malaise. I'm lulled by the sea, drugged by the sun, yet more alive than I've been since your father died. I feel my body heat rise and fall with the thermometer, feel my body fluids rise and fall with the tide.

I put my fingertips to a cold, sweaty glass and am scarcely surprised to see that I leave no prints there. My fingertips go cold with the glass, frost on frost, yet when I touch my cold hand to the warm arm of my chair, I leave no moist prints there either. I think I left my fingerprints behind, somewhere along the seacoast between Texas and here, shed the skin off my fingertips, my old identity.

Lest you fear for my sanity, I assure you I have not taken leave of my senses. I am, as they say, of sound mind and body. I think I know what I am doing, which is all anyone can say, right? Avery, God love him, made all my decisions for me. After he died I suppose I expected you to take up where he left off. I thank you for not doing that. I'm not old enough for you to become my worried parent. It is not always easy to allow ones you love to change—that can be very upsetting. But I want you to know that I am undergoing a change—a sea change (I know, that's awful, but appropriate nonetheless). I've met an interesting man with whom I've been spending a good deal of time. I remember how angry I was when you married Jeanette. I was sure you were making a mistake. Avery, wiser than I, as always, said you had a right to make your own mistakes. Now I understand that. And when you and Jeanette divorced I was angry all over again. Do you recall telling me that in spite of the hurt you felt, you felt a measure of excitement, a sense that you might have a life altogether new, redemptive, you said. At the time I listened and nodded and thought I was indulging your melodramatic sense of yourself. Now I feel much the same sense of rebirth.

I want you to know that this man is unlike any man I have been with before, unlike (I'm sure) any man you would expect me to take up with. (Lord knows he is not what I would have expected for myself.) To begin with (and this may be the least of it), he is much younger than I. He is, to get it out, about your age, Coleman. And there is much more that I *do not* know about him than there is that I *do* know. He's a bit mysterious and not (I suspect) altogether honest (with me, with himself). I find, in my wise (and selfish) old age, that I can afford to be quite honest—in fact, I refuse not to. This may seem strange, coming from your mother, but—especially because of your recent divorce and your present romance—I want to acknowledge that, so far at least, the main attraction he (he calls himself Adam Smith) has for me is his mysteriousness and a very irrational sexual chemistry I feel from him (like static electricity, he zaps me with even casual touches). I know that a woman alone takes her chances. I appreciate that you have tried, since Avery's death, to let me figure my own odds. Believe me, I am aware of the risks, but that is most of the pleasure in the game—especially when it gets close to closing time.

Well, enough of my tired metaphors. I just wanted you to know your old mother is still very much alive and, right now at least, enjoying kicking. No more and no less. I hope Rachel continues to make you happy and that her ex-husband does not knock you off. Ha. You see, I do know that you can take care of yourself. And I think I can too.

Write me, phone me, from time to time, so I'll know I'm not wrong.

For the foreseeable future I'll be here at the Turret Inn, in Hollywood. I love that there's a place like this, in Florida, called Hollywood. I've never been to the real Hollywood, in California, but there is a kind of faded style here that I associate with those white letters on the mountain in California, HOLLYWOOD, that you always see in movies and on TV. This place is *funky*, you know, glitz for old folks—like me. Where else would you find a place called the Turret Inn? My apartment is up in the turret, natch.

I don't remember the exact address—it's on Arizona Street—or the telephone number, and I'm writing this stretched out on a beach towel a good hike from my room. If you need to phone me, you'll have to get the number from information. I do remember that the area code is 305. I'm in Apartment F.

Adam is taking me to dinner tonight, and the weatherman said we'd have a full moon, so I figure Adam might grow hair on his hands and face and start howling. Do you have a silver bullet I can use if things get out of hand? Ha.

Having actually written all this down, I am going straight to the post office, where I will feel a delicious panic when this letter drops out of sight.

With much love,

Mother

10

IN late-afternoon light in her east-facing room, Julia stood naked before a full-length mirror. Accordion music and several voices singing a bouncy song in French came through her open windows.

Julia was sixty-two years old. Her face was what men of her generation had called handsome, never beautiful. The new brown rinse took off a few years. She had a little girl's sprinkling of freckles over her nose. She was fortunate not to have put on weight; she still wore a size ten dress. Her shoulders were more rounded than they used to be, but her skin was still smooth. For the first time in her life, she had been wearing a two-piece bathing suit. Her breasts and the skin between them were white as the white mask around the eyes of a raccoon; her dark chocolate-colored nipples, the shining pupils of those eyes. She had smallish breasts that would never sag more than they had when she was twenty. She held a cube of ice against first one, then the other nipple, and the chocolate-brown flesh tightened and reddened, the tips of her nipples rose. There were a few lines of loose skin along her rib cage. Her belly, while not fat, was a little puffy. She turned and looked over her shoulder at her bare backside. Not bad. She would always have the little lightning-bolt scars on her butt, from the time her dress caught fire. Some lumpiness, the Pillsbury Doughboy, in the backs of her thighs. Below her knees small veins were visible, but fewer, now that she had a tan.

She lay on the carpet and did ten sit-ups, ten minutes of leg lifts. Yesterday she'd done only eight sit-ups, no leg lifts.

Steaming water sloshed over the top of the tub when Julia lowered herself in. The hot water stung her ankles and the backs of her thighs, but she let herself down until water covered her chin, and more water slopped onto the tile floor. She raised an arm into air made cool by the warmer water. She moved a razor up and down like a paintbrush stroking on a smooth coat of fresh pink beneath her arms. She rinsed the razor and lathered a leg, resting her heel on the cool tile wall. She shaved each leg and then shaved around the edges of her dark pubic hair. Billowing in the water, the hair was soft and silky. She rubbed in shampoo and then conditioner. With tweezers she jerked out a wiry gray hair. The next time she put the brown rinse on her head, she'd do down there too.

Julia spent a long time at the mirror. Her eyes were brown, almost black, a little slanted. That almost Oriental look kept bags from under her eyes. She'd bought new makeup she rubbed over her cheeks and into small wrinkles at the corners of her eyes. She'd read an article about eye shadow and liner; now she practiced holding the tiny pencil. When the clerk at Macy's had rung up the charges, Julia had been shocked, but she'd smiled and told the clerk to give her another lipstick too.

Julia's mouth was wide, too big, she told herself, but she had perfect, straight teeth, all original equipment. She had never had long fingernails, but now she pressed on perfect almond shapes she'd bought. As she painted them Tahiti Mauve, one by one, she forgot they were not real.

She sat on the floor, the tiles cool beneath her skin, and held first one foot and then the other against the tub and painted her toenails Calypso Pink. She wished she had done her toes before her fingers; the new, long fingernails made it hard to hold the brush.

The white pumps had spike heels, higher than she was used to; they made her calves look good. Stockings smoothed the backs of her thighs, and the simple white sundress set off her tan.

She heard Adam's knock and gave herself a last look. Watching herself in the mirror, she reached back and unhooked her bra, slipped it out from under her arm, through the side of the sleeveless dress. Her nipples made delicate imprints against the cotton dress, like the nipples on mannequins at Macy's.

Through the screened door, Adam's shape was smoky and indistinct; the top of his head pressed dark against the screen. Julia opened the door and stepped through, pulling the metal front door closed behind her and pushing Adam gently backward against the balcony railing.

"I'm ready," she said.

Adam's forehead bore red crosshatches from the screen. The

setting sun turned the sand orange, and Julia's white dress glowed against her suntan. Adam's eyes (purple in the sunset) covered every inch of her. As he looked, she felt heat spread from behind her ears into her cheeks. She hoped the orange sunlight and her tan concealed her blush. Her nipples tightened against the front of the dress, and she almost expected Adam to put his fingertips there. But he took her hand instead. As it had been last night, his hand was warm, almost hot, but dry.

"You look lovely," he said, and he led her down the steps and across the walkway to a side street, where he opened the door of a white late-model Lincoln. Julia slipped in and leaned back against white leather seats. The heavy door closed with a solid *tunk*. It was very quiet inside the car. Adam walked around the hood, framed in the tinted windshield, and got in beside her. Wordlessly he started the engine and pushed a cassette into the stereo. Julia heard the muffled grinding of gravel beneath the fat tires, then music filled the car—something she had never heard before, yet she felt she recognized it: light, jazzy, saxophone, the raspy whisper of brushes on drums, the clear *plink* of individual piano keys followed by a throaty female voice singing soft scat, rolling repeated meaningless syllables in a meaningful melody. The sun, level with the highway, slipped in and out of spaces between buildings and cast light on the car's hood that, through the tinted glass, looked like the Tahiti Mauve on Julia's fingernails.

Adam drove south. He spoke the names of beaches, bodies of water they crossed in a succession of bridges. Julia looked down at the purple sizzle of sunset on the water. She looked up at lighted windows in high-rise hotels and condominiums. She couldn't quite believe all these people lived in this small space. The condos were a variety of boxes and tubes, wedges and curves, straining and twisting to offer ocean views. She had read ads in the Sunday classified, knew that many of the condos were totally self-sufficient, contained grocery stores, restaurants, dry cleaners, dress shops, pharmacies, you name it. A person could live the rest of her life in one of these tall towers and never have to go outside. It seemed funny, all these old people from the Northeast selling everything to relocate down here, drawn by the weather, the sun and the ocean, and then they never ventured outside. They breathed freon-cooled, filtered air and walked not on sand or in salt water but over thick carpet. On the one hand, this prospect depressed Julia; on the other hand, she imagined a swanky apartment way up high, huge windows looking out at the sky and miles of ocean, and it had a certain appeal. She wondered if sand was a popular color for carpet down here.

Adam took her down Highway 1, through Miami, to a restaurant in Coconut Grove. They ate outdoors, by the sidewalk, and watched people parade by.

"It's a kind of promenade," she said.

"Saturday night in the Grove: it's a tradition. Everyone gets all swacked out to make the scene. Women buy outfits at wild boutiques here in the Grove, then don't have anywhere they can wear the stuff except back where they bought it."

"But it is fun," she said. "All these different people, there's a nice give-and-take." As she spoke, a tall, very pink-skinned boy with spiked corn-silk hair, long, dangly earrings, no shirt, and skintight leather pants walked by holding hands with a muscular black man wearing a white suit, a turquoise T-shirt, and turquoise tennis shoes.

"Sometimes," Adam said, "the give-and-take is not so nice. Sometimes there is more take than give."

"My husband, Avery, used to say things belong to those who want them most."

"Did he also say the best things in life are free?"

Julia ignored Adam's sneer. "No," she said. "He knew you paid a price for everything. But that the coin of the realm might not be money. Money is not the only root of evil."

She could see she had puzzled him. "If," he said, "money is a root, it's the taproot; it goes deep down to the center of the world." He stared at a piece of uneaten meat on Julia's plate.

Julia said nothing. A girl, strikingly pretty, eyed Adam from another sidewalk table. Incognito in her suntan and sundress, Florida tourist, worldly traveler, Julia was less self-conscious about being with a man so good-looking and so much younger than she. It's what he says, she thought, more than how he looks, that makes him seem too young.

He looked up as if he had just waked from a nap. A smile fixed itself on his face, and he said, "Julia, I'm glad you're with me."

Had he read her thoughts? She laughed and shook her head.

"No, wait," he said. "I mean that. I'd rather be with you tonight than anyone I can think of. I feel comfortable with you. I value experience a great deal. And you are a very handsome, sensual lady."

"You barely know me, Adam. We haven't ever, really, talked about anything."

"I trust my instincts. Why don't you, too?"

Julia didn't know if it was her instincts she was trusting or something else. Was the physical desire she felt for Adam instinctive? Or were instincts responsible for the uneasiness she felt? *Something* was certainly urging her on, but something else was attempting a warning. Whatever urged her on also suppressed her apprehensions. For now, she thought, she did not want to think about it. She had always thought too much. She had always been the one to go back inside to make sure she had (though she was always sure she had) turned off the gas range, the electric iron, the water faucet. She was an attractive woman alone in vacationland, and she refused to think.

Scant hours later, Adam held Julia close. She was floating on air. They were in an elevator, rising silently, high up in an expensive condominium on Key Biscayne. Adam said the condo belonged to a business associate. The moment they crossed the threshold, Adam began kissing her, and something started. Something was being born in Julia the moment Adam's lips covered hers and his hot breath entered her mouth and filled her lungs. Her hands moved beneath his jacket, pressed against his back. Through his shirt his skin burned. Then his words came out like a hot wind in the cool, quiet room.

"Kneel down in front of me." It was a command Julia obeyed. Her hands trembled as she followed other commands.

She was frightened and excited.

The apartment was quiet. Julia heard Adam's breathing and her breathing and the *clink* of Adam's belt buckle and the *tump* of shoes hitting the floor and all the whispering together of Adam's shirt and her dress and Adam's trousers and her stockings and Adam's underwear and her panties.

White carpet covered the floor of every room. There were ocean views from every window. But Julia was not looking at the ocean. She was looking at the carpet, up close, smelling the fibers, watching the wiggly shine of nylon threads that sprouted regularly among the thicker wool pile, something you'd see only with your cheek against the carpet, a worm's-eye view. Julia's face, shoulders, breasts, elbows, knees pressed against the carpet, her toes dug into the carpet, her bare buttocks up in the cool air. Above her, Adam Smith stood naked, his legs spread, bowed. Like a rodeo rider, he held one hand tight against her crotch (where he was pushing himself into her from above and behind), held his other hand high above his head. As he slid completely inside her, a sword into a scabbard, he brought his upheld hand down, hard, and she heard (more than felt) the slap against her skin, which was wet with his sweat. He slid the sword almost out, then slammed it in to the hilt and slapped her harder. He pulled back, slammed close again, and his arm came around, over her shoulder, and pulled up against her throat. His fist pressed against her jawbone. His other hand came around her and squeezed first one, then the other breast, his fingers pulling and kneading her nipples.

Julia smelled scorched hair, as from a blow-dryer. Adam Smith's lips, wet and burning, stung the edge of her ear. His saliva slid down the side of her neck.

His tongue and lips moved against her ear. He spoke words that had never meant anything to her, but as she read the movement of his lips, felt deep in her ear canal the hot currents of air his cheeks shaped, those common vulgarities got inside her and rushed down into her lungs and heart, dropped like hot coals through her stomach down toward him, where he was stirring her insides with a branding-iron-hot poker. He spewed words down into her, words as incendiary as the globs of heat he ejaculated up into her, and she burned and burned.

He had not turned on any lights, and now, wordless, they dressed in the dark living room. Julia had carpet burns on her knees and elbows. There were sore, tender places on her body, where, she knew, the skin would turn purple. She held her panties out and bent to step into them. Her legs trembled and she thought she might fall, but she maintained a wobbly balance.

"No," Adam said. "Leave them off. Do not ever wear panties again when we go out."

She did not think. She handed Adam the panties, and he put them in his trousers pocket. Between her legs she burned.

On the drive back, Adam reached over and pulled Julia's dress up around her waist, exposing her from the belly down. Not far from the Turret Inn, they stopped for a traffic light. A van pulled up beside them, and Julia smoothed her dress down.

"No. Pull it back up," Adam said.

The driver of the van looked down into the car. He stared at Julia. Her hand shook, but she gathered the hem of the dress in her fingers and lifted it. Adam slid his fingers in and out of her, while the man in the van watched. They, she and Adam in the Lincoln and the man in the van, sat through two more light changes before Adam drove on. The rest of the drive back to the Turret Inn seemed to take forever, yet when Adam turned off the engine and opened the car door, she felt as if the evening were just beginning, as if they were not returning but just starting out.

Adam came inside with her and slowly undressed her. Then he pulled down the covers of her bed and told her to lie on her back.

Still dressed, he stood over her and worked his fingers in and out of her until her body was rigid. Then he kissed her on the forehead and ran his wet fingers over her lips.

"Taste yourself, Julia. See how warm and sweet you are." One at a time, he slipped each finger into her mouth, and when he had his entire hand in her mouth, he spread his fingers and touched her teeth gently. "Good night, Julia. I wanted you very much tonight, and I was not disappointed. I want you again, right now, which is how I want to leave you." He took her hand and pressed it against the fly of his trousers, hard as a wooden stick or a length of iron. "This is how I want you to make me every time I see you."

Julia spoke his name in the dark, but he was gone. For the first time in hours, she heard the ocean. Naked on the bed, she did not cover herself. Air moving across her skin was restful. She closed her eyes and listened to the waves. This time of night, early in the morning, was the tide coming in or going out? She emptied her mind as she did when she lay on the beach in the sun. She lay still and let the darkness beat down on her exposed skin. She was burning. She was turning darker and darker. She must not let herself think about this. In the darkness, everything is changed. She willed herself to let go, to give in to the waves and let them lull her. She wanted to float and bob and let herself go under.

She opened her eyes. Had she slept? The room was still dark, the night not yet over. She remembered sitting at the light, the man in the van staring down at her, and her ears and the back of her neck flushed hot with shame. But the longer she made herself suffer the shame, the less shameful it felt. And as she relived the moment in her imagination, some part of her responded and she felt the faint echo of desire.

Oh, Julia, what are you doing? What awful pleasures are you learning? After living so long with your Martian, the Ruler of the Elves, are you turning now to the Prince of Darkness?

11

COLE drove through town with fishermen and newspaper boys. He had WACT's early-morning gospel show and a dented steel thermos full of fresh coffee to get him on the road. He headed southeast and watched the dark horizon for the first signs of the sun.

Honeyed voices on the radio harmonized with certainty, singing directions to a blessed promised land. The songs told how all sinners traverse a route of twisting, rough roads and unexpected detours, a lonely journey through dark tempests and over stormy waters, a travail of travel through the wayside of life where hordes of the devil's highwaymen wait to waylay every pilgrim.

An hour later the sun was up, and "Ask the Authority" was coming on through increasing static: *Ask the Authority, he'll tell you what to do / Why don't you ask the Authority, he's got some good advice for you.* The disc jockey who hosted the program said good morning and asked the Authority, "How you feelin' today?"

"I'm feelin' fine, feel like we gonna have another warm day."

"Oh, yeah, it's gonna be a warm one," the host agreed. "You feelin' like givin' out some good advice this mornin'?"

"Oh, I'm feelin' fine. I like this weather, feel summer hangin' on," the Authority said.

"Well, let's take our first caller."

A third voice came on: "I want to ask the Authority what kind of a rat is it around my toolshed. He's white all but his head, and can the Authority tell me a trap I can catch him in?"

"I don't know what that could be," the voice of the Authority said. "Might not be a rat at all. Could be one a those blackjack possums. Or he could be a albino, but looks like he'd have white on his head."

"What color *is* his head?" the host asked. There was a silence. "Guess he don't know what color is his head," the host said. "Could be a albino rat."

"Whatever color he is, rat or not, we can take care of him," said the Authority. "We can use a snap trap for him, or one of those pellet guns or maybe a high-powered twenty-two—that works out pretty good. There are lots of good poisons, got all kinds of good poisons at Bama Feeds Store. You might want to go both ways, with a snap trap *and* a good poison."

"Let's take another call," the host said.

A woman, her voice fading and mixing with static, said, "Tell the Authority a storm was in the vicinity of the Heights last night. We had a good one."

"There we go," said the Authority.

"The Heights got some," said the host. The static got stronger, and Cole lost the next caller's question. Then he heard the Authority saying he didn't go by the almanac.

". . . time to plant is when you got time to plant—when you want something planted you got time." A long sneeze of static was followed by a woman's voice singing, *why he left,* and another woman's voice, ". . . today is not a good day to plant . . . ," *still love him so.* Cole turned the volume up and heard singing, *for poultry, hogs, cattle, and dogs,* and then the Authority, ". . . but hurry, we got just a minute . . ." and then the static got stronger, the voice of the Authority weaker. Finally, Cole gave up and popped an old Bob Dylan tape in, Dylan singing "It Takes a Lot to Laugh, It Takes a Train to Cry." Who could argue with that?

West of Tallahassee he hit Interstate 10 and started making better time. Tallahassee didn't seem like Florida; it was hilly and crowded with live oaks that dripped Spanish moss. Beyond Tallahassee, Cole took Interstate 75 south, headed straight down. At Lake City, a cluster of motels and fast food, he pissed away some of the coffee he'd been guzzling and got a Whopper and fries at a Burger King. An hour and a half later, he got his toll card for Florida's Turnpike. Near Orlando he began to pass orange groves. Most of the license plates were New York and New Jersey. He stopped at the Yeehaw Junction service area and gassed up the truck, took another leak. The sky had taken on a greenish glare, and the landscape was changing; there were trees he couldn't identify.

He had not told his mother he was coming. He wasn't sure

what he was going to do when he got there. He wasn't sure he should be going. It was, after all, Julia's life. What right did he have to interfere? He did *not* care about the money, his inheritance. If blowing all the money, however much there was, made her happy for however many more years she lived, it would be well spent. What difference that this man she had been seeing was just Cole's age?

Right after Jeanette left him, ran off with Chip, while he was hurting bad, Cole had told his mother, "One thing, for sure, I won't ever get involved with a married woman. I couldn't stand to be responsible for hurting someone the way Chip and Jeanette hurt me." Then, as soon as he ran off to Greece, he found himself coveting Philip's girl, April. And now he might be falling in love with Rachel. Of course, Bobby was not Cole's friend. Bobby and Rachel had been having problems for years—*Cole* certainly wasn't breaking up their marriage—but they were still, legally if not emotionally, *married.* So there he was, just where he said he wouldn't be. At least he knew enough now about affairs of the heart to know he would never make any more promises, not even to himself. He had not known the possibilities, the power of real passion. Cole recognized his own hypocrisy. At the same time, he was worried about his mother. So here he was, a fool rushing in. But easy—he would go easy. Just poke around at first, see what there was to see. He had noticed how, after a child grew up, became an adult of a certain age, the child often behaved like a parent. At a certain age, a son or a daughter turned the tables on a mother or a father. *This hurts me more than it does you,* a son said, and took away his mother's car keys (she might kill herself, or someone else); a daughter insisted her father stop smoking, drinking, eating whatever he liked best (it's for his own good); a son took over his widowed mother's financial affairs (in her best interest), and, ultimately, sons and daughters shipped their fathers and mothers off to nursing homes (it's not so bad, quite nice, really, and twenty-four-hour medical attention). Cole was determined *not* to make these assumptions. But he *was* here, poking into his mother's life. He wasn't sure where the impulses and obligations of love turned into some kind of self-protective meddling. But he wasn't going to deny the former for fear of the latter.

South of Fort Pierce, he began to feel as if he were sinking into some kind of thick, humid bog. All the way down into Florida he had had a sense of foreboding, wondering what he was getting into. But he was going with the flow. Traffic headed south was bumper to bumper at seventy miles an hour.

Every now and then there was a series of signs along the

turnpike, Burma-Shave fashion, with macabre safety limericks. The official green signs warned:

DRIVER WHO SNOOZES

WRECKS IN A LAKE

EVERYONE LOSES

PLEASE STAY AWAKE

Cole knew a guy who had written his dissertation for a Ph.D. in American studies on Burma-Shave signs. Cole and Dalt used to joke about it.

The coffee, almost gone, was going right through him. He killed off the thick black dregs, then pulled in at another service area to piss again. Jogging in place on the hot asphalt, he looked north, up the multilaned highway. From here at the bottom of Florida the view was distorted by the curve of the globe, a fish-eye lens. America was a red-white-and-blue balloon, Florida the stretched rubber end of the balloon, Miami the rubber knot that tied off the air. The air was hazy; light bouncing off sky and ocean was the green of tinted glass. Cole felt as if he stood in the bottom of some empty, Brobdingnagian Coca-Cola bottle. The small, round opening was high above him.

He took the Hollywood exit, followed signs To BEACHES, and got a room at a Howard Johnson's right on the ocean.

He was going to spy on his own mother—cops and robbers, hide-and-seek. Was he fooling himself, playing games? He left his pickup in the parking garage and rented a brown Toyota she wouldn't recognize. The .38 rode in the clip-on holster inside his jeans. He had brought his binoculars and camera. He bought a telephoto lens, charged it to his Visa card. Feeling whimsical, he bought a disguise, a gray detective's hat right out of a 1940s movie, and bent the brim down over his forehead. Then he staked out the Turret Inn.

The binocular lenses smeared the edges of Cole's vision and put a blue tint over Julia's face. She was the kind of woman the Bible called *comely:* seemly, graceful, pleasing. She did not look like his mother, not like anyone's mother. Several times she lifted her head and held her gaze steady, as if she were looking right down the double barrels of the binoculars.

Had Cole been a P.I., he would not have had any hard evidence to report to his client. Adam Smith came and went frequently, always expensively dressed, in different expensive automobiles. There was something unnatural in Adam Smith's walk. He wobbled a little, as if he wore built-up soles or stood on socks stuffed down into his shoes to make him look taller. Maybe he was tipsy, or on drugs?

Cole got the film developed at a one-hour place on U.S. 1. Adam Smith's face was a face from a thousand magazine ads, a perfect, anonymously handsome face. A smooth, unwrinkled forehead, skin tanned a deep red, as if the photo had been tinted or Adam Smith's skin dabbed evenly with makeup. He wore a small, fixed smile—the smile of a successfully casketed corpse. In each photo, his eyes were red, glinted like an animal's night eyes caught in headlights.

Cole got good at tailing. Sometimes he drove in front of Adam Smith and watched him in the rearview mirror. The man always used his turn signals far in advance, as if he wanted to make it easy for Cole to anticipate his direction. But Cole was certain Adam Smith never saw him. Adam Smith seemed completely at ease. He radiated relaxed self-confidence.

Cole followed him to a car-rental company—the same place where Cole had rented his Toyota. He risked a ploy; he drove in right behind Adam Smith and complained about the brown Toyota, said it was running rough. While he spoke to the clerk, Cole watched Adam Smith through plate glass. He was returning a Lincoln.

"That's a nice-looking car," Cole said.

"Sure; double the rate you're paying," the clerk said.

"So why's he trading it for that Cadillac?"

"That's Mr. Holcombe. He's thinking about buying a new car, wants to try the models he's considering. Smart move—rent one, check it out before you buy. He puts it all on a charge card, writes it off as some kind of business expense. You want his Lincoln?"

Cole was tempted. He pictured himself looking beneath the seats, along the dash, in the trunk, finding evidence. In that car, with the heavy doors closed, the windows sealed shut, surely he would smell Julia's perfume, see her fingerprints; surely he would learn something. But, instead, he traded the brown Toyota for a blue one. Something less conspicuous than the Lincoln, something he could afford. He didn't have Mr. Holcombe's line of credit.

Adam Smith left Julia's apartment and walked around the back of the building to the office. He was going out of his way to be invisible from Julia's windows. Cole walked along the boardwalk and stepped across the patio to a drink machine near the open office window. He stood, frozen, as in that kids' game Statue, his fingers poised at the coin slot with two quarters.

"Ayala . . ." a voice began.

"Smith," Adam Smith said.

"*Mr.* Smith. I'm sorry."

"This is for you, Percy." Adam Smith sounded like a TV newsman; no accent, some rhythm that had nothing to do with the meaning of his words. Cole couldn't see inside, didn't know what Adam Smith (Ayala?) gave the man.

"You must be scoring good, hey?" the voice said.

"Shut up, please," Adam Smith said.

The office door opened, and Cole dropped the quarters into the machine. He punched a button, and a can of Mountain Dew clunked out. When he turned, Adam Smith had vanished. Cole dropped the unopened drink into a wire trash basket on the boardwalk. He hated Mountain Dew.

That night, Cole stopped at a liquor store for a fifth of Jack Daniel's and got some extra-hot tacos from a carry-out place. He ate the tacos in his motel room and then phoned Rachel.

"Cole, why haven't you called? I was worried. I miss you."

"I miss you too."

"How's your mother?"

"Fine. I don't know. I mean she looks fine. But something's wrong down here. Bad wrong, I think."

"What does she say?"

"I haven't talked to her." Rachel said nothing. Cole went on: "I didn't know what to say. I guess I'll have to call her now, though. I don't know what else to do."

"What have you been up to?"

"Just checking things out. Following this guy Adam Smith—"

"Spying on your own mother? Cole, you're weird sometimes."

"Yeah, I know. Guilty as charged."

"You've got to call her, go talk to her. I thought you two were close. Won't she understand?"

"I don't know. She doesn't look the same. Maybe she's not the same." Again Rachel was silent. "But I know you're right," he said. "I'll phone her tonight; let's don't talk about it. What've you been doing?"

"I'm fine. Shots is fine. I went over to your house this afternoon and checked her food and water. She hasn't eaten much since you left. She misses you. *I* miss you."

"Has Bobby said anything about *us*, about *me?*"

"No. I don't think he wants to say your name out loud. He was polite, not very friendly. Of course, he wouldn't say much until the divorce is settled. He's just protecting his interests."

"I love you," Cole heard himself say.

Cole told Rachel good night and set the receiver back in the cradle. The room was stifling and too quiet. He got up and turned down the thermostat; he needed the air-conditioning, the moving air, the noise. Out the window, red radio-antenna lights blinked above a condo. He switched the TV on low, stared at a woman in a red dress. He opened the fifth of Jack Daniel's, peeled the plastic wrap off the top of a glass, and poured it half full. He sat on the edge of the wide bed and dialed the number for the Turret Inn. He asked for Julia Marrs. There was a long pause, then the click of the switchboard. Was the manager listening? Cole held a swallow of whiskey in his mouth until it burned.

"Hello?" The voice was his mother's, but it sounded different, deeper, more expectant. Cole knew *his* was not the voice she had anticipated. He swallowed whiskey.

"Mother?"

"Cole? Is that you?"

"I'm in Miami—at the airport. There's an American studies conference in Tampa and I had your letter from Hollywood and it was just as easy, same price, to fly to Tampa via Miami. I thought I'd miss my connection on purpose, rent a car, and buzz up to see you, if that's all right." He hadn't planned the lie; it just came out. He didn't want her to know he was here on her account. But something in her voice made him feel guilty, as if she saw right through his story. When he was younger, she would have said so. Now, he knew, they'd both keep up the lie.

"You mean tonight, right now?"

"If that's all right." Was she disappointed? Did she hate to give up an evening with Adam Smith? He took a quick slug from his drink.

"Of course it's all right. It's terrific, a great surprise. We can go out to dinner. I have room here, if you want to sleep on the couch."

"No, I'll have an early-morning flight out. I'll get a room at the airport hotel, rent a car, and drive up. Take me at least an hour to get there."

Up close, Julia looked better than she had through binoculars. Cole had to admit she didn't appear to be a woman who needed anyone's help. She'd done something new to her hair; her fingernails were long and painted hot pink. No one would believe she was sixty-two. She looked as good as she had in years, and he told her so.

"I *feel* good," she said. "Where'd you get that hat?"

"You like it?"

"The hat, yes. On you, no." She took the hat and put it on top of a lampshade. "How are you?"

"I'm fine."

"And your Rachel?"

"I talked with her tonight, before I left the airport. She's fine." Cole wanted to steer the conversation away from himself, wanted his mother to talk about Adam Smith. It was easier than he'd expected. She set two clean glasses on the kitchen counter and filled one glass with ice.

She took a bottle of Stolichnaya vodka from the freezer and poured about three fingers into the empty glass. Then she poured Jack Daniel's over the ice in the other glass and handed it to him.

"I want you to meet Adam. I asked him to come over. I hope you don't mind."

"Of course not. I want to meet any man you're interested in."

Her eyebrows rose, and she gave him a quick look but didn't say anything. She held a pepper mill over her glass and ground it once. A flurry of black flakes floated on the vodka. She gave the vodka a swirl, and Cole saw his father's, Avery's, shaved whiskers, black specks swirling down the lavatory drain.

"When did you start drinking vodka?" He sounded like a suspicious father: *When did you start drinking that stuff?*

She shrugged, smiled, lifted her glass to his.

"Tell me about Adam Smith," Cole said.

"Well, he's not like your father. Nothing like him," she said. "No man on earth is like your father," she added.

Did she mean *he* was not like his father? Cole knew that. He took a slug of the whiskey, thankful for the sweet and bitter way it humped the back of his tongue. He let it burn slowly down his throat.

"Adam is a lot like *you,* actually."

"Like me?"

"Don't get Freudian on me. I mean he's about your age. And he reads a lot. Quotes poetry, even." She laughed, a soft snort. "And you know what? We've done drugs together."

"You've *done drugs*—you sound like an old hippie."

"Marijuana, cocaine. Adam couldn't believe I lived in this world ignorant of such common substances." She nodded, smiled. "You should see your face, Cole. My, my. Have you or have you not smoked marijuana and done cocaine and, I imagine, tried a few other things? And didn't you always tell me, and Avery, that marijuana wasn't nearly as bad for you as alcohol or overeating? And as long as you've got that shocked look on the front of your open mind, I may as well tell you—not that it's any of your business—that I've been having sex with Adam. I recall a lot you've had to say about sex with or without the sanction of marriage."

"Okay. You've made your point. It's none of my business. Except that I love you and don't want you to get hurt."

"Give me a little credit. I'm not just another lonely widow, easy pickings for the first goldbricker or gigolo or whatever who comes along. I can take care of myself. Now, you let me."

There was a knock at the door. Saved, or lost, by the bell. Adam Smith was about to make his entrance. Well, by God, he could handle Adam Smith. He'd have to. She was abso-fucking-lutely right. He was glad he had come. Glad, even, that she knew exactly *why* he had come. He'd dispatched his obligation—shown her he *did* care—and now he could show her he respected her and trusted her. It was, by God, her own life, and she had a right to live it, fuck it up, any way she chose. She was clearly as competent, as sound of mind and body, as he was.

"Coleman." The man (Adam Smith? Holcombe? Ayala?) wore the slight smile Cole had caught with the telephoto lens. "An unexpected pleasure." He extended a hand that had the same even tan as his face.

Cole shook the hand, surprised at how warm to the touch, almost hot, it was, and how firm the grip. What had he expected, a damp, limp-wristed touch? Just because the guy wore a gold chain around his neck didn't mean he wouldn't know how a man is supposed to shake hands.

Julia fixed Adam a drink, Stoli, neat, with ground pepper, and the three of them sat in the small living room.

Smith, Ayala, Holcombe, whatever his name, was a professional gentleman. He made polite, intelligent conversation. He did seem, somehow, to order Julia around. He didn't actually give commands, but there was a way in which he made suggestions—*Julia, open these curved windows you love so much and let your son hear the sound of our surf . . . Julia, your son's glass is almost empty. And*

232

we are out of vodka . . . Julia, we should go now; our reservations are for nine—that put him clearly in control. Cole had to admit the man had a certain audacious charm. Before the three of them left for dinner, he made another of his suggestions—*Julia, we are suffering for your special glow, bring me the mirror*—and he brought out a brown vial and a gold coke spoon and laid down six thick lines on the mirror. He rolled up a hundred-dollar bill and, staring into Cole's eyes, he held the mirror and rolled bill out to Julia. She quietly took one line up each nostril and gave the mirror and bill back. Now Adam Smith watched Julia, his small smile in place, as he gave the mirror and bill to Cole, *our guest.* Cole had to lean up in his chair to take the mirror. The pistol pressed against his tailbone. For an instant he considered taking the pistol out and shooting Adam Smith. He thought of knocking the mirror from the man's hand, or of smugly saying, *No, thanks.* That, he realized, was what Adam Smith would most like him to do. That would put a seal on Cole's hypocrisy. He held the bill against his lower lip and took the cocaine not up his nose but beneath his tongue, one small gesture of contempt for the man's control. Did Adam Smith's small smile twitch? Cole could not be sure. But when he took the last two lines, Adam Smith also took them beneath his tongue.

Julia lifted Cole's gray hat off the lampshade and started to drop it on his head, but she hesitated. She smiled and set the hat on Adam Smith's head. "Perfect fit," she said. "On Adam I like it."

The man stood and held the mirror out. He cocked the hat down at a jaunty angle. "Do you think it suits me, Cole?"

Cole stood to go. Julia looked up at him with slitted eyes.

"Wear it in good health," Cole said. "A gift."

Cole drove his rental car and followed his mother and Adam Smith to the restaurant. It was logical, since they thought he would be going on to the airport hotel. It also meant he would not get to be alone with his mother before he left, unless he came back later and admitted the lie he knew she already suspected about his conference in Tampa.

Which is what, later that night, he decided to do.

After dinner, he said his goodbyes and drove off in the direction of the airport. Then he took I-95 back up to Hollywood and parked the Toyota at the Howard Johnson's, where he had a drink in the bar. A good-looking woman with short, dark hair sat alone at the bar, and he thought vaguely that he'd like to try to pick her up, take her to his room, and spend the night forgetting about Adam Smith.

There was a fatalistic, take-your-chances quality to a night of anonymous sex that would be delicious in its lack of responsibility. Maybe the woman would still be here when he got back from the Turret Inn. She smiled at him as he left, and he wondered what Rachel was doing right now. Maybe she was thinking of him.

He got his truck from the parking garage—no reason to let Adam Smith spot the Toyota—and drove to a parking space beside the Turret Inn. The rented Cadillac was across the street. Cole turned off the ignition and was surprised to see Adam Smith come out of Julia's apartment. The hat made him easy to spot. Cole scrunched down in the seat and rolled his window down a couple of inches. He heard the heavy door of the Cadillac close, then Smith drove away. Lights were on in Julia's apartment.

The door was open. Cole knocked and the door opened wider, but Julia didn't answer. He went inside.

"Mother?" he called. "Mother, where are you?" He checked the kitchen, went into the dark bedroom. He was about to turn on the bathroom light, when he heard her come in the front door. She was singing, and that was probably why he didn't call out immediately. She was singing "Bewitched, Bothered, and Bewildered," the way she had sung to him when he was a child, and he wished she would go on singing forever.

Then he heard laughing, diabolical laughing, a monster in a horror movie. The laughing stopped and the apartment was quiet, then the laughing again, and this time Julia was laughing too.

"You devil," she said, and laughed again. "One second we're walking along the boardwalk, and the next second you've disappeared. Where'd you go?"

"We needed more vodka."

Cole stepped back against the wall. Across the small space of the living room, he watched his mother and Adam Smith go into the kitchen. Adam Smith had a silver case under his arm, one of those metal Samsonite cases that look like an Airstream trailer.

"I have a little work in here, Julia." Adam Smith put the case on the kitchen table and opened it. He took out a full bottle of Stolichnaya vodka and a clear plastic bag that contained what looked like white rocks. Cole thought of NASA, not far up the coast, white lunar chunks, moon rocks displayed in a plexiglass case. Adam Smith handed the liquor to Julia and lifted a shiny metal apothecary scale and a hospital-green funnel out of the silver case. "Give me a few minutes," he said.

Julia put the vodka in the freezer. She leaned over Adam Smith and kissed his ear. She came out of the kitchen and headed toward the bedroom, where Cole stood in the shadows.

The closet door was ajar, and Cole slipped inside. He heard his mother go into the bathroom and close the door behind her. When the toilet flushed, Cole knelt and pulled the closet door closed. He put his eye to the keyhole. His mother came out of the bathroom and stood in the backlighted doorway. Light through fabric gave an x-ray impression of her legs, dark and shapely beneath her skirt. She flipped on the bedroom light and looked at herself in the mirror, touched the back of her hair.

The room went dark again, and Cole realized Adam Smith was standing right against the keyhole. As the man moved away from the closet, approached Julia, he came into focus. He was completely naked. He must have undressed in the living room or kitchen while Julia was in the bathroom. Julia turned to face him, also facing Cole. Her hand went to her throat, where it rested a moment, trembling, before it started opening the buttons of her blouse.

Cole dropped his eyes. The light through the keyhole burned the center of his forehead, the same burning spot of light he had focused through a magnifying glass when he was a boy torturing a cricket. The bright slit of that keyhole both lured and repelled Cole's eye. Through that opening was knowledge of the unknowable; there flamed the burning bush no man could bear to look at directly; there bobbed the Gorgons' three snaky heads and six eyes, any one of which would turn a mortal to stone; there burned a total eclipse of the sun that would blind naked human eyes; there for the looking was all the hard evidence Cole needed, more than he wanted to know. He had already seen more than he would be able to forget. He had seen enough to take out the .38 and poise just one breath away from a completely irrevocable motion. There could be no justification for being where he was; he could never be innocent. Then his mother cried out—not just in pain, but also in pleasure. Cole avoided the flaring opening of the keyhole, but he couldn't keep the cries and the whispered words from blasting through the walls and closet door.

Cole would have said there were no words left to shock him, but he heard the most ordinary words screamed and breathed, and the words wounded him. He heard a man use the words to command his mother, and he heard her use the words to obey the man.

Cole didn't know how long he crouched in the closet, avoiding the bright keyhole. After a while the noises and the words stopped, and there was just the sound of ugly breath. He sat in the soft odors of his mother's dresses and blouses and skirts and the pairs of her shoes stained by the sweat of her feet down close to the baking heat of sand and concrete, and he just let time pass.

He pictured himself finding a shoehorn on the closet floor and using it to dig, to tunnel through the floor, down through the first-story wall of the apartment building, through the foundation, into the sand beneath the beach, until he was far out beneath the sea, where nobody would see him come up and swim away with the fishes. If he could have, he would have taken the shape of a dress or a shoe and let his mother put him on and wear him out onto the boardwalk, where he would have jerked and flapped in the sea breeze till he came loose and was blown away, free of her body. But since he had no other way, he finally opened the door of his darkest closet and crawled quietly out. The light was off, the room dim.

On his hands and knees, he stared at the bed. Adam Smith was gone. Cole had not heard him leave. The windows were faintly light; the sun would soon be up. Cole stood, his legs quivering as they did when he barely avoided an accident in the truck.

His mother lay on her side. Her wrists and ankles were red and raw. Red welts marked her bare stomach, dark green and purple bruises clouded her breasts and one thigh. Bruises didn't form over-night. She breathed deeply, her mouth open, air rasping in and out.

Cole lifted the sheet and covered her up to her neck. She didn't stir.

On the bedside table was the flat mirror and a single-edged safety razor. Soft light from the windows moved onto the mirror. Cole looked close and saw the convolutions of fingerprints, his mother's small smudges and the larger whorls Adam Smith had left behind. The prints turned bright blue and floated in the darkness before Cole's eyes. A wave of nausea rose, and he held the bedside table to steady himself until the nausea passed. The edge of the mirror was cool under his thumb. Cole ran the tongue-moistened tip of a finger along the mirror's edge. Cocaine dust on the mirror coated his finger. He rubbed it over his gums and felt them go numb. Now his blood absorbed the same fuel that ran Adam Smith. Cole was making a pact. He lifted the edge of the sheet where Adam Smith had lain and held it to his nose. He wanted the man's scent.

12

JULIA woke without opening her eyes. She lay in the bed and thought about what she would see when she did open her eyes. She was alone in the double bed, a Hollywood bed (she smiled at the name) on a movable frame with no headstone or footstone. No—head*board*, foot*board*. What kind of slip was that? Oh, Lord, how many clues did she need to see the writing on the wall?

The room, she knew, was a mess. Worse, the whole apartment was a wreck. On her back, she lifted her head, her chin on her chest. She smelled sour and yeasty. She opened her eyes.

A faint purple bruise covered the side of her left breast and disappeared into the dark crevice of her armpit. She sat up in the middle of the bed, and the covers fell away. No breeze blew through the open windows. The sheets were heavy and clammy. Her skin was gritty with salt and sand from the open windows. Three bright spots pulsed near the ceiling. She lay back down and closed her eyes again. The dots went away, but now the bed was spinning. She rolled onto her side and worked her legs over the edge of the mattress. She stood, and her head started pounding. Dizzy, she grabbed the bedside table and knocked the mirror to the floor. Beside her foot, her own face, small, stared up at her. She knelt, and her face in the mirror got larger, swollen and puffy. She lowered her face until it blurred into a shape of brown and the weight of her head rested against the cool mirror. She felt a soft giving in, as the mirror cracked in two the way a cookie breaks gently apart. She touched the bridge of her nose and peeled off the flat, single-edged razor that had stuck to her skin. Each half of the broken mirror was fogged with her breath, evidence she was still alive. The curse of a broken mirror reassured her; she had at least seven more years.

Before planets and seas and heaven were created, Avery had told her, all was Chaos. Then God separated heaven from earth. "We've been trying to bridge that gulf ever since," he said. The fiery parts of Chaos were the lightest and became the skies; land, heavier, fell; and the oceans sank beneath and buoyed up the lands. Lesser gods were made, then stars and animals and, next to last, man. Prometheus and his brother Epimetheus, Titans, were given the duty of making man and providing for him. Prometheus went to heaven, lighted a torch at the chariot of the sun, and brought back fire to man. Woman was made last.

Jupiter made Pandora, the first woman, in heaven. Apollo gave her the gift of music, Venus contributed beauty, Mercury gave her persuasion. Jupiter gave Pandora to Prometheus and Epimetheus to punish them for stealing fire, and to punish man for accepting it. Prometheus warned Epimetheus they must be wary of Jupiter's gift. Epimetheus had a box in which were sealed all the noxious elements man did not need in his new world. Pandora was told to stay away from this box, but the more she was warned away, the more she burned with the desire to learn what was inside. Eventually Pandora opened the box, and every noxious element in the world escaped, all diseases of the body and mind—plague, fear, envy, spite, hatred, lust, and revenge. Pandora tried to replace the lid, but every evil had escaped. One thing, only, remained at the bottom of the box, and that was *hope*.

From the beginning, Avery had told her, *hope* was sealed in a box with every imaginable evil.

As if her body were some object that needed to be shaken, slapped, scrubbed, folded, straightened, wiped dry, put out, put right, put away (an old quilt, a worn chair, a china serving platter), Julia carried herself into the bathroom and tossed down three aspirins and a megavitamin, brushed her teeth, washed her mouth out with Listerine, stepped into the shower, and turned the water on full force, icy cold then scalding hot. She soaped herself all over, dug soft soap up under her toenails and the glued-on fingernails, washed up the insides of her legs, washed her red and tender labia and up into her vagina, slid the bar of soap between the cheeks of her ass and then bumped it up her rib cage and lathered beneath her arms and over her sore breasts. She rubbed shampoo into her hair and poked sudsy fingers into her ears. Her nostrils were stopped up, and she blew mucus into a washcloth and inhaled warm steam. When she had soaped her skin from feet to head and had scrubbed every orifice, she stood under hot water and let it beat against the beating in her head. As hot water went warm, she cut back the cold faucet until only the hot was on, and she stood under it until every drop of heat was gone and her skin was squeaky and tight, pebbled with goose bumps, her palms pink and wrinkled. She was just as thorough with a thick, clean towel, rubbing her skin red as newborn.

She put on a cotton sundress and soft leather flats. On the kitchen counter, beside an orange squeezer, was a pink plastic radio. The dial was a luminous, glow-in-the-dark arch, a miniature rainbow in the morning light; the needle was black and sharply pointed, a speedometer's needle, a compass needle. She wasn't sure the radio would play. She'd listened to the ocean, to accordion music from the boardwalk, to Adam Smith's husky words, but now she needed music to sweep herself clean. She twisted the knob and there was a long pause, then the pink box hummed like a loud bee. She turned the needle and found a classical station: a symphony of Charles Ives. She turned up the volume, and the music filled the air. She stood in the middle of the kitchen and let the music run over her as the hot shower water had run over her. Ives's music cleansed her spirit and lifted her heart. Starting in the kitchen, she went through the house, filling a green plastic garbage bag with empty bottles, glasses, sections of newspapers, paperbacks and magazines, the broken mirror, the razor blade, Adam Smith's and her own damp bathing suits. She pulled the sheets and pillowcases off the bed, averting her eyes from whatever stains might have taken shape there, and stuffed them into the bulging plastic bag. She put all her clothes back into her suitcases. She raked the cosmetics she had bought, another package of false fingernails, hair dye, in on top of the sheets. Her toothbrush and paste, her comb, she tossed into a suitcase. She scrubbed the tub with cleanser and threw away her wet washcloth and damp towel. She filled another garbage bag with the few items in the refrigerator and what food was in the cabinets. Finally, to the lively tempo of Ives, still pouring out of the little radio, she took up a broom. The broom moved with the symphony the way a fairy tale broom moves. Julia followed its lead and let it dance her from room to room. This was all Annabelle's doing.

In two hours the apartment was clean, looked vacant. Julia's suitcases, packed and locked, lay on the bare mattress. She lugged the garbage bags to a Dumpster behind the building and walked on down the boardwalk. She went into Howard Johnson's and ate a tossed salad and a plate of roast beef and mashed potatoes. She had chocolate ice cream and coffee. Then she went back to the Turret Inn, where she put the telephone on the coffee table and sat on the Early American couch and looked out at the ocean while she waited for Adam Smith to call.

She was going to tell him to come over immediately. When he came in, she was going to remember how she had felt this morning, remember the bruised skin beneath her blouse, and she was going to look at him and make him hold her in his arms and kiss her, and then she was going to know that she *could* leave, as she wanted, or she was going to make him fuck her—that *was* the word—on the bare mattress and she was going to know that she *would not* leave, and she would exchange the motion of the sea for the smaller motion of the Hollywood bed on its hard plastic rollers.

13

OLE turned in the rented blue Toyota, and a girl from the car rental place drove him back to the Howard Johnson's. He took a fast, hot shower and put on a clean, faded pair of jeans, a long-sleeved soft chambray work shirt, and tennis shoes. He got his gear and checked out. The sky was deep blue, and the sun cast a hot bright glare over everything.

Cole had no idea where Adam Smith, Ayala, lived. He waited in the truck and watched the door to his mother's apartment at the Turret Inn. Just after noon, Adam Smith showed up. He was in the Cadillac from the night before. It was hot as hell, but he wore a suit and tie. He had on Cole's gray hat and carried his silver Samsonite case. As he had before, the man walked behind the building, out of sight of Julia's windows, to the office. The dark shape of Percy Fox filled the office window. Cole rested his neck on the back of the seat and waited.

In five minutes Adam Smith left the office, walked behind the building back to the Cadillac, and drove away. Cole followed him down A1A to Miami Beach. In south beach, Adam Smith parked in a loading zone and went into a run-down hotel, the Aztec. Less than twenty minutes later, he came out again. He'd changed into plaid bermuda shorts, boat shoes, and a white knit shirt. He fanned his face with Cole's gray hat. He looked like a tourist or a golfer. Cole followed him over the causeway onto the Dolphin Expressway. Off to the south was the Orange Bowl. West of the Miami airport, he headed north on the Palmetto Expressway. Near Hialeah, Cole followed the Cadillac off the expressway and into the parking lot of a shopping mall. When Adam Smith parked, Cole eased past him, watching in the side mirrors of the truck. Cole turned down a row of parked cars and stopped. Adam Smith walked over to a silver Mercedes and pushed something like a small screwdriver into the door lock. Then he opened the door and released the hood latch. He lifted the hood and disappeared beneath it momentarily. Then he got in the car. Cole made a U-turn. A moment later, the Mercedes, hot-wired, backed out of the parking place. The whole operation had taken about two minutes. Cole stayed a couple of cars behind the silver Mercedes, headed northwest on Okeechobee Road. The car swung into a narrow drive that opened into a large parking area in front of a blue metal building where a portable sign, a movie marquee on wheels, outlined with red and white flashing bulbs, advertised:

TOTALLY NUDE DANCERS

"TASHA IS BACK"

Cole pictured the scene inside the big blue building. After this bright Florida sun, it would be so dark you'd have to wait for your eyes to adjust, or you'd walk into a chair or collide with a waitress carrying a tray of drinks. Only the stage, splashed bright blue-white by spotlights, would be clearly visible. And there a body would be twisting and swaying to the beat of rock-and-roll. Right after Avery's funeral, Jeanette had flown back to Alabama, but Cole remained in San Antonio a couple more weeks, until he thought his mother would be all right alone. Time had been heavy on his hands and he'd taken the car one afternoon and gone up to Austin to visit an old friend who taught at the university. In Austin he did not phone the friend but went, instead, to a place called the Classy Pussycat. The Classy Pussycat *was* classier than any strip joint Cole had been in. A sign at the door forbade cutoffs and shorts. Cole was amused that the customers had to be completely covered to watch the dancers uncover. Cole sat at the stage runway and ordered a draft. Behind him, surrounding the runway, were tables with white tablecloths, where drinks in stem glasses were placed by attractive hostesses in long, dressy gowns. The decor was chrome and glass. Girls in skimpy white togas circulated among the tables. For twenty dollars you could buy a "table dance." The girl of your choice would undress and dance right beside your chair.

A loud, expensive sound system made the music come out of the walls and up out of the floor. Cole's feet and legs vibrated with Bob Seger's sultry "Night Moves." From his seat at the runway, Cole stared at a dancing girl's feet. A lithe, darkly tanned blonde with a foldout's hourglass figure, the dancer couldn't have been more than twenty or twenty-one. She wore black, open-toed, spike-heeled shoes, with a strap over the back of her foot; her Achilles tendon flexed as she moved. She almost kicked over Cole's beer. He was so close he saw scuff marks on her shoes and slivers of tan where the dark-red polish had worn off one of her toenails. He looked up her long, bare leg, looked above the black G-string she wore, up to the undersides of her bare breasts bouncing with the music. Looking up her body was like looking up a terraced hill, like looking up the front of a mountain—mounds, cavities, protrusions. The close, high angle made her top-heavy, reflected her in a carnival mirror. In a garter on her right thigh was a green ruffle of dollar bills. Men came to the stage with dollars, and she knelt for them to insert their money. Each contribution bought a slow, up-close look and a kiss.

Cole held up a dollar bill, folded lengthwise like the ones the blonde wore under the garter. She walked, taking her time, toward the money. She stopped, stared down, and smiled in a practiced, sultry way, posing, her lips pouted. Cole met her gaze, stared at her eyes to keep from staring at her nipples. Slowly she brought her tall body down and squatted there on the edge of the runway. Cole's beer stood suggestively between her thighs, which she closed against the full glass. A guy behind Cole whistled, someone gave a whoop. The dancer's eyes never left Cole's. His ears went warm; he was completely self-conscious. Then she reached down, unsnapped her G-string, and opened her legs. The elastic straps bounced against the firm muscles along her thighs. She smiled at Cole and waited. He did not know what was expected. He reached to lift the triangle of black fabric, and the woman stage-slapped his face and, with exaggerated movements, lifted his hand away from her crotch. Then she jerked the G-string off and tossed it, like spilled salt, over her shoulder. She stretched the garter open and Cole poked his dollar in with the others. The light-brown hair between the woman's legs had been shaved into the shape of an elongated heart. She leaned to give Cole his kiss, a quick peck that tasted of tobacco and lipstick, then quickly stood and danced after another dollar.

Cole stayed through two other dancers, another draft beer. He watched table dancers lean so close their nipples almost grazed men's shirts, but there was no touching. No one broke the rules, no one even tried. So very, very close, yet so far, far away.

Before long Cole realized his mind was wandering. He was not paying close attention. The completely nude bodies of pretty women seemed familiar, ordinary. He was almost bored. But when he stepped from the dark, smoky room with the pulsing stage lights and the loud vibrations of the music, when he walked out into the bright November glare of the parking lot, he was immediately sad. As soon as he was outside, he wanted to go back inside. As soon as he left, he felt a renewed sexual curiosity about what secrets waited inside, what secrets lay beneath the white togas, the sequined tops and silky G-strings.

He drove directly to a record store to see if he could find the Bob Seger song. He looked in *Rock* and in *Male Vocalists* but didn't see it. When a clerk asked if she could help him, Cole said no, he was just looking. That had always irritated Jeanette—his unwillingness to ask for or accept assistance. "Night Moves" was the title cut of a new album he finally found under *New Releases*. He bought the cassette and played it in his mother's car, his dead father's car, over and over, as he drove back to San Antonio.

Now, nearly six years later, the flashing marquee still had its allure. TOTALLY NUDE. "TASHA IS BACK." Cole wondered where she had been and if she was glad to be back. He'd like to go inside that dark place and drink a cold beer and see if Tasha lived up to her name. There would be others to see: Brandy, Cherry, Ginger, Honey, Sugar, Cinnamon—a secret recipe for something sinfully delicious.

Cole drove past the strip joint and pulled into an auto-parts place. An orange wrecker hid Cole's truck but allowed a good view of the Mercedes, its passenger door left open. In two minutes Adam Smith came out, carrying a valise that looked like a bowling ball bag.

Cole pulled back onto Okeechobee Road behind the Mercedes. Traffic thinned, and Cole dropped farther behind. They crossed under the turnpike extension and headed into the edge of the Everglades, on a narrow road that ran alongside a canal.

The Everglades stretched endlessly, wetland grasses faded into the blue horizon as in a watercolor. Above the Mercedes Cole saw the moon, pale-white whorls of a thumbprint. Mars has two moons, named, Avery taught him, for the sons of Ares, the Greek god of war. Deimos, which means "terror," is the outer moon; Phobos, which means "fear," is the inner moon. Phobos, *fear*, rises and sets several times a day. Cole gripped the steering wheel with both hands, all his knuckles white.

Adam Smith turned onto a white shell road, and Cole followed a white cloud of dust. This road ran straight down a ridge beside another canal. On one side the roadbed—fill dredged up to make the canal—dropped off to the water, on the other side, to thick brush. Ahead, the Mercedes negotiated a narrow bridge over the canal at a point where water spread into a swampy area. Cole pulled off in the cover of tall Australian pines. Through the trees he watched the Mercedes creep off the road down the incline toward the canal.

Clouds of mosquitoes made Cole glad he had on jeans and long sleeves, in spite of the muggy heat. At the far side of the bridge he knelt behind an abutment. In the white glare, the silver automobile and the surface of the water reflected light and mirrored the sky in the same way, so that Cole saw the automobile as a pool of water, an offshoot of the canal. Then the car door opened, and a green van emerged from a stand of trees. When the van was parallel to the Mercedes, Adam Smith carried the valise over, and the side of the van slid open. The valise disappeared; Adam Smith took a brown square—a manila envelope. The van curved up the slope toward Cole and the road. For a split second Cole considered hanging from the bridge abutment to hide himself, then the van continued its curve and crawled onto the road, headed away from him. The van had an Alabama license plate, "Heart of Dixie," the numbers too mud-splattered to read. Cole watched the van down the road until it merged with the gray and green of the horizon and disappeared into the Everglades. He heard something and looked beneath the bridge to see a huge alligator slide off a ledge of mud into the water. The back of his neck tightened involuntarily; he pictured an animated version of himself— Captain Hook–style—hanging from the bridge while the 'gator— tick-tock, was that how it went?—snapped at his legs.

Adam Smith, his back to Cole, leaned into the opened trunk of the Mercedes. Cole lifted the .38 from the holster inside his jeans. He took long strides to absorb the slope. Eight to ten feet behind Adam Smith, Cole stopped. He stood canted to one side, his left foot a little in front of his right—*Make yourself as small a target as possible.* Cole gripped the pistol in his right hand, which he held firmly in the palm of his left hand. Adam Smith must have heard him, but he did not speak or turn around. He reached down with both hands to swat at his bare legs. It was such a spastic-looking action that it took Cole a second to realize mosquitoes were giving the man fits.

"Turn around," Cole said, his voice soft, muffled-sounding.

"Hello, sonny boy," Adam Smith said. "Miss your flight to Tampa?" Adam Smith did not turn. "Now that you have me, what are you going to do with me?"

"I don't know," Cole said. "I don't know. I have to keep you away from my mother."

"But Mommy *likes* me, sonny Boy. I make Mommy *bad,* and that makes Mommy feel *good.*"

"Shut up." Cole's voice sounded like a voice he had never heard before.

"C'mon, sonny, you've had her for years. It's nice to share."

"I said *shut up.*"

"I'm going to tell you *everything* Mommy and the bad man do together . . ." Adam Smith's hands disappeared behind the lip of the trunk, and he was turning. He grunted, *"Sonny boy,"* and Cole heard the *crack—hiss* in the same instant he saw the little dark-green alligator on the knit shirt. Cole moved deliberately. He raised his arms and aimed at the little alligator and squeezed off two shots, *one, two.* His ears rang, and blue spots danced in front of his eyes like a blue ball on a drive-in screen bouncing a tune over words: "Here Comes Peter Cottontail." Cole took a breath and tried to find the knit alligator to aim two more shots—*If you don't hit the fucker with two rounds, you better start over.* Adam Smith was on his back in the trunk. His bare knees were up, his shins hung straight down over the bumper, both feet bare in the air. Cole pulled his elbows snug against his rib cage and gripped the pistol.

He approached the car. He waited for Adam Smith to jerk upright and lunge at him, but the body did not move. On the ground, behind the car, lay the rifle Adam Smith had dropped—a bolt action .22. Cole wondered if it was Adam Smith's or if it had just been there, a kind of gift, in the trunk of the stolen car. Adam Smith looked as if he had just replaced the bulb that came on beneath the rear deck when the trunk was opened, the bulb that now cast a bright-yellow light over his face, his wide-open eyes. Into the white knit shirt a dark-red stain spread slowly, the way spilled juice (tomato, cranberry) spread into the absorbency of a fresh paper towel. The boat shoes Adam Smith had worn sat, side by side, beneath the car's bumper, like shoes placed on the floor beside a bed when someone goes to sleep.

Cole touched nothing. He got no closer to the car than a couple of feet. Then he walked to his truck and drove back in the direction from which he had come. In fifteen minutes he was on Highway 27, headed north. Ten more minutes brought him to a gas station and grocery store, a telephone booth.

He drove past the phone. He might do fine with the police, fine with the courts, but how would he do with his mother? He could no more be the son who killed his mother's lover than he could be the son who hid in a closet and heard his mother cry out to answer something dark and unknowable that thrashed in her bed.

Maybe someone had seen him. Maybe someone would con-

246

nect him to Adam Smith—Percy Fox at the Turret Inn, the guy at the car rental place, someone in the shopping mall parking lot who saw his truck follow the Mercedes, a fisherman on one of the canals—anything was possible. Cole had read that there were whole companies of Vietnam veterans who lived in the Everglades, unable to wake from their own continuous nightmares. Maybe they knew everything that happened out there, had hidden sentinels, scouts on patrol. If they did, wouldn't they recognize the enemy? If there was money in the envelope Adam Smith had taken from the van, and surely there was, the Army of the Everglades could use that money to resupply. But Cole knew he was his only witness, and, somehow, he knew he would never be caught. But what he had witnessed he would see always.

How hard would the police try to solve the murder of a car thief and drug dealer? Now there was one less to worry about. How often did those guys kill one another in the streets of Miami, in the maze of the Everglades: the perfect place to leave a body—might be days, weeks even, before anyone happened along. Dead men tell no lies, but what truths do they speak? A ballistics test would say Adam Smith was killed by two shots from a .38 at a distance of about eight feet. Bennie said the *average* shooting in America was over a distance of about six feet and *on the average* one-point-nine shots were fired. Nothing greatly out of the ordinary here. Cole left no fingerprints. There must be plenty of different tire tracks on that road, if it was soft enough to take an impression. Contrary to movies and TV cop shows, Cole knew, something like 60 percent of the murders in America went unsolved. An alligator might see those bright bermuda shorts, those bare knees, bare feet hanging down close to the damp grass. A Florida panther might lope up in the dark and catch Adam Smith's scent. No more corpse. *Corpus delicti,* the body of the crime, hard evidence, missing for everyone except Cole. But it was Cole's mother who would miss the body most. It was Julia he had wounded most painfully. That was done, no matter what he did now.

She might never know the man was dead. Adam Smith might simply join the world's long list of disappearances. How much coverage did an *average* killing get in the Miami media? Julia didn't watch TV; did she read the papers? It was possible, likely even, that she would wait to hear from Adam Smith, and when he never called, never showed up, she'd admit what she must have already suspected, already known at least with her heart—that he was something other than what he seemed.

So am I, Cole thought. *So are we all.*

247

If, somehow, they traced some clue back to Cole, if someday a plain, dark Ford pulled up at Cole's house, or at the university, and two men in suits said they wanted to speak to Coleman Marrs, well, he'd deal with that then.

Cole followed Highway 27 around the south end of Lake Okeechobee and just at dark stopped at a phone booth beside a closed gas station. A simple white sign gave the name of the town: VENUS. Rachel's voice in the telephone sounded close and familiar, but not being able to see her or touch her emphasized the space and time between them.

"Where are you?" Rachel said.

He laughed. "Venus."

"Venus?"

"Venus, Florida. The son of a Martian, back in our solar system after a trip into deep space. Headed home fast as I can pedal."

"I can't wait. I need you, Cole. And I've got some great news. I was going to wait till you got back, to tell you in person, but now that I have your voice I can't wait."

Rachel had his voice. His mother would wait for Adam Smith's voice, but it was gone. What dark words had Adam Smith whispered to her that now drifted forever out into space? Words Cole had whispered to Jeanette, words Jeanette whispered to Chip, were out there too, drifting forever for those with ears to hear.

"Cole, we can see each other now. We don't have to worry about the lawyers."

"How so?"

"Bobby's got a girlfriend. I *saw* them. I was driving down Riverside and saw them. She was sitting right against him."

"How does that change things?"

"Don't you see? He can't bring *you* into a divorce fight now, because he knows I'll bring *her* into it. This means we can see each other openly."

"You said Bobby would kill me if he ever saw us together."

"You've got your pistol, don't you? You haven't forgotten how to use it, have you? Now, if anything *does* happen, he looks just as bad as we do. In the eyes of the law, I mean."

Rachel sounded dispassionate, her voice unfamiliar.

A long silence passed, the seashell sound of ocean in Cole's ear. He stood in a phone booth that stuck up into space above the curve of the earth. From the receiver, pressed hard against his ear, a cord ran into the phone; a wire ran from the phone to the top of a pole, where it connected to more wire, insulated cable strung from pole to pole, for miles and miles, through mysterious routing stations and substations, to another pole, down a line and into a room inside a house where a cord went into a phone and another coiled up to a receiver tight in Rachel's hand. Her words and his breath hurtled through wire, under dark skies, between the limbs of trees, beneath the feet of birds, over moving car lights and bright neon, into and out of rain, swayed but not garbled by shifting winds. As the wire from the tape deck had connected Cole to April on a beach in Greece, an electrical umbilical cord carried the charge of words, declarations sought and made, between Cole and Rachel. Contact: he had dialed a certain sequence of numbers, and now he was connected to that woman. The toll for the call would come on his regular bill. He might forget (though of course he would not) and read the list of charges and wonder, *Who do I know in Venus, Florida?* When the bill came he'd remember, and then he'd pay.

Rachel said she couldn't wait to see him, to phone her the instant he got home, no matter what time it was.

"I love you," she said.

"I love you, too" he heard himself say.

That was a pledge he had always taken seriously. When, he wondered, had he first declared his love for another? More than likely, as a child, to his mother. His list of loves was shorter than his list of lovers. First there was his mother; later, with a little boy's masculine embarrassment, Avery; when he was fifteen, his first real girlfriend, Sweet Robin Browne (and that was true, he thought); Jeanette, that wild week of Mardi Gras and marriage; and now (finally? he wondered) Rachel. As a child, had he ever made that pledge in his prayers? And if he voiced his love to God, was that no more, and no less, than an acknowledgment of his love for himself? His mother's voice, measured and clear, spoke over the distance of years. He leaned against her, the side of his face rested against her bare arm. Her skin was cool and her round bicep where his cheek rested was smooth and firm, almost like the curved, polished bedpost against his bare leg, but smooth and firm as only a mother's body can be. He smelled the winter smell of the floor furnace, the bleached-clean sheets, and her perfume, Je Reviens (he asked her the name so many times he would never forget, and once he gave her a quarter of an ounce). The perfume was as blue as the ocean. The tiny bottle, round and flat like a fifty-cent piece, cost him two months' paper route pay.

Julia had read to him from the book of Matthew, Christ's warnings about good and corrupt fruit:

Either make the tree good, and his fruit good; or else make the tree corrupt, and his fruit corrupt: for the tree is known by his fruit.

I love you. Rachel had said the words like a recitation, but still Cole had hated to hang up, hated to lose the sound of Rachel's voice. If he weren't tethered to Rachel his feet might lift and swing up into the air, he might jerk free of the earth's pull and be sucked into space, the globe smaller and smaller, the surrounding darkness larger and larger.

How many times had Rachel said *I love you,* and to whom? Julia had said those words to Huldah and Annabelle, to Garner, never to her real father but probably to her young half-brother, George junior, never to Larry Otto, and most often to Avery and to Cole. Had she ever spoken those words to Adam Smith? Among the dark whispers Cole had heard as he knelt, hidden in his mother's closet, were words enough, but not those three. Cole remembered Christ's warning, from Matthew, in his mother's voice:

. . . out of the abundance of the heart the mouth speaketh. . . . every idle word that men shall speak, they shall give account thereof in the day of judgment. For by thy words thou shalt be justified, and by thy words thou shalt be condemned.

Through the plexiglass door of the phone booth Cole read the sign again: VENUS. Another world. He feared he might never find his way back to the world he had left only a few hundred miles behind, a few days ago.

Minutes after midnight, a new day, Cole barreled west on Interstate 10 and crossed into the central time zone. Midnight became the eleventh hour; he was to relive an hour. A day in his life on which he took another life was to be a twenty-five-hour day. On Mars, Cole remembered, every day is thirty-seven and a half minutes longer than every day on earth.

Cole turned north and crossed the state line back into Alabama. He had an outlaw's relief at entering a different jurisdiction—this time, familiar territory. His eyes burned, and south of Ozark he pulled into a rest area, removed his contact lenses, and slept for three hours.

By sunup, Cole was at the outskirts of town. He punched the radio to WACT. Flatt and Scruggs were singing on the old-time gospel show again, singing "Troublesome Waters." Cole fine-tuned the radio. The song was about a lonely pilgrim struggling to stay afloat in life's stormy waters. The pilgrim cried to his saviour and felt the touch of His hand guiding the boat safely through the tempests of life to the shining beaches of heaven. As the song ended, Cole was turning off the highway at the intersection by the new mall. He looked up at the traffic light, which had just turned yellow, and did a double take. There was Bobby, a billboard bigger than life, his face sideways, his big ear filling Cole's windshield: TALK TO BOBBY. . . . HE'S LISTENING. Cole laughed, then sang out loud, mimicking an old Ray Stevens song, "Santa Claus Is Watching You."

Cole drove up in front of his house, and the "Ask the Authority" theme song came on. Cole turned off the engine, then turned the key back a click so the radio would play: *Ask the Authority, he'll tell you what to do / Why don't you ask the Authority, he's got some good advice for you.* Then, before the Authority's familiar voice came on, Cole switched off the key. He sat and stared at the house he rented. It wasn't much. Paint was peeling; grass needed mowing. The dark windows of the vacant-looking house made him lonely. He had a deep longing to telephone his mother, but knew he could not.

At least Shots would be there to greet him. He'd get a hot shower and lie down on cool cotton sheets. Maybe he'd call Rachel. Maybe he'd get her to drive over right now. Maybe he'd wait awhile. He'd have to call before evening, when she'd be coming over to feed Shots and check her water. He wasn't very anxious to see her. Mainly, he was bone weary. Bobby and his threats were not going to be the same now that Cole had a notch on his pistol. He wondered if the Authority had anything to add to the advice in Matthew about good and corrupt fruit. He wondered whether the Authority would agree that the conditions had recently been favorable for planting someone down in the Everglades, close to heaven's bright shore.

14

JULIA sat on the couch and waited all afternoon for the phone to ring. She knew that if it did, Adam would be on the other end. He and Cole were the only people who knew where she was, and she did not expect to hear from Cole again for a while.

That evening, when it got dark, she left the lamps off and lay in the light that came up from the boardwalk. Sea breezes kept the curtains softly whipping into the room. Eventually, lulled by the waves, she slept on the couch.

The next morning she went back to the Howard Johnson's and had a traveler's breakfast of ham and eggs, hash browns, toast, and plenty of black coffee. Then she took a slow stroll down the board-walk to the pink Hollywood Hotel and back. She loaded her car and checked out. Mr. Fox was surprised to see her go.

"Want me to give Mr. Smith a message for you? A forwarding address, phone number?"

"No. He could have reached me at this number if he'd wanted."

She was, she thought, not surprised, and only a small, curious, dark part of her was sorry that Adam had not called. No regrets, but time to move on. She'd waited as long as she was going to wait. She goosed the car good, headed north, somewhere.

15

COLE dreamed about Adam Smith night after night. In each dream came a moment when Cole touched Adam Smith's bare skin: Cole reached to turn on a car radio, and Adam Smith's fingers were there, on the knob, where they had not been before; Cole picked up a knife to cut his steak, and he felt Adam Smith's fist gripping the knife handle; Cole stumbled over broken sidewalk, Adam Smith caught him, and Cole's lips brushed against Adam Smith's cold skin. When he touched the man, Cole woke and could not get back to sleep. Awake, he heard, again, sounds that had come from his mother's bed, and he was in a panic to do something about that man, before he remembered what he had done.

In the middle of the night, Cole resolved to drive back to the Everglades and find that narrow road; he knew he could drive right to the spot, return to the scene of the crime and see if Adam Smith still lay, resting on his back, looking up at the opened casket cover of the trunk lid. It was enough of a nightmare to have never happened. If Cole was the only witness, how could he verify that it *had* happened? *I think, therefore I am?* What was the solipsistic riddle: *If a tree falls in a completely uninhabited forest, does it make any noise?* Must there be ears to hear, eyes to see? He'd once read a story in which fictional characters existed on some planet, an actual, flesh-and-blood existence, so long as a reader somewhere kept the characters alive in his or her imagination. Were that true, Adam Smith was very much alive, for at least as long as Julia and Cole were alive.

Cole went to the university library every day and read the Miami *Herald,* which arrived two days late. He had checked it beginning with the day he followed Adam Smith out into the Everglades.

So far there had been no mention of a body found in the Everglades, nothing remotely connected with the man Cole had shot and killed. There was no mention of a stolen Mercedes either.

Every time a patrol car drove down his street, Cole pictured it stopping before his house. In traffic, after a university football game, a cop blew his whistle and Cole hit his brakes, ready to surrender. The cop yelled, "Clear out, buddy. Hubba hubba," and gave Cole a friendly salute.

Cole's phone rang, and he lifted the receiver expecting the man's voice: *Hello, sonny boy.*

He turned on the television, and shots rang out in his living room.

He picked up a newspaper. KILLER SOUGHT, the headlines screamed.

He tried to grade a set of papers but couldn't keep his mind on the work. He'd missed a couple of classes and needed to get caught up. He thumbed through the text, a collection of essays, and read something from Governor William Bradford:

> For summer being done, all things stand upon them with a weather-beaten face; and the whole country, full of woods and thickets, represented a wild and savage hue. If they looked behind them, there was the mighty ocean which they had passed, and was now as a main bar and gulf to separate them from all the civil parts of the world.

Three hundred sixty-six years later, Cole knew how that felt.

Everything Cole saw, heard, read, seemed connected to a death in the Everglades: this small, synchronous world.

Sunday morning Cole went to the campus Presbyterian church. He hadn't been inside a church, except for weddings and funerals, since he'd been a kid in Texas. It was a small church, and Cole recognized a few faces—students, a history professor he knew. The congregation stood and sang a hymn he'd never heard. In unison, they read a Prayer of Confession printed in the order of worship: "Gracious God, through water and the Spirit, you have claimed us as your own. . . ."

During the Silent Confession, Cole's ears rang with the blast of a .38. He tried to *confess* that he had killed a man, Adam Smith. But why name him at all? If God was God, Cole was not his only witness. God knew the name, knew the man's *real* name.

Cole had long been a sucker for the finger that jabs a spinning globe, the eye that falls on Scripture in a randomly opened Bible, the

254

divination of destination and of destiny. He listened to the First Lesson, from Exodus, expecting divine revelation:

> . . . there shall no man see me, and live . . . I will put thee in a cleft of the rock, and will cover thee with my hand while I pass by: And I will take away mine hand, and thou shalt see my back parts: but my face shall not be seen.

Had Cole seen those back parts stripped bare, seen them through the eye slit of a keyhole, guided by the sight of a pistol barrel? Adam Smith tangled in Julia's sheets, that frozen face, that blood-soaked shirt—were those sights of God's backside, the dark side of the moon, the underbelly of a snake, the bottom of a rock, the evil that men do?

The Second Lesson was from Luke:

> The light of the body is the eye: therefore when thine eye is single, thy whole body also is full of light; but when *thine eye* is evil, thy body also *is* full of darkness. Take heed therefore that the light which is in thee be not darkness.

Cole understood degrees of darkness, understood how the light in him had burned bright when it was dark.

The sermon was about true repentance. Perhaps he *had* been led to church, perhaps this sermon *was* especially for his ears. On the other hand, pick, *at random,* just about any church on any Sunday; the odds are pretty good you'll hear someone preach repentance. With good reason, he thought; there's no doubting what we need most.

A baptismal ceremony followed the sermon. The mother, thin and pale, with straight dark hair, carried a baby, still and quiet as a doll. The minister and the mother read statements, made declarations. When the minister put water on his round head, the baby wailed, a throaty caterwaul that resonated beneath the high, vaulted ceiling. "In this water we are buried with Christ in his death. From this water we are raised to share in his resurrection, reborn by the power of the Holy Spirit."

Members of the congregation turned to touch the hands of those beside them, those in front, those behind. Straight, outstretched arms, fingers pointed like pistol barrels at Cole. People whispered, mumbled like jungle-book natives or cowboy-movie Indians; their hands touched him, warm, moist, sticky hands.

"Peace, brother."

"Peace, murderer."

"Peace be unto you."

"And unto your victim."

Cole trembled. Heat flashed bright through his body; his body blinked cool, flickered dim, went frigid black. His mouth filled with wool. Their eyes would not meet his.

Row by row, the congregation filed out into the aisle and went to the altar to stand in a wide circle, hands linked. Bread was blessed, wine poured. *Body of Christ.* A little boy reached up to press a bit of bread to Cole's dry lips: "Cole," the boy whispered, "this is the body of Adam." "Eat, and be completely satisfied," the minister said. *Blood of Christ.* The boy's lips, stained red, whispered, "Cole, this is the blood of Adam. Drink." *In remembrance of Him who died for thee.*

Cole drove into the country. He pulled off the highway and got out of the truck. A car roared by, blowing dust and warm air. Cole held down a loose strand of barbed wire and stepped over a fence into a wooded area. Dry, brown leaves rattled against his boots. He walked beneath trees and stepped into the brightness of a cleared field. Hit by an unmistakable stench, he covered his nose and breathed the soapy scent of his hand. Hand-washers—Pontius Pilate, Lady Macbeth. Flies lifted, black lace blown back from the head of a dead calf.

He needed company, normalcy. He stopped at the mall and phoned Rachel, asked her to meet him at the cafeteria for lunch with the after-church crowd. She couldn't; she had to color and wash her hair; it would take all afternoon. Cole sat on a bench in the mall. People in Sunday clothes lined up outside the cafeteria. He envied young couples with babies in strollers, kids tugging at their arms. He envied middle-aged men and women in line with white-haired parents and teenaged sons and daughters. What if he and Jeanette had had a kid? Eyeing your eye in the face of a child might make all the difference in the world. Maybe he and Rachel could have a baby. Was he too old? His mother was sixty-two; how would he feel about her if she were eighty?

A woman who looked to be his mother's age stood alone in line. She wore a snazzy red skirt, a black wool sweater. Her low heels were red. Her gray hair was up in a soft bun. Did she smile at him?

The woman raised her right arm as if she were a student with a question. "Here, honey," she said. For an instant Cole thought her endearment was directed at him, then he followed her dark-brown eyes to a big man in a camel-hair jacket, a shock of gray hair bouncing on his forehead. Cole stepped back as the man leaned to embrace the woman. She gave the man her cheek and clamped her red fingernails into his woolly arm.

Cole went home and turned on the TV and made a cheese sandwich. A panoramic shot from high above the Orange Bowl panned the Miami skyline, then zoomed out toward the Everglades. He stared at a network of canals, gray lines on the screen. What the devil was going on? It looked like the canals of Mars. He peered close, wondered if he would see Adam Smith's body. The camera rose from the Everglades to the blue sky; one of the Goodyear blimps filled the screen. Pro football, the Dolphins playing the Jets.

Cole drove to Dalt's.

"Sonofabitch," Dalt said. "I figured you'd fallen off the edge of the planet. Come in."

They sat in Dalt's dim kitchen and drank cans of cold Tecate beer with lime wedges. A bit of lime pulp clung to Dalt's beard. Like a sliver of glass, it held light from the sink window; and when Dalt talked, the piece of light danced. He told Dalt he'd gone to Miami to check on his mother. He told him he'd met her "friend" Adam Smith, but he left out everything else.

"Anything you want to talk about, *compadre?*" Dalt asked.

"Like what?"

"You tell me. Something ain't right."

He wanted to tell *someone,* and Dalt was as good a friend as he had. *While I was out of town, I killed this guy, see.* He thought the words, worked up to speech—his mouth and lips flexed, trying to shape the first word. But words wouldn't come.

Dalt got up and went to a knotty-pine cabinet. He held a bottle of Herradura tequila by the neck, two shot glasses on the ends of his fingers like thimbles. He set the tequila on the kitchen table between them and clicked the glasses together: castanets. "Confession's good for the soul," he said.

Cole could say nothing.

Dalt plunked the shot glasses side by side on the table. He lifted the bottle and his left eyebrow at the same time and filled both glasses. "You still get the tequila," he said. "It's also good for the soul."

Tequila was the taste of a tenpenny nail between Cole's teeth, his tongue tip against the smooth, round nailhead, the day he and Jeanette helped frame in his daddy's houseboat. Up on a ladder, the bright sun and limitless summer sky above him, Avery had looked as young as Cole—a boy with a dream.

"I wish my father had not died," he said. "For the usual reasons, but also because I'd like to fight with him about some things, and it's hard to do battle with a dead man." Dalt poured them each another shot. Cole studied the Herradura label: an upside-down blue horseshoe arched over a man digging into the heart of a huge agave with a tool that resembled a long-handled tennis racket. "The horseshoe's turned wrong. Good luck spills out that way," he said.

"Yeah, it spills down into this bottle, so we can drink it," Dalt said.

"You know what I did this morning?" Dalt waited for him to tell him. "I went to church." He emptied his beer and leaned his chair back so he could reach Dalt's refrigerator without getting up. He got another Tecate and drank it without lime.

"Amen," Dalt said, in a tone that was difficult to read.

"Are we getting old, Dalt?" Cole said.

Dalt got up and went to the bathroom. "We are. We surely are," he almost whispered. He left the door open, and Cole heard his steady stream hitting water. Dalt's voice echoed from the bathroom, boomed with authority. "We are every one of us dying, Cole. That's why it's important to have good fellowship while we can. This whole dying lifetime." Dalt came back from the bathroom and held up a vial. "Help me kill the last of McLeod's L.A. coke?"

"I think I'll pass," he said.

Dalt raised the eyebrow again but said nothing. He emptied the cocaine onto the edge of his fist as if it were salt, snorted it, and chased it with a shot of tequila.

The two men sat in the kitchen and drank until long after dark. Dalt insisted on driving Cole home. Cole left his truck, and they took the Volvo. Dalt was as drunk as Cole was, another case of the blind leading the blind. The Volvo gurgled and farted and rumbled but got them to Cole's. They leaned against each other and lurched up the steps.

Cole took out the last two beers in his refrigerator.

"I don't really want one," Dalt said, but took the beer anyway. "I'm looped enough to say something I been wanting to say I know I shouldn't."

"Shoot," Cole said.

"Interesting choice of words."

"What do you mean?"

"I mean for a guy who's been packing a rod." Dalt took a long pull on the beer. "I got this bad feeling about you and Rachel." Cole started to say something, but Dalt held his hand up. "Wait, let me say it all. Do you really believe this husband—"

"Ex-husband."

"Ex-husband—this local-businessman type—would actually kill you? I mean he's never even approached you, has he? All those threats of his you got from Rachel. Right? Doesn't that strike you— doesn't that strike you as odd? If he's mad enough to kill you, looks like he'd threaten you in person. At least on the goddamn phone. If Rachel thought he was a psychopath, would she let you risk your life? I know I'm outa line, but seems she likes melodrama. She's got you carrying a fucking pistol. Why take the risk? You ain't the type."

Cole heard Dalt as if he were outside, talking through a closed window. Dalt's lips moved, but the words sounded far away. *Not the type?* If only Dalt knew.

"Tequila's doing some of my talking, but I worry about you. You know about kissing by the garden gate. I hate to see you blinded by love."

"Okay. Message sent, message received. Leave it at that. I'm feeling pretty okay tonight; I don't want to blow it."

"You're not pissed?"

"No."

"Okay. I got one more thing to tell you."

Cole held up his hands.

"Hang on," Dalt said. "Different subject. My last obligatory message. Jeanette's pregnant. She and Chip . . . the baby is due around Christmas."

"Season's greetings," Cole said. "Does that mean they *had* to get married?" He laughed.

Dalt laughed with him and shook his head, shrugged. "Who's counting? Who cares? What goes round comes round. *Qué será*, et cetera." He chugged the rest of his beer, slapped Cole on the shoulder, and left.

Cole turned off the lamp and stood in the dark living room until the rumble of the Volvo faded.

Maybe it was just because he was drunk, but he didn't feel much affected by the news of Jeanette's pregnancy. He'd wrestled with his dark angel out in the Everglades. He may have won, but he'd been lamed. He had to, he knew, heal himself. He wished Jeanette the best.

He wondered if Rachel had called while he was at Dalt's. He considered calling her. He didn't want to look at a clock, but he knew it must be after midnight. He put George Jones on the stereo and lay down on the couch. When "He Stopped Lovin' Her Today" came on, Cole smiled and sang softly with the record.

16

SHOTS'S tail bounced just above the tops of tall weeds and against bushes and under low tree limbs like a feather duster cleaning up around the lake. Cole coveted her energy, her joy.

He was fly-fishing for *Lepomis macrochirus,* bluegill, called, in the South, bream, and pronounced *brim. McClane's New Standard Fishing Encyclopedia* had reminded him, in a lyrical entry under PAN-FISH, "There . . . always will be many things to learn with a cane pole which escape modern philosophers."

The sun ran up the brown length of the fly rod. He brought the rod forward and *pushed* the green line a good forty feet across the water. The tiny popper, at the end of an invisible monofilament leader, settled like a bug on the surface. He looked through polarized sunglasses beneath the lake's dark surface. A lunar landscape of bream beds, a honeycomb of craters, was scraped by the males where the females laid thousands of eggs. When bream were on the beds you could catch a mess of them, but it was too far into fall for that. He waited for a slow count of ten, then gave the rod a delicate twitch that just perceptibly moved the popper. A soft kiss puckered the surface where the artificial bug had been. He pulled, set the tiny hook. The motion had its parallel in shooting a pistol—*Squeeze, don't jerk, the trigger.*

Taut line cut through water at right angles from the rod tip. The line and rod and Cole's arm hummed like a tuning fork as a fish baffled the tea-colored water with its flat body.

Anticipation was heightened by the possibility that he wouldn't get a bite, by not knowing from one instant to the next if the next would be the instant something happened. By the time he realized it was happening it might already be over—you couldn't hook every fish that hit. The entire short time he fought the fish, he feared losing it—not because he cared so much about landing the fish, but because he didn't want to lose the vibrations in his arms. The moment he cast again, he forgot what it felt like to have a fish on the line and wanted it as much as he had before. From the moment a fish hit until Cole took it off the hook, for that length of time he would not see Adam Smith's eyes staring up under the rear deck of the Mercedes; for that length of time he would not wonder when he would next hear from his mother; for that length of time he would not have ambivalent feelings about Rachel; for that length of time he wouldn't have ambivalent feelings about anything.

Cole wet his hand in the lake so his dry skin wouldn't peel the protective oils off the fish, then slid his palm from the bream's little O of a mouth back to where its body widened, combing fins down flat. If you weren't careful, they pricked like the devil. He used needled-nosed pliers to get the hook out of the fish's gullet.

The bug had taken a beating; raw wood showed through white paint, and the hook was loose. Cole bit the end off the tippet and tied on a new, chartreuse popper with an orange feather. He worked his way down the shoreline, casting beneath low-hanging limbs. The line unfolded smoothly, and the bright bug landed under the cover, as if a bug had dropped from a tree.

He twitched the popper, harder than he intended, and the concave end of the wooden body cupped air against water and made the loud *pop* for which it was named. To say the water exploded would not be a fish story. Something black and green and silver; something like a giant tree stump Walt Disney had animated, pulling, roots and all, free of earth; something like the famous cow, dappled black and white, jumping like any silver rocket ship into space on its way over the moon; something like a cannonball shot from a sunken gunship—*something* fired up out of the lake and *ker-blam* hit the water again: a boulder thrown from a high cliff, Bluto himself doing a belly-buster off the high-dive. A fucking whale had taken that itty-bitty popper and headed for Davy Jones's locker. Line stripped off, burned Cole's hand. He hoped his knots held, the line to the backing, the backing to the reel. He tightened what drag the reel had, but the fish wasn't fazed. Then it stopped, and he cranked furiously to take up slack. He got half the green line back on the reel, and still had slack. The fish must have shaken the hook. He reeled again; the line wouldn't budge. He must've hung on an underwater limb. Then his breath caught as the fish exploded once more. The fish, a real lunker, was so big it scared him. The biggest bass he'd ever hooked, and he had it on a bream bug with a one-pound-test leader and a trout tippet. He kept the rod tip up and tried to work the fish away from shore. It took a good ten minutes to get the fish off the cover. The fish's head broke the surface and was skimming in easily. It was almost a disappointment that the fish had planed out. *Woof.* Shots sounded like a guard dog. Cole heard her sliding down the incline behind him. She hit the water, making a beeline for the bass, proving for the first time in her life that she was a genuine retriever.

"No," he yelled.

Sudden slack in the line gave the fish ideas; it went straight for the bottom. Confused by Cole's yell and the sudden disappearance of the fish, the dog made a wide U-turn and swam back toward shore.

Hard as it struggled, the spent fish did not have much fight left.

Shots stood up, ankle deep in the lake, and shook herself, spraying Cole, splattering leaves behind him, and dimpling the surface of the lake.

He had the fish in shallow water, and he knelt to grip its open mouth between the thumb and fingers of his left hand. The char-treuse bream bug was hooked firmly in the tough, colorless tissue inside the edge of the fish's mouth. It was a beautiful bass, dark-green along the top down to a lateral line of black spots, fading to silver-white below.

Shots came over, calmer now, shy-acting.

"Come here, girl," he said. "You're my only witness." With the pliers he backed the small hook out. His fist disappeared easily into the wide mouth. The dog wagged her tail and thrust her nose forward, but when the fish jerked against air she jumped back, splashing water up Cole's leg. "Sit," he said. The dog sat in the shallow water and cocked her head.

He carried the fish back to the grassy spot where he'd left his tackle box. He got out the "de-liar" scales he'd never used. He was afraid the flat, C-shaped, stainless-steel crook wouldn't hold the fish, but it did. The scale read a little over seven pounds—the biggest largemouth he'd ever caught, and he'd done it on a fly rod with a one-pound leader and a bream bug.

He waded out, knee deep, leaned over, and lowered the fish into the lake. Water gave back some of the color the fish had already lost. He barely held the fish, one hand at the mouth, one gently holding the caudal fin, but when he let go, the fish leaned over sideways and did not swim away.

Shots stood and walked up to her haunches in the water, her nose against the back of Cole's knee, and watched him move the fish steadily back and forth in the water.

He released the bass again. It floated, suspended just beneath the surface. The pectoral fins trembled, and the fish swam a foot or so forward and stopped. Then the big bass swam away, the dark top of its body vanishing in the dark water.

To say Cole was happy would not be entirely true, but he was a good kind of tired. A blister was rising where the butt of the rod had rubbed his palm, and his skin stung where the line had burned him. Even after a hot shower and a good soaping, his hands would keep the smell of fish. His jeans, socks, and boots were soaked, his steps heavy with that weight. He bent to feel muscles stretch; his arms and shoulders ached sweetly from pleasant exertion. Tonight he might be able to sleep without Adam Smith's cold cheek beside his on the pillow, might be tired enough to drift away without first getting whiskey-blurred.

He stood a long while, watching the water. Nothing moved. His arm hung at his side, his hand on Shots's head. He moved his fingers and felt, beneath the soft fur, the firm but fragile line of dog skull. The dog stared out over the lake. What did she see? Cole saw only wide water and no way to cross.

Clouds were moving in from the north, the lake going from gray-green to ultramarine. Ultramarine pigment is made, he had read somewhere, from powdered gemstone, pulverized lapis lazuli. As Huldah taught Julia, beauty is not easy.

A gust of wind rattled trees behind him and scattered yellow and brown leaves on the water. He shivered. The wind was shifting, a storm brewing, blowing winter in. Not many fishing days left. Shots stood in the shallow water and looked at Cole. Thunder rumbled in the distance, and the dog's whole body trembled. Watching for lightning, Cole sloshed up out of the water toward dry land.

17

THANKSGIVING DAY, Cole grilled amberjack he'd bought off the back of a truck parked in a deserted filling station, glad he wasn't about to eat the big bass, glad it still swam free. The old man's sign said: FRESH FROM FLORIDA. Cole had phoned the Turret Inn, to wish Julia happy Thanksgiving, but she'd checked out. He tried not to worry about her. Rachel opened a bottle of pretty good white wine and made a green salad. They ate on a card table on Cole's porch.

Bobby had agreed to everything Rachel wanted, but she still clenched her jaw every time she said his name. Had Cole been able to work up a good hate for Bobby, it would have been easier to sympathize with Rachel's anger, but Cole's hatred for Adam Smith seemed to have used up his quota. Bobby, at least, had a reason for his anger. Though Cole was no longer sure Bobby had done or said all the things Rachel had reported.

By the time they finished supper it was dark. They went inside and watched a public television special on endangered species. The show included (coincidence or divine intervention?) a segment about the alligator, *Alligator mississipiensis*, about to be taken off the endangered list (after a remarkable comeback in Texas, Louisiana, Alabama, and Florida), and a segment about the Florida panther, whose future did not look so good. As the video tracked through the Everglades, Cole watched for the silver Mercedes. An alligator whirled in shallow water and hissed like an old locomotive blowing steam. "Ticktock" again, the alligator from *Peter Pan* opened the red wedge of his mouth, the bottom jaw dropped, deadly drawbridge, and one eyelid lowered too, a sly wink, sharing the secret flavor of Adam Smith's flesh.

The muscular Florida panther crouched, its deep, gravelly purr amplified when the camera moved in for a close-up. The panther's yellow eyes stared at Cole, a look of recognition, then the panther turned and merged with the landscape, his goodbye snarl fueled and lubricated with Adam Smith's blood.

Cole glanced at Rachel. She stared not at the TV but at him. She watched every move he made, her eyes following him as the panther's eyes did. They had not made love since he'd gotten back from Florida. He had not seen her the first few nights; he'd been too haunted. He'd told her he was exhausted. She asked him out to Forest Lake, but he didn't want to hold her in the bed where she and Bobby had lain together so many times.

"Don't you want me to stay here?" she asked.

"Not tonight. I have papers to grade, lots of work to catch up on." It sounded lame to him, but Rachel flashed a smile and said she understood. She said for him to do his work and get some rest. She pecked his cheek and left, humming. He listened to the MG whine away as Rachel wound out the gears.

He picked bones out of the amberjack Rachel had left, untouched, on her plate. He fed the fish to Shots, who inhaled it and then watched him put dishes into a sinkful of hot, soapy water. Let the suckers soak overnight. He turned off the lights and carried the half-full bottle of wine and Rachel's glass, her lipstick smile on the rim, to the couch. The television threw different colors across the dark room. He pulled his boots off and let them drop. They landed akimbo, the uppers under the edge of the couch, the feet sticking out as a mechanic's feet stick out from under a car. He spoke to the boots: "Hey, buddy, fix me up. Change my oil and filter, give me a tune-up." He heard a familiar voice and looked up to see Bobby Vickery smiling at him, the big ear: *Talk to Bobby*. . . . He pushed a button on the remote control, and the television and the room went dark. He leaned over and punched the stereo on. Music blasted out, some new-wave band. Before he killed the volume he heard a woman sing *dirty invitation to a new world,* or at least that's what it sounded like. He listened to his favorite Bob Dylan tape, and as he sang along on "Bob Dylan's Dream," he took out his contacts and splashed water on his face. Shots followed him from room to room, finally lying down with a heavy sigh against the couch. Cole found a Patsy Cline tape and put it on, turned out the lamp, and lay back on the couch with his wine as the darkness filled with Patsy's guttural, heartbreaking "Crazy."

Shots's low growl woke him. Someone was tapping on the front door. Patsy was singing "I Fall to Pieces." The tape had reversed itself (how many times?), Patsy singing one side, then the other. The tapping was as relentless as an alarm clock. Cole reached for the pistol, then remembered it was in the dresser drawer. He had not worn it since he got back from Florida. He did not go to the bedroom to get it. He put on his prescription sunglasses and went to the door.

As soon as Cole saw her standing there, he realized he'd been half expecting her. It was drizzling, and her hair stood out in fine, damp points around her head.

"Mother, come in. What time is it?"

"It's nighttime. Don't you have lights?"

18

THE clock in the kitchen range said 2:20. The darkest hour, Julia thought, is just before dawn. Shots's tail swept the linoleum; Julia rubbed between the dog's ears. Cole ran water for a pot of coffee. In the dark glasses, an empty mug in his hand, he looked like a blind beggar.

"Are those the only glasses you have?"

"Yeah, I broke the other pair. I wear my contacts all the time; these are all I have."

Julia shook her head and laughed. She wore a white sweatshirt with a blue unicorn on the front; she'd bought it on the boardwalk in Hollywood before she left. Beneath the unicorn, red letters: ONLY IN FLORIDA.

Cole told her about Elizabethan slave traders who had explored Florida. They carried horns the Florida Indians said were from unicorns back to England and reported there were unicorns and lions all over Florida. The horns from the Indians proved the unicorns, and the unicorns proved the lions, because, lions being the natural enemies of unicorns, where one is, the other cannot be missing.

Julia smiled but felt sad. "You know," she said, "you know a lot of fanciful stories."

"Guess I got that from my ol' dad."

"Avery's stories were mythological; they explained things. Day after tomorrow, you know, is the anniversary of his death." She looked around the small kitchen as if she might find there some explanation for the passage of time, the disappearance of loved ones.

Cole shook his head, then he poured them each a cup of fresh coffee.

267

She had, she told him, decided to leave Florida, though she might go back. She intended to follow the ocean, after this detour to see him. She was here—she smiled—to check on her only child.

"The way," Cole said, "I checked on you in Florida?"

"I want to know if Rachel is the real McCoy," she said.

Cole shrugged and refilled her cup.

Julia did not mention Adam Smith. She said she was going to stay on the road, keep close to water. She might go up the east coast, survey the beaches. Might go all the way to Nova Scotia. Then, if she still felt like moving, there were the Great Lakes, and out in Minnesota, at Lake Itasca, the mighty Mississippi was a little stream even her old bones could jump across. She could puddle-hop some of that dry, big-sky country to the Pacific, an ocean she'd never seen.

Cole paced back and forth in the kitchen. He was different. He acted as he had when he was a child and knew something he didn't want her to know. In the fluorescent kitchen light he looked tired; her son, for the first time in her memory, looked *old*. Julia saw her slanted eyes, her nose and square chin in his face. There were wrinkles around his eyes that she did not have. She wanted to touch his face, to smooth the skin back and feel his face baby soft beneath her fingers.

He looked at her looking at him. She shook her head, and he smiled a sad smile. She spoke:

"Mother—Huldah, you know—used to tell me, when I was a little girl, that beauty was not easy. You have to *suffer* to be beautiful, Mother said. Even after I was grown I thought she meant skin-deep beauty. I had to get to be an old woman, like her, before I could understand what she really meant."

Cole nodded.

"Adam," she said, "seems to have vanished off the face of the earth. The night you met him was the last night I ever saw him." She waited, but her son had nothing to say.

They went out onto the front porch, where the tablecloth on the card table was wet from blowing rain. They sat for a while without talking and drank their coffee. The rain had let up, but lightning still flickered in the distance.

After a while some of the awkwardness Julia felt faded, like the thunder she could no longer hear behind lightning that still threw shadows across the porch. There was a secret between them now, and she didn't know what it was, but there would always be love there too, to flash like lightning into whatever dark spaces angled around and between them.

Cole got up for more coffee. The porch shook with a sudden, close explosion of thunder, a simultaneous flash of lightning. Intense, blinding illumination covered the retina like a bright stain that only slowly let the darkness return. Blinded, Cole walked into the chair where Julia sat and shot out his hand to steady himself. Julia's arm jerked up in a reflex of self-protection.

Lightning flashed again, thunder boomed, and the two, mother and son, son and mother, stared at each other. Cole's eyes were hidden behind the dark glasses, his lips curled back in a tight grimace, his teeth bared. This face, frozen ghostly white as an image in a negative, was the face, the photograph of Cole, that replaced all others, a look Julia would remember always.

Epilogue

1

I N the dream, Cole knew he was dreaming.

He was in the kitchen of Rachel and Bobby's house. The ceramic fruit on the wall—maroon apple, blue grapes, long, yellow banana—glowed in fluorescent light. Rachel stood in the center of the kitchen wearing a pink wrapper and slippers fashioned as furry, pink mice; pink rubber mouse whiskers twitched at the toes of the slippers, and two plastic eyes looked up at Cole from each foot. Rachel took from the freezer a package of ground hamburger. She tilted the package in one hand, the meat purple, then orange, changing the way those iridescent shirts, popular in the sixties, change color; changing the way a bikinied girl in a plastic key chain winks her eye (open, closed, open) as the key chain dangles in the light. Rachel put the meat into a brown covered casserole dish. She did not notice Cole watching her.

In his darkly paneled den, Bobby sat, his face hidden behind a newspaper. Cole walked toward him, but Bobby did not seem to hear. Cole stood over Bobby and looked down behind the newspaper. Bobby's head was tilted, displaying his large ear, from the TV ads: *Talk to Bobby. . . . He's listening.*

Then, without walking there, Cole was in the dining room. In the polished top of Rachel's black Oriental table Cole stared up at himself. Reflected on either side of Cole's face were Rachel's fixed smile, Bobby's inclined ear.

"Sit here, Cole," Bobby said. He pulled back a black chair from the head of the table. Cole sat, and Rachel, who had, apparently, disappeared, now reappeared carrying the covered casserole. She placed the heavy dish in front of Cole, and with a flourish from a commercial, Bobby smiled and lifted the lid.

Raw meat jiggled like a mold of jello, bright and glistening. Small individual cylinders of the ground meat began to pulse and move, pink-orange worms, jerking grubs the shapes of elbow macaroni.

Cole reached for the casserole's cover to hide the writhing meat, but he could not get hold of it. Each time he reached, the cover moved of its own accord. Cole's hand was led back and forth across the tabletop as if it were being pulled over a Ouija board. The alphabet appeared in an arc of perfect block letters beneath his fingertips.

In the dream, Cole struggled to wake from the dream. He was desperate to wake himself before he spelled out a word, before any message could take shape. He strained to rouse himself, as a swimmer forces his body toward the bright surface, trying to rise faster than the panic racing up inside his chest.

His hand rested momentarily on the letter *N*. As his hand moved again, he fought with all his strength for consciousness.

Finally, he woke, shaking his head back and forth, continuing to shake his head for several moments after he realized he was out of the dream. He was hot, his skin sticky. His heart beat fast, high in his throat. The room was dark and quiet. It took him several seconds to get his bearings.

Shots lay against the screen door, sleeping quietly. Cole remembered his mother's visit, the thunderstorm. Without calling out, he knew she was not in the house. Where had she gone? The refrigerator motor cycled on and hummed in a familiar way. The world went right on.

He didn't need a soothsayer to interpret his dream. He didn't care what the dream *meant,* what someone might say its parts represented. He did care about the look on Rachel's face, her fixed smile. He cared that that was how his unconscious mind's eye saw her. It was bad enough that Adam Smith's body must lie between Cole and his mother from now on. It was also there between Cole and Rachel. That secret, and other things too. Cole had enough unanswered questions to deal with; he didn't need to wonder about Rachel. Dalt was right; a lot of things didn't add up.

Was it really passion that had directed his life lately, or was it something more perverse? A friend had written him months ago, after his divorce from Jeanette was final. The friend had urged him, based on the friend's own experience, to give himself at least two years to deal with the divorce before he got involved with someone else.

"Don't do anything irrevocable, don't do anything you might regret. You've got plenty of time."

What perversity had lured him so quickly into bed with Rachel, into Rachel and Bobby's house that night when Bobby almost caught him there, and down to Florida and into Julia's closet, into her life, then, finally, lured him onto Adam's trail and out into the wilds of the Everglades from which, he realized, he might never completely return. Was it perversity—a curious tendency toward risk, mystery, the dark side of things—that had caused Jeanette not only to leave him but to betray him?

Cole realized then, for the first time, that before he could live with what he had done in Florida, he had to live with what he had *not* done for so many years before. He would take some time, however much time it took, and begin to make his life new. All his life he'd had the examples of his own, decent parents. Maybe, he thought, that was why he'd been led to perversity. Maybe decency created longings for indecency. Had Julia's perfect marriage led her, somehow, to Adam Smith? Well, he *still* had the example of his mother. She was starting over for at least the second time. At her age she was on the road, going somewhere.

He switched on a lamp. Shots lifted her head and watched to see what he would do. There on an end table was his mother's empty wineglass, and propped against her glass was the message she had left him. Without his contacts or the prescription sunglasses, he held the paper close and read:

Cole,

We do whatever we have to do. You know that.
Whatever you do, I forgive you. Others, too, forgive you. Now you have to forgive, and/or forget, yourself.
I'm gone. Can't let the sun catch me snoozing. I'll send you postcards from paradise—every single one I find.

Love,

Mother

He got up from the couch and peeled off the clothes he'd slept and sweated in. Shots thumped her tail steadily and waited. Naked, Cole headed for the kitchen to see what time it was. He'd fix a big breakfast. He wanted the smells of coffee brewing and bacon sizzling. The cool bare floor felt good under his bare feet. The dog rose and stretched and followed him.

275

2

IN Bessemer, Alabama, Julia passed steel mills, their insides flaring fire in the near-darkness of dawn. Chimneys belched smoke, which drifted in the still morning air into low orange clouds. Sulfurous fumes stung Julia's eyes and nose. A hot wind pricked her cheeks like sparked flint and burned her throat. Fire and brimstone. She thought of the priest, Father O'Brien, who had married Cole and Jeanette and then gone away to work— he called it a lay ministry—in a factory town. She wondered if he was still there, up near Chicago, this morning, breathing air that smelled like this air. The skyline of downtown Birmingham quivered through refracted light the way stars twinkle at night. Off to the south, a huge metal statue of Vulcan looked down from the top of a mountain. Julia pressed down on the accelerator, and the black car sped like a cinder spewed from one of Vulcan's giant furnaces.

North of Birmingham, the highway stretched out for a long, slow climb up between mountain ridges. Red rock faces fell between pine forests. Julia had the highway to herself. The eastern sky was streaked with red. *Red sky at morning, sailor take warning.* The highway curved around a mountain's swollen hip, the car squatting a little with the lean of the land. The speedometer was on 90, but it didn't feel nearly fast enough. She felt as if she were barely moving, as if she were some dark speck on the pavement, some dark whorl in a stratum of slowly shifting rock, glacial motion, mindless geologic time.

A billboard invited her to visit Lookout Mountain and see four states. Another said: See Ruby Falls. Hadn't someone made a song out of that, in which some lonely Ruby falls for the wrong man? Ladies love outlaws; when a woman says *no* she means *yes;* a woman doesn't have the same desires, her *needs* are not as strong as a man's—more bedtime mythology.

Yet another sign, high on the side of a mountain, advertised the Chattanooga Choo-Choo. In 1942, not long after Pearl Harbor, before they married, she and Avery danced to Glenn Miller, "The Chattanooga Choo-Choo," at the Kit Kat Klub in San Antonio. And "Bewitched, Bothered, and Bewildered" and "I've Got Sixpence" and "My Adobe Hacienda" and "Deep in the Heart of Texas."

She was crying. She looked up at her eyes in the rearview mirror. Tears ran down both her cheeks and streaked her face. She wiped her cheeks with the back of her hand, just as she had before she left Cole's a couple of hours ago. He had fallen asleep on the couch, his head resting on his folded arms, just his ear and cheek visible. She had leaned over to kiss him goodbye, and for a moment, he was her baby again; then a lightning flash from the storm that had passed earlier lit up her memory and she saw, again, the blue-gray skin, the blue-gray teeth, the tight, fixed grin of a dead son.

Julia tilted the rearview mirror down for a better look, and now she was crying and laughing at the same time. What else could she do?

She turned off the highway onto a blacktopped road and faced directly into the just-risen sun. The brightness glistened in her teary eyes, and pine needles shot off green and gold rays.

There was a picnic area ahead, and she pulled off the road and stopped beside a wooden table. Here, the air was fresh and cool. She wiped her face with her sleeve and stretched. The picnic area ended where a dense pine forest began, running high up a mountain ridge. A trail disappeared into the forest; Julia followed that trail.

She walked on a thick padding of brown pine needles in the cool shade of tall trees. After about a mile, steadily climbing, the trail became rocky, and the pines thinned out. Soon she was in bright sunlight, and the trail was switching back and forth as it went almost straight up.

Julia stopped to get her breath. Below, she saw the highway, but the picnic area and her car were hidden by trees. She went on, higher. By the time she was again out of breath, the trail had leveled off and she was on a grassy ledge. She went out to the edge, where a guardrail of steel pipe ran through thick creosote posts sunk in the rock face of the cliff. Her hands wrapped around the sun-warmed pipe. The sun shone on the creosote posts, which had black, wet-looking streaks down them that gave off a faint railroad smell.

On the highway, a semi the size of a child's toy was inching along a grade. At this distance the diesel engine was soundless. All around her was peacefulness, bird songs and breeze ruffling the tops of trees. Far beyond the highway were more ridges, green turning blue with distance, wave after wave of mountain ridges, blue to blue to blue until the sky took over.

Julia stood on the edge and felt its pull. But the inclination to jump, this leap, lured her no more than any other precipice.

She thought of Adam Smith and realized it was the first time today.

"The Widow Marrs," she shouted, "has no regrets." She waited, but there was no echo. Good. She'd said it, it didn't need repeating. She felt at peace with the world and everyone in it—in a state of grace. *For by grace are ye saved through faith; and that not of your-selves.* Oh, Huldah, Mother, you are with me always. Beauty *is* difficult, but the peace that passeth understanding is effortless beauty. I miss you. I miss Annabelle and Garner. I miss Cole, my only begotten son. And I miss Avery, miss my Martian, which is almost like missing myself. I do not miss Adam Smith, but Lord God, I would do every-thing again just as I have done. I repent nothing. *Amen,* she whis-pered.

The way back down the trail was easier than walking. Gravity took over, and her feet glided over rocks and red clay. Wildflowers bright-ened the edge of the trail near the entrance to the piney woods. Had she simply not seen them on her hike up, or had they only now opened their blossoms? When she came out of the dense pines, she shaded her eyes against the sun and smelled on her hands the metal pipe that marked the boundary she had left behind.

A ragtag-looking man trudged along the shoulder of the highway, his thumb halfheartedly out for a ride. Julia pulled over and opened the passenger door. The man peered in, the floppy brim of an old brown fedora hiding his eyes.

"Where you headed?" he whispered.

"On," Julia said.

The man shook his head and stuffed what looked like a bedroll into the small space behind the bucket seat. He got in and reached across his shoulder for the seat belt, pulled it over, and slipped it into the lock as if he were an experienced race driver. Then he reached down and expertly lifted the lever to recline the seatback. He gave his rear a little wiggle, left to right, right to left, as someone shapes a seat for himself in the sand when he stretches out on a beach. He sighed, and apparently comfortable and satisfied, settling in for a long ride, he lifted the fedora and gave his head a shake that imitated exactly the motion of his hips. Long, shiny, gray-streaked hair spilled from beneath the hat, and wide, dark eyes met Julia's questioning look.

"My name's Amanda, but my friends call me Mandy," the woman said, and she offered Julia her hand.

"My friends call me Julia."

"Julia, I was mighty glad to see you stop. I been walking this road a long, long while. It ain't the walking I mind so much as the sound of my own voice. A body needs some other body to talk with."

"I'm glad for your company," Julia said. She rolled her window up so she could hear Mandy better. In the quiet, closed car the woman gave off a sweet, grassy aroma.

"This is a nice day for traveling. It seems like winter isn't coming," Mandy said. "Of course, winter always comes—just sneaking up on us this year."

Julia nodded and they rode in silence for a few miles.

"Look at that," Mandy said. She put the tip of her finger near the top of the windshield. Something silver flashed in the sun. It seemed to come out of the top of a mountain.

"It looks like a flying saucer," Julia said.

Mandy didn't laugh. "No," she said, "that one's a jet from the air force base. But I've seen flying saucers before. On this very road."

"So you believe there's life up there?" Julia said.

"Oh, we're not alone in the universe. Some of them, spacemen, Martians, know all about us. I read in a paper I found not long ago about one of those flying saucers having a Confederate flag on its bottom. And, sometimes, one of those flying saucers will land and take someone away to another world."

The silver shape disappeared above the roof of the car, but both women still stared at the blue space where it had been.

"*You* believe in stuff like that?" Mandy asked.

"Sure I do," Julia said. "Why not? Anything's possible."

About the Author

Allen Wier was born in San Antonio, Texas, and grew up in Texas, Mexico, and Louisiana. He is the author of three previous books—*Blanco,* and *Departing as Air,* novels, and *Things About to Disappear,* a collection of stories. He has been a Guggenheim Fellow in fiction and has received a grant from the National Endowment for the Arts.

Mr. Wier lives with his wife, Donnie, and son, Wes, in Tuscaloosa, Alabama, where he teaches in the writing program at the University of Alabama.